WANT YOU DEAD

Peter James was educated at Charterhouse then at film school. He lived in North America for a number of years, working as a screenwriter and film producer before returning to England. His novels, including the *Sunday Times* number one bestselling Roy Grace series, have been translated into thirty-six languages, with worldwide sales of fifteen million copies. Three of his earlier novels have been filmed. His novella *The Perfect Murder* and his first Roy Grace novel, *Dead Simple*, have both been adapted for the stage. James has also produced numerous films, including *The Merchant of Venice*, starring Al Pacino, Jeremy Irons and Joseph Fiennes. He divides his time between his homes in Notting Hill, London, and near Brighton in Sussex.

Visit his website at www.peterjames.com
Or follow him on Twitter @peterjamesuk
Or Facebook: facebook.com/peterjames.roygrace

WANT YOU DEAD

PETER JAMES

PAN BOOKS

First published 2014 by Macmillan

This edition published 2014 by Pan Books
an imprint of Pan Macmillan, a division of Macmillan Publishers Limited
Pan Macmillan, 20 New Wharf Road, London N1 9RR
Basingstoke and Oxford
Associated companies throughout the world
www.panmacmillan.com

ISBN 978-1-4472-0319-3

3 5 7 9 8 6 4

A CIP catalogue record for this book is available from the British Library.

Typeset by Ellipsis Digital Limited, Glasgow
Printed and bound by CPI Group (UK) Ltd, Croydon, CR0 4YY

Visit **www.panmacmillan.com** to read more about all our books
and to buy them. You will also find features, author interviews and
news of any author events, and you can sign up for e-newsletters
so that you're always first to hear about our new releases.

For my wonderful agent and friend

CAROLE BLAKE

1

Wednesday, 23 October

Karl Murphy was a decent and kind man, a family doctor with two small children whom he was bringing up on his own. He worked long hours, and did his very best for his growing list of patients. The last two years had been tough since his beloved wife, Ingrid, had died, and there were some aspects of his work he found really hard, particularly having to break news to patients who were terminally ill. But it never occurred to him that he might have made enemies – and certainly not that there might be someone who hated him so much he wanted him dead.

And was planning to kill him tonight.

Sure, okay, however hard you tried, you couldn't please everyone, and boy, did he see that at work some days. Most of his patients were pleasant, but a few of them tested him and the staff in his medical practice to the limit. But he still tried to treat them all equally.

As he stood at the clubhouse bar on this late October evening, showered and changed out of his golfing clothes, politely drinking his second pint of lime and lemonade with his partners in the tournament and glancing discreetly at his watch, anxious to make his escape, he realized for the first time in a long, long while he was feeling happy – and excited. There was a new lady in his life. They hadn't been dating for long, but already he had grown extremely fond of her. To the point that he had thought today, out on the golf course, that he was falling in love with her. But being a very private man, he said nothing of this to his companions.

Shortly after 6 p.m. he downed the remains of his drink, anxious about the time, quite unaware that there was a man waiting outside in the blustery darkness.

His sister, Stefanie, had picked the kids up from school today and would be staying with them at his home until he arrived with the babysitter. But she had to leave by 6.45 p.m. latest, to go to a business dinner with her husband, and Karl could not make her late for that. He thanked his host for the charity golf day, and his fellow teammates in turn congratulated him for playing so well, then he slipped eagerly away from the nineteenth-hole drinking session that looked set to go on late into the night. He had something that he wanted to do very much more than get smashed with a bunch of fellow golfers, however pleasant they were. He had a date. A very hot date, and the prospect of seeing her, after three days apart, was giving him the kind of butterflies he'd not had since his teens.

He hurried across the car park, through the wind and rain, to the far end where he had parked his car, popped open the boot, and slung his golf bag inside it. Then he zipped the small silver trophy he had won into a side pocket of the bag, totally preoccupied with thoughts of the evening ahead. God, what a ray of sunshine she had brought into his life! These past two years since Ingrid had died had been hell and now, finally, he was coming through it. In the long, bleak period since her death, he had not thought that would ever be possible.

He didn't notice the motionless figure, all in black, who lay beneath the tartan dog rug on the rear seat, nor did he think it odd that the interior lights failed to come on when he opened the driver's door. It seemed that almost every day another bit of the ageing Audi ceased working, or, like the fuel gauge, only functioned intermittently. He had a new A6 on order, and would be taking delivery in a few weeks' time.

He settled behind the wheel, pulled on his seat belt, started the engine and switched on the headlights. Then he switched the radio from Classic FM to Radio 4, to catch the second half of the news, drove out of the car park, and along the narrow road beside the eighteenth fairway of Haywards Heath Golf Club. Headlights were coming the other way, and he pulled over to the side to let the car pass. As he was about to accelerate forward he heard a sudden movement behind him, then something damp and acrid was clamped over his mouth and nose.

Chloroform, he recognized from his medical training, in the fleeting instant that he tried to resist, before his brain went muzzy and his feet came off the pedals, and his hands lost their grip on the wheel.

2

Wednesday night, 23 October

He held his binoculars to his eyes, in the darkness, focused tight on the woman he loved so much. The night-sight for his crossbow, which he used to keep watch on her when she turned out the lights, lay on the table beside him.

She was drinking a glass of white wine – her fourth tonight – and dialling a number on her phone, again, looking anxious and edgy. With a brief toss of her head, she flicked her red hair away from her pretty face. It was something she always did when she was uptight or nervous about something.

He won't answer, my love, my sweet, really he won't.

3

God, men! What was wrong? Was it her? Them?

There are some things you do in life, Red thought, that are really, really dumb. They don't seem that way at the time; it is only when they go wrong, you realize. It had taken her two years – two years of ignoring the advice of her family, her friends, and ultimately the police. Two years before she had realized just how dangerous Bryce Laurent, the man she had met and fallen in love with from her lonely hearts advert, was.

If she could only wind the clock back two years, with the knowledge she now had.

Please, God.

She would never have joined that online dating agency, and certainly would not have placed that stupid message on it.

Single girl, 29, redhead and smouldering, love life that's crashed and burned. Seeks new flame to rekindle her fire. Fun, friendship and – who knows – maybe more?

Most of the replies had been complete dross. But then she had been warned by her girlfriends that a lot of the men who replied to these things were liars – married guys after a quick shag and not much else.

Well, she had replied to those friends, she wasn't interested in a *quick* shag but she could do with a *long* shag! That wasn't something she'd had for most of the years she had wasted on that introspective dickhead Dominic, who was normally back to checking his emails thirty seconds after a thirty-second bonk.

Besides, Red had reckoned she was smart enough to tell the difference between the shysters and someone decent.

Wrong.

Very badly wrong.

Even more wrong, at this moment, than she knew.

She was unaware that she was being watched, as she took another sip of Sauvignon Blanc and listened to the phone, counting each ring. Three. Four. Five. Six. Then voicemail. It was 8.30 p.m. He was an hour and a half late for their date. Where the hell was he?

She hung up without leaving a message this time, feeling angry and hurt.

4

Wednesday night, 23 October

Van was *the man!* Oh yes. Oh yes, indeed! Van Morrison's 'Queen of the Slipstream' was blasting from his big black Jawbone speaker, flooding his tiny apartment with all those beautiful words he had once felt about Red.

The grumpy old shithead above him banged on the ceiling with his walking stick, as usual when he played his music late at night. But he didn't care.

She had been the Queen of the Slipstream. His queen.

Queen of Hearts.

Red.

The colour of the Queen of Hearts.

And she had rejected him.

And humiliated him.

Did it hurt? Oh yes, it hurt. Every minute of every day and night. Every second.

He had been lucky to get this apartment, with the view it had. Some things were meant to be. Like he and Red had been meant to be. Taking the binoculars from his eyes, he rocked his head from side to side, fury twisting inside him. Okay, so some bad stuff had got in the way of their relationship, but that was all history now – it was too far gone.

He watched her cute lips as she took another sip of her wine. Lips he had kissed so tenderly, so passionately. Lips he had drawn in the cartoon sketches he had made of her, one of which – of her lips pouted in a provocative smile – was framed on the wall. It was captioned, *I'm a five-a-day gal!*

Lips that had kissed every part of his body. The thought of these lips kissing another man was too much to bear. They were his lips. He possessed them. The thought of another man touching the soft skin of her body, holding her naked, entering her, was like an endless bolus of cold water surging through him. The thought of her eyes meeting another man's just as she climaxed made him shake with helpless rage.

But not so helpless any more. Now he had a plan.

If I can't have you, no one will.

He closed the curtains and turned the lights back on. Then he continued to watch her for some moments on one of the screens on the bank of monitors on the wall. She was redialling. Bugging her phone had been simple, with a piece of software, SpyBubble, that he had bought over the internet and secretly installed on her mobile phone. It enabled him to listen to all her conversations, wherever she might be, and whether she was using the phone or not, as well as receive automatically all texts to and from her, the numbers of every call she made or received, all the websites she looked at, all her photographs, and, very importantly, through GPS, know her exact location all the time.

He stared around at the framed photographs of himself covering the walls. There he was in a pink Leander jacket wearing a straw boater at the Henley Regatta, looking pretty much like a young George Clooney, with Red on his arm in a floaty dress and a huge hat. There was another of him in a leather flying helmet in the cockpit of a Tiger Moth. A studious one of him in the Air Traffic Control Centre at Gatwick Airport. Another of him looking rather fetching in a mortar board and gown at his graduation from the Sorbonne in

Paris. Another, also in a mortar board and gown, of him being awarded his doctorate from the School of Aviation in Sydney. There was one he particularly liked of himself in his firefighter uniform. Next to it was one of him shaking hands with Prince Charles. Another shaking hands with Sir Paul McCartney. Impressive? Impressive enough for a queen?

And she had rejected him.

Poisoned against him by the lies of her family. Poisoned by her friends. How could she have listened to them and believed them? She had destroyed everything through her own stupidity.

He turned the music up, drowning out the thoughts raging in his head, and ignored another *blam, blam, blam* on the ceiling from Mr Grumpy.

Then he picked up his binoculars again, switched off the lights, made his way over to the window, and opened the curtains a fraction. It was much nicer to watch her in the flesh, rather than on the screens showing images with sound from every room in her place. He could feel her pain better that way. He looked out and down towards the second-floor window across the alley. Her living-room light was on and he could see her clearly. She was holding her phone to her ear and looking very worried.

So you should be.

5

Wednesday night, 23 October

'Don't do this to me, please,' Red said, as the mobile phone again went to voicemail after six rings.

'Hi, this is Karl. I can't answer just now, so leave a message and I'll call you right back.'

She'd left three messages, and still he had not called *right back.* The first one had been at 7.30 p.m. – half an hour after the time he'd said he would pick her up. They'd planned to have dinner at the China Garden. She'd left a second message at 8 p.m., and a third, trying not to sound angry – which had been hard – shortly before 9 p.m. It was now 10.30 p.m. She'd even checked her Twitter messages and Facebook page, although Karl had never before used them to communicate with her.

Terrific, she thought. *Stood up. How great is that?*

Splitting up with Bryce had been a nightmare that still stayed with her. In those first few weeks after she had thrown him out, with the help of the police, she would often come home to find his Aston Martin parked right outside her old flat. He would be nowhere around, but the sight of the car was enough to give her the creeps. He'd stopped doing it after the time she had got really pissed off at him and let all four of the tyres down. But even after that, sometimes during her solitary training runs for the Brighton Marathon, in aid of the Samaritans, she would spot him watching her, always from a distance, either on foot or in a moving car. For a while it had put her off, particularly the evening runs she used to love across the Downs in the falling darkness.

On the advice of the people she had talked to at the Sanctuary Scheme, she had moved out of her flat into this temporary accommodation, rented under an assumed name they had given to her. The second-floor flat, chosen for its position, had no windows that were visible from the main road, and a reinforced front door. It was in a gloomy, tired converted Victorian mansion block that had once been a grand private residence, close to Hove seafront. Her view from all the main windows was out onto the fire escape of an ugly 1950s apartment block, across a courtyard and an alleyway that led to the car park and lock-up garages behind her building.

Although she was meant to feel safe here, the place depressed her. It had a narrow hallway, dingily lit, that led through into a small open-plan living/dining area, with an old-fashioned kitchen that was little more than a galley separated by a breakfast bar. There was a small bedroom off the hallway that she had made into her den, and a larger bedroom, with a window that looked down onto the lock-up garages and wheelie-bin store at the rear.

She'd given the whole place a lick of white paint which had brightened it a little, and hung some pictures and family photographs, but it did not feel like home – and never would. Hopefully, she would be out of here soon and moving into her dream flat, thanks to the sale of her old place going through, and some financial help from her parents with the deposit. It was airy and spacious, on the top floor of the Royal Regent, a Regency house conversion on Marine Parade in Kemp Town, with a huge suntrap of a balcony facing the English Channel, and fabulous views of the marina to the east and Brighton Pier to the west.

She had been advised by the police not to drive her beloved 1973 convertible Volkswagen Beetle, as it was too conspicuous. So it now sat, forlornly, in a lock-up garage she had rented nearby, and she took it out only very occasionally to keep the battery charged and everything turning over.

She poured the last of the bottle of Sauvignon Blanc she had opened earlier, when it was obvious she wasn't going anywhere tonight with Karl. *Men*, she thought angrily. *Sodding, bloody men*.

But this was so out of character.

After the nightmare of these past years that she had been through, Karl Murphy had seemed a total breath of fresh air. She'd been introduced to him by her best friend, Raquel Evans, a dentist. He was a doctor in the same medical centre as Raquel, and a recent widower. His wife had died from cancer two years back, leaving him with two small boys. According to Raquel, he was now ready to move on and start a new relationship. Raquel had had a feeling the two of them might hit it off, and she'd been right.

Early days, but they'd had dinner a few times, and then last Saturday, with his sons staying overnight with his late wife's parents, they'd slept together for the first time, and spent much of Sunday together. Karl had told her, with a big grin, that he must be quite sweet on her to have sacrificed his regular Sunday-morning golf game.

It was a little bit early in their relationship to be a golf widow, Red had replied, with an equally big – but pointed – grin. They'd spent Sunday morning in bed, then they'd gone to the Brighton Shellfish & Oyster Bar, under the Kings Road Arches, for a seafood brunch of oysters and smoked salmon, followed by a blissful long walk along the esplanade. In the late afternoon, Karl had left to go and collect his boys, and they'd arranged their next date for tonight, Wednesday. He had planned to take the day off to play in a golf tournament and would be over straight after, he had said, to pick her up at 7 p.m.

So where was he? Had he had an accident? Was he in hospital? He hadn't told her which golf course he was playing at, so she had no idea where to begin phoning. She suddenly realized how little she actually knew about him, despite having checked him out. And probably how little about her he had told anyone.

She toyed with phoning the police, asking if there had been any accidents, but dismissed that. They'd heard enough from her over the past few years, with her frequent 999 calls after yet another of Bryce's violent attacks. The hospitals? *Excuse me, I'm calling to see if by chance Dr Karl Murphy has been admitted.*

She realized, though, from her past experience with men, that she was probably being too charitable. He was more than likely pissed, propping up the bar at the nineteenth hole of some clubhouse, and had forgotten all about her.

Sodding men.

She drained her glass.

Her fifth, counted the man watching her.

6

He continued to sit in the darkness, his binoculars to his eyes; she was still wearing a wristwatch that looked like it had come out of a Christmas cracker. What kind of a cheapskate was Karl, her wonderful new lover, not to have bought her a more expensive one? She'd returned the Cartier Tank watch he'd given her, along with all the other jewellery, when she'd dumped his bags out on the street and changed the locks on him.

Everything except the thin silver band on her right wrist.

He drew the curtains shut and switched the lights on again, then sat at the small round table and picked up a deck of cards. He fanned them out with just one hand, snapped them shut, then fanned them out once more. Practise. He needed to practise for several hours a day, every day, on his existing repertoire of tricks. Tomorrow he had an important gig, performing his close magic, table to table, at the Brighton estate agents' dinner.

Maybe Red would be there. He could give her a nice surprise.

Now you see the queen, now you don't!

Once my queen.

Still wearing the bracelet I gave you!

He knew what that meant. It was very Freudian. She needed to hang on to something he had given her. Because,

14

even though she might refuse to admit it, she still loved him.

I bet you're going to want me back, aren't you? Won't be long until you come begging, will it? You really do find me irresistible, but you just don't realize it. All women find me totally irresistible! Just don't leave it too long, because I won't wait for you for ever.

Just kidding!

I wouldn't take you back if you came crawling and begging. You and your hideous family and your ghastly friends. I hate the whole shitty little world you inhabit. I could have freed you from all that.

That's your big mistake, not to recognize that.

He looked at his watch. 11.10 p.m. Time to rock 'n' roll. He placed his mobile phone on the sitting-room table and picked up the keys of the rented Vauxhall Astra. He had parked it in his lock-up garage two streets away, and fitted it earlier with the false number plates copied from an identical car he had found in the long-stay car park of Gatwick Airport. Then he donned his black anorak, checking the pockets to ensure he had everything he needed, pulled on his black leather gloves, tugged a black baseball cap low over his face, and slipped out into the night.

7

Karl rolled around inside the pitch-dark carpeted boot of his car. He had a blinding headache, and he was shaking with fear, and with anger. He was determined not to panic, breathing steady calming breaths through his nostrils, doing his best to think clearly, to work his way out of the situation.

He was trying to figure out where he was and how long he had been here – and why the hell this had happened to him. Mistaken identity? Or had his assailant taken his keys and was now robbing his house? Or worse, going after his beloved children, Dane and Ben?

Jesus, what the hell must Red be thinking? She was at home waiting for him to pick her up. If he could only phone her . . . But his phone was in his trouser pocket and he was unable to move his hands to get to it.

He occasionally heard a vehicle passing, and guessed he had to be somewhere near a country road. They were becoming less and less frequent, which indicated it was getting later. Whoever had done this to him knew about bindings; he was unable to move his legs or his arms, or spit the gag out of his mouth, and he was suffering painful cramps. Nor did he know – and this frightened him a lot – how airtight the boot was. He was just aware that the faster he breathed, the more oxygen he would use up. He had to stay calm. Sooner or later someone would rescue him. He had to make sure his air lasted.

His mouth was parched and he had long since given up trying to cry for help, which made him choke on the gag, held tightly in place by some kind of tape which felt as if it was wound all the way around his head.

For Chrissake, there had to be a sharp object in here somewhere, surely? Something he could rub against and use to saw through his bindings? He nudged closer to his golf bag, heard the clubs rattle, and slid his arm bindings up against the edge of one of the irons. But each time he tried, the club just spun around without traction.

Help me, please, someone.

He heard the roar of a car, and the swish of tyres on the wet road. Hope rose in him. Then the sound receding into the distance.

Someone stop, please!

He heard the roar of another engine. The swish of passing tyres, then the squeal of brakes. *Yes! Oh God, yes, thank you!*

Moments later he felt a blast of cold air as the boot lid raised. A blinding light in his eyes. And his joy was short-lived.

'Nice to see you again, my friend,' said a suave male voice from behind the light. 'Sorry to have kept you, I've been a bit tied up. But not as much as you, eh?'

Karl heard the sound of something metal striking the ground, then a liquid sloshing around. He could suddenly smell petrol.

Terror swirled through him.

'You're a doctor, aren't you?' the suave voice asked.

Karl grunted.

'Do you have any painkillers on you?'

Karl shook his head.

'Are you sure? None anywhere in your car? You're a doctor, surely you must have some?'

Karl was silent, trembling. Trying to figure out what the hell this was all about.

'You see, doctor, they're for you, not for me. You'd be better off taking some. With what's about to happen to you. Please understand this is not your fault, and I'm not a sadist – I don't want to see you in agony, that's why the painkillers.'

Karl felt himself being lifted, clumsily, out of the boot, carried a short distance, then dumped down on wet grass. Then he heard the slam of his boot lid closing. 'I'm going to need you to write a note, Karl, if that's okay with you?'

He said nothing, squinting against the bright light of the torch.

'It's a goodbye note. I'll free your right arm so you can write it – are you right-handed?'

The doctor continued to stare, blinking, into the beam. He was close to throwing up. The next moment, there was a searing pain on his face as the tape was ripped away. Then the gag was tugged out of his mouth.

'That better?' his captor asked.

'Who the hell are you? I think you've got the wrong person. I'm Dr Karl Murphy,' he pleaded.

'I know who you are. If you promise not to do anything silly, I'll free your writing arm. Left or right?'

'Right.'

'Now we're making progress!'

Karl Murphy saw the glint of a knife blade, and moments later his right arm came free. A pen was thrust into his hand, then a sheet of lined notepaper was held in front of him. It was from a pad he recognized, that he kept in his medical bag in the car, clamped to a clipboard. He caught a glimpse of his captor, all dressed in black, with a baseball cap pulled low over his face.

The next moment he felt himself being dragged across the grass and propped up against something hard and un-yielding. A tree trunk. The clipboard, with the torch shining on it, was placed in front of him.

'Write a goodbye note, Karl.'

'A goodbye note? To who?'

'To *who*? Tut tut, Dr Murphy. Didn't they teach you grammar at school? To *whom*!'

'I'm not writing any damned note to anyone,' he said defiantly.

His captor walked away. Karl struggled, tugging desper-ately at his bindings with his free hand. Moments later his captor returned, holding a large, dark object. He heard the sloshing of liquid. The next instant he felt liquid being poured all over his body, and smelled the unmistakable reek of petrol again. He squirmed, trying to roll away. More petrol was tipped over his head and face, stinging his eyes. Then he saw, in the beam of the torch, a small plastic cigarette lighter, held in a gloved hand.

'Are you going to be a good boy, or do you want me to use this?'

A tidal wave of terror surged through him. 'Look, please, I don't know who you are or what you want. Surely we can discuss this? Just tell me what you want!'

'I want you to write a goodbye note. Do that and I'll go away. If you don't, I'm going to flick this and see what happens.'

'Please! Please don't! Listen – this is a terrible mistake. I'm not who you think I am. My name's Karl Murphy, I'm a GP in Brighton. I lost my wife to cancer; I have two small children who depend on me. Please don't do this.'

'I know exactly who you are. I won't do anything if you write the note. I'm going to give you exactly ten seconds. Write the note and that will be the end of it, you'll never see me again. Okay, the countdown starts. Ten . . . nine . . . eight . . . seven . . .'

'Okay!' Karl Murphy screamed. 'I'll do it!'

His captor smiled. 'I knew you would. You're not a fool.'

He straightened the clipboard and stood over him. A car was approaching. Karl stared, desperately hoping it might stop. A thicket of trees and shrubs and the man's handsome face were fleetingly illuminated. Then he could hear the sound receding into the distance. Thinking hard, Karl began to write.

When he had finished, the clipboard was snatched away. He saw the torch beam jigging through the trees, and again, alone in the darkness, tried desperately to free himself. He felt a twinge of hope as he picked at the plastic tape and a small amount came free, then tore away. He dug with his fingernails, frantically trying to find the join again. Then the torch beam reappeared through the trees.

Moments later, he found himself being hoisted into the air, slung over his captor's shoulder in a fireman's lift, and carried away, unsteadily, into increasing darkness.

'Put me down!' he said. 'I did what you asked.'

His captor said nothing.

'Look, please, I need to phone someone, she's going to be worried about me.'

Silence.

The journey seemed like an eternity, occasionally lit up by stabs of the torch beam into the wooded undergrowth ahead.

'Please, whoever you are, I wrote the note. I did what you asked.'

Silence.

Then his captor said, 'Shit, you're a heavy bastard.'

'Please put me down.'

'All in good time.'

A short while later Karl suddenly felt himself being dumped into long, wet, prickly undergrowth.

'Arrivé!'

Hope rose in him as he felt his captor begin to loosen and remove his remaining bindings.

'Thank you,' he gasped.

'You're very welcome.'

As his legs finally became free, although numb, he gave a sigh of relief. But it was short-lived. He saw his captor step out of his overalls and discard them on the floor. An instant later he felt himself being shoved hard over onto his side, then shoved again, and he was rolling, over and over, down a steep slope, for just a few moments, before he felt himself squelch on his back into mud.

Then a waterfall of liquid was tumbling onto his face and all over his body. Petrol again, he realized, in almost paralysing terror. He tried to sit up, to haul himself to his feet, but the petrol continued to pour down. Then in the darkness above him he saw the tiny flame of a cigarette lighter.

'Please!' Karl screamed, his voice yammering in fear. 'Please no! You promised if I wrote the note, you promised! Please no, please no! You promised!'

'I lied.'

Suddenly, Karl saw a sheet of burning paper. For an instant it floated like a Chinese lantern high above him, then sank, fluttering from side to side, the flame increasing as it fell.

Bryce Laurent stood well back. An instant later, a ball of

21

flame erupted, rising above him into the darkness. It was accompanied by a dreadful howl of agony from the doctor. Followed by screams for help that faded within seconds into choking gasps.

Then silence.

It was all over so fast.

Bryce felt a tad disappointed. Cheated, almost. He would have liked Karl Murphy to have suffered much more.

But hey, shit happened.

He bent down and picked up his overalls, which reeked of petrol, and walked back to his car.

8

Although it had been over three months now, Anthony Mascolo's sense of pride had still not worn off as he reversed his Porsche into the parking bay marked RESERVED FOR CAPTAIN.

Haywards Heath Golf Club, a few miles north of Brighton, was one of the county's most prestigious courses; becoming Captain had been his dream, and he felt a real sense of achievement at having accomplished one of his life's ambitions. Plus, as a bonus now that he had retired from running a hairdressing empire, he was able to devote all the time this demanding role required. It was such a joy to be able to play on a Thursday morning, like today, or indeed any other day of the week, without the guilty feeling that he was skiving off work.

He savoured the scent of freshly mown grass as he removed his golf bag and trolley from the boot of the car. It was just after 8 a.m. on a glorious, late-autumn morning, the fairways sparkling with dew, and the sun climbing low through a steely blue sky. There was a chill in the air and a sense of anticipation in his heart. If he could play again today the way he had been playing for the past two weeks, he had a real chance of his handicap dropping, for the first time ever, into single figures.

That would be such a damned good feeling!

Twenty minutes later, fortified by coffee and a bacon roll, he stood with three friends and fellow members beside the white tee of the first hole, practising his swing with his driver. *Thwack! Thwack! Thwack!* Oh yes, the lessons he'd been having with the club pro throughout the summer had improved his game no end, especially getting rid of his tendency to hook the ball left. He felt confident this morning, sublimely confident.

'Four-ball better ball, tenner a head?' his partner, Bob Sansom, suggested.

The other three nodded. Then Anthony Mascolo teed off first. A cracker, straight off the sweet spot; he raised his head and watched the dead straight flight of the Titleist 4. The ball rolled to a halt in the wet, shorn grass, a good two hundred and fifty yards ahead, smack in the centre of the fairway.

'Nice shot, Anthony!' all three of his companions said, with genuine warmth. That was something he loved about this game: it might be competitive, but it was always friendly.

His second shot took him to the edge of the green, and he sank it in two putts for a very satisfying par on the first hole.

As he knelt to retrieve the ball, he smelled, very faintly, the aroma of barbecued meat. Probably coming from one of the houses surrounding the wooded course, he thought, although it was a tad early for someone to be cooking a roast. But, despite his recent bacon roll, the smell was making him feel hungry. He patted his stomach inside his jumper, aware that he had put on weight since his retirement, then concentrated on filling in the score card.

As they reached the end of the second hole, which the Captain won again, the aroma of cooked meat was even stronger. 'Smells like someone's having a barbecue,' Bob

Sansom said. 'Pork chops – there's nothing like barbecued pork chops!'

'No, you want a rib of beef on the bone,' Anthony Mascolo said. 'The pink bits and the charred bits, they're the best!'

Terry Haines, a retired stock-market analyst, frowned and looked at his watch. 'It's a bit bloody early! Who's having a barbecue at 8.30 a.m.? I didn't think the halfway hut was open this early.'

There was a catering shack at the start of the tenth hole, which was open on most fine days, selling hot dogs, bacon sarnies and drinks.

'It's not,' Anthony Mascolo said.

'Hope it's not bloody campers again!' said Gerry Marsh, a retired solicitor.

They'd had problems on a couple of occasions during the summer with young holidaymakers camping illegally within the grounds of the club, but they had been politely moved on.

Anthony Mascolo teed off first; but, distracted by the smell, he sliced the ball, sending it way over to the right into a dense clump of trees and shrubbery, where there was only a slender chance of ever finding one's ball, let alone playing out of it.

He waited until the others had teed off, then played a provisional, again slicing it, but not so badly this time. It rolled to a halt a few yards short of the hedgerow and trees.

'Fuck it!' he murmured to himself, then strode off, his electric cart propelling itself along in front of him. His companions, all of whom had played decent shots landing on the fairway, strode over to help him look for his ball.

Taking an 8-iron from his bag, Mascolo stepped into the thicket, probing his way through a cluster of dying nettles, peering hopefully for the glint of white dimples that might be his ball. The smell of barbecued pork was even stronger here, and that made no sense to him. He lifted some brambles out of the way with his club head, trying to calculate from the path of the ball just how far it might have gone in – and what it might have struck and bounced off. Then, to his gloom, he saw the deep ditch on the far side.

It would be just his rotten luck that the ball had rolled into that. Then there really would be no recovery, and he'd have to play his provisional, which meant his next shot would be his fourth. No chance of a par on this hole.

'This smell is making me really hungry!' Bob Sansom said. 'I didn't have any breakfast because I'm trying to lose weight – now I'm bloody ravenous! I'm hallucinating roast pork and crackling!'

'Lucky for you I've got a jar of apple sauce in my bag!' joked Gerry Marsh.

'And I've got gravy and potatoes!' said Terry Haines.

Anthony Mascolo hacked his way through dense brambles to the edge of the ditch and looked down into it, gloomily expecting to see his ball lying at the bottom, probably half submerged in muddy water.

Instead, he saw something else.

'Oh my God!' he said.

Gerry Marsh joined him and peered down also. When he saw what his companion was looking at, he turned away, his complexion draining to sheet white, and moments later he threw his breakfast up over his two-tone golf shoes.

'Oh Jesus,' Terry Haines said, backing away shaking, his face drained of colour. 'Oh God.'

In the perverse way the human brain sometimes works, as Anthony Mascolo pulled his mobile phone out of his golf bag and dialled 999, he was thinking, *Hey, we're going to have to abandon our game here today, so I don't have to worry about screwing up this hole!* As the full horror of what he was looking at struck home, and the reek of Gerry Marsh's vomit hit him, he continued to stare, mesmerized, shaken to the core, then backed away, unable to look further.

A disembodied voice said, 'Emergency, which service please?'

It was coming from his phone.

He didn't know which service. He really didn't. 'Fire,' he said. 'Ambulance. Police.'

His phone slipped from his hands into the undergrowth, and he turned away. His head was spinning. He felt giddy. He clutched a thin tree trunk for support.

9

Detective Superintendent Roy Grace sat in his office on the second floor of Sussex House, which housed the Force Crime and Justice Department and the Brighton HQ of the Surrey and Sussex Major Crime Team. He was sipping the remnants of an hour-old coffee, which was now somewhere between lukewarm and tepid. Several stacks of paper lay on his desk, which, along with some sixty emails in his inbox, he had been steadily working through since 7 a.m., with his tired and addled 'baby brain'.

His son, Noah, now almost four months old, was not allowing him or his beloved Cleo much peace at night. But he didn't mind, he was still overwhelmed with joy at having become a father. Although just one night of unbroken sleep would be nice, he thought – and soon, hopefully, he would have four!

Saturday week, in just under ten days' time, he and Cleo were getting married. They'd originally planned their wedding, which had been subsequently postponed over legal difficulties in getting his long-vanished wife, Sandy, declared dead, to take place in a country church in the village where Cleo's parents lived; but they'd now decided on the pretty church in Rottingdean, a coastal village annexed to the eastern extremity of Brighton, because they both liked the vicar, Father Martin, who they had met on various occasions through their work.

They were heading off for a short honeymoon the following Monday to a surprise destination for Cleo – four nights in Venice. She had mentioned a couple of times in the past how much she had always wanted to go there. He was so much looking forward to that time with her, although he knew they would miss Noah badly – but not the sleep deprivation.

However, despite his intense love of Cleo, his joy was tinged with a dark shadow. Sandy. He could not escape the guilt that continued to haunt him; the fear that just maybe, while he was getting on with his life, and happier than he had ever been, Sandy might still be suffering somewhere at the hands of a maniac who had captured her and was keeping her prisoner – or that she had died, suffering a terrible death. He did his best to push these thoughts aside, in the knowledge that he had done everything humanly possible during the past decade to find her. He turned his attention back to his workload.

One stack of paper in front of him, the smallest and least urgent, had a yellow Post-it note on the top, with the wording, written in his new Lead Management Secretary's handwriting, *Rugby stuff*. He was President and Secretary of the Police Rugby Team, and needed to sort out several forthcoming fixtures. Another pile, also labelled with a Post-it note, contained a list of queries and requests from Nicola Roigard, the recently appointed Police and Crime Commissioner for Sussex. In addition to being the county's second most senior homicide detective, Grace also had responsibility for the ongoing work and reopening of many of Sussex's cold cases, and had to give her regular updates.

She was pleasant to deal with but sharp, and missed no tricks.

The third and most pressing stack – as well as the largest – was the paperwork he needed to complete, with the help of financial investigator Emily Gaylor, previously from the Criminal Justice Department, for the trial of the perpetrators of his most recent case, Operation Flounder, a nasty tie-up burglary in Brighton earlier in the year, in which the victim had died.

On his iPhone notepad he had a 'to do' list, which was the reserve list for their wedding. There was a limit on numbers, so every time they had a refusal they'd been able to add someone else from the waiting list. There were so many people he would have liked to have asked that it was really worrying him. What should have been a joyous occasion had turned into a major headache for them.

But one thing he was looking forward to was this evening's poker game, which he had played most Thursday nights for the past fifteen years with a group of friends, several of whom were police colleagues. It was his turn to host the game, and Cleo had been hard at work preparing snacks and cooking a coq au vin for the meal they always had halfway through the evening.

With particularly bad timing, he was the duty Senior Investigating Officer for this week, and he sincerely hoped that none of the average thirteen homicides a year that occurred in the county of Sussex would happen today and mess up his plans.

He dealt with the rugby club correspondence and then made his way to the tiny kitchenette that housed a fridge and a few basics to make himself another coffee. As the kettle came to the boil his mobile phone rang.

'Roy Grace,' he answered. Instantly, he recognized with dismay the voice of the duty Ops-1 Controller, Inspector Andy Kille.

It was not good news. Such calls never were.

10

Thursday morning, 24 October

'You okay, Red?'

No, I am so not okay, she thought. But that was not what her boss, Geoff Brady, at Mishon Mackay, the estate agency where she worked as a negotiator, would want to hear. Still not a word from Karl.

Bastard.

You complete bastard.

Why did you lie to me?

She looked up from the property details in front of her that she had been tasked with writing. It was a new instruction and a horrid little place in her opinion. A tiny terraced house, overshadowed by an industrial estate next to it, on a busy hill with endless traffic day and night. It fronted straight onto the road, had no parking facility outside, and a sunless backyard just about big enough to exercise a lame gerbil in. 'I'm fine,' she said.

Geoff Brady smiled. He always smiled. Forty-five years old, a dapper dresser with an Irish accent, he exuded charm. If he'd been told the world would end tomorrow, he would have kept smiling, and still managed to sell a property to someone. 'You've a worried look on your face,' he said.

'I'm good.'

He peered down at what she had written on her computer screen.

Period bijou terraced cottage within five minutes' walk of Hove station, close to the recreation ground and all the amenities of the much sought after Church Road district. In need of some modernization, this period property comprises two ground-floor rooms, a separate kitchen and cloakroom, and two bedrooms upstairs, with separate bathroom, all nicely proportioned. A unique opportunity to acquire a city-centre property.

'Hmm,' he said thoughtfully. 'Mention that it's handy for the buses.'

It was, she thought. There was a bus stop almost outside, so close the engines made every room shake. 'Okay, good point.'

'*Charming*,' he said. 'People always like that word. You have two *periods*. Change the first one to *charming*.'

'*Charming* bijou terraced cottage?'

'Yes,' he said. 'I like that. That has a nice ring to it. What about photographs?'

She clicked to bring them up, feeling proud of her artistry with her camera. Brady peered at them. 'These are terrible – who took them?'

'I did,' she said, a tad crestfallen.

He pointed. 'Look, the toilet seat's up in that one! There's a bottle of bleach on the draining board there. There are clothes strewn everywhere in that bedroom. You can't put photographs like that on any property details. The place has to look immaculate.'

'I'm sorry,' she said.

'You'll get the hang of it. But you'll need to retake those. How many viewings do you have today, Red?'

'Twelve so far,' she said. 'I'm working on some more.'

He nodded. The daily target was fifteen viewings for each negotiator. 'Okay,' he said, and moved on.

The large open-plan office was themed in white, and partially screened off from the front of the premises by a low wall. A giant clock was fixed above them as if there as a reminder never to waste time, and on one wall was a gridded whiteboard captioned, with a thick blue marker pen, *COUNTDOWN £164,000 to go!* It was the target remaining for commission for this branch of the estate agency chain to try to achieve before the year-end. Running down the left was a list of properties, starting from £165,000 and rising to £3,500,000, with the number of viewings to date listed alongside.

The negotiators all adhered to a strict dress code – the men in suits and ties and pale shirts, the women in conservative clothes and shoes that were suitable for endless climbing up and down staircases. It was early still; they'd just had their morning meeting and now everyone was settling down to the business of the day. The place smelled of a combination of coffee and a whole range of colognes, aftershaves, eaux de toilette and perfumes. Outside, the rush hour was just winding down. It was 9.30 a.m.

There was a team of nine altogether in this branch, and the firm was doing well, but Red was a relatively new kid on the block, having spent the last twelve years doing a variety of secretarial jobs before finding her niche, and she was still learning. Through the window, if she sat up straight, Red could just about see out onto the wide, busy shopping precinct of Church Road in Hove and the Tesco superstore across the road.

She yawned. Her eyes felt raw from an almost sleepless night waiting for the phone to ring. Or a knock on the door. She was in denial, she knew, about having been stood up by Karl. Dumped. But it was totally out of character, or so she thought.

She really had thought that Karl was different. Unlike dickhead Dominic, then Bryce, who had been totally possessive about her to the point of obsession, Karl seemed so gentle and normal. He always asked her how her day had been, what she had done, and seemed to really like hearing about the properties she had shown to clients. Bryce had only ever been interested in telling her about *his* day, and sometimes trying out a new magic trick that he was working on. Then flying into a temper and lashing out at her at the slightest thing.

Men were shits, shits, total shits.

She had actually allowed herself to think that she and Karl might have a future. He was the first man she had met whom she could imagine having a child with. From the way he talked about his children he seemed to be a wonderful father. At least that's what she had thought up until only yesterday.

But not after being stood up.

She read through the details of the property, then added in the word that her boss had suggested. *Charming* bijou terraced cottage.

She felt a pang in her heart. In spite of her anger and disappointment, she was missing Karl, dammit. She pinged him a text.

What happened? I waited all night. R u ok?

Then, for good measure, she sent him an email as well.

Karl, I'm really worried. Are you okay? If you've dumped me, at least let me know.

Ten minutes later she dialled his number, and again it went straight to voicemail. She left yet another message. 'Karl, it's Red, please call me.'

Then she froze.

Bryce was standing outside, in a hoodie, staring in. Staring at her.

An instant later, he was gone.

She dashed from her desk, ran to the front door, and out onto the pavement. A bus roared past, followed by a delivery lorry. She looked up and down, saw other shoppers, but no sign of Bryce. He had a distinctive swagger of a walk, like he owned the pavement, which always made it easy for her to pick him out in a crowd. A taxi in the Streamline livery suddenly pulled away from the kerb a hundred yards or so to her left.

Was he in that?

Or had she imagined this?

No, she was certain, she had not. He was clever, wearing a hoodie so she could not recognize him clearly. But then he had always been clever. If only he used his brain for something constructive, instead of just finding endless – and sometimes ingenious – ways to make her life hell, he might be a happier person himself.

But as her father, a retired solicitor, told her, someone like Bryce would never change. Which meant she would have to spend the rest of her life looking over her shoulder.

And through windows.

11

Bryce Laurent yawned. He was so excited by the successful activities of last night that he'd barely slept a wink, and his breakfast shift here in the kitchen doing the laundry had started at 5 a.m. He didn't need the money and he loathed the work, but he had a very definite purpose. It was physical, hot, and the smell and chemicals were not pleasant. Several times since starting here he had gone home with a raw throat and a headache from the fumes.

But not for much longer, if all went to plan. And he had every reason to believe all would go to plan. He'd practised in his workshop several times, simulating the same conditions, and he had prepared for today with fastidious care. He was looking forward to it a lot.

The thought made him smile, and not a huge amount had done since . . .

He winced.

Sometimes it was just too painful to think about. In his mind, his life was carved up into three distinct segments. The years which it seemed, in retrospect, he had sleepwalked through before he had met Red. Then with Red he had come alive, truly alive. It had been the most intense, magical, thrilling time ever. And now this kind of colourless, angry half-life. This unbearable segment of his life – post-Red. The endgame. The closing weeks of her life, and his.

There were big lessons to teach her and her nasty parents before it was over for them all. Before she would be ready to say the words he now wanted to hear so much. The last words she would ever utter:

I'm sorry.

12

Thursday midday, 24 October

A fire engine, two police cars and a paramedic's car were parked on the grass on the third fairway of Haywards Heath Golf Club.

Roy Grace radioed the local DI, Paul Hazeldine, who had requested his attendance and, accompanied by newly promoted Detective Inspector Glenn Branson, followed the agitated Club Secretary on foot. Ahead, he could see a strip of blue and white crime scene tape fluttering in the breeze, with a uniformed PCSO scene guard standing in front, and a small Crime Scene Investigators' changing tent nearby. The tall figure of Detective Inspector Hazeldine appeared, in a protective oversuit, and ducked under the tape.

The smell of burnt human flesh messed with your mind, Roy Grace thought. It reminded you of roast pork, which made you feel hungry, until you saw the human cadaver. Then it twisted your mind inside out, making you feel guilty at such a terrible thought. Yet still hungry at the same time.

They passed a group of golfers standing with their bags and trolleys by the clubhouse, and Grace heard an indignant voice.

'Look at the bloody ruts! Did they have to drive over the fairway? What if a ball lands there? And when the hell are they going to let us back on the course?'

Resisting the temptation to turn and give the man a

piece of his mind, they walked across to the DI, who greeted them with a grim expression and brought them up to speed.

Hazeldine had urbane good looks, and normally an irrepressibly cheery demeanour. Roy Grace had once crewed with him in a Response car in Brighton way back when they had been uniformed PCs.

'Good to see you, Roy, and thanks for coming out.'

'Good to see you, too, Paul.'

Hazeldine peeled off a glove and shook hands with both men.

'So what have we got?'

'Single body, heavily burnt. There's a petrol can nearby. We're conducting a search of the immediate area.'

'Do we have a name?' Grace asked.

'No, not yet.'

Grace and Branson went into the tent, sat on plastic chairs and wormed their way into protective oversuits and then overshoes.

Branson sniffed several times. 'Long pig,' he said.

'*Long pig*?' Grace replied.

'You don't know about *long pig*?'

'No.'

'You mean, I actually know something you don't?' He grinned.

'What is it?'

Branson shook his head. 'It's what cannibals in Papua New Guinea call white men. Apparently you taste like pork.'

'Thanks a lot. And what do you taste of?'

'They don't eat black men.'

The pair signed the scene guard's log and ducked under the blue and white police crime scene tape. They then followed DI Hazeldine along the route that was marked by more tape, through the brambles to the edge of a ditch.

And looked down.

'Shit!' Glenn Branson said.

Roy Grace said nothing, absorbing the sheer horror of what he was staring at.

'Did you ever see *A Nightmare on Elm Street*?' Glenn asked, a touch irreverently.

Grace knew what he meant. What lay in the ditch was like a prop from a horror movie.

He so wished it was a prop.

The body lay on mud, with burnt undergrowth all around, fists raised in the air as if about to punch some unseen adversary.

With the blackened skin, hairless skull and empty eye sockets, it looked like some gruesome modern sculpture that had been stolen from an art gallery.

Except for the smell of cooked meat. And the petrol can nearby.

Bile rose up in Roy Grace's throat and he took a step back. He'd not thrown up at the sight of a corpse since his very first post-mortem as a fledgling police constable at Brighton and Hove Mortuary. It had been when the mortician had held the rotary bandsaw, ground its teeth through the skullcap of the deceased lying on the steel table, severed the optic nerves with a Sabatier carving knife, and lifted out the brain.

He'd done then what over half of police officers attending their first post-mortem do. Turned bright green and staggered out of the room. After a cup of sugary tea and a digestive biscuit he'd regained his composure and seen the rest of the post-mortem through. But that evening when he had gone home, he had gulped down three whiskies in a row, and when his then wife, Sandy, had arrived home, he'd looked at her with X-ray eyes, seeing her coiled intestines, as well as the rest of her internal organs. It had been a good two weeks before he had been able to make love to her again.

In the ensuing years, he had got over it. But there were some homicide victims that still got to him. One had been the remains of a man in a burnt-out car on Ditchling Common – the victim of a gay hate crime. He had found it really hard to get his head around the knowledge that the twisted, charred, hairless sculpture had once been a living human being.

Like this one below him now.

He stared at one detail, the large wristwatch, charred and melted beyond recognition. Fixating on this inanimate possession as a way of avoiding looking at the body itself, he turned to Hazeldine. 'Who found this person?' he asked.

'Some members playing a round of golf, Roy.'

Grace had taken up golf some years back, but had not found it easy. Sandy had resented the amount of time it took on top of the long hours he worked and, in fairness to her, he had agreed and given up, deciding reluctantly that it wasn't his game. 'Where are they?'

'In the clubhouse. I asked them to wait. They're not too happy.'

'The person in the ditch isn't either,' Grace retorted drily. He resisted the temptation to climb down and take a closer look, not wanting to contaminate the scene any further. And besides, what he could see confirmed what he had been told.

Hazeldine's radio crackled. He spoke into it, then turned to Roy Grace. 'It seems like we've found a car half a mile up the road, which may be linked to the victim, although as yet we do not have any positive ID.'

'Yes?'

'Apparently the keys are in the ignition and there's a suicide note in the car. The Crime Scene Manager David Green's at the vehicle,' Hazeldine informed him. 'He's currently checking over the car. Crime Scene Investigator Claire Dennis had a brief look around the body, but hasn't found anything to indicate foul play. There's some petrol left in the can, and there is a search team on their way to see if we can find a match or a lighter.'

Grace shook his head. 'Christ, what a hell of a way to go. I think if I was going to top myself, I hope I'd have the presence of mind to find a less horrible way.'

Hazeldine nodded. Glenn Branson did too.

All the time, Grace's mind was in overdrive. Suicide? Someone had once told him that barbiturates were the best way to kill yourself. You just went out feeling pleasantly woozy.

Self-immolation in a muddy ditch?

How agonizing would that have been? Shit.

He turned away and said to DI Hazeldine, 'Let's go and see the car.'

Grace and Branson followed the DI along a network of paths, passing a sign saying, BUGGIES THIS WAY, through a clearing in the woods, and arriving at a narrow country lane. An Audi estate, encircled in blue and white crime scene tape, was parked on the grass verge, with a uniformed PC scene guard in front. The tailgate was open and a figure in protective clothing was carefully inspecting the contents of the rear of the car. Another SOCO was taking photographs of the exterior of the car.

'How are you doing, David?' DI Hazeldine asked.

The Crime Scene Manager turned and flipped back his hood as he saw Roy Grace. 'Hi Roy!' he said, with a broad smile. 'Didn't know you were a golfer! What's your handicap?'

'Not my game. Had a go a few times but I was rubbish.'

'Me too – water hazards get me every time.'

Grace gave him a wry smile. Humour was what got all coppers through the grimmest stuff. 'So what do you have in the car?'

'We've just had confirmation of the car's owner from the PNC. A Dr Karl Murphy. Address in Brighton. There's a golf bag and shoes in the back. And a suicide note on the front seat. Shit handwriting, but that's doctors for you.' He went around to the front, opened the driver's door and pointed.

Roy Grace saw a note inside a plastic evidence bag lying on the front seat. He snapped on a pair of gloves from his pocket, picked up the bag and studied the note. It was on lined paper, torn from what looked like a ringed notepad.

I am so sorry. My will is with my executor, solicitor Maud Opfer of Opfer Dexter Associates. Life since Ingrid's death is meaningless. I want to be united with her again. Please tell Dane and Ben I love them and will love them for ever and that their Daddy's gone to take care of Mummy. Love you both so much. One day, when you are older, I hope you will find it in your hearts to forgive me. XX

He felt moisture in his eyes. Could this ever be him? If something happened to Cleo, would Noah one day be handed a note telling him that his daddy had left him?

God forbid.

He read it through once more with a frown. Then he laid it back on the seat, pulled out his phone, took a photograph of it and also used his scanner app.

He turned back to DI Hazeldine. 'It does appear at the moment that this is a suicide, and not something for us. But I'd like you to get the note tested for prints. Get it copied and then send the original to the lab at Sussex House. I'll leave

DI Branson here, and send someone from Major Crime Team over to assist him with making enquiries, but my sense is it's a divisional matter that you can deal with locally. But I'd like to have the car lifted and secured in case we need to do a fuller forensic examination of it after the PM findings.'

'I appreciate you coming over, Roy. And good to see you again. We should have a beer sometime and catch up.'

'That sounds like a plan,' Grace replied. He was feeling relieved. If this had turned out to be a murder investigation, he would have had to cancel his boys' poker game at home tonight, which would have meant he would have been eating the coq au vin that Cleo had prepared for several days to come.

Thank God, he thought a tad irreverently, she had not decided to give his poker boys roast pork.

But at the same time, something was bothering him.

Before he'd left the scene, Roy Grace had got Dave Green to conduct a cursory search of the body, which had resulted in the recovery of a charred mobile phone, which he'd had sent to the High Tech Crime Unit for analysis.

Deep in thought, Roy headed back to Sussex House, leaving his colleagues at the scene. Something troubled him about the suicide note, but he could not put his finger on what it was exactly.

13

'Take a card,' Matt Wainwright said, knowing he needed to keep practising. 'Any card, any one you like! Don't let me see it!' Then with a flick of his hand he fanned the entire deck out, presenting them to Bobbie Bhogal, one of his fellow fire officers on the Blue Watch at Worthing Fire Station.

'Remember it, okay?'

Bhogal nodded.

'Now put it back!'

Bhogal slipped it back.

Instantly, Wainwright flicked the fanned-out cards back into a neat stack. 'All right, all right, now tap the top of the deck for me, will you?'

Bhogal tapped the top of the deck.

Moments later a card jumped out of the pack, flipped over a couple of times, and landed on the floor, face down.

'Wait! Don't touch it! Tell us all which card you took out, Bobbie.'

'The queen of hearts.'

'Turn it over!'

He leaned forward and turned the card over. It was the three of clubs.

All ten of the fire officers in the room laughed. 'Guess you screwed up, Matt!' Darren Wickens, the Blue Watch Commander, said.

'Oh yes?'

'Unless you're brain dead, Bobbie here chose the queen of hearts. That's the three of clubs. In case you're blind!'

Another roar of laughter.

'Tap the deck again, Bobbie!' Matt said.

Bobbie Bhogal obliged. Another card jumped out of the pack and flipped over, again landing face down.

'Turn it over.'

Bobbie Bhogal reached down, then held the card up for them all to see. It was the jack of spades.

'You're so full of shit, Matt!' another colleague said.

'Got any more tricks?' said another. 'Do that one you did last week where we all had to remember three of them?'

Wainwright said nothing for some moments, then he turned to Bobbie Bhogal. 'What do you have in your pocket?'

'Cigarettes.'

'Anything else?'

Bhogal patted his breast pocket. 'Yeah, my wallet.'

'Open it.'

'Careful!' someone shouted. 'Watch the moths fly out!'

There was another roar of laughter.

Bobbie Bhogal pulled out his wallet and held it up.

'Tell us the time, Bobbie,' the magician said.

Bhogal looked at his wrist. 'Shit! Where's my fucking watch?'

'Can you describe it?'

'It's a Casio, with a brown leather strap.'

Matt Wainwright held up his wrist. He was wearing a Casio with a brown strap. 'Might this be it?'

Bobbie Bhogal glared at it, hating to be made a fool of.

'Now, Bobbie, look inside your wallet. Tell me what you see?'

Bhogal pulled out a playing card and looked astonished.

It was the queen of hearts. 'Shit!' he said. 'Bloody hell! How did you do that, Matt?'

'If I tell you, I'll have to kill you!'

Moments later the siren went off. Three lights flashed up on the wall above them. One light signalled one appliance was required – for something small such as a vehicle on fire. Two required both duty crews. Three meant the reserve appliance was also required. That only happened for major incidents. The reserve was manned by volunteers who lived and worked within four minutes' drive or bike ride of the station.

All of them instantly leapt to their feet, hurried out of the mess deck, past the sofas and armchairs, and the rarely used snooker table in the recreation room. The Watch Commander, who had gone first, opened the door to the pole hatch, then in turn they slid down into the muster room, and ran out to the huge garage where the fire engines – the big red toolboxes, as they called them – sat. At the start of the shift, they had each placed their uniforms and boots at their allotted stations outside the vehicles, their boots tucked into their trouser legs like children's.

Less than one minute and fifteen seconds after the alarm had first sounded, all of them except the drivers, because they could not drive in boots, had changed into their fire-fighting kit; the garage doors slid upwards and the first two engines, blue lights strobing, sirens wailing, pulled out onto the forecourt, and then, as the traffic stopped for them, out onto the road.

14

'Shall we start upstairs?' Red said, as brightly as she could. She'd been feeling terrible all day.

The young couple nodded in unison.

'I love these houses,' Red continued, as she led the way. 'The Edwardians knew how to build solid homes that would last. And Portland Avenue is such a lovely street!'

'Which are the local schools?' asked the heavily pregnant woman as they reached the landing.

'Well, the New Church Road area is really well served, Mrs Hovey. There are several schools including Deepdene, a private nursery school, and St Christopher's, just five minutes' walk away, which is also private and has a terrific reputation.'

Her husband peered around with a dubious expression. 'Rather a small landing, Sam,' he said.

'Ah, yes,' Red replied. 'The thing is, the architect clearly felt the size of the bedrooms was more important. I'll begin with the smallest.' She pushed open the door and waited for them both to enter. 'It would make the most perfect room for your baby, don't you think?'

It was pleasant, with a south aspect onto the side wall of the neighbouring house.

'It would!' the pregnant woman exclaimed. 'Delightful!'

'Not much light,' her husband said.

He was a good-looking man, dressed in a nice suit. His wife was pretty and sparky. Red felt a pang of envy as she saw them hold hands, evidently much in love. They'd sold their flat and were cash buyers, and this was within their price range. She could see them setting up home here, in this semi-detached three-bedroom house just north of New Church Road, a quiet residential area of the city that was close to the sea and within walking distance of a large shopping area. She could see them pushing the buggy around these streets.

She could happily live in a house like this herself. Up until yesterday, she could have imagined living here with Karl, and being pregnant with his child. How amazing might that have been? Her parents hadn't met Karl, but she knew they would have really liked him. Her mother, a life coach, was an astute judge of people. She had disliked Bryce from the get-go, but back then Red had been totally smitten with him, and all her mother's words of warning had fallen on deaf ears.

She and her mother had fallen out big time over Bryce, and later he had blamed her parents for being behind their break-up.

It wasn't until her mother had showed her the evidence that she had finally been forced to realize the truth. That everything about Bryce was a lie.

She had been a lot more careful with Karl, surreptitiously checking out his background – which had made her feel sneaky, but safe.

'Now, this is a really nice size spare bedroom – with its own en suite bathroom,' she said, saving the stunning master bedroom – one of the property's best selling points – until last. She held the door open.

'Yes!' Mrs Hovey said.

'Your parents would be happy with this room when they come to stay,' her husband said.

Promising, Red thought.

Then she led them across the landing to the pièce de résistance. She opened the master bedroom door, waited until they had entered and were absorbed in looking around, then tapped the Sky News app on her phone, hoping desperately, forlornly, for some news of Karl.

'Wow!' Mrs Hovey said. 'You're right, this is a stunning room!'

'The bathroom's a bit disappointing,' her husband said.

'We could change it, darling. It's a fabulous bedroom!'

Red wasn't listening. She was staring at the news. Unable to take her eyes off the screen.

15

The charred body lying in the ditch at Haywards Heath Golf Club looked even more eerie under the glare of the spotlights, if that were possible, thought Glenn Branson. He was standing with DS Bella Moy, who Roy Grace had dispatched from the Major Crime Team to join him. Both of them were feeling cold in the chilly autumnal air behind the screens that had been erected to enable the Home Office Pathologist, Dr Frazer Theobald, who was conveniently in the area for another post-mortem, to view the body in situ. Although it looked very much like suicide, foul play had to be ruled out.

A little earlier, he'd had to deal with an irate Club Secretary, James Birkett, who felt the police were being over the top in closing down the entire golf club, and demanded to know when his members could resume playing. He had been extremely unhappy when Glenn had told him, apologetically, that it would depend on whether or not the pathologist was satisfied there was no foul play. If he was not satisfied, it meant it could be several days before this part of the golf course at least could reopen.

In an attempt to mollify him, and masking his irritation, Glenn Branson had asked the Secretary how he would feel if this man was a member of his family – would he not want the police to do everything possible to find the perpetrator, and not take the risk of golfers trampling a vital piece of evidence into the ground?

Under the harsh lights the corpse seemed even more like a prop from a horror movie, and despite all his experience, Glenn found himself having to remember that this was a human being, someone's son, and, more than likely, someone's loved one. As the pathologist worked his painstakingly thorough, methodical, slow way around the body, Glenn tentatively put an arm around Bella's shoulder. You had to be so careful in the police in this new politically correct age. One false move and you could find yourself up on a disciplinary charge of sexual harassment.

He fancied Bella like hell. Although his wife, Ari, had died only a couple of months ago, they had been living apart for over a year and before her sudden death, following a bicycle accident, she had started divorce proceedings. Even beneath the blue hood of her crime scene protective over-suit, Bella looked attractive. In her mid-thirties, she was not conventionally beautiful, but she had something about her face, and a good figure, and Glenn believed that if she would allow him to organize a total makeover – as he had once done with Roy Grace – she would really blossom.

There was one fly in the ointment, however. It seemed that at the moment she was dating one of his colleagues, Detective Sergeant Norman Potting. It was hard to understand what she could see in a four-times divorced, shabby, balding, pipe-smoking male chauvinist in his mid-fifties, and Glenn was determined to make a play for her. He felt her respond, a little, to the pressure from his right arm, and she moved closer, snuggling against him.

'I am soooooo cold!' she said. 'And starving.'

'Can't offer you any pork scratchings, I'm afraid.'

She shuddered. 'Yech! Thanks, Glenn.'

Suddenly her phone rang. She answered and Glenn strained to hear the voice of the caller, but was unable to. As Bella stepped away her whole demeanour changed. Her face was alive, animated. 'I'm just attending a rural suicide with Glenn. Call you later, depending on what time we get finished?'

Glenn watched the pathologist take a ruler measurement on the upper part of the victim's right leg. It never ceased to amaze him quite how different all the pathologists he worked with were. Short, tubby and jolly. Slender and beautiful. Tall and cynical. Wiry and deadly serious. This particular one, Dr Frazer Theobald, was a short, stockily built man in his mid-fifties, with beady nut-brown eyes; he sported a thick Adolf Hitler style moustache beneath a massive hooter of a nose and an untidy, threadbare thatch of wiry hair on his head. It was Roy Grace who had first mentioned it, and he totally agreed: Theobald would not have needed much more than a large cigar in his mouth, to have gone to a fancy dress party as a passable Groucho Marx.

After Bella had hung up, Glenn gave her a quizzical look, but she deliberately avoided eye contact. 'Glenn,' she said, 'if you need to go home, don't worry – I can stay on.'

'I'm okay,' he said.

'What about your kids?'

'Ari's sister is babysitting. They adore her, it's all cool.'

Then she looked at him tenderly. 'And you're okay, are you? It must have been terrible for you – your wife—'

She was interrupted by his phone ringing.

'Glenn Branson,' he answered.

It was quiet, methodical Ray Packham from the High Tech Crime Unit, who had stayed late in his office, with another colleague, to work on the charred phone that had been recovered from the victim.

'We've got lucky, Glenn,' he said, 'with the phone. If it had been an iPhone, which are encrypted, we'd have been stuffed. But this one's a Galaxy S11, and we're able to read the chip off the main board. We're still working on it, but I thought it might be helpful to you to know that someone has called this number several times in the past twenty-four hours.'

'Do you have the caller's number?'

Sounding very pleased with himself, Packham said, 'I do!'

16

Thursday evening, 24 October

There was a cool blast of air in the downstairs room of Cleo's townhouse, where Roy Grace sat around the makeshift card table with his poker buddies. Like some of the others, he had a cigar smouldering in the ashtray beside him. He checked the two cards in front of him – an ace of diamonds and a nine of clubs – as Sean Mcdonald, a recently retired Public Order Specialist Constable, dealt the flop.

The queen of hearts, ace of clubs and nine of spades.

Two pairs, aces on nines. This was potentially a good hand.

A pile of gambling chips lay in the centre of the table. Alongside each of the six players were tumblers of whisky or glasses of wine, piles of cash and chips, and a couple of overflowing ashtrays surrounded by fragments of crisps and nuts. There was a fug of smoke in the room which the draught from the open window was helping to clear. Cleo was upstairs, working on her Open University philosophy degree, with Noah asleep, his door shut against the cigar fumes, up in his bedroom.

Grace stared ruefully at his diminished pile of chips. He was too distracted to focus tonight. But with a hand like this he had to play. He tentatively put down two one-pound chips.

Bob Thornton, to his left, a long-time retired DI in his

mid-seventies, was by a wide margin the oldest of the group of regular players. They took it in turns to host an evening every Thursday, week in week out, year in year out.

The game had been going on long before Grace had joined the force. Bob was a frequent winner and, true to form, there was a mountain of chips and cash in front of the man right now.

Grace watched Bob hunch his shoulders as he checked his two hole cards, keeping them close to his chest, peering at them through his glasses with alert, greedy eyes. He opened and shut his mouth, flicking his tongue along his lips in a serpent-like manner. Grace, who reckoned he could read the man's body language, knew immediately he didn't have to worry about Bob's hand – unless he got lucky on either of the next two cards, the turn and the river.

But to his surprise, Bob Thornton matched his two pounds and raised him three. Grace eyed the rest of his companions. Gary Bleasdale, wearing a sweatshirt over a T-shirt, was a thirty-four-year-old detective in Brighton CID; he had a serious, narrow face beneath short curly hair; he was peering at his cards impassively.

Next to Gary sat Chris Croke, a motorcycle cop in the Road Policing Unit. With lean and wiry good looks, short blond hair, blue eyes and a quick-fire charm, Croke was a consummate ladies' man, who, thanks to having married a wealthy woman, seemed to live the lifestyle more of a playboy than that of a cop. He was a reckless and unpredictable gambler, and in seven years of playing with him, Grace found his body language hard to decipher. He never seemed to care whether he won or lost; it was much easier to read people who had something at stake. Croke now doubled the ante by raising a full five pounds.

Grace turned his focus on Frank Newton, a quiet,

balding man who worked in IT at Brighton police station. He rarely bluffed, rarely raised, and as a result rarely finished any evening up. Newton's giveaway was a nervous twitch of his right eye – the sure-fire signal that he had a strong hand. It was twitching now. But then, suddenly, he shook his head. 'I'm out.'

It was back round to Grace. He either had to raise his bet or drop out. He had two pairs and there were two more cards to come. No other aces or nines were showing. He tossed in a further eight pounds.

Then his mind went back to the suicide note which he had photographed on his phone and now knew by heart. And could not stop thinking about. He'd dealt with his share of suicides over the years, as well as two homicides in the past that had been set up to look like suicides. The pattern for every suicide was different, and who the hell knew what truly went on in the mind of someone about to take that terrible step?

From the little he knew about the victim so far, he was a well-liked and respected family GP. Dr Karl Murphy had gone to play in a golf tournament, and had played well. His sister had collected his two small sons from school, and had been waiting for her brother to return. He had confided to her that he had a date that night and was excited – and had a babysitter arranged.

The mindset of someone on the verge of suicide?

Another card had appeared face up on the table. The three of clubs. No sodding use at all to him, he thought. He looked again at the four cards on the table. With his hidden ace and hidden nine he was still in reasonable shape. There was a total bag of nails in terms of numbers and suits on the table. So it was unlikely anyone was holding a run or a flush in their hand. He pushed a five-pound chip forward, then, as he sank back into his thoughts, his phone rang.

Looking at the display, he saw it was Glenn Branson.

Stepping away apologetically from the table, he answered it.

'Sorry to wake you up, old timer.'

'Very witty!'

'Our suicide victim at Haywards Heath, yeah?'

'Tell me.'

'Frazer Theobald can't confirm it's suicide, at this stage, but he'll know more tomorrow after the post-mortem.'

'Is he suspicious?'

'No. But he needs to do a post-mortem before he can be certain.'

'Okay. Where are you? Still on the golf course?'

'I've been working on my handicap.'

'Haha!'

'Yeah, too fucking funny. It's bloody brass monkeys out here.'

'Roy!' someone called out. 'Are you in?'

Grace ended the call and returned to the table, and saw the final card, the river, was lying face up. It was the nine of hearts.

And suddenly his adrenaline was surging. With his concealed ace and nine he now had a full house. Nines on aces. He looked at the five open cards carefully, thinking hard. There was virtually nothing that could beat him, from what was showing. The only possible higher full house was if someone had two aces as their hole cards. He looked at his fellow players, then raised the bet to ten pounds.

Bob Thornton, tongue flicking again, raised to thirty pounds. Everyone else folded.

Grace studied the old detective for some moments. He

was bluffing, he was sure. He matched his bet and raised him by a further thirty pounds.

Thornton moved a further thirty pounds of chips forward. 'See you,' he said.

Grace flipped up his two hole cards triumphantly.

But his triumph was short-lived.

Thornton flipped his cards to reveal a pair of queens. 'Full house,' he said. 'Queens on nines.'

Grace grimaced as Thornton scooped the pot over towards his already massive pile of chips.

Thornton grinned at him, then flicked his tongue mischievously.

Bastard! Grace thought, realizing he had been out-smarted. The canny sod had worked out, somehow, that Roy had picked up on his little giveaway and had just now used it against him.

At that moment Cleo appeared. 'Supper's ready! How's everyone doing?'

17

Thursday evening, 24 October

Red sat in front of her television with a glass of wine in her hand, mesmerized by the images of the blazing restaurant, Cuba Libre, on the edge of Brighton's Lanes.

And deeply dismayed.

It was her favourite restaurant in the city, and it was where, in happier times, Bryce had taken her on their first date. It had a big, airy interior, with a great bar, comfortable sofas and a terrific menu. Karl, by coincidence, had also taken her there on their first solo date.

On the screen she watched a helicopter circling above the building. A reporter standing in the road, mike in her hand and surrounded by strobing blue lights, was shouting to the camera that the blaze, which had begun in the kitchen, was now out of control.

Red drained her glass, refilled it, and although she was making an effort to quit smoking to please Karl, she lit her third cigarette of the evening.

Then her doorbell rang.

Please God, be Karl!

She ran over to the intercom and stared at the tiny black-and-white video screen. And her heart sank. She saw two uniformed police officers.

She pressed the *speak* button. 'Hello?'

'Ms Red Westwood?' The female officer spoke. 'This is

Sergeant Nelson and PC Spofford from Sussex Police. I'm sorry to trouble you so late. Is it possible to have a word?'

Red's heart was pounding. Constable Spofford had been to see her on many of the occasions she'd called the police when Bryce was being violent to her, and she had met Sergeant Nelson before, too.

It was 10.30 p.m. Her nerves had been shot to hell after being with Bryce. Some months ago, at the suggestion of her friend, Raquel, who had read about the charity in the *Argus*, she had turned for guidance to the Sanctuary Scheme. On the day she had finally plucked up the courage to throw Bryce out, they had arranged the securing of the front door and windows, and the installation of a spyhole in the door. They had recommended she make a formal report to the police and press charges, but she hadn't wanted to do that and risk angering Bryce further.

Despite these precautions, she had still been concerned, which was why she had moved to temporary accommodation in this flat, in the hope that he would not be able to find her.

She walked out into the hall, past her expensive Specialized road bike, which she kept inside her flat after having had the previous one stolen. She had a second bike for getting around town, which she referred to as her *shit bike*, padlocked down in the hallway. If that one got stolen, it wouldn't matter too much.

'Come on up.' She pressed the buzzer, peered through the spyhole, because she could never be totally sure who might be out on the landing, then removed the safety chain, turned the key in the two deadlocks and opened the reinforced front door.

The stairwell light came on. She heard footsteps. Moments later she saw the familiar uniformed figure of Rob Spofford, his tall, trim frame almost dwarfing the petite figure of uniformed Sergeant Karen Nelson following behind him. She had wavy fair hair that bounced down as she took off her hat, and despite a composed demeanour she had a distinct presence of authority about her, Red thought, that no one sensible would want to mess with.

Her colleague had a friendly face beneath close-cropped dark hair that made him look much younger than his twenty-nine years, and gave him the air of a listener. And boy, Red thought, had he listened! On the frequent visits he had paid her, responding to her 999 calls, and then checking up on her during the days and weeks that followed to ensure she was okay, she had talked and he had listened and offered his wisdom. She liked him enormously, and he seemed wise beyond his years.

Red invited them in and closed the door behind them, then looked at them anxiously. 'What's . . . what's happened?'

'We need to ask you a few questions, Ms Westwood,' Sergeant Nelson said.

'Yes, of course. Would you like a drink? Tea, coffee, a glass of wine?'

The sergeant shook her head. 'No, thank you. But perhaps we could sit down.'

Red led them through to the sitting room, grabbed the remote and muted the television. 'Terrible, that fire,' she said.

'My wife's favourite restaurant,' Constable Spofford said. 'Not that we can afford to go there, except on very special occasions.'

The three of them stared at the silent images for some

moments after they had sat down. 'It's nice to see you, Rob – Constable – Spofford,' Red said, wondering if it was inappropriate to use his first name in front of his superior.

'Been a few months,' he said. 'All's quiet?'

'Yes. Maybe Bryce has moved away – or hopefully found someone new.'

'Good, I'm glad to hear it.' He looked a tad uneasy.

'Ms Westwood,' Sergeant Nelson said, 'records we've obtained from the O2 phone company indicate you've made numerous calls to one particular number during the past twenty-four hours.' She gave her the number. 'Is that correct?'

Red nodded hesitantly, suddenly feeling sick in the pit of her stomach. 'Why . . . why are you asking?'

The two police officers glanced at each other in a way that made Red feel extremely uncomfortable. Then the sergeant responded in a bland, impersonal way.

'The registered owner of this phone is a Dr Karl Murphy. Do you mind if I ask how you know him?'

The flickering images on the television screen were too distracting. Red grabbed the remote and switched the television off. 'Why? What . . . what's he done? Has something happened to him?'

'Can I ask what your relationship with Dr Murphy is?'

Spofford's phone started ringing. He removed it from his pocket, looked at the display and silenced it, giving his colleague and Red apologetic glances.

'We're going out together,' Red replied. Then she shrugged. 'He was meant to pick me up at seven o'clock yesterday evening and he never showed up. Why? Has he had an accident?'

'How long have you been seeing each other?'

She thought for a moment. 'About six weeks.'

'Without being too personal, Ms Westwood, how would you describe your relationship with Dr Murphy?'

'What is all this about?' Red asked, her nerves making her irritable. She looked at Spofford, but only got a blank expression and uncomfortable body language back from him.

The sergeant stared sympathetically at her and for a moment Red thought she was softening. But then she responded with the distancing, formal tone of a professional copper.

'I'm afraid you might want to prepare yourself. We've found a body, in strange circumstances, that might be Dr Murphy, and we think you might be able to help us.'

'A body?'

'I'm afraid so, yes.'

'What do you mean? He's dead?'

'We don't have formal identification at this stage. But we're pretty certain it is Dr Murphy.'

'It's not him, not Karl,' Red said emphatically. 'You've got that wrong. What makes you think it could be him?'

'Did you have any kind of falling out with him?' the sergeant asked.

Red shook her head resolutely. 'Absolutely not. Far from it. I thought that we . . .' Her voice tailed off.

Karen Nelson looked at her expectantly. After some moments she prompted, 'You thought what?'

Red shook her head. 'For one brief moment in my life, I thought that Karl might be different from other men, that's all. Then he stood me up last night.' She gulped down some wine, picked up her pack of cigarettes and shook one out. 'Mind if I smoke?'

'It's your home,' DS Nelson said.

'I love the smell,' Spofford said. 'Please go ahead.'

'Want one?' She offered him the pack.

'I'd love one. But no thanks.'

Red lit the cigarette. 'Please tell me what's happened? You said you found a body – has Karl had an accident?'

The two police officers exchanged yet another glance. And that glance told Red all she needed to know.

'Please tell me something, tell me what you know!' Red pleaded. 'Has he had an accident? Please tell me at least that!'

'Can we establish when you last had contact with Dr Murphy?' Sergeant Nelson replied.

'The last time I saw him was on Sunday. But we spoke every day – several times a day. I last spoke to him on Tuesday evening. He . . .' She hesitated. 'He told me he adored me.'

'Would you say that Dr Murphy was depressed at all?'

'Depressed? No! Well, let me qualify that. Yes, he told me he had been very depressed after his wife died. He told me at one point he had felt suicidal because he loved her so much. But he would never commit suicide, he said, because of their children. He couldn't do that to them.'

'He talked about suicide?' the sergeant pressed, and made a note on her pad. 'What exactly did he say?'

Red shook her head. 'He didn't talk about it in a serious way. He said it had gone through his mind – in the immediate aftermath of her death. But he totally dismissed it.'

'How sure are you of that?'

'That he couldn't kill himself? One hundred per cent. He's a bright guy, very positive. And he lives for his children. They are the world to him.' She felt engulfed in a dark cloud. 'Why . . . why are you asking me about suicide?'

'I don't want to cause you unnecessary distress, Ms Westwood,' Karen Nelson said. 'But the body that has been found that may be Dr Karl Murphy appears to be a suicide victim. We can't be sure at this stage, but the mobile phone recovered from the scene is the one you have been ringing.'

Red closed her eyes. 'Oh God no, please no, please don't let it be Karl.'

Sergeant Nelson raised her hands apologetically. 'I will give you more information as soon as I can, I promise.'

'Just to confirm, Red,' Spofford said. 'All has been quiet with Bryce Laurent for how long now?'

Red thought for some moments. 'Since we split up,' she said.

'Okay, good.' He made a note in his book. 'You've heard nothing at all? Not seen him anywhere?'

'Nothing, not a call, and I haven't seen him – well, I thought I might have seen him outside my office this morning, but I'm not sure. You were very helpful in bringing all that to an end, and I really appreciate it.'

'You thought you saw him this morning? Despite the exclusion order? He's not allowed within half a mile of you. Did you report it?'

'No,' Red said gloomily. 'I wasn't one hundred per cent sure. I might have imagined it. I went out and couldn't see any sign of him.' She shrugged.

The two officers stood up and Red showed them to the door. 'I think you have the wrong person,' she said. 'Karl and I were talking about, you know, the future. He wouldn't have committed suicide, believe me, please believe me. You have the wrong person.'

'I'll be in touch as soon as I have any more news,' Karen Nelson said.

PC Spofford gave her a sympathetic but helpless smile as he followed his colleague out. Red did not respond. She felt numb. She closed and locked the door carefully. Inside she was a mess of jelly.

18

Van *the man* was playing 'Someone Like You' on the stereo, and he was watching two different shows, both muted, on his twin fifty-five-inch Samsung screens. On one was the news, and on the other was all the television he needed, most of the time – except tonight.

Red loved this song. They had danced to it on their second date. *Someone like you!* he had whispered into her ear, and kissed her on the cheek. Then they'd kissed on the lips and they'd danced the entire song out, in a Brighton nightclub, without their lips ever parting.

He watched her return to her living room after seeing the cops out, pour a large glass of white wine, and light another cigarette.

Tut, tut, you are smoking too much, baby. But don't worry, smoke on! It's not going to kill you. Something else is going to get you long before those thin white sticks with the filter tips.

He watched her pick up the remote and turn up the volume on the news, but the fire at the Cuba Libre was no longer showing. Now it was the Prime Minister, in some factory that made soup, wearing a silly-looking protective hat and protective gloves, nodding approvingly as he supped from a large spoon.

Red was crying.

Bryce was crying too. He was staring at his laptop screen, looking through all the emails and texts she had sent him back in those early days when they had been so much in love.

> You're incredible! I miss you so much, my darling Bryce. I can't wait to see you tonight XXXXXXXXXXXXXXX

> God, my darling Bryce, what have you done to me? Every second without you is pure torture. I crave you. XXXXXXXXXXXXXXXXXXXXXX

> Did I tell you that you are the most amazing, incredible, smart, beautiful man I ever met in my life. I want you so badly. Just get over here as quickly as you can. I'm naked inside my clothes and waiting for you. XXXXXXXXXXXXXXXXXXX

You stupid girl, he thought, sniffing and dabbing his eyes. *You stupid, stupid girl. Remember that time we went to see* Othello *at the Old Vic in London? Remember that line? Like the base Indian who threw a pearl away, richer than all his tribe?*

Remember?

19

Two years earlier

Red had chosen her dress carefully, with the help of her best friend, Raquel Evans, who had accompanied her, for several hours that June morning, on a trek around Brighton's fashion shops. She'd finally settled on a simple black A-line dress from a boutique in Dukes Lane that both the assistant and Raquel, who was also a redhead, told her looked stunning – without being overtly sexy.

Black always suited her, and she had followed the Maître d' confidently across the floor of Brighton's elegant Cuba Libre restaurant, beneath the huge rotating bamboo ceiling fans, to a table in the corner.

Mr Laurent, he apologized, had not yet arrived. But as she reached the table she saw, to her surprise, a bottle of champagne in an ice bucket, and a red rose lying on the plate in front of the chair to which she was guided.

Would madame like a drink while she waited?

'I'm fine,' she had said, although in truth she was a bag of nerves and could have done with a seriously large cocktail.

She did not have to wait long. Within a few minutes, an apparition strode towards her. He was tall, with short black gelled hair, and looked like a young George Clooney. He wore a beautiful black linen jacket over a white open-neck shirt, expensive-looking jeans and dark-coloured loafers, and he had the most confident smile she had ever seen – with flawless white teeth. He was even better looking in the flesh than in his photograph.

'You are here before me – that is unforgivable of me! I am so sorry!' His voice was strong, with a faint transatlantic drawl. He took her hand and kissed it, and she smelled his very sexy, musky cologne, then he settled opposite her and said, smiling again, 'Wow! You are so not what I expected!'

She smiled at him. 'Oh?' She was thinking the same. How come such a gorgeous hunk needed to join a dating agency?

'No, really, I mean . . . I had a feeling, from your photo on the site . . . and all the ones on your Facebook page, that you would be lovely. But wow . . . not this lovely!'

'Well, to tell you the truth, you are a very nice surprise, too!' she said. 'And thank you for the flowers. That was really thoughtful of you.'

'You like champagne?'

'If you really twist my arm,' she said with a grin.

He raised a hand in the air and waved, and almost instantly a waiter came over and began opening the bottle.

'It's vintage,' Bryce said. 'Only the best for you.'

When their glasses had been filled, he raised his. 'So,' he said with a smile that almost melted her heart. '*Single girl, 29, redhead and smouldering, love life that's crashed and burned. Seeks new flame to rekindle her fire. Fun, friendship and – who knows – maybe more?*'

'God!' she said. 'It sounds so cheesy, hearing it back.'

'Not at all,' he said. 'It's what caught my eye. It's why we're here! I'm already having a good time. Are you?'

'I'm having a *very* good time.'

They clinked glasses.

He drank some and then said, 'You know, I've been a bit presumptuous. I'm told the menu here is very good, but I thought for our first dinner we should have something a little special. In one of your emails you said you liked shell-fish?'

'I do.'

'Excellent. I phoned and asked the manager to get us two lobsters. And to start, I thought we'd go off-menu also and I asked him to bring us Beluga caviar – does that suit you? It's the finest in the world.'

This all seemed so amazing, for a moment she wondered if it was a set-up. Had Raquel – or one of her other friends – done this? Like a Mr Hunk date-o-gram or something? But why would they? They'd never be so cruel, surely. She looked at his face and his eyes smiled back at her, full of laughter and life. This was real. Totally over the top, but definitely real.

'My God,' she said. 'Wow . . . but – I – I've actually never had caviar before – not real caviar. Just that lumpfish you get in jars.'

'Nothing is too good for you,' he replied. 'You are stunning, do you know that?'

'Thank you, but no, I don't.'

'Well, you are!'

They clinked glasses again.

Who was this Adonis of a man? It was like a dream. She'd kissed an awful lot of frogs since Dominic. Had she finally met a prince? She couldn't be intoxicated, not from just one sip of champagne, but she was definitely feeling a little bit tipsy. There was something about him she found deeply charming – and very sexy.

And yet, a caution bell was ringing in her mind.

'So in your emails, you never told me what you do?' he said.

'I work as a PA for a structural engineering firm,' she

said. 'Although, actually I've always fancied becoming an estate agent.'

'I've got contacts with several estate agents in the city. Just let me know and I can put you in touch with them.'

'Thank you! And what about you? What do you do?'

'Well, I used to be a pilot for United in the US, then I got a job as a private pilot for a Texan oil billionaire. Unfortunately my wife became sick with advanced breast cancer and I couldn't be away all the time my job required. I felt I needed to be around to look after her. She was from England, and she really wanted to come back here to spend her last days near her family. I managed to retrain and get a ground job as an Air Traffic Controller at Gatwick.'

'Like in the film *Pushing Tin*?'

'Yes, except it is not like that at all in reality.'

The caviar was served. It arrived in a silver bowl surrounded by ice, with tiny blinis and a mound of sour cream. The eggs were the size of miniature peas, a silver grey colour. She had never seen anything like them. They reminded her of large frogspawn.

Bryce showed her the way to eat it, by putting a tiny smear of the cream on a blini, then spooning the eggs on top, and popping it in his mouth with his fingers.

She copied him, then tried to mask her shock at the taste. Her first bite evoked the memory of her mother spooning cod liver oil into her mouth when she had a cold as a child. Then she felt the silky texture of the eggs themselves melting, and experienced a sudden frisson of excitement, realizing she was eating the world's most fabled and expensive delicacy.

'So?' he asked.

'Amazing!' she replied.

'You're amazing,' he said. Then from his inside pocket he suddenly produced a deck of cards, and with a flick of his wrist fanned them out perfectly so that every single card was visible.

'Wow! That's pretty impressive.'

He turned the fan away so that only she could see them. 'Select one. Just choose and touch it, but don't show it to me.'

She touched the queen of hearts. 'Okay, done.'

With another flick he snapped the deck shut. And with another he fanned them open again. 'Do you see the card?' he asked.

It wasn't there. She frowned and glanced down at the table wondering where it was. 'No,' she said. 'I can't see it.'

'Open your handbag.'

She leaned down, picked her handbag off the floor and popped the clasp. She opened it and gasped. The queen of hearts lay there between her lipstick and phone. She lifted it up.

'Was that the one you chose?' he asked eagerly.

'That's incredible! How did you do that?'

He shrugged. 'It's my hobby,' he said. 'I do close magic for fun. Have you heard of the Magic Castle in Los Angeles?'

Red shook her head.

'Have you ever been to LA?'

'No.'

'Maybe I'll take you there one day. Who knows?'

She grinned. 'I'd love to go to LA.'

'Are you missing anything?'

'Missing anything? I don't think so.'

He dug his hand into his side pocket and pulled out a watch. It was her white Swatch.

'How the hell?' she exclaimed.

He handed it to her and she clipped it back on her wrist. 'Okay, I'm impressed!'

'I'm impressed too,' he replied. 'With you.'

Against all her principles – and Raquel's advice – and partly because she was smashed at the end of the meal, she invited him up for coffee when, leaving the taxi waiting, he walked her to the front door of her building.

He stroked her face and ran his fingers through her hair, held both her wrists gently, then gave her a single light kiss on her lips. 'Not tonight,' he said. 'We've both drunk too much. When we make love for the first time, I want it to be special.'

She closed the door behind her, walked along the communal corridor, past her chained-up bicycle, and floated up the three flights of stairs. It wasn't until she entered her third-floor flat, in a modern block beside the River Adur with its view out over Shoreham Port, that she noticed the bracelet on her right wrist.

It was a narrow silver band, completely circling her wrist, which fitted snugly. Too snugly to have been slipped over her hand. She stared at it, bemused, wondering exactly when he had put it on. Just now, when he had held her wrists outside?

But more puzzling still, there was no clasp. It was solid, all the way around. She examined it carefully, tugging at it, but there was no join, no seam that she could find. On the surface she saw tiny engraved writing. She had to squint to read the words. *Queen of Hearts.* Followed by a heart symbol.

Then her phone pinged with an incoming text. She pulled it out of her bag and looked at the display.

WANT YOU DEAD

If you want it removed, you'll have to wait for our next date.

She texted back, **XXX**
And almost instantly the reply came. **XXX**

20

Friday, 25 October

Red sat at her tiny breakfast bar, red-eyed from a sleepless night and her chest feeling raw from having smoked far too many cigarettes. Her flat was a mess – its usual state. Her CDs and DVDs were strewn around on the floor beneath the television and stereo stack. She needed to have a good tidy-up, but at the moment that was the furthest thing from her mind.

Her laptop was open, displaying the front page headline of the *Argus* online. **Brighton restaurant destroyed in blaze**. There was a photograph of the Cuba Libre surrounded by fire engines, its beautiful grey facade blackened. It was 8.20 a.m. and she stared at the television, waiting for the local news to come on, spooning porridge into her mouth with no appetite and sipping her coffee. Outside it was pelting with rain, making her dismal view of the fire escape opposite even more dismal.

Suicide?

It wasn't possible. It was *so* not possible. It had to be mistaken identity. Whatever had happened to Karl, he had not killed himself. No way on earth.

She felt terrible. October was always a grim time of the year, with the prospect of months of winter ahead. And the prospect of a lousy weekend in front of her. Karl had talked about them going away to a hotel he knew in the New Forest.

That was clearly not going to happen now. Unless, miraculously, he contacted her.

Otherwise, Sunday lunch with her parents loomed. Red, the saddo single, and her elder, hugely successful sister, married and very smugly pregnant.

She felt she was the lame duck of the family. Margot, in addition to being married to a successful London hedge-fund manager, had her own meteoric career in a City law firm.

And here she was, struggling to write sales copy for a grotty little house that no one in their right mind would want to live in. And living in hiding herself.

Stalked by her ex, and her most recent date dead.

Could Bryce have had anything to do with that?

Absurd. She stared down at the bracelet. The one Bryce had slipped on her wrist, unnoticed, that very first date at Cuba Libre restaurant. She remembered that on their second date, when she had told him she could not remove it and asked him how the hell he had ever put it on, he had grinned and told her a magician never reveals his secrets. He would only take it off, he said, when she was no longer his.

The tarnished thin silver band had been on her wrist for so long she rarely noticed it. But she stared at it now. She had lost over a stone in weight in the past few months from worry, and the bracelet hung looser on her wrist. But still nowhere loose enough to slide it over her hand. She had toyed with going to a jeweller and asking them to cut it off, but something held her back from doing that. Fear?

Fear that if Bryce saw her in the street without it, it might antagonize him further?

Then she heard the words *golf course* on the television, and instantly looked up at the screen. She saw a cluster of police vehicles in front of a wooded area. Crime scene tape.

Officers in blue protective oversuits and a large screen. A male presenter, holding a microphone in his hand, hair matted by the rain and looking like he would rather be anywhere but here, said, 'Sussex Police have not yet released the identity of the charred body of a male found in a ditch, close to the third tee of Haywards Heath Golf Club yesterday.'

Red felt a tightening in her gullet. Was this Karl? God. Was it? She grabbed her phone and dialled Raquel's surgery number. But the answering machine kicked in. It was out of hours. She hung up and dialled Raquel's mobile number. She'd left messages the night before, but her friend had not got back to her.

'Sorry to call so early, Raq. Can you just tell me something – has Karl Murphy been in the office? I mean, was he in yesterday?'

Raquel's voice sounded strange. 'Sorry about last night, we were out at a dinner. No – no, he wasn't.'

'Maybe I'm going out of my mind . . . but I think something has happened to him. The police came and saw me last night about a body that's been found.'

'You're not going out of your mind. I think you could be right.'

'Why – why – what – why are you saying that?'

'I had to come in early – at the request of the police. Karl's a patient – they've asked for his dental records.'

On the television, the scene suddenly cut to a conference room. Against a curved blue backdrop of a display board bearing the web address www.sussex.police.co.uk and an artistic display of five police badges on a blue background – with Crimestoppers' number prominently displayed beneath – a slim, suited man, with short gelled fair hair and blue eyes, looking very serious, was speaking. Along the bottom of the screen ran the caption, *Detective*

Superintendent Roy Grace of Surrey and Sussex Major Crime Team.

'We are hoping to have a formal identification of this man later today,' he said. 'However, at this time the post-mortem results are inconclusive. I would appeal to anyone who was either on Haywards Heath golf course or in the vicinity between the hours of midday Wednesday and 9 a.m. Thursday, who saw anything suspicious, or who noticed any motor vehicle parked out of place, to come forward and phone the police, or Sussex Crimestoppers, on the following numbers . . .'

21

Bryce Laurent also had his television monitors on. All six of them. On one screen was breakfast television news. But it was a different one that interested him more. Red Westwood on the phone, talking to her best friend, Raquel.

He'd been out for meals with Red, Raquel and her husband, Paul, a local GP, as well as to the cinema and the theatre; they'd even spent a weekend away together, the four of them, in Bath. Raquel and Paul were all right. He hadn't exactly warmed to them, but they'd not been negative about him. Not the way Red's parents had been. Especially her bitch mother.

Dental records.

It wouldn't be long now.

And then, soon after, she would find out this was only just the beginning.

22

Roy Grace had barely slept all night. He had ended the poker game two hundred and fifty pounds down, one of his biggest ever losses in the game. He often found it hard to sleep after his poker evening, but last night had been worse than usual. It wasn't the loss that bothered him – over the years it all evened out, and it was the camaraderie of the poker evenings that he enjoyed even more than the game itself. It was the suicide note that did not feel right, that had kept him awake.

Now he sat at his desk, at 8.30 a.m. on Friday morning, sipping his second ultra-strong coffee of the day, staring at the overnight serials – the log of all reported incidents in the city – of which the major one was the Cuba Libre restaurant blaze. He felt a twinge of sadness about the restaurant. It was one of Cleo's favourite places, and they'd had some great evenings there.

But his thoughts continued to be dominated by the suicide note, which he had photographed on his iPhone.

I am so sorry. My will is with my executor, solicitor Maud Opfer of Opfer Dexter Associates. Life since Ingrid's death is meaningless. I want to be united with her again. Please tell Dane and Ben I love them and will love them for ever and that their Daddy's gone to take care of Mummy. Love you both so much. One day, when you are older, I hope you will find it in your hearts to forgive me. XX

There was something very clinical about it. It was carefully thought out. Was that consistent with someone who pours petrol over themselves? Who in hell would choose that kind of a death unless it was someone trying to make a statement, like a political or religious protestor? Surely a family doctor like Karl Murphy would have to be in a deranged state of mind to have done this? And if he was in that state, would he have written such a concise note?

He picked up the phone and called one of the regular members of his Major Crime enquiry team, Detective Sergeant Norman Potting. He asked him to obtain a sample of the doctor's handwriting from his secretary, then find a graphologist on the books of the College of Policing – which was now the principal research resource all forces used – and get it analysed, along with the suicide note, to establish for certain that they were both written by the same person.

He glanced at his watch. Just a few minutes before financial investigator Emily Gaylor was due in to continue working with him on clearing up Operation Flounder. Cleo had been asleep when he had left, much earlier this morning. It was strange, he thought. He had always loved his work, and it had come above everything else in his life. But now, since becoming a father, he found himself resenting having to be away from his son. He dialled Cleo to say good morning and to see how Noah was.

She answered on the third ring. 'Hi darling,' she said, sounding distracted.

'You okay?' he asked.

'Just giving Noah a feed. How was the poker in the end?'

'Don't ask!' he said. 'But the boys all loved the meal – they said to thank you.'

'They're a nice crowd.'

'They are.'

Suddenly she shouted out an agonized, 'Oww!'

'What's happened?'

'Noah just sucked my nipple really hard! It's as sore as hell!'

'God, there is so much they don't tell you about being parents. I just wish I could help you more.'

'Try growing some breasts!'

'Okay, I'll get hormone tablets!'

She cried out in pain again, even louder this time. 'Shit!' Then she said, 'You know what the weirdest thing is?'

'Tell me.'

'This might sound strange. But I was looking down at Noah in the middle of the night and I suddenly thought, you know, one day you might be pushing me around as a frail little old lady in a wheelchair!'

'Hopefully not for a few years yet!'

'You're right, darling. There's so much they don't tell you about becoming a parent.'

'True, but one day Noah's going to learn that he won life's lottery. He has the best mother in the world. Just remind him of that next time he bites you.'

'Owwwww!' she cried out in pain. 'Shit, that hurt!'

There was a knock on his door.

'I have to go.' He blew Cleo a kiss down the line, then hung up, smiling. He was filled suddenly with an almost overwhelming feeling of love for Cleo and for his son. Then he looked back at the suicide note once more. It was a big reality check.

It was really bothering him.

'Come in!' he called out.

23

Friday, 25 October

There were several things that Glenn Branson had in common with Roy Grace. High up on that list was the dislike of attending post-mortems. In modern investigations, although the crime scene was a major focus for all homicides, it was the mortuary – and the pathological laboratory – that were in many ways the crucible of any investigation.

But at 8.30 a.m. on a cold, wet Friday October morning, with its grim, grey tiled walls and stark overhead lighting, there were few more depressing places to be than the PM room of Brighton and Hove City Mortuary, Glenn thought.

The Detective Inspector stood, gowned up in green, feeling distinctly queasy at the sickly sweet roast pork smell, tinged with petrol, emanating from the charred corpse that lay on the steel table in the centre of the larger of the two areas separated by a square archway. The smell almost blocked out the normal reek of Trigene disinfectant and Jeyes Fluid that he associated with this place.

Over to his left, in the adjoining room, were three elderly people laid out, naked, on similar tables, their skin the colour of alabaster, buff tags hanging from their toes. They had been prepped by Darren, the Assistant Anatomical Pathology Technician, helped by the locum who was standing in for Cleo whilst she was on maternity leave.

The skullcaps had been removed with a bandsaw, their scalps peeled back and hanging over their faces, exposing their brains. Their sternums had been taken out and laid across the pubis of each of them in a nod at protecting their modesty, exposing their yellow, fatty internal tissue and their coiled intestines. They were awaiting the arrival of the duty local pathologist, who would conduct a far less rigorous post-mortem than the one currently being carried out on the charred victim from Haywards Heath Golf Club, whose arms were still raised in the air as if in a final gesture of defiance.

He remembered something, irreverently, that Roy Grace had whispered to him in here at a previous post-mortem, shortly after he had split up with his wife, Ari, and when he was feeling terrible. *Matey, no matter how shit you are feeling, you are going to have a better weekend than any overnight guest in here.*

And, for one of the few times since his wife had died, he found himself grinning. Then, after a few moments, he focused again on the present situation.

The moment anyone died they became the property of the local Coroner, who made the decision whether a post-mortem should be carried out or not. The principal criterion was whether the death needed explanation, or whether they had died from illness whilst under the care of their doctor. When the cause of death was obvious, such as from recurrent heart trouble or cancer, no post-mortem would be required. But if the death was sudden, either from unknown causes or from an accident such as a fall from a ladder or a car crash, then a post-mortem needed to be carried out to eliminate foul play.

But it was different for the victim in front of Glenn Branson now, where a more thorough examination was required to confirm whether it was indeed suicide, as the evidence pointed to, or something more sinister.

There were thirty Home Office pathologists in the UK who specialized in possible homicide victims and who were highly paid, on a per body basis, for their work. Dr Frazer Theobald, also gowned up in green, was one. He raised something that Glenn recognized as a human lung, with large forceps. 'This is very interesting,' he said, then dictated some technical jargon Glenn Branson did not understand into a small machine he held in his other gloved hand.

On the wall on the far side of the room were weighing scales and a chart itemizing the name of the deceased, with columns for the weights of their brain, lungs, heart, liver, kidneys and spleen. All that was written on it so far was, *ANON. MALE* and *7.5* against the brain.

In addition to Glenn Branson, Darren and the locum, in the room were James Gartrell, the CSI photographer, who was steadily working his way around the body, and the Coroner's Officer, Philip Keay. He was standing in a green gown, blue mask hanging from its tapes just below his chin, dictating into a machine with a worried frown.

'I think you all need to see this,' Frazer Theobald said. 'Because of the implications.'

Glenn, along with Gartrell and Keay, moved forward. He tried to avoid looking at the exposed, partly charred brain inside the open skull. But his eyes kept being drawn towards it.

'The left lung,' Theobald said. 'If our victim had set fire to himself, I would expect to find that he had inhaled both flames and smoke. There is clear evidence of fire and smoke damage to the thorax and lungs.'

'Can you explain the significance of that, Dr Theobald?'

Glenn Branson asked. 'Are you saying this is consistent with him setting fire to himself?'

He peered at Glenn, his beady nut-brown eyes the only part of his face that was visible. 'Yes, I am. This is all pointing to suicide.'

'But why in a ditch, several hundred yards from his car?' Branson queried.

Theobald shrugged. 'Who knows what goes on in the mind of someone deciding to kill themselves? That's not for me to speculate. All I can tell you is this does not have the appearance of foul play, in my opinion, at this stage. But I need to examine the body in more detail and conduct some blood tests.'

Glenn Branson stepped out of the room and called Roy Grace to tell him the news. But, to his surprise, instead of sounding grateful, his boss, and mate, sounded strangely distant – and dubious.

24

Dr Judith Biddlestone, the counsellor Red had been recommended by Rise, the Brighton charity that helped victims of domestic abuse, was in her late forties. Before becoming a counsellor she had been a clinical trainer for the National Health Service, and she now worked out of a basement consulting room in the trendy North Laine district of Brighton, with burning candles around that made it smell like some kind of temple, Red thought. She had a lean, athletic figure, short blonde highlighted hair, a cheery freckled face, and was dressed in jeans and a thin black T-shirt, despite the autumnal day.

Red had pedalled across town, on her *shit bike*, after leaving work later than planned. The couple she had showed around the Portland Avenue property yesterday had suddenly appeared in the office, panicking that the weekend was coming up and that they might lose the house. They had wanted to put in an offer, and Red had not wanted to miss out on the chance of her first sale.

So now, over half an hour late for her appointment, at 6.35 p.m. on Friday afternoon, she and the psychologist sat opposite each other on beanbag chairs, sipping mint tea while a stern crimson Buddha cast a watchful eye over them from the mantelpiece. This was her sixth session with Dr Biddlestone.

Red started by bringing her up to speed on Dr Karl Murphy, then finished by saying, 'I do wonder if it's all my fault.'

'Tell me why you think that, Red.' She spoke with a trace of a Newcastle accent.

'I don't know. I . . . it seems . . . well . . . it sort of feels like I'm just useless. Everything I do seems to turn to shit. Maybe I'm just shaken up at the moment. I feel so down.'

'Bereavement plays havoc with the human mind, Red. Tell me why you feel you are useless.'

'I suppose . . . you know . . . I failed in my relationship with Bryce.'

'That's how you see it?' Judith Biddlestone frowned at her. 'That you're the one who failed, not Bryce?'

'I go round in circles in my thoughts. But yes, I do feel that sometimes.'

'What I want to do, in the short time we have, is I'd like us to recap on your relationship with him, Red,' the psychologist said, 'because there are so many gaps. Let's go right back to the beginning of your relationship with Bryce Laurent. I feel you are blocking important things out – not deliberately – but try really hard to remember all that you can.'

Red thought back, hard. It had been three days after their first date that they had first slept together. And that had been truly amazing. They had made love, it had seemed, almost all through the night. Never in all her life had she been with a lover so passionate and attentive. She felt totally, utterly and intensely ravished.

She woke on the Saturday morning in his arms, in her flat, and they made love again. And again a short while later.

They spent most of the weekend in bed, ordering in first

a pizza, then a Chinese, watching old movies on television while drinking more vintage Roederer Cristal champagne, which he had nipped out and bought from an off-licence. He liked her skin, he told her. He liked her hair, her teeth, her smell, her humour.

She liked everything about him.

'The following weekend he took me away,' she said. 'To a gorgeous country house hotel. He picked me up in his car, a beautiful Aston Martin convertible – which I later found out was rented.' She closed her eyes and remembered how she had sat back in the soft seat, cocooned in the rich scent of leather, with warm June air blowing on her face.

They'd slept in a suite with a four-poster bed, gone for long walks along sandy beaches, and lunched and dined on endless glasses of vintage champagne and rich white wine.

She told the psychologist all of this.

'So when did it start to go wrong, Red?' Judith Biddle-stone asked when she had finished.

Red shrugged. 'God, that's a big one. I think the truth is, it went wrong way back before we ever met.'

The psychologist waited.

'He had issues in his childhood.'

'What issues?'

'I think he was abused.'

'What makes you think that?'

'Something he let slip a couple of times. It just made me wonder.'

'What did he let slip?'

'Well, it wasn't much really. Sometimes when he was angry he would make a comment about his *bitch* mother. He hates smoking – I tried not to let him see me smoking. But I remember one time he saw me and said I was just like his fucking mother. But he wouldn't talk about her. I did try to get him to open up to me, but he would get angry, almost instantly, whenever I did. And violent. So I stopped.'

'When you tried to talk to him about his childhood generally, he became instantly angry and violent?'

'Yes.'

'And you believe that is because he was abused?'

'Well . . . that is what happens, isn't it? Abused children grow up to become abusers?'

'On occasion, but it's much more complex than simple cause and effect. I'm interested that you made sense of Bryce's behaviour that way. Why do you think you did that?'

'He was a total control freak, and had a tidiness obsession – he was always tidying up.' She gave a wan smile. 'Bird shit on his car drove him mental – he'd wash and then polish and then re-polish the whole car whenever that happened – and living close to Brighton seafront, with gulls everywhere, that happened a lot.'

'What was that like for you?'

'Awful. I felt like I was walking on eggshells most of the time. Trying not to do anything that would set him off.'

'And you told yourself he was like that because of his past?'

'I've just remembered he once said I would understand him better if I knew about what his parents had done to him.'

'Do you want to tell me about that?'

'He kept telling me I was no good. That I couldn't cook, that I was a useless lover. He told me once that making love to me was like screwing a dead fish. My esteem was on the floor; I guess it still is. He made me feel worthless. But then after abusing me and hitting me, he would start sobbing, begging me for forgiveness, promising to change. It was during one of those outbursts for forgiveness he said I would understand him better if I knew about what his parents had done to him.'

'Did he tell you what he meant?'

'No, he wouldn't talk about it. I figured it must have been really bad, though.'

'You called the police numerous times during the latter part of your relationship, didn't you tell me?'

'Yes. There was one particular officer, Constable Spofford – Rob Spofford. A young officer on the Response Team who was particularly kind to me. He's now on the Neighbourhood Policing Team, covering my area. He told me that he'd regularly seen his own father be violent to his mother. He was the one who put me in touch with the Sanctuary Scheme. And who kept trying to convince me to end it with Bryce.'

'Do you have any understanding of what prevented you taking PC Spofford's advice and leaving Bryce at that point?'

She shrugged. 'I don't know. Bryce's constant bullying got to me, and he was always so remorseful afterwards. I guess I really believed I could help him.'

'Ahh. So might it be your belief that Bryce had been abused as a child that kept you in the relationship?'

'Stupid, huh?'

'Why be so harsh with yourself?'

'I didn't learn, did I? I thought I could help him. I thought if I could just get him to open up about his childhood, he would be nicer to me. But the more I tried to get him to talk, the angrier he got.'

'Just notice how little compassion you have for yourself right now and how at odds that is with your very evident compassion for the hurt you believe Bryce experienced.'

'See, I can't even get that right.'

'Is that how Bryce made you feel? As if you got things wrong the whole time?'

'Constantly! I thought I was going mad a lot of the time. The more I tried to get things right, the more I messed up. I'd have done almost anything to have him be nice to me.'

'And did you put up with almost anything in the hope that he might eventually be nice to you?'

'I've been thinking about that,' Red said. 'The thing is, the making-up part was so incredible. Suddenly, the person who hated me and hurt me so much turned into a gentle, loving creature. He would make me think that the row had all been my fault, because of my inadequacies.'

'*Your* inadequacies?'

Red laughed. 'Yes. I've got a whole list. Do you want to hear them?'

'I suspect we can use the last of our time together today much more profitably than reinforcing Bryce's distorted take on reality. I've got a copy of a report PC Spofford sent to the Sanctuary team in your file. Did you see it? It followed a discussion of your case at a MARAC meeting.'

'MARAC?' Red queried.

'Yes, it's a fortnightly meeting attended by the Police Anti-Victimization Unit, the Housing Service, the Health Department, the Education Department and various welfare and medical agencies, to look at all those at high risk in domestic abuse situations. It stands for Multi Agency Risk Assessment Conference.' Judith Biddlestone opened the red plastic folder and pulled out several sheets of printout. 'You signed an authorization for me to obtain this report. I'll just read you a little of it. This is what he wrote:

'*I'm extremely concerned about Ms Red Westwood. I believe she is in an abusive, violent relationship which is a real threat to her future safety and well-being and that Sussex Police need to take action. I can see the pain inside her eyes, I can see someone inside her crying out. She is terrified.*'

Tears welled in Red's eyes as she listened. She nodded. 'Yes,' she said, her voice barely above a whisper. 'I was terrified. I couldn't see any future. I couldn't see any life beyond Bryce. I guess . . . you know . . . with Karl . . . I was just starting to feel that, maybe, some kind of happiness was possible.'

The psychologist handed her a tissue and Red wiped her eyes, then sobbed for some moments. 'Shit. What the hell's wrong with Bryce? He has all this charm, charisma and real talent, but it's like he – he's got – this may sound strange – it's like he's got a failure gene, if there's such a thing. And he's spent his whole life kicking against it.'

'What do you mean by a *failure gene* exactly, Red?'

'I guess . . . the thing is, he's got so much talent. He's actually a brilliant artist – he can draw really well – and he's a really talented cartoonist. He's tried to get work published in newspapers, magazines, but he never has so far. He did nearly get a cartoon published in *Private Eye* a couple of years ago, but they wanted him to make a minor change and he refused. He told them to go to hell. I tried to convince him to do what they wanted; that . . . you know . . . the change was no big deal, and it would make him a published artist and that more might come of it. He just lost it, raged at me, told me I didn't understand the integrity of his art and went berserk. He totally lost the plot. He threw wine in my face, then he started hitting me – he just went wild. I really thought he was going to kill me.'

'Uh-huh.'

'I tried to get out of the flat. I was hysterical. He wouldn't let me go, he grabbed me – he's very strong, he works out obsessively. I locked myself in the toilet and dialled the police. Then he started crying, telling me no one had ever loved him before, no one had understood him. Begged me to forgive him.'

'It's a memory, Red. You are safe now.'

'But it feels so real, like it's going to happen all over again.'

'I know. But it ended. You do know that, right? Tell me how it ended?'

'The police turned up – it was PC Spofford and a woman officer. I let Bryce do the talking. He told them it was all a misunderstanding; they asked me to confirm this, and whether I wanted Bryce removed. I told them yes, it was a misunderstanding and I wanted him to stay.'

'Of course you did. To disobey Bryce wasn't smart, right?'

Red was silent for some moments. 'Yes,' she said finally. 'I felt he was so mixed up.' She shrugged. 'I – I thought maybe it was love that he needed. That if I loved him enough, I could change him.'

'You know what they say about when a man and a woman fall in love?'

'No?'

'The woman always hopes she can change him. The man always hopes she will stay the same for ever.'

Red gave a thin smile. 'Is that why all marriages end in disappointment?'

'Not all. But many.' She smiled. 'So, Bryce's failure gene – it's his ego that's held him back?'

'He has a massive ego, that's for sure. He's a good magician, too – he specializes in close magic. He used to tell me he was better than anyone else and one day he would be more famous than Siegfried and Roy, and David Copperfield. He really believed that. When I first dated him he had several gigs a week, but they started dropping off – I think because he kept losing his temper with people who weren't paying attention, or when one of his tricks didn't quite work. Oh, and he was also obsessed with Houdini. He said he was a better escapologist than Houdini. He used to make me tie him up and handcuff him, and he would escape within minutes.'

'He *made* you tie him up? You didn't want to?'

'No, I'm not into bondage.'

'This was more than escapology then? Did the bondage always involve him being tied up, or were you tied up by him also?'

Red whispered, 'Mostly he tied me up, and that really scared me. He pushed it constantly to the limit, when I really thought I was going to suffocate.'

'Just notice your breathing, Red. You are safe now.'

She took a few moments to calm down before she went on. 'I get so scared when I think of him and the things he used to do to me.'

'I know. Breathe – it helps.'

Red breathed in and exhaled several times. Then she gave a humorous laugh. 'It's silly that just remembering him makes me feel like I am suffocating again. I'm so stupid!'

'It is not silly and you are not stupid.'

'I loved him. I really did. I was intoxicated by him. I thought for a time, in those early days, that we were soul-mates, I really did. He used to tell me we had met before in a previous life, and – this may sound stupid or naive – I believed him.'

'It doesn't sound stupid or naive, Red. Often when people meet and fall in love, that's what they feel. A connection that is so incredibly powerful. That was you and Bryce?'

'It was. Yes. I thought I had met the man I would have children with, and with whom I would spend the rest of my life. Shit, I was so dumb.'

'You're being harsh with yourself again, Red. Let's talk

about the fact that you did get out of that relationship. Something even you couldn't label as *silly*, *stupid* or *dumb*. What was the turning point?'

'My mother. I think I told you she was – is – a prison visitor, and also a life coach?'

'Yes, you did.'

'My mother irritated me so much. She kept saying she didn't like him, didn't trust him. You know what I thought?'

The psychologist shook her head.

'Well, it may sound strange, but I thought she might be jealous.'

'You thought your mother might be jealous of your boyfriend? That's not uncommon, you know.'

Red shrugged. 'My mother confided in me, years ago, that the spark had gone out of her marriage to my father. She and I were always very close – we talked about these things. In the early days, Bryce seemed so perfect, so attentive, and she had told me how attentive my father had been to her when they were courting. I started to feel that maybe it was bringing those memories back for her.'

'So you discounted your mother's misgivings about Bryce?'

'Possibly . . . I don't know. I was truly besotted with him. I'd never met anyone like him who was so into me. I worshipped the ground he walked on. He was sometimes so kind, such fun to be with, and – God, this is embarrassing to say – but he was so incredibly sexy in bed. He pushed all my buttons – and found some I never knew I had. It wasn't until after we had moved in together that I began to realize what a control freak he was. It seemed okay at first; he would take me shopping, and decide on my outfits – and pay for them. I was flattered, for a while. But then he started questioning me about every second of my day. Demanding to know where I had been. If I had been out with friends, he wanted to know what I had drunk, what I had eaten, who had paid.'

'Right now, as you tell me all of that, what are you aware of?'

'How stupid I feel that I lived with him for all that time.'

'Notice, Red, that you simultaneously tell yourself that Bryce was a controlling, violent man because he himself was abused as a child, and also that you are stupid for having stayed with him. Both beliefs exonerate Bryce of responsibility and both place significant responsibility upon you.'

'That's because it was partly my fault.'

'Do you know, I don't think I've ever met a woman who was abused who didn't believe, to some extent, that it was her fault. Do you think it could have been all of their faults?'

'Of course not!'

'What makes you different then?'

'I knew things weren't right even before he became violent. One morning when I got up to go to work, Bryce had taken all my shoes. He wouldn't let me have any back until I had sworn my undying love for him.'

'How did that make you feel?'

'Well, at the time, although I was furious, I was flattered! I liked the idea someone loved me so much that he would do that. Call me naive. But it went downhill rapidly from there. The real turning point for me was – I didn't know she had done this – but my mother had secretly hired a private detective to look into Bryce's past. Bryce told me he was working as an Air Traffic Controller at Gatwick Airport. My mother gave me the detective's report. Bryce had lied. He'd never worked in Air Traffic Control at all. He'd had a job, a couple of years earlier, on the ground staff at Gatwick, in the fire training area, and had been sacked after apparently endangering the life of another employee – and then punching his manager. He'd been deported from the US after getting in a fight with a previous girlfriend and doing a three-year jail term there for violent assault. He'd also said he used to be a pilot in the US. But he's never had a pilot's licence.'

The psychologist shot a discreet glance at her watch. 'I'm aware of the time, Red. We have just a few minutes left and certainly not enough time to unpack all that you have just told me. Can we bracket it and put it on the agenda for our next session?'

'Sure.'

Dr Biddlestone spent the last couple of minutes of the session making sure Red felt sufficiently well grounded to cycle home, then she said, 'I'll see you on Monday, Red.'

'8.30 a.m.?'

'8.30 a.m.'

Bryce, who had listened to every word, transmitted from her bugged phone, made a note in his electronic diary to be sure to be listening in then.

25

Friday, 25 October

Today was going to be a busy shopping day, and did he have a long list to get through! He needed supplies for all his plans. Quite a bit of the stuff he could buy online, but that could be traced easily. Better, he knew, to buy all the gear from shops, paying cash. He had plenty of that thanks to his dear, sweet mummy obligingly dying much earlier than she, or he, had expected.

Loads of the stuff! Seven hundred and fifty thousand pounds of it, net, after the thieving estate agents had taken their commission and the thieving solicitor had had his sticky paws in the jar. He had plans for them both, but they could wait.

His first stop was the hardware store, Dockerills, on Church Street in the centre of Brighton. He had selected it because it was always busy, and no one was likely to remember a man in a baseball cap buying pliers, bolt cutters, a blade cutter, duct tape and a small hammer.

Next, he drove in his rented van to an electrical supplies warehouse just off Davigdor Road in Hove, where he bought an assortment of timers, mostly ones with a range of one thousand metres and more, four digital relays and one thousand metres of nichrome wire. Next stop was RF Solutions on the Cliffe Industrial Estate, outside Lewes, where he bought a selection of relays and switching units.

Then he drove across to Lancing Business Park and bought three car batteries, from which he could obtain sulphuric acid, and some specialist adhesive tapes. And from a newsagent on the way back, he bought an assortment of AA and AAA batteries.

He also bought a burger from a mobile roadside stall on the main road back to Brighton, where he was unlikely to be remembered. All this shopping had given him an appetite.

After lunch he bought, from a garden centre a couple of miles away, several sacks of sodium chlorate weedkiller.

Then, tugging a baseball cap low over his face, he drove out to Gatwick Airport and entered the long-stay car park, collecting a ticket from the automatic gate. He followed the signs for today's vehicles, winding around the rows and rows of parked cars. A bus passed him, stopped a short distance away, and several people, lugging suitcases, boarded.

Happy holiday, he thought, with a twinge of sadness, looking at one couple, who exchanged a kiss before climbing up the steps. That could have been him and Red, jetting off to some sunny paradise. Maybe the Maldives.

A suited businessman, carrying one of those overnight bags with a built-in suit holder, boarded also.

Have a good trip! Come back with that deal!

He reversed into an empty bay, switched off the engine, and waited, looking around for any CCTV cameras. He saw one some distance away, but there were no others. Then he waited as dusk slowly fell. The weather was closing in. Drizzle falling from a darkening, rain-laden sky. Perfect! Someone drove a brand-new Jaguar XF in, which was of no interest to him. Then came a one-year-old Mazda MX-5. Again of no interest. Then a Porsche Cayman. No good. A Ford Focus. Too recent a model. Followed by a small Lexus saloon. Too recent also.

Then bingo!

A ten-year-old BMW 5 Series. And, almost unbelievably, it reversed into the bay directly opposite him.

Meant to be!

He watched the middle-aged couple get out, dressed in summer clothing in which they looked ridiculous in this weather. The man was wearing a panama hat, and the obese woman was wearing what looked like a floral wigwam. The man removed a briefcase from the rear seat, and his wife a large handbag. Then the man popped the boot lid and removed two enormous wheeled suitcases, locked the car, and they headed off towards the nearest bus pick-up point.

Maybe they had both been beautiful young things once, he thought. Like him and Red.

Ten minutes later they boarded a bus.

Happy holiday! he thought. *You ugly fuckwits.*

As soon as it was as dark as it was going to get, he left his car, pulled the hood of his raincoat over his baseball cap until it almost totally obscured his vision, then grabbed the tools he thought he might need from the rear of his van. With their stupid clothes, and all their luggage, that couple were going away for a while for sure. He had all the time in the world.

With a single blow of his hammer he smashed the side window of the BMW, reached inside and yanked the door handle. The alarm parppp-parppped. He ducked inside, yanked the bonnet release handle, raised the bonnet and rapidly cut the alarm wires, silencing it. Then he looked around, warily, his nerves jangling. But no security guard came running. Apart from an empty bus making its rounds like a forlorn robot searching for a soulmate, the car park was deserted.

He clamped a protective locking disc, which he had

stolen from a fire engine's equipment at the airport, over the BMW's steering wheel. It was designed for firefighters to cut people out of crashed cars when the airbag had not deployed to prevent it doing so accidentally. Then he ducked under the wheel, and with his blade cut away the protective outer shield of the airbag. Next, being careful to avoid the trigger sensors, he sliced into the airbag itself, and allowed the salt-white sodium azide crystals to fall into the plastic beaker he had taken from a filling station on the way here.

Sodium azide was one of the most toxic chemicals in the world. It was far more rapid acting than cyanide and, unlike cyanide, where the poison could be neutralized with amyl nitrate, there was no antidote. It was tasteless, and would bond with the haemoglobin in the blood causing death within minutes. And it had the bonus of being virtually undetectable, unless you were specifically looking for it.

He wasn't sure he would need it, but it gave him another option. You could never have enough options!

Oh baby, oh Red, you should never have driven me to this, really you shouldn't!

I'd hate to think of you swallowing sodium azide. Really I would. But I guess, if the truth be known, I would prefer that to seeing you screw Dr Karl Murphy.

But sodium azide. It's not a nice death. Not nice at all.

Mercifully quick, that's the upside.

But after what you did to me, would I really want it to be quick?

If you want to know the truth, Red, I would really like to see you suffer. To hear you scream out how much you love me. How desperately badly you want me back. That you would do anything to get me back.

That you would swallow sodium azide, if that's what it took.

Then I could look into your eyes and say to you, 'Sorry, Red. There is no antidote. If you'd stayed with me, you would be looking forward to a whole long future. Kids. Grand-children. Family Christmases. Happy old age. All that stuff.

Now all you have is less than a minute.

Moments to contemplate your regrets.

Moments to think about how sorry you are.

Moments to think how good it could all have been for you and me.

People often say that's how it goes in life. Shit happens. But you know, that's a cop-out. You know what the reality is? Shit falls from its own weight.

Think about that.

He flipped back through the early texts from Red on his phone. Stopped at one.

God, I so love what you do to me ☺))) I'm so full of sweetness and love when I think of you, and I like that! Actually I LOVE that! These feelings are awesome. Wish you were here right now, holding me naked in your arms and deep inside me.

Shielding the cup against the falling rain, he hurried back to his van, and eased himself back into the driving seat, put the cup into a plastic bag, and carefully knotted the top, sealing it.

Sodium azide would kill someone, agonizingly, within sixty seconds. It was only found in older car airbags, and when they deployed in collisions, the other chemicals in there neutralized it.

By the time the ugly couple returned from their holiday, and found their BMW had been broken into and the airbag tampered with, he would be long gone.

And maybe the sodium azide would be long gone, too.

God, Red, I can't live without you. And I can't watch you with another man. Really, the pain would be too much for me to bear.

Blame it on your parents. That poet Philip Larkin got it right, didn't he, when he wrote: They fuck you up, your mum and dad. They may not mean to, but they do.

Oh boy, Red, yours really did. Royally.

26

Roy Grace sat at home, on the sofa, with the initial post-mortem report on Dr Karl Murphy lying beside him and Humphrey asleep on his back, paws up, at his feet. He was watching Cleo giving Noah his supper, and making another check on the list of wedding acceptances. Noah, in a red and white striped top, had a mush of food in front of him on the white plastic tray.

'Noah having supper!' she said, breezily, as she spooned some sweet potato purée into the baby's mouth. 'Hello Noah, what are you eating today? Yum!'

It reminded Grace he needed to fill Marlon's food hopper. The goldfish was eleven, still forever circumnavigating his bowl. Every morning when he came downstairs, he half expected to see the fish floating lifeless and was always relieved to see it was still active, still as mournful-looking as ever. But it was a link with Sandy, the only living link he had. He'd won it at a fairground with her. And he was heartened to find, on an internet trawl, that the current record for longevity for a goldfish was thirty-four years.

Using two of his fingers and his thumb, Noah tried cramming some mashed banana into his mouth. As he sucked, bits dropped down, some bouncing off the tray and falling onto the mat below him, and a thin stream of dribble slid down his chin.

'Mmm, yum yum, Noah!' Cleo encouraged him, dabbing away the dribble.

There were times when Roy Grace found himself unable to take his eyes off his son. Scarcely able to believe this was his child, his and Cleo's creation. The emotions he felt for him were completely overwhelming. And he felt moved almost to tears by the love and happiness he could see in Cleo's face.

He reached down and rubbed Humphrey's belly for some moments. The black Labrador-Border Collie cross made a happy grunting sound, his right hind leg jigging. Then Grace picked up the post-mortem report and looked at one section which he had ringed in red ink. Traces of the anti-depressant Paxil were present in Murphy's blood, on which there had been a fast-track analysis. The pathologist had made an annotation that there was a possible, but unproven, link between this drug and suicides.

Suddenly turning to him, Cleo said, 'Any joy, darling, with that clue?'

The Times, open on the crossword page, lay on the sofa beside the wedding list, along with a book of sudoku. Cleo was struggling with her studies for an Open University degree, at times unable to concentrate during these first months of Noah's life but determined to continue. So to help keep her brain active, she had taken to doing crossword puzzles and sudoku.

Grace looked down at the clue in *The Times*, for 4 across, eight letters, which had been marked in red by Cleo. It was three words. *Percussionist be calm!*

Grace tried to think. 'Doldrums?' he suggested.

'Doldrums?' she repeated, frowning.

'That's an area of ocean around the tropics where sailboats often get becalmed for days.'

'It can also mean down in the dumps, can't it?' Cleo said. Then she gave Noah a chiding as he spat mashed banana onto the floor beneath him. 'Tut, tut, tut, naughty Noah!' She turned back to Roy. 'Yes, doldrums, I like it. I think you're right, and it fits!' She wrote it in.

As he watched her, he remembered how when he was a child his mother had been keen on crossword puzzles, but he never cared for them much, especially now, with his work on major crimes – they tended to be puzzles enough. His thoughts returned to the suicide of Karl Murphy, which he was continuing to fret over as he read through the pathologist's report again very carefully. Karl Murphy's sister had been interviewed earlier in the day and she had stated that the doctor had talked of killing himself several times after the death of his wife, although just recently he had seemed more cheerful.

So far the evidence for suicide was stacking up convincingly.

So why, Grace wondered, was he still not convinced?

27

Sunday, 27 October

At 3 a.m. the alarm went off. Bryce sat bolt upright, shaking sleep out of his head. He climbed out of bed, padded through into his bathroom, ran the tap, filling a glass with water, and swallowed two anabolic steroid tablets.

Then, naked, he settled down into the rowing machine on his floor, and worked feverishly for fifteen minutes. Afterwards he lay on his stomach and did one hundred press-ups. All the time thinking of Red. Thinking of being inside her. Then he did fifty sit-ups, feeling the tightening of his abs. He followed it with twenty minutes of crunches with the weights. When he had finished, he went back to bed and lay there.

Thinking about Red's beautiful, thick strands of hair. About the scent of her body. About all the things she had said to him.

> **God, Bryce, I can't keep my hands off you. I feel you so intensely, craving you every second we are apart. I'm feeling the craving growing stronger and stronger every second we are apart. 42, 180 seconds until we are together again. 42, 176 now! God, I want you. Sooooooo much ☺))) XXXXXXXXX**

And then you dumped me. Threw me out of your flat. Gave me back the beautiful watch I'd given you.

You didn't mean to do that, did you, Red? You were poisoned, weren't you? By your toxic mother. It wasn't your fault. I should forgive you, shouldn't I? Really I should.

But I don't think that's possible now. Killing you is the only option.

He looked up at the bank of monitors. The infrared camera in Red's bedroom showed her stirring. *You're so troubled, aren't you, so troubled? They shoot wounded horses out of kindness. It will be an act of kindness to kill you, too.*

28

Sunday, 27 October

Red woke up crying. The clock by her bed said 3.52 a.m. She had cried for most of Saturday. She felt so confused and scared, and most of all sad. A terrible sense of loss and help-lessness. In reality, they had been lovers for such a brief time, and although she had secretly checked him out, she felt she hardly knew Karl Murphy. *Shit, how do you grieve for someone you barely knew?* She had never met his parents or any of his family, and did not know how she might contact them. Yet she felt a deep sense of loss.

And she felt a terrible sense of guilt. Was there some-thing she could have done, should have done? Should she have noticed the signs and reached out to him? What was it that had pushed him over the edge? What was the inad-equacy in her that had failed to change his mind about life not being worth living?

She lay in the darkness, thinking through all the conver-sations they had had. Sure, he had talked about his love for his children. And the intense sadness he felt about his wife. Yet, all the things he had said to her about moving on, about the importance of being strong for his children and giving them a proper family life, just did not chime with him com-mitting suicide.

Karl had told her on more than one occasion that,

deeply though he had felt the loss of Ingrid, his obligations lay with his children. To ensure they grew up loved. The connection Red had felt with him was very definitely less passionate than in the early days of her past relationship with Bryce Laurent; it was more gentle, more of a friendship. He was such a sweet guy. She wracked her brains, as she had done continually during the past days, for any clues, for anything he might have given her, anything at all he had said, that gave an indication that he had felt suicidal.

But she could find none.

He had told her how much he loved his children, and that they would always come first in his life.

She'd now heard he had mentioned suicide to his sister a couple of times, in the early days after his wife had died. One concern was that he had been taking anti-depressants, and she had read that there were some kinds that could suddenly, without warning, send people into a suicidal spiral. Had that happened to him?

She fell back into a deep, dreamless slumber, and woke again at 6.15 a.m. Knowing she would be unable to sleep any more, she got up, pulled on her jogging kit, went downstairs and let herself out of the front door, then ran down in the darkness to the seafront. She crossed the Kingsway, normally busy with traffic but deserted at this hour on a Sunday morning, ran down past the bowls club and onto the promenade, where she turned right. She jogged past the Hove Lagoon, the Deep Sea Anglers club building, and then past the terrace of white, elegant Moorish-style beachfront houses, home to a number of local celebrities, including Adele, Nick Berry, Norman Cook and Zoë Ball, and on along the perimeter of Shoreham Harbour.

Suicide?

He was a doctor. He was smart. He would have known which anti-depressants not to take.

Surely?

29

Shortly after 11.30 a.m., Bryce, dressed in jeans, work boots and a fleece jacket over a sweater, turned left off the road that led up to Brighton's Devil's Dyke onto the bumpy cart track that wound down for half a mile, south, past the farmer's house, then on through farmland and towards the cluster of once derelict outbuildings that now housed his workshop and stores, and which he rented under a false name. The same name this vehicle was registered under.

The dark green Land Rover Defender bounced and lurched along the muddy track on its hard, sturdy springs. The vehicle suited him well; it was a true chameleon – like himself. It looked as much at home parked on a city kerb as it did in a rural field; it was the kind of workhorse that was a familiar sight to most people, and was therefore unlikely to raise eyebrows wherever he was.

And therefore unlikely to be remembered.

He skirted a tumbledown barn with an ancient plough entwined in brambles, and a short distance on passed a rotting railway carriage that looked as if it might once have been converted into a dwelling, and which sat incongruously here in the middle of nowhere. Then he drove down a short incline, past an abandoned horsebox trailer that sat on four flat tyres, a pile of rusty scaffold poles, and patches of scorched earth where he had conducted some of his experiments. He pulled up on the hard surface between his three small, well-secured buildings – a barn that was a former grain store, a large workshop, and a disused dairy – and climbed out.

A mile to the south was the residential sprawl of the Hangleton area to the west of the city of Brighton and Hove, with Southwick and Portslade beyond, and Shoreham. He could see the tall smokestack of the power station, and on a clear day he would have been able to see the English Channel, if he had cared. But there was a steady drizzle falling, and the sky was misty with rain. And the view did not interest him. It might have done once, in former days, in another life.

Life with Red.

Everything had interested him then. He had seen the world through different eyes. He had seen beauty in everything when he had been with her. With Red it had truly been a world of colour. Now it was all monochrome. He had never brought her here, to his secret place. Sure, he had planned to, to the place where he developed his conjuring tricks and his escapology tricks. He had learned about explosives during his time as a sapper and bomb disposal expert in the Territorial Army – before they had thrown him out. And he had learned about electronic security systems in his time installing alarms for a Brighton security company called Languard Alarms, before they had – totally unjustifiably – fired him.

But that was then.

He jumped down from the Land Rover and hurried through the rain to the workshop, which had bars across the frosted glass windows and a sign on the front door which read: PT FIREWORKS LTD.

As a registered fireworks manufacturer he was able to

order all kinds of explosives without any problem. He unlocked the heavy-duty padlock and the two deadlocks, went inside, closing and double-bolting the door behind him, and switched on the lights.

As always he began with a quick check that everything was in order, as he had last left it. His eyes roamed around the plywood-panelled walls; the tanks of oxyacetylene gas, oxygen, nitrous oxide; a lathe; a chest freezer filled with dry ice; a fridge full of chemicals; the racks of Dexion shelving stacked with computer equipment, instruction manuals, cylinders of chemicals, dials, gauges, tubing; and one shelf piled high with tarnished silver cups he had won for his magic tricks at conventions around the country.

Oh yes, he was good. He was damned good! Other people recognized that. But not Red's mother. And Red never gave him the chance to show it. One day she would be sorry, they both would. He was the best. The best ever. Eat your fucking heart out Houdini, David Copperfield, Siegfried and Roy.

But what consumed his thoughts right now was the bank of television monitors on the wall. He hit the power switch to activate them, and moments later they flickered into life. He saw Red at her desk in her spare bedroom, typing on her computer. Sending emails? Facebook posts? Tweets? He'd check all that out when he got back home – everything she typed got emailed, every fifteen minutes, to the computer in his flat.

She was dressed in conservative clothes. A black roll-neck sweater, a tweed skirt, black leggings and boots. All set for Sunday lunch with her mother – the witch – and her father. And her older sister who intimidated her with her successful career and her perfectly planned pregnancy and her pompous husband. *Poor you! But with luck, you'll be spared! All sorted!*

And she was again wearing that cheap watch she had worn on their first date. The one he had replaced with the Cartier, which she had returned when she dumped him.

Not good, Red, he chided silently. *You are one classy lady. You should be wearing a Cartier, honestly. Whatever else may have happened between us, I so want you wearing a quality watch.*

He punched the code into his iPhone and checked his texts, hoping as ever there might be one from Red. But there was nothing. His heart heaving, he scrolled back through all the texts she had sent him, which he had never erased. Scrolled right back, with tears in his eyes, to those earliest days, when she had been crazily in love with him. And he with her. When he had been on his way to her flat.

Can't wait to see you, my gorgeous Red! ☺ XXX 3 mins!

And her reply:

Can't wait that long! XXX

Two mins now ☺ XXX

I'm going to have to start without you! XXX

One min! XXX

God, Bryce remembered that night so clearly. And so many nights like it, when he'd driven, often at mad speeds, angry at everyone in his way who slowed him down, to see Red. He'd text his ETA as he got closer, until with minutes to go he'd text a final countdown. When he reached her doorstep, he'd buzz her flat; there would be a click and he would enter the communal porch of her apartment building, and run up the stairs. Her door would open and their lips would meet. They'd be entwined in silence, kicking the door shut, tugging at each other's clothes, staring, grinning, lusting into each other's eyes, and making love on the carpeted floor in her hallway, unable, because of the crazed grip of their desire for each other, to get beyond the threshold.

Now, as he stared at the monitors showing the interior of her current flat, he saw memories of their short time together everywhere. The rug that had been on the living-room floor which they had made love on. Where she had once held him in her mouth as he had crouched, his trousers and pants pulled down by her, staring into his eyes with such trust and love as he had dug his hands into her hair.

The oak table from her old kitchen on top of which he had once taken her so hard and harshly and incredibly erotically. The perspex Ghost chair on which they had made love with her sitting astride him. Staring into his eyes. Telling him to come with her eyes open, staring into his.

Where did it go wrong?

He knew. Of course he knew. Her bloody scheming mother. Her bloody weak father.

So sad what I'm going to do. But I have to move this on. As long as you are out there, Red, as long as I have the know-ledge that you are kissing someone else, that you are letting someone else come inside you, I cannot live. It's not that I really want to harm you. You need to understand that. It's that I need to move on. And I can't do that so long as you are seeing other men.

I can't bear the pain.

Sorry about your car, that's just to teach you a lesson. You need to be punished first. Then you die.

But I'll explain all that to you soon, in another life. In our next life, you and I will be entwined for ever. Just like the lovers in that Keats poem, 'Ode on a Grecian Urn'. The one I read out to you that you loved so much. You said to me that was us. Two lovers, frozen in marble, about to kiss, but not yet having requited their love. They never had and they never would. They would forever remain in that moment of anticipation, total adoration.

And no disappointment.

God, Red, why did you disappoint me? Why the hell did you ever listen to your bitch mother?

Bryce stared around his treasure trove. He felt at peace here, in his workshop, with the rain pattering down on the roof. There was no one within earshot, or sight, of this building.

No one to be bothered by the occasional explosion. Or the occasional bursts of flame as he tested his latest incendiary devices, some of which were home-made, others bought in.

The stuff he planned to use.

She was standing up now. She walked towards the front door, grabbing her raincoat off a hook, and her umbrella.

You're in for a surprise, my angel. I'm doing it for you, to save you the humiliation of Sunday lunch with the sister and brother-in-law you hate, and your goddamn awful parents.

Trust me, that is not the way to be spending one of the last Sundays of your life.

30

At midday, Red left her apartment, hurried across the road through the light drizzle, then made a right turn into Westbourne Terrace Mews. After a couple of minutes, she reached the lock-up garage where she kept her beloved yellow and black 1973 Volkswagen Beetle convertible. Bryce had so not been impressed with it. The car was dangerous, he told her. It had no airbags, and with its almost fluorescent colour, he said it looked like a giant seagull had shat on it. He wanted to buy her a modern Golf convertible, but she had refused. She loved this car.

And, she'd told Bryce in no uncertain terms, the car had *soul.*

She unlocked the garage door and hoisted it up. The Beetle sat there, gleaming from the loving polish she had given it three weeks ago. She opened the door, climbed in, pushed the key into the ignition and twisted it. As ever, the engine turned over faithfully, clattering into life behind her, settling into its reassuring whirring sound. She loved the familiar smell of the car, a mixture of old paintwork, fabric cleaner and slight dampness.

She reversed out of the garage, got out and shut the door, then pulled on her seat belt and drove along the seafront, turning left at the statue of Queen Victoria. The rain hardened, suddenly drumming down on the fabric roof, and the windows were misting.

As she crossed over Church Road and headed up The Drive, the heater started to kick in, a steady blast of increasingly warm air against the October chill. The traffic lights at the junction with Old Shoreham Road were red, and she halted behind a row of cars. She put the gear lever into neutral and pulled on the handbrake. Music was playing on the radio from Juice FM. A Lucinda Williams song that Bryce had loved.

And which she had loved too then.

This song is all about you and me, Bryce had said.

And yes, it had been.

Not a day goes by ... You left your mark on me ...

She felt a deep twinge of pain. He had. In those early days he had left his mark like no one she had ever met before. He was the man, she had believed then, she would spend the rest of her life with.

Shit, Bryce. God, what the hell happened? Why? Why did you do it? Why didn't you tell me the truth about you from the start? Maybe it would have all been so different if you had.

Suddenly, she could smell burning. The lights turned green and the cars in front moved off. She yanked off the handbrake, put the Volkswagen into gear, and pressed the accelerator, but the engine died. Someone behind hooted. She raised an apologetic hand and twisted the key. The engine turned for some seconds, a whining metallic rattle, then stopped. Wisps of smoke curled from behind her.

Shit. Shit. Shit.

More smoke was coming out from the footwell, rising up in front of her. It had a toxic, acrid smell.

The car behind hooted again, louder, more angrily.

She coughed, feeling sudden panic. The smoke was

thickening. She flung open the door, and instantly there was a sickening crunch and it flew back on its hinges as a white van thundered past, ripping it almost clean off, then screeching to a halt with a slithering sound. She stumbled out into the road in a cloud of smoke, and a car swerved around her.

'What the fuck are you playing at?' someone yelled at her. The driver of the van, she realized through her confusion. Then he said, 'Oh, bloody hell. Hang on, love, I've got a fire extinguisher.'

She could hear a crackling sound.

The driver ran back to his van and returned moments later holding a tiny fire extinguisher in his hand. 'How do you open the engine cover?'

She pulled the key out of the ignition, ran to the rear of the car, rammed the key in and pushed the button. Trails of smoke were rising from the grille.

'Open it slowly!' he said. 'Careful!'

Cautiously, Red lifted the cover a few inches. Smoke poured out either side.

'Call the fire brigade!' he shouted, then took over, hoisting up the cover further.

Almost mesmerized in her panic, she watched him disappear in a cloud of smoke. She hurried around to the side of the car, leaned in and grabbed her handbag, then pulled her phone out and dialled 999.

She saw the van driver, a short, tubby man in his forties, spray a jet of foam into the engine compartment.

'Emergency. Which service please?' a disembodied voice asked.

'Fire,' she gasped. 'My car's on fire.'

She could see flames leaping from the engine compartment now. She was dimly conscious of vehicles on both sides of the street stopping. Someone jumped out of the front of a bus holding another fire extinguisher, and ran across the road towards her. He joined the van driver spraying the contents into the engine compartment. But it seemed to make the fire worse. Flames leapt into the air, forcing both men back.

She stared helplessly in horror as she waited for the fire engine to arrive, and the entire car turned into a fireball.

31

Bryce Laurent had Red's mobile phone on loudspeaker in his warehouse. He was busily opening a crate of slow-burn fuses that had been delivered from China earlier in the week.

You poor thing, Red, you sound so upset because you've lost your car. You need a present, don't you? I think a present would cheer you up. I'll give it a think. A nice present to take to the grave with you.

32

Pond Cottage was a long, narrow thatched house, with low beamed ceilings, part of it dating back to Tudor times. It was situated down a winding country lane to the north of Henfield, a large village eight miles from Brighton, and it had been Red's family home – and refuge – all of her life.

It sat behind a tall, immaculately trimmed yew hedge, topped with a row of topiaried birds, which her father kept trimmed with almost obsessive care. To the rear of the low-roofed house was an equally immaculately tended garden, with a duck pond that had an island in the middle, an acre of perfect lawn, and a view over miles of farmland beyond. Since his retirement as a family solicitor in Brighton, her father divided his waking hours between working on the garden and, with her mother, sailing their small cruiser, *Red Margot*, in all weathers. The boat, named after her and her sister, was her parents' real passion. Red and her sister had spent many childhood weekends and chunks of their holidays on board, sometimes reluctantly, sometimes happily, exploring the ports of Devon, Cornwall, Normandy, Brittany and the Channel Islands.

Red loved the pride her parents took in that garden, and the sight of the house now, even in the falling rain beneath a dismal sky, cheered her a little. Although in truth she wasn't particularly excited by the prospect of seeing her sister and her tosser of a husband. She and Karl had planned a long, lazy Sunday morning in bed, then a drive out to one of his favourite country pubs, maybe The Griffin at Fletching or The Cat at West Hoathly, or perhaps The Royal Oak at Wineham, for lunch.

Arriving here today she felt even more of a failure than ever. She paid the taxi, pulling the banknotes from her purse with shaking hands, and gave the driver a large tip because he had been so kind and sympathetic to her over her car. Then she climbed out into the rain, still feeling flustered and shaken, and hurried up to the front door, pulling her key out of her handbag, conscious of just how late she was for Sunday lunch. It was 2.45 p.m., and her father was a stickler for sitting down at the table at 1 p.m. on the dot.

Her parents, her sister, Margot, and her brother-in-law, the odiously pompous Rory, were seated around the oak refectory table eating crumble and custard when she entered the kitchen/dining room. There was a cosy heat from the Aga, and the sweet smell of a log fire, which she knew would be burning in the inglenook in the sitting room.

'You poor darling,' her mother said. 'What a trauma. I'm sorry we started without you, but the lamb would have been ruined.' In her early sixties, with a tangle of shoulder-length flame-coloured hair and dressed in a baggy sweater and jeans, her mother was still a very attractive woman. But shit, Red thought, how could she still, after all these years, not be able to get her head around the knowledge that her daughter did not eat lamb? she wondered. Red had been traumatized, at the age of nine, when they had been stuck in a traffic jam behind a lorry crammed with sheep being taken to Shoreham Harbour, and had refused to eat it ever since. For much of her childhood, out of principle, she had been a vegetarian, and although she occasionally – and reluctantly – did eat some meat now because she found herself sometimes craving it, she steadfastly refused to touch lamb.

She stared at her mother, her temper already frayed enough without this thoughtless comment. Why couldn't her mother remember that fins were fine with her, but fur, paws and hooves were mostly not. *The lamb was pretty badly ruined the day someone killed it and chopped it up, Mummy,* she nearly said, but kept her cool. She was in no mood to have a row right now, and nor did she have the strength.

Her father, hair awry as ever, dressed in shapeless trousers, plimsolls and a Shetland sweater over a Viyella shirt, was right behind her, thrusting a glass of champagne into her hand. 'Kept it chilled for you, my angel!' he said, giving her a kiss.

'Your car caught fire?' her elder sister said. 'That old wreck? It's hardly surprising, it was bound to happen one day.'

Margot had always managed to make Red feel inadequate from earliest childhood, and her cutting, supercilious smile was doing it again right now. Four years older than her, Margot had always been the apple of her father's eye. Margot was the one who got the high scores and the great reports at school, followed by a double first at Oxford.

She was now a high-powered lawyer in the City earning, their mother had confided, close to £1 million a year. She sat at the table, with her short, razored black hair and sharp features, smartly dressed as ever in her designer maternity wear. And now, of course, she was the one who was pregnant. Seven smug months pregnant. With her immaculate, brand-new 5 Series BMW smugly parked in the driveway. Not a car that would ever catch fire.

Rory, who worked for a hedge fund and was related to a Tory cabinet minister – and harboured political ambitions of his own – was as far up his own backside as was possible without his head actually appearing out of his own throat, Red liked to tell her friends. An old Etonian with aristocratic antecedents, he was a tall, chinless wonder with a lock of floppy fair hair, dressed today in a pink shirt, red cords, and black suede Gucci loafers. 'You're bloody lucky it happened where it did, Red,' he said, ever the crass politician before even becoming one. 'Just imagine if that had happened on a major road in rush hour? Could have caused delays to hundreds – maybe thousands of people. Classic cars belong in museums, Red, not on public roads.'

Or up your rectum, Red nearly said.

'It's a pretty car, darling,' her mother said. 'But not practical, is it, for everyday use?'

'Actually, I disagree,' Red said. 'There's an argument classics are much greener than modern cars.'

'Your mother and I are so relieved you weren't hurt,' her father said. 'So what happened?'

'The fire brigade reckon it was probably caused by the wiring – they said it happens with old cars sometimes. The car's destroyed.'

'Apart from the car, darling,' her father asked. 'How are you? How's the new man in your life?'

'New man?' Margot suddenly looked interested, in the way of a vulture spotting fresh roadkill.

'He sounds really nice,' her mother said. 'A doctor! Quite a contrast to that awful liar, Bryce.'

Red felt her heart twist.

'Tell us about this new man,' Margot said.

Red sipped her champagne, thinking. She hadn't told her family the latest news, and she didn't feel like telling them at this moment.

'We're all so bloody relieved you have Bryce out of your life. He really was a horrible little man,' her father chipped in. 'Of course, we could never have said that to you at the time. But what a total conman. Thank God we found out in time!'

'You really had a lucky escape,' Margot said. 'God, how close did you come to marrying him? Darling Red, we all love you and want the best for you. But that creep, Bryce whatsisname, honestly! He was the pits!'

'I loved him,' Red said defiantly, draining her champagne. She wasn't driving now, and could drink as much as she liked. And one thing she really liked about her parents was their shared love of booze. 'At the time, I really loved him.'

'Out of desperation?' Margot asked.

Red glared at her sister, then reached for the decanter of claret and filled her wine glass. 'Is that why you married Rory?' she said, her anger starting to boil over. 'Because you were thirty and desperate not to be left on the shelf?'

'I don't think that's the case at all, Red,' Rory said indignantly.

Her mother broke the awkward silence that followed. 'Margot, darling, I'm sure Red didn't mean that,' she said, looking pointedly at Red. 'Did you?'

'None of you seem to understand that I did actually love Bryce then. Yes. Totally and utterly. I'd have done anything for him.' She shrugged, and drank some wine, then looked at her sister. 'Okay, so maybe I fell for Bryce because I was desperate. I was never Miss Perfect like you, okay?'

'Shall we change the subject?' their father said. 'Let's talk about something more cheerful. This flat you've found, Red. It sounds perfect for you!'

'I want to hear about this new man in your life,' Margot said insistently.

Red downed her glass of claret in one, and refilled it. Getting pissed, she decided, was the best option today. She had so badly wanted to tell them all about Karl's death, but now something held her back. Maybe it was the fear of adding yet another item to the long list of failures and disasters that seemed to catalogue her life to date. Or maybe it was simply that after the nightmare of the past couple of hours she was badly in need of some TLC from her family.

'I really did think Bryce was the one,' Red said. 'I owe a lot to Mum for finding out the truth about him. God knows what would have happened if she hadn't been so perceptive. I could have ended up marrying a monster.'

'But you are moving on now, aren't you, darling?' her father said. 'You've found this new flat that you like?'

'I'm hoping to exchange contracts soon. I'd love you to see it.'

'Where is it?' her sister asked.

'Quite close to where I am now – along Kemp Town seafront. It's gorgeous. The top floor with a balcony overlooking the sea – a real suntrap, and I think a good investment. It needs some renovation, but I'm fine with that because it'll be a good project for me.'

'When can we go and see it, darling?' her mother asked.

'Pretty well anytime. The owners are away in Australia. Perhaps next weekend, either Saturday or Sunday, if you're free? I'll arrange to get the keys from the agent.'

'Are we free, darling?' her father asked, looking at her mother for confirmation.

'Sunday would be best,' her mother said. 'We're meant to be bringing the boat back on Thursday or Friday, if the forecast is right, and we have a lot to sort out on it at Brighton Marina on Saturday.'

'Ah yes,' her father said. 'We're bringing her back from Chichester to the marina for the winter. So Sunday would be best. Look forward to it.'

33

Sunday, 27 October

Seething as he listened to the conversation, Bryce Laurent made a note in the large lined Moleskine notebook titled *Red File* into which he transcribed every conversation that Red and her family had.

Her totally fucked-up family.

He could picture the dining table exactly. He'd sat there himself through several painful lunches and dinners with Red and her evil parents. And on two occasions with her equally toxic sister and her dribbling turkey of a husband.

But Red's sister and her husband were just a sideshow. Her mother was the truly evil, poisonous one. Supported by her vacuous fool of a husband.

I could have ended up marrying a monster.

He wrote down the words.

Really, Red? I'm a monster, am I? Well, if that's what you think, then a monster I shall be! But I don't think you really meant that, did you? Maybe you are just upset over losing your car? It was a bit of a dodgy vehicle. I did warn you about it. You really should not have been driving something that old with none of the modern safety features in it. Good riddance, I say. But hey, I understand you're upset. You need cheering up. A nice gift might cheer you up, perhaps? Yes?

I have good thoughts about this.

A gift would be a nice touch.

Bryce looked at his watch. He had dated Red for almost a year when they had been walking, arm in arm, down Bond Street in London, and had stopped to look in the window of Cartier. She'd told him then that she thought they were the most elegant watches in the world.

He remembered the look of total joy on her face the day, just a few weeks later, he had slipped the Cartier Tank watch on her wrist.

But that was then.

He turned his focus back to the conversation, just one of the communications sent to him regularly throughout the day and night by the SpyBubble software, then replayed it from the start, listening intently.

Especially to the parts where they were talking about him.

'*He sounds really nice. A doctor! Quite a contrast to that awful liar, Bryce.*'

That was her mother's voice. Camilla Westwood.

Camilla!

Oh, you smug cow, Camilla. Don't you realize how much I loved your daughter? I loved her in a way I've never loved anyone before. She was my light, my laughter, my sunshine. She was, quite apart from being the sexiest creature I've ever met, my soulmate. Your daughter was the woman who told me, who whispered into my ear while we were making love, that she wanted to spend the rest of her life with me.

And I responded, 'Right back at you!'

Three days later, she dumped me.

Poisoned by you and your husband.

I'm a monster, am I?

Okay, I'm fine with that, I can live with that. So long as you understand what monsters do. They kill people. They rip them to shreds. Happy with that?

Happy knowing you are going to die?
You really should not have said that.
'*I owe a lot to Mum for finding out the truth about him.*
God knows what would have happened if she hadn't been so
perceptive. I could have ended up marrying a monster.'
Do you remember the last text you sent me, Red? When
you were still as crazily in love with me as I was with you?
Before your toxic parents poisoned your mind?

Every part of me is thinking of you. It is totally the best
feeling. I want it to stay with me for a long, long time.
Am high on you and what you do to me, and I looooove
the time we spend together, even if it is just staring at
each other. I feel so lucky we feel like this. I've never felt
anything so strong and I totally adore it. And I totally
adore every inch of you. I go to sleep dreaming of you
and I wake in the morning craving you – and counting
the hours until I see you again. XXXXXX + XXXXXXXX +
XXXXXXXXXXXXXX

Oh shit, I adore you.

PS did I tell u I adore you? XXXXXXXXX

PPS did I tell you just how much I adore you?
XXXXXXXXXXXXXXXX

You sent this just two days before you dumped me.
Nobody changes their mind that fast. Not unless their
mind has been poisoned.
And I'm really sorry – but no one can mess with another
human's emotions in that way. There's a Rubicon in every
relationship that we cross. You and I crossed it a long while
ago. We crossed it, I thought, the day we were making love and
you asked me to come with my eyes open, staring into yours.

That was the night our souls intertwined.

Can you even begin to understand the anger I am feeling now?

It's why I have to kill you. Because I cannot live in a world in which you are with some other man. My heart just won't take it. I'm sorry, Red. Really I am. We could have had such a great life together. Instead, we're just going to have to settle for a great death.

Single girl, 29, redhead and smouldering, love life that's crashed and burned. Seeks new flame to rekindle her fire.

You wanted fire, Red? You've got it.

34

Monday, 28 October

At 8.30 a.m. on Monday, Red sat once more in the basement consulting room of the terraced house, close to Brighton station, with the crimson Buddha staring benignly down at her from the mantelpiece. The room felt chilly, the ancient two-bar electric fire in the grate giving out scant heat.

'So how was your weekend, Red?' Judith Biddlestone asked.

'Let's not go there.'

'Oh dear, I'm sorry. Any parts of it you want to talk about?'

'My car caught fire.'

'Oh my God. Are you okay?'

'I'm fine. I managed to get out, thank goodness, before it burst into flames. Afterwards I had to endure more sarcasm from my sister at Sunday lunch. It wasn't the greatest weekend. I kept thinking how Karl and I had planned to spend it.'

'Your older sister, Margot, who you describe as *successful*?'

'And who has never stopped letting me know it, all my life.'

'I don't think she's ever helped your confidence, has she?'

'Probably not. No.'

'Do you want to talk about your weekend or shall we revisit what we bracketed at the end of the last session?'

'Let's keep talking about Bryce. That's why I came to see you in the first place.'

'You told me that the private detective your mother had secretly hired found out that Bryce lied to you about what he did for a living, and about his past. How did he learn about what you had discovered?'

'I confronted him with it.'

'How did Bryce react?'

'With total denial. He said the detective had the wrong person.'

'What happened then?'

'I said I needed some space to think about our relationship and our future. He didn't want to know. He kept insisting that we were engaged, and we were going to spend the rest of our lives together.'

'And were you engaged at this point?'

For some moments Red was hesitant in replying. 'Well, in his mind, yes. We were having dinner in Cuba Libre – the restaurant where we'd had our first date – when he suddenly put a little box on the table. He took out a ring and slipped it on my wedding finger, and then asked me to marry him. Actually, I didn't like the ring, it wasn't my taste at all – it was very bling. And I was already uncertain about him at this stage. There were so many ups and downs, good times and bad. I told him I would have to think about it. That triggered another row when we got back to my flat – he went bananas. I ended up calling the police. And PC Spofford came. They arrested Bryce and took him away because I was scared to have him in the house. But they had to release him on police bail the next day because he hadn't hit me or anything. He'd just been abusive, and I didn't want to press charges.'

'He was taken into custody the night he asked you to marry him, due to his rage. You told him you needed time to think, and yet he believed the two of you to be engaged. How did you make sense of that?' the psychologist asked.

'That's how things were with Bryce and me. What he wanted, he got. I learned not to contradict him. I knew I hadn't accepted his proposal but calling the police hadn't worked – he was back the next day, being nice and acting all *loved up* because we were engaged. I just went along with it. It was important not to give him a reason to get angry.'

'What the detective had uncovered, I'm sure, would have fallen squarely into the category of things that would give him a reason to get angry?'

'Definitely! Things just went from bad to worse. The detective said Bryce had told me a pack of lies about his background, and that he had a conviction for serious assault in the US. Part of me wanted out, but whenever I tried to broach this with him, he would burst into tears, throw his whole unloved childhood baggage at me, tell me that I was the only person who had ever given him a feeling of self-worth in his life. And he swore he would change. He said he knew he wasn't perfect but that the detective had got the wrong man and that he hadn't lied to me about all those things. He was very convincing. I wanted to believe him.'

'When you think about that now, why do you think you wanted to believe Bryce?'

'I felt such a fool when I heard what the detective had found out and especially that my mum had been right not to trust Bryce. I – I guess I'd put so much of myself into the relationship it was difficult just to walk away.'

The psychologist said, 'Of course it was difficult, Red. I liken the incongruity of hating the way you are treated in a relationship yet not wanting to leave it to the experience of newly trained troops.'

'How so?'

'Basic training for the British Army is tough. Recruits are treated, on the whole, pretty harshly and I've never met one that said they had a nice easy time of it. Usually they were hurt and in pain – physical or emotional, or both – every day, and were humiliated and broken in the process. Yet, having given so much of themselves, they tend not to take kindly to a bystander suggesting that if the Army has been so *unkind*, they maybe ought to leave and join the Royal Navy instead.'

'That makes a lot of sense to me. I felt that I had invested so much of myself that I had more to lose by leaving than by staying. And he kept convincing me that if I broke up with him, I'd never find another man. And – this may sound pathetic – I believed that. He'd made me believe that. I suppose I let him stay out of some kind of desperation. You have to understand that he has immense charm and is very persuasive – very manipulative.'

'I do understand that. Do you? Do you allow yourself to truly know how well he manipulated you?'

'He was a prize manipulator. He even managed to be nice for a long while after I challenged him about the private detective. I actually began to think maybe he had changed. I was going to leave him, but he begged me to stay, and foolishly I gave him another chance. Then one night a few weeks later something I said seemed to pull a trigger in him and he went loopy again – totally berserk.'

'Trigger?'

'He was admiring himself in the mirror – naked. He's obsessed with his body. He gets up in the middle of the night, takes steroids and does weight training. I just joked – quoted that Robbie Burns line – as he stared at himself with, like, absolute approval. I said, "Would that the world could see us the way we see ourselves." And that was it. He smashed the mirror, then turned on me, screaming and shaking. He picked up a shard of broken glass and came at me with it. I actually thought I was going to die. Somehow I managed to get out and ran into the street, barefoot, screaming. A guy walking his dog stopped and called the police for me, and Bryce was arrested.

'I decided then and there to throw him out, while he was in custody. I packed all his stuff in the two suitcases that he had arrived with, including the ghastly, vulgar bling ring and the Cartier watch, then I asked Constable Spofford to come to the house the morning he was released on bail because I didn't know what would happen. Rob – Constable – Spofford put all his stuff outside the front door, and he told Bryce when he turned up that I did not want to see him, and he wasn't to go in.'

'And how did Bryce react?'

'He didn't say a word. Just took his stuff and went off quietly, like a lamb, apparently.'

'Curious. With what you know of Bryce is that what you would have imagined he would do?'

'At the time I remember feeling relieved that he hadn't made a scene but after a few hours I started to feel really scared. Other people kept telling me it was over but I knew it wasn't. I don't think Bryce will ever let me go.'

'Tell me why you think that.'

'Because in his head I belong to him. I had an anonymous email with an attachment a couple of days later. I opened it. It was a cartoon drawing of a playing card – the queen of hearts. I knew it was from him. I wasn't sure what to make of it; but it seemed, maybe, his way of saying goodbye.'

'And then?'

'Nothing. Total silence. I thought that perhaps he had finally got the message and moved on. Several of my friends tried to fix me up with new men, but I wasn't in the right frame of mind to meet anyone. Then my best friend, Raquel Evans – a dentist – said there was a very good-looking young doctor called Karl Murphy in the medical centre where she worked, who was a widower with two small boys. I agreed to go on a blind date with him, Raquel and her husband, Paul. Something clicked – or sparked – between us. I really liked him, and suddenly, after all the darkness of Bryce, I could see light again. We had fun together. It wasn't the intensity of passion I had with Bryce, but I felt comfortable with him, safe, for the first time in as long as I could remember. And I really liked him. I could see a future with him. I actually liked that he had young children – he seemed to care about them so much, and that made him seem a good person to me. We were starting to make plans.'

'And now you think he might be dead?'

Red shook her head. 'I know for sure now, he's dead. His body's been identified by his dental records. He committed suicide. Doused himself in petrol – self-immolation, they call it. Can you believe a doctor would do that? Cover himself in petrol, then set fire to himself? Surely a medic would know what a painful death that would be? Why didn't he just take pills, which he could have prescribed for himself?'

'How are you processing this, Red? What sense are you making of it all?'

'I still cannot believe he killed himself.'

'You don't think it was suicide?'

'I'm told the post-mortem strongly indicates that it was. But why? Why would he have done that?'

'Are you asking me why?'

'Can you explain it? I cannot make sense of it at all.'

'I couldn't possibly comment without having known him, Red. I am interested in how you are making sense of what has happened, given that you did know him.'

'I thought I knew him. Do you think I should go to his funeral?'

'What do you think about that?'

'I don't even know when it will be, or where – I'm hoping to find out today – but I wonder if it will seem more real if I do go. Maybe I'll get some closure?'

'Funerals can be helpful for closure. But it depends on how you feel.'

'I wish I could get some closure with Bryce,' Red said, abruptly changing the subject. 'I still have it, you know, the guilt. That it was my fault, all the abuse. That I brought it all on.'

The psychologist looked through her notes. 'You said that in our last session on Friday. Why do you feel that?'

Red thought for some moments. 'I guess that's how he made me feel – that I let him down all the time. In the kitchen. In bed. That I couldn't live up to his expectations.'

'You wanted to live up to his expectations?'

'Of course.'

'Were you clear about what they were?'

'I'm not sure I understand,' Red replied.

'I apologize, I wasn't clear. Curious, that I would become unclear as we were talking about Bryce and his expectations. What I meant to say was, did Bryce's expectations stay the same regardless of his mood or the situation?'

Red laughed bitterly and said, 'No, never. One day he would be pleased with me and the next I'd do exactly the same thing and he would fly into a rage.'

'Did he do that in company? If you were with his friends, for instance?'

'That's something I realized was very weird about him. He had no friends. None. I thought all men have a best mate, don't they?'

'Normal men do, Red. Yes. He had none at all? No former work colleague? Childhood buddy?'

'No one. I was all he had. In the early days I was so proud of him, I wanted to show him off to all my friends. I arranged evenings out in bars and restaurants with some of them. But he got insanely jealous if I talked to any other man. One time at a party in Brighton, I was just having an innocent chat with the husband of a friend of mine when Bryce came up and asked him just what the hell he thought he was doing chatting me up. He was so furious I had to restrain him from hitting the guy, and then took him home. We had a terrible row that night. He called me a whore, a slut, all kinds of names. Then he tied me up, gagged me and raped me. I thought he was going to kill me. He left me tied up and gagged all night.' She fell silent.

'You're safe now. Such a terrifying ordeal and it's over. You survived. Are you still with me, Red?'

'Just about.'

'Okay, stay with me. You don't need to go back there.'

'It feels so real when I remember.'

'I know.'

'In the morning he was sobbing, begging me to forgive him. He told me he had only done it because he loved me and was scared of losing me. He would only untie me after I had promised not to call the police. When he finally did untie me he got mad at me again because I'd wet myself.'

Judith Biddlestone nodded, her eyes softening and her mouth forming an upside-down smile.

'I was so ashamed.'

'The shame's not yours, Red. Who benefited most from you feeling ashamed?'

'I guess Bryce did. I could never have told the police about the demeaning things he did to me. I can hardly bear to tell you.'

'And yet you have, and in doing so have placed some of that shame back where it belongs. With Bryce.'

Red was silent for some moments, then she asked, 'Do you think it's a good sign that I haven't heard from him since we split up? Apart from that queen of hearts email a few days after?'

'What do you think, Red? It's more than four months now. Do you believe it's over?'

'I want to believe it is. But I can't believe he would let me go so easily. I did think I saw him on Thursday, outside the office, but maybe I was imagining it. I ran outside and couldn't see any sign of him.'

Oh no, my lovely Red, Bryce thought, as he listened. *You weren't imagining it at all.*

35

Bryce sat, his earpiece plugged in, his whole body tight with anger; a muscle in his face was twitching the side of his mouth. *Monster. Ghastly. Vulgar. Bling.*

Four months, counsellor? What do you know about time in hell, lady? Linear time is a meaningless construct. Why should four months be any different to four minutes? Four days? Four years? It doesn't hurt any less; it hurts more. The pain builds every day. It's pretty crass of you, a counsellor of all people, to assume I've moved on. You might measure your time in minutes, days, months. But it all blends into one continuum of pain to me. Four months of pain. I feel it like a weight, crushing me.

Crushing me like those hurtful words.

I'm a monster am I, Red?

Vulgar, ghastly, bling. Is that what you thought of it, Red? It's a beautiful ring. I had it specially made for you by one of the best jewellers in Brighton. It cost me over ten thousand pounds of my inheritance.

Vulgar? Ghastly? Bling?

You know what, Red, I'm starting to think I had a lucky escape from being stuck with a spoiled brat. Maybe I should be grateful to you for that. Really, I mean it. In fact, the more I think about it, the more grateful I am that you let me go.

I'm going to give you a present, to show you my gratitude.

36

Monday, 28 October

Shortly after 10 a.m. on Monday morning, Roy Grace was working through the stack of paperwork for the prosecution of Lucas Daly – one of the offenders under arrest from the recent Operation Flounder. Daly's assets were steadily being tracked down and seized, under the Proceeds of Crime Act, by financial investigator Emily Gaylor.

Grace had a ton of paperwork he wanted to clear by the end of the week, before his wedding day and the short honeymoon next week. But distracting him was the wedding file, efficiently prepared by Cleo, which was also on his desk. It contained the documentation for the booking of the church and the reception after, the catering contract, the order form for the drinks, canapés and meal. The biggest headache of all was the seating plan. Who to invite and not invite had been bad enough, and they'd had to make some tough decisions. But now trying to decide who should sit where was a complete nightmare.

There was a knock on his door and without waiting for a reply, as usual, Norman Potting ambled in. 'Morning, chief. Got some information back for you,' he said, clutching a brown envelope and looking pleased with himself. Recently the Detective Sergeant had been diagnosed with prostate cancer. Around the same time, Grace had noticed, Potting appeared to have had something of a makeover. The comb-over was still the same, but his previously sparse grey hair was now an unnatural-looking shiny black. The horrible tweed jackets with leather-patched elbows and grey flannel trousers that he favoured had been replaced with dark grey suits, fresh shirts and ties that no longer showed what he'd eaten for breakfast. And instead of reeking of stale pipe tobacco, he smelled quite fragrant.

'Have a seat, Norman.'

Potting used to shuffle along, but today he walked across the floor with almost a spring in his step. He sat down and looked, for a moment, a tad shy.

'I've been meaning to ask, Norman, what's the latest on your prostate?'

'Well, so far so good. The old PSA levels have dropped quite substantially – the quack's pretty pleased.'

'That's good news. What does your doctor think is the reason?'

'He's not sure. I've got a good sex life at the moment. Maybe that could be it.'

Despite that being rather too much information, Grace nodded, and grinned. 'Well, good news, Norman. Keep it up – as it were.'

'Oh, I am, chief! Oh yes!' Then he looked almost coy. 'Actually, chief, that's one of the reasons I came to see you. It's about your wedding.'

'Yes?'

'I'm well chuffed to be invited.'

'Cleo and I are delighted you can come.'

'The thing is . . .' Potting blushed. 'I just wondered . . . you know . . . if you are doing a seating plan . . . would it be possible to sit next to DS Moy?'

Grace stared him in the face, and grinned. 'Oh? So are

the suspicions I've been having over the past few months correct?'

'Suspicions, chief?'

'I couldn't help noticing the body language between you two. Something going on, is there?'

'There's no regulations against it that I'd be contravening, are there, chief?' Potting looked worried for a moment.

'About relationships between staff? No, none. So, you and Bella – you're seeing each other?'

'You could say that, chief. Actually, it's gone beyond that stage. We're sort of, um, a bit of an item, actually.' He blushed. 'I've asked Bella to be my wife – last night, actually – and she's accepted.'

Grace grinned. Despite them being the most unlikely couple imaginable, he was pleased for both of them. Bella, who was in her mid-thirties, had been stuck at home for years looking after her ailing mother, and leading what seemed to him to be a totally joyless life beyond her work. And Norman, despite being his own worst enemy at times, had been ruthlessly conned and exploited by his scheming Thai bride and had recently been dealt a shitty blow by Mother Nature. 'So she will become Mrs Norman Potting the fifth?'

'Fifth and last, I hope!' Potting said.

Then both men fell silent as the darkness behind the possible truth of that comment, Norman's prostate cancer, sat between them like an elephant in the room.

'Well, she's a lovely lady. Let's hope you have a long and happy marriage,' Grace said. 'You both deserve a break in life. I'll make sure you sit together. And congratulations!'

'Thank you, I appreciate it.' Potting gave a sad, wintry smile. 'Right, business.' He shook out the contents of the envelope, several printed pages clipped together, and passed them across the desk to Grace. 'You asked me to have the suicide note of Dr Karl Murphy checked out by a graphologist? To have it compared against samples of his normal handwriting?'

Grace nodded. 'Yes. And?'

'This is the full report. It's pretty detailed. In summary, there is little doubt Dr Karl Murphy wrote the note. I was able to get the work fast-tracked as the guy owed me a favour.'

'Good work, Norman, thanks.'

'But there is one slightly odd thing,' Potting said. 'The graphologist said that Murphy's normal handwriting has a right – forward – slant. This note has been written in a left slant – rearward.'

Grace frowned. 'Do doctors use handwriting much these days or do they type everything on keyboards?'

Potting thought for some moments. 'Well, I've been seeing more of doctors just recently than I really want. A few write prescriptions by hand, but pretty much everything is done on computers now.'

'You need to talk to his secretary, get her to go through all his files, see if there are any other examples of left-slant handwriting. If not, it could mean something.'

'That he was trying to send us a signal? A message, chief?'

'Possibly.' Then Grace thought for a moment. 'You're a bit of a crossword puzzle man, aren't you, Norman?'

'Done the *Telegraph* every day for years – well, tried to do it anyway. Why?'

'Well, I'm speculating wildly here, but I've found out Dr Murphy was a keen crossword man. If he wrote this in a backward slant, perhaps to signal he was writing under coercion, then possibly, just possibly, he left something cryptic in these words. Maybe you could analyse it word by word from a crossword perspective?'

Potting frowned. 'I'll try.'

'This is probably not going to go anywhere, but I want to make sure. So far every bit of forensic evidence, and the graphologist's findings, point towards suicide. But . . .' Grace shrugged.

A few minutes later, as Norman Potting left his office, closing the door behind him, Roy Grace's phone rang. It was his new Lead Management Secretary.

'Roy,' she said, 'I've just had a call from the Chief Constable's staff officer. Tom Martinson's asked if you can come over to see him late afternoon. I have you booked in for a cold cases review meeting, but you are free after then. Would 6 p.m. suit you?'

Instantly, the sky outside seemed to cloud over. He had hoped to get home early tonight, to help Cleo put Noah to bed. It didn't matter that Roy was both a grown man and a highly experienced police officer. A call from the Chief Constable could still set his nerves jangling. His first thought was what he might have done wrong to merit a reprimand. But he couldn't think of anything. It might be for some transgression he had not even realized he had committed. Or to brief him on some forthcoming event. Or a change in policy on some aspect of policing in Sussex.

Whatever.

'Did he give a clue what it's about?' he asked.

'None, I'm afraid.'

Grace had a feeling it was not going to be good news.

He was right.

37

The headline on page six of the *Argus* newspaper online read: **Top copper to wed on Saturday.**

Sandy Lohmann, seated in front of the computer screen in her Munich apartment in the little room she had made her study, with its view down onto the turbulent water of the River Isar just beyond the waterfall, stared transfixed at the screen.

> The wedding of Detective Superintendent Roy Grace, of Surrey and Sussex Major Crime Team, and Cleo Morey, Senior Anatomical Pathology Technician of Brighton and Hove Mortuary, will take place at St Margaret's Church in Rottingdean at 2.30 p.m. on Saturday, 2 November. Many senior police officers, including Chief Constable Tom Martinson, are expected to attend. The marriage will bring to a close the detective's years of sadness following the unexplained disappearance of his former wife, Sandra (Sandy) Christina Grace, over ten years ago, who was formally declared dead in August of this year.

'Mama?'

She turned to her son, Bruno, trying to hide her irritation at being distracted. 'Ja, mein Lieber?'

He was hungry. She would make him supper in a few

minutes, she promised. 'I just need to finish this,' she said, in her fluent German.

He padded off, disgruntled, returning to his computer game in which he was killing futuristic warriors on an inter-galactic battlefield.

Sandy logged on first to Lufthansa, and then to British Airways. Then she went onto expedia.com. This was good timing. It was a holiday for German schools next week, so it would be no problem to take her son – their son. Within five minutes she had booked flights to London and a bed and breakfast hotel in Brighton, called Strawberry Fields, for the two of them.

How very convenient to have had me declared dead, she thought, with anger rising by the second. *Getting married, are you, Roy Grace? I don't think so.*

38

Monday, 28 October

Mondays had never been Red's favourite day of the week, and this particular one had proved no exception. On Saturday she had shown fourteen different clients around properties the agency had up for sale, and seven of them had contacted her today to say they weren't interested. Then, to add to her despondency, the couple she had shown around the Portland Avenue house on Thursday, for whom she had had such high hopes, had called to say they had found somewhere that they liked better with another agency, and they had withdrawn their earlier offer.

She left the office at 5 p.m., although ordinarily she would have stayed at her desk for at least another half hour. Raquel Evans was taking her to a hot yoga class this evening, which her friend thought would do her some good. And she was quite looking forward to doing something different.

As was her normal daily routine, she stopped at the convenience store on her way home to buy herself something to bung in the microwave for her evening meal. She looked along the chilled cabinet section and pulled out a fish pie, then grabbed a pack of frozen beans and dropped them into her basket. As she did so, she was dazzled by a brilliant flash of light.

She heard a scream.

A boom that popped her ears.

Suddenly she was enveloped in a cloud of noxious black smoke that stung her eyes, almost blinding her with tears. Her instant thought was, *Shit, is this a terrorist attack?* More and more smoke billowed around.

She turned to run down the aisle towards where she thought the door was. But crashing into someone, she stumbled away, backing into a stack of tins which clattered down around her. She turned, totally disoriented, holding her breath, trying to work out which way the door was. An alarm was screeching above her. She stumbled forward and her legs bashed painfully into something. A shelf? She breathed out, then breathed in the vile smoke.

In a wild panic, coughing and choking, her throat feeling like it had been stuffed with burning cotton wool, she fell to her knees. She had read somewhere that in a fire, the closer to the ground you got the better off you would be. There were screams all around her. Her eyes were watering so much she could see nothing. There was another explosion. Then another. The alarm continued like a banshee. Suddenly she felt cold water spraying on her head. The banshee continued, mixed with terrified cries, shouts, screams.

Oh shit, Red thought. She dropped her basket, thinking only of survival. Where the hell was the exit? Somewhere close to her, a mobile phone rang.

She felt the heat of flames on her face. Burning. She spun around, keeping as low as she could. Crawling. Collided with something hard that smacked her cheek. A trolley.

Then a hand grabbed hers. Pulled. Pulled.

'Help me!' she said.

The hand pulled her up, silently, and she scrabbled along on her knees, gripping the hand, feeling – knowing – that her life depended on it. The siren and screams continued in the choking darkness all around her.

Then suddenly she felt a blast of cold. Heard the swoosh of electric doors. She was outside. Still on her knees. Gulping down fresh air. A cacophony of wailing sirens. She turned to look at the chaos behind her. Fire engines were arriving. People were staggering out, falling over. Slivers of blue light slid past her along the pavement, like ghosts.

I'm outside, she thought, coughing again. *Thank God, I'm outside!*

In terrorist attacks they set off one bomb to get you outside and then another to hit all the rescue workers, she remembered from news reports. *Got to get away. Fast.*

As police cars and ambulances arrived, followed by more fire engines, in a cacophony of screaming sounds, Red staggered to her feet, retrieved her bike and stumbled away in panic and terror, gulping down air.

Get away from here!

She hurried along New Church Road, pushing her bike, her chest hurting, then turned left into her street, Westbourne Terrace. The thick, choking smoke was in her lungs and her nostrils. She coughed with every step until finally the steady, cooling sea breeze had replaced most of it.

She was shaking.

Shit.

What happened?

What the hell happened?

Terrorists?

It was all she could think of.

Her hand was shaking so much, she struggled for some moments to get the key in the lock of her front door. Then she went inside, pushed her bike along the hallway, and secured it with the padlock. Popping the timer switch for the stair lights, she climbed up to her second-floor apartment.

Again she struggled with her keys, finally inserting them.

She went in, snapped on the hall light, slammed the door shut behind her and, exhausted, leaned against it, thinking, gathering her thoughts.

Something did not feel right.

It took her some moments before she realized, and stared down, frozen in sudden fear. At her left hand.

At her third finger.

At the vulgar, diamond-encrusted engagement ring which she had returned to Bryce Laurent when she had thrown him out.

The ring that was now back on her finger.

39

Monday, 28 October

Red stood, shivering in fear, beneath the bare, feeble glow of the long-life bulb hanging from a flex that looked like a fire-hazard-in-waiting above her head. She stood, rooted to the spot. Staring at the ring on her finger, staring down the hallway, one hand on the door, ready to jerk it open and run back out onto the landing.

Was Bryce in here?

Her eyes darted nervously down the corridor at each of the doors. One was closed, the other slightly ajar.

Was he behind one of them?

Or in the living room beyond the end of the hallway?

In the bathroom?

There were two deadlocks on the front door, which the woman from the Sanctuary Scheme assured her could not be picked. The windows were all double glazed with toughened glass and locked. No one could get in from the outside, certainly not easily.

How the hell had the ring been put back on her finger? Was it the silent person who had held her hand and guided her out of the convenience store and then vanished? Had that been Bryce?

Had he set fire to the store deliberately? In order to create a diversion to put the ring back on her finger? He had once told her, in happier times, that pickpockets worked by creating a diversion by confusion.

If it had been Bryce, there was no way he could be here already, ahead of her. Was there? She pulled her phone out of her handbag, found PC Spofford's mobile number in her 'Favourites' and hovered her finger above it, ready to press it and set it dialling in an instant. But she held off, concerned that she had already called him out so many times in the past months on false alarms. Instead, she slipped off one of her heeled shoes and brandished it in her right hand. Holding the phone in her left hand, with a finger poised, she took a few paces as quietly as she could along the corridor, then turned the handle of her den door and pushed it open so hard it banged back against the wall.

Her laptop sat on her desk, lid closed as she had left it. The den was empty. 'Hello Constable Spofford,' she said loudly, but without having dialled him. It was for the benefit of her unseen visitor – if by chance he was here. 'I have an intruder. Could you come right away? Five minutes? Thanks, I'll stay on the line.'

She pushed open the louvred door to the little toilet at the rear until she could see in. Nothing.

She crept further along the corridor, then, with a shiver of fear, kicked open her bedroom door. The room was also empty, undisturbed, the bed neatly made with the white candlewick counterpane on top, and her two ragged teddy bears from her childhood, Moppet and Edward, lying back against the nest of cushions, holding paws.

Next she checked the bathroom, entering and sliding back the privacy door for the toilet. Nothing.

Then, holding the shoe high, heel forward, she strode into the main open-plan living/dining room.

Empty.

Her breakfast coffee mug and cereal bowl lay on the bar, as she had left them this morning, along with her Kindle on which she read *The Times* every morning. She hurried back down the hallway and secured the safety chain, then twisted the lever of the internal bolt.

Finally she felt secure. She coughed again, then again went through to the kitchen, poured a glass of cold water, sat at the table and gulped it down, then began twisting the ring, trying to pull it off. But it would not move.

Then her sense of devastation at the loss of Karl Murphy suddenly welled up and she began crying. She went to the fridge, pulled out a bottle of Spanish white Albarino wine – one of the few things Bryce had given her a taste for that she still enjoyed – opened it and poured herself a very large glass. She drank a gulp of it, then another. Her heart felt like it had weights hanging from it. She stripped off her clothes, which reeked of smoke, put her skirt and top into a bin bag to take to the dry-cleaner's, and the rest she shoved into the washing machine.

Then she walked, naked, into the bathroom, opened the glass door and switched on the really strong power shower – one of the very few features she liked about this place. She checked the temperature with her hands, and when she was happy with it, she stepped inside the cubicle.

For several minutes she luxuriated in the strong jet, cleansing the smoke from her hair and from every pore of her skin. She soaped her finger and finally wrenched the ring off and put it in the soap dish. Her thoughts were a jumbled mess. Karl was dead, and she still could not get her head around that. How the hell had the ring been put back on her finger? By whom?

By Bryce. There was no other possible explanation.

Was he in the minimart tonight when the fire broke out?

Fire was one of his party tricks.

Connections started forming inside her head. Cuba Libre? Her car? Was she just being fanciful? Now, this evening, her convenience store?

Still deep in thought, she stepped out of the shower and wrapped one of her hugely expensive hotel-size towels around herself. She had been in the shower for so long the mirror had totally steamed up. She opened the window a fraction, and the door, and slowly the mirror began to clear.

She massaged leave-in conditioner into her hair, then night cream on her face. Then, as she stared at her reflection, she froze.

A distinctive shape was forming in the centre of the mirror.

A vertical rectangle, with hearts in each corner of it. And the silhouette of a woman's head, wearing a crown.

The queen of hearts.

40

It was shortly after 6 p.m. when Roy Grace was ushered by Tom Martinson's assistant into the Chief Constable's spacious, elegant office. It occupied a corner of the first floor of the Queen Anne mansion that gave its name to the Sussex Police headquarters complex, Malling House. The chief officers of Sussex police were all located within this handsome, imposing building.

Roy Grace's nervousness was not improved by noticing that the Chief looked uneasy himself. Martinson jumped up from behind his huge, polished-wood L-shaped desk and hurried across, his arm outstretched, and shook Roy's hand. 'Thanks for coming to see me, Roy,' he said, his normally cheery, precise voice sounding a tad less assured than usual, ushering him over to one of two black sofas arranged in a corner, with a coffee table between them.

Grace sat on the edge of one sofa, and the Chief settled on the edge of the other. He was a fit-looking man of fifty, with thinning, short dark hair and a pleasant, no-nonsense air about him, dressed as usual in his uniform of white shirt with epaulettes, black tie and black trousers.

Grace observed him wring his hands. 'Can I offer you something to drink, Roy? Tea? Coffee? Water?'

'I'm fine, thank you, sir.'

'Good, right. Look, I thought I ought to give you a heads-up. I think you know that Assistant Chief Constable Rigg is moving on?'

'I do, yes, sir. He's been promoted to Deputy Chief Constable of Gloucestershire?'

'Yes, correct. Well, we've appointed his replacement, who will be starting here next Monday – I think while you are on honeymoon, correct?'

'Yes sir.'

'Judith and I are very much looking forward to your wedding on Saturday, by the way. Should be a jolly occasion.'

Grace smiled. 'Cleo and I are very honoured that you and your wife are coming.'

'We're delighted to be invited! And Rottingdean is a beautiful church – what an idyllic venue for a wedding.' Martinson smiled fleetingly, then looked serious again. 'The thing is, we had a number of applicants for this post. But the one who stood out as by far the best qualified is someone I think you've had a few issues with in the past. I just want you to understand that his appointment is in no way any reflection on how much I value you.'

Grace frowned, wondering whom he might be talking about. There was one person he could think of, but instantly dismissed.

As if reading his mind, Martinson said, 'Chief Superintendent Cassian Pewe, from the Met.'

'Cassian Pewe?' Grace echoed lamely, as if hoping that somehow he had misheard.

'He really does have outstanding qualities for this role.'

Grace felt like an insect that had fallen into a draining sink, that was swirling around and about to be sucked down the plughole. *Cassian Pewe?*

'I know the two of you have had issues in the past, but he assures me these are completely forgotten now.'

Grace had originally met Cassian Pewe when, as a London Metropolitan Police Public Order Inspector, Pewe had come to Sussex to run a public order training course. A year later, Grace had a run-in with the deeply arrogant officer when the Met had sent in reinforcements to help police Brighton during the Labour Party Conference. Then, eighteen months ago, Cassian Pewe had been brought in as a Review Superintendent by Grace's previous ACC, Alison Vosper. Pewe's first task had been to organize a police search team to dig up the garden of Grace's house on suspicion that Grace had murdered his wife, Sandy, and buried her remains there.

Roy Grace could never forgive him for that. The man preened and strutted, always acting as if he was in charge, even when he wasn't. The Chief was well known in the force for his dislike of arrogance – he could not be serious, surely? Roy was amazed that a man of Martinson's judgement could have done this. He was appointing this total shit as his boss?

Just over a year ago, Roy Grace had saved Cassian Pewe's life, risking his own in the process, when Pewe had been in Grace's car which, after being rammed in a chase, had almost gone over the cliffs of Beachy Head. After that incident, Pewe had applied for a transfer back to the Met. And out of his life, Roy had hoped.

He could not believe this man was coming back. And now as his boss. Chucking caution to the wind, he said, 'I'm really not happy about this, sir.'

'I appreciate that you might not be,' Tom Martinson said. 'If it makes you too uncomfortable, I could see if we could get you transferred to another role when something comes up, but I would hate to lose you from Major Crime. Perhaps stick it out for a bit? He categorically assures me he has nothing personal against you.'

Grace thought hard for some moments before replying. Of all the roles in Sussex Police that he knew of, few – if any – could match his. Investigating homicides was what he loved. There weren't many days that he woke and did not look forward to going to work.

But Cassian Pewe as his boss?

Shit.

41

'Shit.'

The towel around Red fell to the floor. She spun round, staring at the closed door behind her in total panic. *Shit, oh shit. No.* She shook in terror. Had Bryce been in here? Was he here now? Had he entered while she had been in the shower?

She rammed home the bathroom bolt, then leaned against the door, staring again at the image of the playing card on the mirror. Then she ran over to the window, and looked down into the deserted alleyway. Two floors up. Too high to jump. Terror pulsed inside her, tightening her gullet. The cold, damp air made her shiver even more.

She felt for some moments as if she was back in a child-hood nightmare, being chased by a monster, trying to scream and no sound coming out. Should she scream now, out of the window, for help?

Would someone hear?

Then her terror turned to anger. *Screw you, Bryce.* She tried to think rationally. She had checked the flat, locked and bolted the front door. There was no way he could have come in while she was in the shower.

Was there?

Shivering, she grabbed her towel, then looked around the bathroom for a weapon. Looked at the loo brush. At the round, free-standing vanity mirror. At her range of bottles of perfume and jars of creams. She settled on the mirror, picked it up, gripping it by the base. Then she unbolted the door and hurled it open.

And stared out into the empty corridor.

42

Monday, 28 October

Bryce, in his flat across the alleyway, watched her on the monitor showing images from the pinhole camera he had concealed in one of the bolts securing the bathroom mirror to the wall. He was grinning.

Nice to see her naked. Nice to see her truly afraid. He watched her step out into the hallway, looking right, then left, vanity mirror held high. He watched her, with deep satisfaction, check every inch of the flat again, flinging open the doors of every room, every cupboard, then finally picking up the phone and dialling.

He knew exactly who she would be calling, and he was right.

'PC Spofford,' the voice answered.

He loved the panic in her voice as she spoke to the constable. The reassuring voice of the police officer saying he would be with her in fifteen minutes. The same little bastard cop who had handed him his packed suitcases outside her front door not so many months ago.

Then he switched his attention to his laptop screen. To the Google Earth map of her parents' house near Henfield. Where her stupid bitch mother and pathetically weak father lived. But not for much longer.

He zoomed in close, studying the windows, the roof.

Then he entered another address into Google Earth. The

Royal Regent mansion block on Marine Parade where Red was buying her dream home. And which she would be showing her parents next Sunday.

Your dream home, babe. Dream on!

43

When Suzy's plane lifted up and climbed away over the east Devon coastline, Matt stayed with her, and went with her to ...

Monday, 28 October

Red, dressed now in black tights, a knee-length black skirt, a grey roll-neck sweater and boots, and trembling with fear, heard the entryphone buzz and looked at the small video screen beside the door. Then relief surged through her as she saw the familiar friendly face of PC Rob Spofford, slightly distorted by the poor lens. She pressed the button to let him in, then waited. After a minute she heard a rap on the door. She peered through the spyhole, slid off the safety chain and twisted open the two locks.

As he stepped inside, she closed the door hastily behind him and slid back the bolt. 'God, thanks so much for coming,' she said.

She'd never seen him out of uniform before. He was dressed in a dark bomber jacket over a T-shirt and jeans, and seemed leaner and more wiry than he did in uniform. 'No problem. I was off duty tonight, but I've been called back in by my sergeant. Tell me.'

'I'm not sure where to begin,' she said.

'You look like you need a drink, Red.'

She nodded. 'I do. Want to join me?'

'No thanks, much though I would like one.'

The quietly assured, gentle police officer had a calming effect on her. She felt safe with him here as he followed her through into the kitchen. She poured herself a glass of

Albarino, got him a glass of water and they went through into the living room. Spofford sat on the tiny sofa and she perched across from him on a hard, beat-up armchair. 'Mind if I smoke?' she asked, craving a cigarette.

'Not if I can cadge one.'

She grinned. 'You're a smoker, too?'

'Yep. Just don't tell my wife!'

She grinned again as she fetched the pack and an ash-tray, then shook one out for him and held up the lighter flame.

'So tell me,' he said.

She lit her cigarette and drew deeply on it. 'Look, this may sound crazy – and I'm not sure where to begin.'

'Go as far back as you like.'

'Okay. The thing is, Bryce, I think I told you, was – is – a part-time magician?'

'You did, yes.'

'A lot of his tricks involve fire. He has one where he hands you his business card and suddenly it bursts into flames.'

'Okay.'

'I may be putting two and two together and making five. But Karl, my new boyfriend, was found burnt to death. Then the restaurant Bryce first took me to – and that Karl first took me to – was burned down. On Sunday I was going to my parents for lunch, and on the way my car caught fire. Today, on my way home, I stopped in my local convenience store and a fire broke out there while I was in it. When I got back here, the engagement ring Bryce had given me, and which I had given back to him, was somehow on my finger.' She pointed to it on the coffee table. 'Then I came home, got in the shower, and the queen of hearts appeared on the bath-room mirror. When I had my first date with Bryce, at Cuba

Libre, he did a magic trick on me, and a queen of hearts playing card appeared in my handbag.'

Spofford frowned. 'Show me the mirror.'

Red led the way through into the bathroom, pointed at the mirror, then stared at it in disbelief.

There was nothing there.

The constable looked at her, then at the mirror, then back at her.

'It was there,' she said. 'I'm not making this up.' She walked over and peered closely, looking for any trace of the queen of hearts. But the mirror was completely clear, as if it had just been carefully and thoroughly cleaned.

'It was there!' Red said. She looked at Spofford, who raised his eyebrows.

'Really,' she said. 'It was. I'm not going mental.'

'Where was it exactly?'

He peered closely as she pointed out the area of the mirror where she had seen the card, starting to doubt herself now.

He studied the mirror for several seconds. Then he looked back at her. 'You've been under a lot of stress, haven't you?'

'Rob, please don't give me that shit. I saw it, I didn't imagine it. Please don't make me out to be a neurotic loony. I saw it, I really did.'

Constable Spofford leaned forward and breathed heavily, several times, on the glass.

An instant later the queen of hearts playing card appeared again.

44

Monday, 28 October

Oh, how very clever you are, Constable Spofford!

Bryce watched his monitors with amusement as the police officer strutted self-importantly around the little flat, checking the windows and the front door, then shaking his head. He could find nothing wrong, he told Red.

Of course you won't!

'Is there any possible way Bryce could have a key?' Spofford asked her.

Good thinking, Batman! But I don't need keys. You probably don't understand that in my sapper training in the TA, picking locks was a major part. I also had a cell buddy in the US who was a master lock-picker. There isn't any lock on any door on Planet Earth I can't open within thirty seconds. Harry Houdini would have had nothing on me. But I'm not going to share that little nugget with you, am I?

So do what you have to do. Fill your boots. Look important to Red. Maybe you're hoping to get a shag out of her? Well, good luck, mate. She's like one of those female black widow spiders. You shag her then she eats you. You end up as a turd on her doorstep.

But that's all you ever were, Constable Spofford, isn't it? A mass of dumb protein, consumed, digested and excreted the following day.

I'll see you in Hell one day. Until then, have a good time on earth, my friend. Go on looking important, giving Red confidence.

But don't imagine for one moment you are going to save her life.

45

Cleo was on the sofa in the living area, in a baggy top, bra strap down over her shoulder, breastfeeding Noah, when Roy Grace entered shortly after 7 p.m. An old episode of *Miss Marple* was playing on the television screen and she immediately muted it as she smiled a greeting. Humphrey raced across to him, tail wagging madly, and jumped up. He gave the dog a distracted hug, and Cleo frowned as she saw the expression on his face.

'How was your day, darling?' she asked dubiously.

'Down, boy,' he said. Then walked across, kissed her on the cheek, and gave Noah a light peck on his chubby arm. 'Don't ask.'

'Daddy's home, Noah! Look!' she squealed in her 'baby' voice, looking down fondly at her son. Then she looked up worriedly at Roy. 'What happened?'

'I'll tell you when I've calmed down. I don't think it would be good for Noah to hear me swearing.'

He went through into the kitchen and mixed himself a larger than usual vodka martini, then downed it in one continuous gulp. He made himself another, went up to the first floor and out onto the terrace, and lit a cigarette.

Cassian sodding Pewe. The biggest shit he'd ever encountered in all his twenty years' service in the police force. Pewe made ACC Peter Rigg's predecessor, the acidic Alison

Vosper, seem a saint in comparison. What the hell was going on? A year ago, Cassian Pewe, after failing to screw him, had left Sussex CID in semi-disgrace and limped back to his old role in London's Metropolitan Police. Now this shit was to be his new boss?

Cassian assures me he has nothing personal against you.

Tom Martinson's words echoed unconvincingly in his head. This was the worst news. The worst possible news ever. He could not remember ever feeling this down. He sat on a wicker chair, staring gloomily all around him. Feeling totally walled in.

Transfer out of Major Crime? Out of the job he loved so much? Hell no. He had never been a quitter and he wasn't going to start now. He'd find a way through this. He *had* to. With the recent merger of Surrey and Sussex Major Crime Teams, his position was already dangerously weakened, as there was currently a surplus of homicide detectives across the two counties. In a sudden flash of paranoia he wondered if bringing Pewe in was a subtle way of getting rid of him. Was the Chief Constable playing games?

He thought back over the past year or so. He'd had some good results, surely? Okay, one killer had escaped, possibly, or drowned in Shoreham Harbour. Glenn Branson had been shot and another officer badly injured in a previous case. Did his face suddenly not fit any more? The only way to shore up his future here was to shine, make sure he was on the Police and Crime Commissioner's radar. Make himself indispensable.

But he needed something massively high profile to get his teeth into for that to happen.

He didn't know it yet, but he was about to get that opportunity.

46

Monday, 28 October

The booze was helping his mood. Cleo had long put Noah into his cot, and was now upstairs herself. Grace sat on the sofa, eating a microwaved Marks and Spencer vegetarian ravioli and watching the news on television. *Sod you, Cassian Pewe. Mess with me again and I'll finish your career, by God I will.*

There was a news item about police force cuts. The Chief Constable, Tom Martinson, was being interviewed and was on the defensive. Nothing would affect the frontline policing of the county, he assured his interrogator.

Grace admired his strong performance. It was, and always would be, impossible to win the fight against crime. There were always going to be villains out there, from every stratum of society, hurting people, destroying lives, and all too often taking lives. Making the public feel safe was a major role for the police. Reassurance, such as Martinson's right now, went a long way.

His work phone rang. Although he was getting married on Saturday, because of two other colleagues being away and one off sick, he was having to do a second consecutive week as the on-call Senior Investigating Officer. He could of course delegate, and that was going through his mind now as he answered.

'Detective Superintendent Grace?'

It was Inspector Andy Kille, the duty Ops-1 Controller in the Haywards Heath Control Room.

'Roy, uniform at John Street, Brighton, are extremely concerned about an individual, Ms Red Westwood. She's currently in a safe house following domestic abuse by her boyfriend. But it would seem the boyfriend has gained access. Uniform attended and PC Spofford would like a word with you. Can I patch him through?'

'Yes, yes,' Roy Grace said, thinking, *Shit*. He should not have had a drink while on call. But he had a Plan B.

There was a crackle of static, then he heard a voice. 'Detective Superintendent Grace?'

'Yes, tell me.'

Grace listened to a litany of the constable's concerns. Red Westwood's history of domestic abuse with her magician lover, Bryce Laurent – and his phoney background. The burnt body of Dr Karl Murphy. The fire that destroyed Cuba Libre restaurant. The fire in the engine compartment of Red Westwood's Volkswagen. The fire in the convenience store. The engagement ring that was suddenly and mysteriously back on Red Westwood's finger. The appearance of the queen of hearts on the bathroom mirror. The certainty that this dangerous man had gained access to her secure apartment.

'I'm not happy with what I'm hearing,' he said when Spofford had finished. 'I knew about the doctor's death, but I wasn't aware of the connection to the other incidents. Can you have someone stay with Ms Westwood? I'm sending someone from the Major Crime Team over to you right away.'

'I'll stay here myself, sir,' Spofford said.

Grace ended the call and immediately dialled Glenn Branson and gave him the details. 'Are you able to attend, matey?'

'Give me half an hour. I'll see if I can get Ari's sister to come over and babysit.'

'You're a good man.'

'Yeah, I know. You sound pissed.'

'I am pissed.'

'Drinking when you're on call?'

'If I go out, I'll arrange a driver. But for now I need a drink and I'll tell you why tomorrow.'

'Is everything okay?' Glenn asked, genuinely concerned.

'No, it's shit.'

'Noah and Cleo – they okay?'

'They're fine. Don't worry, I'll tell you all tomorrow.'

47

Red sat on the sofa, holding a glass of wine and sipping slowly, aware she needed to keep sober and alert, and trying to watch the *Ten O'Clock News* on television as a distraction. The engagement ring now sat on the coffee table in front of her, and she was tugging at the bracelet, trying to remove that too. Having lost so much weight, it was so loose on her wrist she could almost – but not quite – get it over her hand. She would definitely go to a jeweller in the morning, she decided, to get the damned thing cut off.

Out in the hallway a locksmith, summoned by PC Spofford, was working on replacing the two deadlocks on the front door. She could hear the constable, who was also out in the hall, on his phone, talking to the skipper in the Anti-Victimization Unit, briefing him on his concerns.

After a few minutes the locksmith, a cheery man in heavy-duty blue overalls whose day job was maintaining the locks at Lewes Prison, came into the room and handed Red two sets of shiny new keys. She knew she would be moving soon, but no date had been fixed and she needed to feel safe in the flat. Safe from Bryce.

'All done!' he said. 'I've also replaced the safety chain with a heavier one, and I've added an extra lock that you can secure when you are in here. I'll be back tomorrow at Constable Spofford's request to turn your spare bedroom into a safe room – a panic room. It will have a reinforced door and walls, and a dedicated mobile phone that goes straight through to the police. PC Spofford's mobile will be on speed dial. The room will keep you safe for an hour, minimum, against any attempt to penetrate it – more than enough time for the police to reach you. Here's my card if you need me in the meantime.' The name on it was Jack Tunks.

'Thanks so much, Jack,' she said.

'You don't need to worry, Ms Westwood. I've been round all your windows and tomorrow I'm going to upgrade the locks on them, too. Not even Houdini would be able to get in,' he assured her, totally unaware of Bryce Laurent watching and listening to every word from across the alley.

Houdini was an old fraud, Bryce said silently. *Of course he would not have got in. Be happy in those thoughts!*

Despite the presence of the locksmith and the police officer, Red jumped in shock when she heard the shrill beep of the entryphone buzzer. Spofford accompanied her along the hallway. On the screen, she could see out in the street below a tall black man, dressed in a bomber jacket and jeans, his head as bald and shiny as a bowling ball.

She pressed the speaker button. 'Hello?'

'Detective Inspector Branson, from Surrey and Sussex Major Crime Team,' he said.

'Come on up,' she said, her voice tight with anxiety. 'The second floor. Thank you so much for coming.'

Bryce Laurent smiled. It was all escalating nicely, all going according to plan.

Oh, Red, how different this could have been! If you hadn't listened to your parents, but had just followed your heart. We could be in bed right now, making tender love, with our whole lives ahead of us. Instead, you and I, we're both history. How tragic is that?

'DI Branson?' Red asked, opening the door to the tall, cheery-looking man-mountain.

'Yep, same name as Richard, but without a billion quid in the bank!' he replied with a smile.

Five minutes later, he was seated opposite her in the living room, sipping from his mug of coffee and making detailed notes on his pad. Constable Spofford, confident she was in good hands, left.

'Let's start at the beginning,' Glenn Branson said. 'As far back as you like.'

She liked the detective instantly. He had a warmth about him, and a nice energy. And at the same time, he had an aura of sadness and vulnerability, as if he had suffered a personal tragedy. She told him the history of how she and Bryce had met, then over the next hour relayed everything that had happened, from her mother first discovering, through the detective, that the entire past history Bryce had given her was false, to the events of the past week.

Branson asked her if she still had the original email correspondence with Bryce from when they had first begun dating. She opened her laptop and showed him the wording of her advertisement on the online dating site.

> Single girl, 29, redhead and smouldering, love life
> that's crashed and burned. Seeks new flame to
> rekindle her fire. Fun, friendship and – who knows
> – maybe more?

He wrote it down, then looked pensive. 'I understand you think a number of fires in the past week might be linked?'

'Yes. To this advert – to my ex. It just seems too coincidental. Each of these fires has some kind of link to me.'

'From what I'm told, Bryce Laurent sounds like he's pretty sick.'

We're dealing with someone pretty sick, are we, Detective Inspector? Well, let's find out how right – and bright – you are! You ain't seen nothing yet, I promise you.

48

Tuesday, 29 October

Matt Wainwright had just been promoted to Crew Commander of the Blue Watch, and this was his first shift in his new role; he had decided to arrive early to make a good impression. Although the shift change was not until 8.30 a.m., at 7.30, as he headed through driving rain along the dark streets towards Worthing fire station, his thoughts were focused on the management of his team during the day ahead.

He was also thinking about a new card trick that he had almost perfected, and how, if it was quiet, he would try it on some of the lads today. He was far too preoccupied to notice the small white van that kept a steady two hundred yards behind him in the breaking daylight.

He turned left, drove along the side of Worthing fire station, and pulled up in an empty bay at the rear. Several of the garage doors were raised and two of the fire engines were out in the car park being cleaned by his night-shift colleagues as their last duty before heading home.

He took a final drag on his cigarette, then tossed it out of the window onto the tarmac. It rolled along, throwing a shower of sparks, before being extinguished by the rain.

One of the biggest excitements about his work was never knowing what was going to happen in five minutes' time. The siren might sound in the station at any moment. When it did, the officers required would be out of the common room, down the pole, into their uniforms and racing out on blues and twos within the target time of ninety seconds.

In fifteen years he'd not met a firefighter who did not passionately love the adrenaline rush from riding in one of these massive red beasts. And no amount of money on earth could replicate the thrill of helming an eighteen-ton fire engine through a city's streets, together with the heightened sense of danger that so often went with it, not knowing what you would be facing at the other end.

He wondered what today might bring. The majority of firefighters, like himself, found domestic house fires, where all kinds of different aspects of your training came into play, the most challenging and the most satisfying. Some preferred cutting people out of car wrecks. Others the theatre of massive industrial building fires, with dozens of crews from around the county attending. But for all of them, the most satisfaction came from rescuing people and saving lives.

And there was one thing a number of firefighters had in common: although the Fire and Rescue Service was their day job, and the fulcrum around which their lives revolved, many of them, like himself, had second careers. He hoped that, at some point, he could make enough money out of his magic to do it full-time. It was certainly heading that way, from the rise in the number of bookings. And with two small children at home, his wife, Sue, would be a lot happier if he no longer had to work the dangerous, anti-social – and often extended – hours that went with this job.

Bryce Laurent, standing in the shadows in the pelting rain, watched Matt Wainwright until he had gone inside. Then he turned his focus back to the cigarette butt on the ground. After some minutes, both fire engines were reversed into the garage and the doors closed. The rear car park was now deserted, patterned with a mosaic of weak light from the windows above.

Bryce, dressed head to toe in black, strode stealthily over to the cigarette, picked it up in his gloved fingers, then carefully placed it in a small plastic bag and slipped it into his pocket. Then, looking around and up, he took the few steps over to Matt Wainwright's Nissan and within a matter of seconds had popped the driver's door open.

Wainwright had been pissing him off for the past three years. Eating his lunch. Fancying himself. Getting gigs he had been after. And which he would have been much better at.

Not any more, dude!

He slipped inside the car, and closed the door.

49

Tuesday, 29 October

'Good morning, old timer. Got a few minutes?' Glenn Branson said, breezing into Roy Grace's office at a quarter to eight on Tuesday. Then he hesitated, noticing the mug of coffee, the opened can of Coke, and the blister pack of paracetamol, with most of them popped open. Roy Grace's tie was at half mast, his normally healthy complexion was pallid and his eyes had the telltale bloodshot look that came from lack of sleep or a hangover.

Or, in Grace's case right now, both.

'You look like shit!'

'Thanks,' Grace said, unsmiling.

'Seriously, I mean it. Did you have your stag night early and forget to tell me?'

'Very funny.' He stared at the DI. Glenn was wearing one of his regular sharp suits, this one a shiny brown, with a tie that could have been seen from Mars. For someone who had lost his wife less than three months ago, even though they were separated, he seemed to have been remarkably cheery these past few weeks. But now he had his kids, his house – and his life – back.

Outside the window, with its view across the ASDA supermarket car park and loading bay, and south over Brighton towards the sea, the sky was a tombstone grey and rain was falling heavily. 'Remember Cassian Pewe?' Grace quizzed him.

'Lovely Cassian Pewe,' he replied. 'The golden-haired Met officer, with his rasping, nasally voice. He was seconded here last year and managed to upset just about everyone in this building and in Sussex CID. Yeah, remember him well, unfortunately. Mr Two Face.'

Grace drained his glass of Coke then topped it up. 'Yeah.' He was remembering him well, too. Which accounted for his drinking binge last night, which he was now regretting in the cold light of day. After Pewe had returned to the Met with his tail between his legs, Grace had found out that Pewe had messed with evidence on a cold case he was looking into, and he had threatened him with arrest.

What he had never known, and still did not, was that Cassian Pewe had had a brief affair with his wife, Sandy.

He told Glenn Branson the latest news about the appointment.

'I can't believe it! Pewe? Assistant Chief Constable?'

'Yeah, well you're going to have to believe it.'

'Remember that movie, *The Sting*?'

'Robert Redford and Paul Newman?'

'And Robert Shaw.'

'What about it?'

Branson shrugged. 'I'll set my mind to it. We'll sort the bastard out, somehow.'

For the first time since he had left Tom Martinson's office last night, Grace smiled. 'Thanks mate, I like your attitude. Maybe I should try a charm offensive first.'

'Got a snake charmer, have you?'

'I should try to find one on Google.' Grace grinned again, then looked serious. 'So, you didn't come to hear my problems. Tell me.'

'You asked me to go and talk to Ms Red Westwood last night, yeah?'

Roy Grace nodded.

'She's a smart lady. Intelligent and rational. I'll give you the full history and I think you're going to agree with me when you've heard it that the doctor at Haywards Heath Golf Club – the burnt body and the suicide note – there might be something more going on there than we think.'

'Meaning?'

'Meaning it might not be suicide.'

'All the forensic evidence indicates he took his own life,' Grace said, taking a sip of his coffee. 'He was alive at the time the fire started. There was flame damage to his mouth and throat, and he had inhaled a lot of smoke.'

'Hear me out,' Branson said, pulling out his notebook, then going through everything he had written down in faithful detail.

Twenty minutes later, Grace scrabbled through the piles of folders cluttering his desk and pulled out the one on Dr Karl Murphy. From it he extracted his copy of Murphy's suicide note. Instantly his eyes went to the one sentence he found so curious.

'How much did this lady tell you about Dr Murphy, Glenn?'

Branson thought for some moments. Through the window Grace noticed a police patrol car slow down, indicating left as it travelled down the hill, then turning in towards the gates to the Custody Centre. He caught a glimpse of a hunched figure in the rear. A prisoner, arrested for some alleged offence, on his way to be processed. In his gloom, Grace's thoughts momentarily digressed to his baby son, Noah. There were so many sodding miscreants out there, and they would only ever arrest a tiny percentage.

How the hell could he ever make this world safe for his child?

As Glenn Branson relayed all that Red Westwood had said about Karl Murphy, Grace made notes. The doctor was a keen golfer – which fitted with his body being found on a golf course – and, from what little he knew of the game, Haywards Heath had a high reputation.

'Red said he liked puzzles,' Branson continued. 'He did *The Times* crossword every day – he'd told her proudly that his record time was just two minutes short of the world champion.'

'You any good at crosswords?' Grace asked him.

Branson shook his head. 'Don't think I'm hardwired that way. Ari did them sometimes, used to ask me for help with some clues. I never understood them, except if they were to do with movies. She said I was thick.' He looked sad suddenly, then shrugged. 'Yeah, she was probably right. She was a lot smarter than me.' He fell silent for a moment. 'We did have good times. Before . . .'

Grace looked at him quizzically. It was the first time in a while that his friend had mentioned his wife. 'Before?'

Branson shrugged. 'Before Sammy was born. That's when it all changed. Suddenly I was no longer number one in her life. Don't let that happen to you and Cleo.'

Grace knew what he meant. He and Cleo had discussed this many times, and they'd both agreed that whilst the birth of Noah had changed things and they loved him truly, deeply, they would always make time for each other. He nodded. 'We're working on it.'

'Work on it hard, mate. Our happiness graph hit rock bottom and stayed there. It got even worse after Remi was born and Ari became depressed.'

He stopped suddenly, with a catch in his voice, and

Grace saw a single tear trickle down his cheek. He leaned across his desk and patted Glenn on his shoulder. 'She gave you hell that you never deserved, mate. Don't forget that.'

Glenn smiled and wiped away his tear with the back of his hand. 'Yeah. I know. But I can't help thinking back.'

'You'd be a strange man if you didn't.'

Glenn nodded and sniffed. 'Okay, let's focus. One other thing, for what it's worth, Red said that Karl Murphy's wife, who died, was German-born, like his mother.'

'Any significance in that?'

Branson shook his head. 'Well, nothing that she's aware of.'

Despite his head feeling like it had been stung by a thousand bees, Roy Grace drummed his fingers on his desktop, and for some moments was preoccupied with his thoughts. 'I don't like what I'm hearing from you about the fires.'

'I didn't think you would.'

'What we have against us is the pathologist's report. But . . .' He read through his notes. 'This connection through the fires. Red Westwood is the one common link in all of them. I think I'd like to get a second opinion from Jack Skerritt.'

Roy Grace was Head of Major Crime, and could make the decision to upgrade the enquiry into Dr Karl Murphy's death into a murder investigation on his own. But because of his uncertainties, and both the time and financial costs to the force of a full-scale murder enquiry, it was normal practice to run his thoughts past his superior – as much to cover his own back as for any other reason, particularly as he knew that ACC Cassian Pewe would be looking for any errors of judgement to give him the chance to haul him over the coals.

He called Skerritt's assistant, to be told he was away today but had a thirty-minute window first thing the next morning.

'I can take over the investigation for you while you're on honeymoon,' Glenn said. 'I don't want this to mess it up for you.'

'My work comes first,' Grace said.

The DI shook his head. 'That's what screwed up your marriage to Sandy, and mine to Ari. Don't let it happen to you again. You've got someone very special in Cleo.'

'Karl Murphy was very special to some people, too,' Grace said. 'We need to find out the truth.'

'I'm not letting you screw your life up, mate. You'd better understand that.'

Grace stared back at his friend and colleague. And saw he looked deadly serious.

50

It was full daylight now, but still raining hard beneath a bitumen black sky. Back in his van, parked a short distance along from Worthing fire station, Bryce Laurent was glad of the cover the rain would give him. He saw the fire station doors rise. Moments later two appliances, blue lights strobing, sirens wailing, pulled out into the rush-hour traffic. It was shortly after 9 a.m. He noticed in the front passenger seat of the second fire engine the figure of Matt Wainwright. Crew Commander. He knew the routine.

Ninety seconds after the klaxon sounded in the fire station, the crews would head out, following the instructions on the slip of paper printed out at the station, and the updates in real time on the computer screen inside the cab. He'd enjoyed his brief time as a Fire and Rescue officer with this crew here.

But he hadn't been so happy when they'd sacked him.

That was so totally not deserved. Matt was a wannabe magician. Laurent had helped him, shown him some of the tricks of the trade. Then the little shit had started taking some of his gigs. That had to be stopped.

And, oh yes, he was going to stop this!

The appliances screamed past him.

And something screamed inside his head.

His mother.

He dug his fingers into his ears.
But still he could hear her screams.
That night.
That night he became free.

51

'Are you ready for Mummy, darling?'

She came staggering into his bedroom, naked except for her red high heels, as he lay reading Dennis the Menace in *The Beano* comic. She had a bent joint in her mouth, with an inch of ash on the tip, and fumes of alcohol filled the air, along with the pungent, rubbery smell of the burning drug.

Moments later she sat heavily on the side of the bed, and looked down in surprise as the ash fell onto the carpet. Her long red hair tumbled around her face like a stage curtain coming down on the first act. She gave him the joint and told him to draw on it. He did so out of duty, then she told him to draw on it again, and slid her hand under the duvet, taking hold of him.

His head began swimming and he felt a tingling deep in his belly. And burning embarrassment. Her grip on him was starting to feel deeply erotic. She slipped her flaccid, wrinkled body under the sheets beside him, and tossed his comic onto the floor, then gripped his penis harder in her hand and began to massage it gently. Despite himself, he felt it enlarging. Until suddenly it was so painfully stiff it hurt.

'Mummy can make that better,' she whispered. 'Oooh, you're such a big boy. So big! So handsome. So many women will want you, but they are dirty women, unclean women. You're too good for the trash out there. You are Mummy's very special boy, Mummy's big boy. Let me feel my big boy inside me.'

Now Bryce was remembering Valentine's night, three months later, when he was sixteen. He had been out drinking, for the first time, with the only person he connected with at school. Ricky Heley. They were tall and mature-looking for their age, and no one had challenged them in the pubs. Ricky was an outsider like himself. He had a pretty face and a clumsy, gangly body. They were the only two boys in the class who didn't have girlfriends – not even a crush – let alone dated a girl. Bryce didn't dare chat any girl up – he was scared of how his mother would react.

That morning he and Ricky had each received ten Valentine cards, much to the apparent astonishment of their classmates. They were filled with individual and deeply personal declarations of love and cravings from secret admirers. For a brief while they were taken in, until the smirks of their classmates gave the game away.

That night he and Ricky went on a drinking binge. They walked through Kemp Town to a series of pubs, several where Ricky said he knew how to get free drinks. In each of them much older men stood them pints and whisky chasers, and chatted to them. In each pub, as soon as they had drained their glasses, Ricky would grab Bryce's arm and lead him away, ignoring the pleas of whoever had bought them the drinks to stay.

It was the first time Bryce had drunk alcohol, and as he staggered home up the steep hill, past Queen's Park, veering unsteadily across the pavement and clinging to an equally unsteady Ricky Heley, he felt anger smouldering inside him. They staggered into Freshfield Road and crossed the wide street to the terraced house where he lived.

'Thanks,' he slurred to Ricky. 'For helping me home. Not sure. Not sure how.' He stopped, his vision blurry. Suddenly Ricky lunged forward, pressing his lips against his.

'Hey!' Bryce pushed him away.

Ricky persisted, cupping Bryce's face hard with his hands, pressing his lips against his mouth and pushing his tongue inside. Bryce responded by bringing his right leg up as hard as he could into Heley's groin. As his friend staggered back, Bryce took several steps forward and punched him on the nose. Blood spattered around his friend's mouth. Heley took a further few steps back and fell over.

'Don't ever fucking do that to me again, you poof,' Bryce said. Then, leaving him lying on the pavement with blood pouring from his nose, Bryce let himself into the house and closed the front door behind him. As he did so, he heard his mother's slurred voice.

'That you?'

'Urrr.'

'Where've you been?'

'Out.'

'You've been drinking?' There was sharp accusation in her voice.

'I'm sixteen.'

'Have you been with any women?'

'I haven't, no.'

'I need you so badly. Come to Mummy!'

He climbed the stairs slowly, unsteadily, reluctantly, hating this, hating himself, hating what the other boys at school would say if they ever found out. He stumbled along the landing and stood in the doorway of his mother's room. She was sitting up in her wide pink bed, a cigarette between her lips, an almost empty glass of wine in her hand, her breasts practically falling out of her low negligee, leering at him. 'Come here, my baby,' she said.

'I'm tired, Mummy.'

'Come and satisfy your mummy! Your mummy needs it so bad tonight, my baby.' Without removing the cigarette from her lips, she drew on it, then snorted the smoke through her nostrils, and tapped the ash into a saucer overflowing with butts on the bedside table. A movie was playing on television, one of the hard-man action thrillers she watched incessantly. 'Bring it here to me, darling,' she said.

And suddenly, as if the anger smouldering deep within him had set light to the kindling, there was a burning explosion inside him. He stared with absolute hatred, clenching his fists. He looked at her mahogany Victorian dressing table. At the mass of perfume bottles and make-up containers, bottles and tubes of cream and lotions, and a canister of hairspray.

The hairspray.

Suddenly, despite his drunkenness, he was thinking with clarity. He dug his left hand into his pocket and wiggled his handkerchief out.

'Come to Mummy!'

'I have to blow my nose.'

She frowned as instead of blowing his nose he wound the handkerchief around his right hand.

'What are you doing, my darling?'

He stumbled over to the dressing table, grabbed the hairspray in his handkerchiefed right hand, pushed off the top with his thumb, then lunged at his mother, pressing the button down hard, directing the jet straight at her face.

She stared at him with a look of total surprise. An instant later, as the spray flared up the burning cigarette, there was a fierce roaring sound and it erupted into flame. She screamed. He kept his finger on the button. Kept spraying as flames caught hold of her hair. She screamed again, wriggled desperately. Her nightdress was on fire now, and the bedclothes. Still he kept the button pressed down. As the flames blackened her skin her screams became less and less strong, turning into a rasping gasp. Until she fell silent, her face all black now, her eyes moving but sightless, two tiny white orbs swivelling in their darkened sockets, her mouth opening and shutting.

The whole bed was burning now. He backed away, and stood watching in the doorway as the curtains caught fire and the flames crept up to the ceiling. He could still see his mother, her body making small movements, and he could smell roasting meat.

Then, with his handkerchief still around his hand, he put the spray back on the bedside table, picked the top off the floor and pushed it back on, then backed out of the room, leaving the door open, and went through to his own room. Keeping the light off, he peered down into the street. Heley had gone. Good. There was no one there. Good. As quietly as he could, he opened the window, letting in the night air. Opened it as wide as it would go. Moments later he heard the roar of flames intensify.

Hastily he removed his clothes, pulled on his pyjamas and dressing gown, with the glow of the streetlamps outside giving him just enough light to see by, pushed his feet into his slippers and staggered, still unsteadily, back out onto the landing. His mother's entire bedroom was now an inferno. The heat was burning his own face. But still he waited, until her door frame started burning and the flames began licking their way along the landing.

He walked slowly downstairs, steadying himself on the

handrail, smiling, removing the handkerchief then cramming it back into his pocket.

He waited at the bottom of the stairs for some more minutes until the entire upstairs was burning fiercely. Then he pushed open the front door and stumbled out, screaming and sobbing for help.

'Fire! God, fire, fire, fire! Help me! Help me!'

He stumbled around to the next-door neighbour's and rang the bell, pounding on the door frantically. 'Fire! Please help, my mother's trapped, please help me!'

52

Detective Chief Superintendent Jack Skerritt was a popular man within Sussex Police, a hard man, an old-school no-nonsense copper who had little truck with political correctness or bleeding-heart liberals. A former Commander of Brighton and Hove, he'd had a high level of experience both in uniform and in the CID. Fifty-two years old, he was due to retire at the end of the year. He had told Grace a few months back, over a drink at another officer's retirement party, that what he looked forward to most of all about retirement was the idea of being able to go into a pub and tell people what he really thought about any issue, without being quoted in the press the following day – and then harangued. His views were, in general, pretty right wing, but he was no bigoted fool.

Skerritt was not in a good mood this morning; he was close to apoplectic over the news of Cassian Pewe's appointment. Grace and Branson sat at the twelve-seater meeting table in his spacious office, along from Grace's office in the mostly open-plan CID area on the first floor of Sussex House, while the Detective Chief Superintendent vented spleen. 'Tom Martinson's a top bloke,' he said. 'I don't get this. I'm going to be having words with him. Bringing that bastard back is like putting a lunatic in charge of the asylum. Shit!'

When Skerritt had finally calmed down, Grace summarized the situation, then allowed Glenn Branson to explain in depth the reasons for his concerns that Dr Karl Murphy's death might not have been suicide.

Skerritt shook his head. 'I hear what you're saying, but I'm not convinced, I'm afraid. I've had my balls chewed off by ACC Rigg over this department's expenses recently, and I can't support you stepping this up to a murder enquiry, with all the costs that entails, from what I'm hearing from you both. If you go ahead, Roy, it'll have to be your decision, with clear justification for it.'

'So what the hell do I need, Jack?' Roy Grace asked fractiously. He seldom lost his temper, but his lack of sleep, combined with Skerritt's intransigence, were taking him perilously close to losing it now.

'You're experienced enough, Roy,' Skerritt replied. 'You have good instincts about when something's a murder. But I don't think you're there with this one. I'm not convinced.'

Grace tapped the side of his nose. 'My copper's nose. That's telling me this is a murder investigation, sir.'

'Despite there being a suicide note, checked out by a graphologist, and despite the pathologist's report?'

'I'm still not convinced about the suicide note. But I haven't got anything to substantiate this.'

'Separately, Roy, has any forensic link between the fires been established?'

'I'm on that at the moment. I'm discussing everything that's happened with the Chief Fire Investigator.'

Skerritt nodded. 'Look, one thing is for sure, no one knows the state of mind of someone in the moments before they commit suicide, Roy. But Dr Murphy was hardly likely to be in a rational state. You don't kill yourself when you have two small children if you're in a rational state.'

Grace looked at Branson, then back at the Detective Chief Superintendent. 'What would it take to change your mind, sir? To support my upgrading this to a murder enquiry?'

'If you can cast doubt on the note, that would change things. If you can convince me it was written under duress, then we'd be getting somewhere.'

Roy Grace smiled grimly. Skerritt wasn't an idiot; he was probably seeing the overview more clearly than he himself was right now. And perhaps it was the right decision for him to make this call based on what he had been told. But in his heart, Grace was still convinced there was more to it.

Skerritt raised both his hands in the air. 'I have to leave it with you. I'm sorry – but feel free to talk to me about it again.'

53

Wednesday, 30 October

Roy Grace and Glenn Branson returned to Grace's office shortly before 10 a.m. in silence. The pair of them perched, pensively, at the small round meeting table.

'Want a coffee?' Grace asked.

Glenn nodded gloomily. 'I'll get them.'

'No, I'll go—'

Branson silenced him with his hand. 'You need to keep up your strength for your wedding night, old timer.'

'Haha!' Then Grace pursed his lips, balled his right fist and thumped his left palm. 'Convince him it was written under duress? So where the hell do we start with that one?'

There was a sharp rap on the door, and Norman Potting barged in without waiting for an answer, holding a sheet of paper in a plastic folder and looking pleased with himself. Then he stopped as he saw the grim expressions on the faces of his two superiors. 'Sorry, am I interrupting something?'

'It's okay, Norman,' Grace said. 'Something urgent?'

'Well, it might be, chief. The suicide note from Dr Murphy that you asked me to look at? I think I may have found something.'

Suddenly he had their rapt attention.

'Tell us,' Grace said.

Potting removed the sheet of paper from the folder and placed it on the table. It was a copy of the suicide note, with several words circled and annotations in blue ink above them and in the margins. He sat down. Grace and Branson followed, moving their chairs closely either side of him.

I am so sorry. My will is with my executor, solicitor Maud Opfer of Opfer Dexter Associates. Life since Ingrid's death is meaningless. I want to be united with her again. Please tell Dane and Ben I love them and will love them for ever and that their Daddy's gone to take care of Mummy. Love you both so much. One day, when you are older, I hope you will find it in your hearts to forgive me. XX

Potting pointed at the name of the solicitor. 'I decided to start by contacting the law firm to have a word with this Maud Opfer, to see if there was anything I could glean from her. That's when I learned there is no such law firm as Opfer Dexter Associates.'

Grace frowned. 'I didn't recognize the firm as being a local one, but I supposed it was either a London firm or one somewhere else in the UK.'

Potting shook his head. 'That obviously alerted me that something was not right. I did wonder about the name Dexter, the character on television who is a serial killer – know the programme I mean?'

Grace nodded. 'Cleo watches it.'

'I've watched a few episodes too,' Glenn Branson said.

'Opfer is a strange name,' Potting continued. 'I wondered what the significance might be, so I tried it in Google Translate – that detects the most likely language of any word or phrase you type in. It came back that it means "victim" in German.'

'Shit!' Branson exclaimed.

'Karl Murphy spoke fluent German,' Potting went on. 'His mother was from Munich – hence his Germanic first name. Now, in crossword parlance Maud is not a big jump to *mord*, the German word for "death". As a keen crossworder, Karl Murphy would probably have known that. Put those two together into Google and up pops "murder victim".'

Grace and Branson were silent for some moments, looking at the circled words and the writing above them.

'I'm speculating, of course,' Norman Potting said. 'But what do you think?'

Grace barely heard him. He had his phone out and was dialling Jack Skerritt's number with a shaking hand.

54

Wednesday, 30 October

Although he was trained both in cognitive witness and suspect interviewing techniques, Roy Grace rarely conducted interviews himself, preferring to leave the lengthy and carefully structured process to other trusted members of his team while he concentrated on the overview of a case, ensuring he had missed nothing. Later he could study relevant sections of the interviews.

He was acutely aware that although twenty years of service in the police had given him a great deal of experience, there was a large red flag that came with all experience, and that was the danger of complacency. It was often the most experienced people who had the hardest falls for that very reason.

He'd read that in many tragic air disasters, the airline's senior captain had been at the helm – including the worst ever in Tenerife, in 1977, when a KLM and Pan Am 747 collided. There was a long history of the wrong limbs being amputated in hospitals by senior consultants being careless through complacency. And then there was the tragic fact that all the world's top avalanche experts had died in avalanches.

It was for this reason that, at the start of every murder enquiry, and continually throughout it, Roy Grace would assiduously write down all his decisions, and reasons for them, in his policy book, and would check his own procedures off against the structured list laid out in fine detail in the *Murder Manual*.

But in this instance he felt it important to see and talk to Red Westwood himself. So at a few minutes before 5 p.m. he entered the tiny witness interview room, a short distance along the corridor of the first floor of Sussex House from the conference room where he held his murder enquiry briefings.

It was a square, bland, windowless box, with three crimson chairs, a small round coffee table, with water, glasses and three coffee mugs on it, a CCTV camera mounted high up, and built-in recording equipment. Glenn Branson was already seated there, next to a nervous-looking woman aged about thirty, who was sitting upright on the edge of her chair. Grace winced at his colleague's tie, and had already chided Glenn about it earlier in the day. Interviewers learned early in their training to dress in the plainest possible clothes, so as to be wearing nothing that might distract the witness. But it was too late to say anything again, so he turned his attention to studying the young woman, and focusing his mind on what he wanted to achieve from the next hour or so.

She had an attractive face, slightly narrow, the narrowness accentuated by long, elegantly cut dark red hair, centre parted, that hung either side of it. She was wearing a thin black roll-neck sweater, a short tweed skirt, black leggings and black knee-length boots. As he entered, she gave him a wan smile, revealing quite beautiful white teeth. But she was looking on edge.

'Red Westwood, Detective Superintendent Roy Grace,' Glenn said. Then he turned to Red. 'Detective Superintendent Grace is going to be the Senior Investigating Officer on this case. You're in good hands, he's the best.'

She smiled, and as she did so her whole face lit up, before sinking back behind the dark cloud that seemed to envelop her. Grace saw, in that moment, a huge warmth in her. He liked her instantly.

He closed the door and sat down. 'Are you happy for this interview to be recorded, Ms Westwood?'

'Absolutely,' she said. She had a strong, confident, slightly gravelly voice, and smiled as she spoke. But he could see the anxiety in her brown eyes, and it was there in the way she twisted a silver bracelet she was wearing with her fingers. She also wore one ring, a silver band on her right thumb, and a thin silver necklace with a crucifix and several silver charms.

Glenn reached across and activated the video equipment.

'Seventeen-o-five hours, Wednesday, 30 October,' Roy Grace said, for the benefit of the recording. 'Interview of Ms Red Westwood carried out by Detective Superintendent Roy Grace and Detective Inspector Glenn Branson.' He looked at Red. 'It's good of you to leave work early to come and talk to us, Ms Westwood.'

'Thank you. I'm going through hell. I'm really grateful to you for seeing me.' She looked at each officer, giving them a nervous smile. She felt safe in this room, in this building. At this moment she would have liked to stay here for ever.

'I know you gave DI Branson a very full statement on Monday night, but would it be an imposition to ask you to go through it all again?' Grace asked.

'Not at all, no. Where would you like me to start?'

'Can you tell me how you met Bryce Laurent?' Roy Grace asked.

She grimaced, and he saw her small, pretty nose crinkle. 'Well, it's a bit embarrassing really. I'd been in a long-term relationship with my then ex – his name's Dominic Chandler. I realized I didn't want to spend the rest of my life with him. We were on different journeys. He wanted to have children, and although I did too, I just knew I didn't want to have them with him. We split up – not too happily, but that's another story.'

'Were there any other issues in that relationship?' Grace asked.

'Issues?' she replied.

'Did Dominic Chandler, for instance, have any history of violence?'

She shook her head resolutely. 'No, not at all. Absolutely not. He was very gentle, in that sense. And he had nothing to fear – I was totally faithful to him in the time we were together.'

'Do you have any reason to feel he might be bitter towards you now?'

'Dominic? No. I bumped into him a few months ago at Hove station. He was very cheerful, told me he was getting married. No, anyhow, he absolutely isn't a violent person.'

Grace and Branson exchanged a glance. Then Grace went on. 'Okay, tell us what happened after you and Dominic Chandler split up?'

'I moved out of his flat and got my own place. It felt good to be out of the relationship but at the same time, I guess . . . you know . . . I was acutely aware of my biological clock ticking. If I was going to have children, then I'd have to meet someone fairly soon. Some of my friends fitted me up with a handful of blind dates, all of them disastrous. My closest friend, Raquel Evans, thought I ought to try some online dating sites. So I put an ad on a couple of them.'

'What did you say?' Grace asked.

Glenn opened his notebook, searching for the page where he had written the words down on Monday night. Red blushed, and dug into her handbag. 'Actually, I've brought it, because it might be relevant.' She unfolded a sheet of paper and read from it: '*Single girl, 29, redhead and smouldering, love life that's crashed and burned. Seeks new flame to re-kindle her fire. Fun, friendship and – who knows – maybe more?*'

She looked at the two detectives. 'A bit cheesy?'

But she could not read either of their faces.

Roy Grace reached out for it and read it himself, then handed it back to her. 'DI Branson told me that you said Bryce Laurent was something of a magician. Did he ever use fire in any of his tricks?' Grace asked.

She nodded. 'Yes. Actually, somewhere in his tangled past he worked as a firefighter. It's possible he still does.'

Both men frowned. 'You think he might be working for the fire brigade – the Fire and Rescue Service?' Glenn Branson said.

'Apparently you are allowed to do other work as a fire-fighter. Especially if you work as a retained officer near an unmanned station. I think you have to work and live within four minutes of it.' She raised her eyebrows. 'But to be honest, he could be doing anything right now – and be anyone. When I first met him he spun me a story of how he'd been an airline pilot in the US and then moved to Air Traffic Control, so as not to be away from home because his wife was sick. That was all a pack of lies. His name wasn't his real name – he's had a whole ton of aliases.'

'Do you know them?' Roy Grace asked.

'Some,' she said. 'Bryce Laurent is one for starters. I've no idea what his real name is – and he's told so many lies about his past, I'm not even sure if he does any more. And I know about some of his previous jobs because of the detective agency my mother employed – behind my back, but I'm grateful she did now. He was in the Territorial Army as a sapper for a while; but as with everything else, he got kicked out. He worked for a security company installing alarm systems, and got the sack from that. He's a talented conjuror – a close magician I think they call it. He started making a name for himself in Brighton, but lost the plot with that, too.'

Grace frowned. 'He seems to have a handy lot of skill sets for everything we're thinking might be connected to him.'

'He's a brilliant artist, too – very good at cartoons.'

'Which of his conjuring tricks involve fire, Red?' Roy Grace asked.

'Quite a few. He used something called *Flash String*, something else called *Flash Paper*, and then there was *Flash Wool*. He was quite into pyrotechnics. He told me he had a sideline business making bespoke fireworks.'

'Oh?' said Glenn Branson. 'How much did he tell you about this?'

'Very little. He said he had an interest in a factory, but I've no idea where. Somewhere in Sussex, I think.'

'You were together for how long?'

'Just under two years.'

'And he never took you to this factory, or told you where it was?' Glenn Branson said, sounding puzzled.

'You need to remember that during that whole time he was living the lie that he worked in Air Traffic Control at Gatwick. He'd come home from his shifts and tell me about his day, and the occasional incidents. He was so convincing I never had any reason to doubt it. Until my mother showed me the report from the detective agency.'

'Okay. It would be helpful if you could think back, and try to tell us as much as you can remember about how you felt when you first met Bryce,' Roy Grace said.

'I was very vulnerable at that point, I suppose. After several years of being with Dominic, Bryce was like a breath of fresh air, at first. He seemed genuinely interested in me. He showered me with gifts. I totally believed everything he told me about his background – I mean, why wouldn't I? I had no reason not to. I got really angry with my mother for being suspicious about him. I guess that's what love does to you. It's so true what they say – that love is blind. I was blind. Totally and utterly blind for months. I should have sussed, because none of my friends were comfortable with him.'

'Do you know where he is living now?' Grace asked.

'No, I don't.'

'There's a court exclusion order on him coming or living within half a mile of you,' Branson said. 'You said you thought you might have seen him outside your office last Thursday. But you couldn't be sure?'

'No.'

'Could anyone have drawn the queen of hearts on your bathroom mirror other than Bryce Laurent?' Grace asked.

'No one,' she said. 'No one comes in my place – not unless I'm there with them, like a plumber. But how could he have got in?'

'He seems a pretty resourceful guy,' Roy Grace answered.

'Oh yes, he's that.'

'One of our first tasks is to see if we can establish a forensic link between Mr Laurent and the death of Dr Murphy, the Cuba Libre restaurant fire, your car and the minimart,' he continued. 'But based on the fact that he seems to have been in your flat yesterday, and he put the engagement ring back on your finger, you are not safe. We can arrest him – if we can find him. But you need to move. I don't think you can consider your flat secure any more.'

'There is a proper panic room in place now, boss,' Glenn Branson said. 'It can only be locked and unlocked from inside – it's impenetrable. That would give Red an hour's protection – enough time for us to reach her.'

'I'm in the process of moving,' Red said to them. 'I should be exchanging contracts soon.'

'Where to?' Grace asked.

'Along the seafront, in Kemp Town.'

The Detective Superintendent frowned. 'When is that due to happen?'

'A month to six weeks or so.'

'I'd really like to move you out of Brighton altogether,' Grace said.

'Move? How do you mean? Where to?'

'Another part of the country. And change your name and identity – until we find this man and have him under arrest.'

She shook her head. 'I really don't want to do that. I've got my job here, my new career, and I'm not going to let that bastard beat me. I'm staying in Brighton.'

'It wouldn't be for ever,' Glenn Branson reassured her.

'I don't want to lose my job, please. Are you saying you can force me to do that?'

Grace shook his head. 'No, but under police guidelines I am going to have to serve you with something called a Warning Notice,' he said, his tone apologetic. 'It's a formal document that will say it is not possible for us to provide you with round-the-clock protection and that we advise you to increase your own personal security, and to consider moving away as one option.'

'We could officially assign you a Witness Protection Officer, although you have that already more or less in the form of PC Spofford,' Glenn Branson said, looking at Roy Grace for approval. 'But he can't guard you around the clock.'

Red felt a deep sinking feeling in the pit of her stomach. Moving away possibly was the right thing. But everything she knew and loved was in Brighton and the surrounding area. She had visions of being all alone in a seaside boarding house in an unfamiliar place at the other end of the country. Away from family and friends. And how could she keep her job if she did that?

'The thing is, Red, that we only have limited resources. We can't give you twenty-four-hour police protection, but we can help you to hide,' Glenn Branson added.

'You've just said yourself that Bryce is resourceful. If he wants to find me, he'll find me – just like he found my flat. If he really is behind all these fires, I think maybe he's doing it just to bully me – sort of punish me. I don't think I'm actually in physical danger from him. If he wanted to harm me, surely he'd have done that by now?'

She saw the two detectives exchange a glance. Then Roy Grace looked her in the eye. 'Do you think it is possible he wanted to punish Dr Murphy?'

'Punish Karl?'

'For dating you?'

Red looked into the deadly serious faces of the two men. The idea made her flesh crawl. She felt like she had a tightening tourniquet in her stomach as she realized the implication of what the detective had just said. It had been at the back of her mind for days, but she had dismissed it. Bryce had a dark side for sure, but he wouldn't have gone that far, would he? Could he have?

'Do you – do you think – think – he—' Her words fell away. She wasn't sure what she was saying. She felt enveloped suddenly in a dark, acrid fog.

Then she heard the black detective's voice. Tender now. 'Red, are you okay?'

She stared at him through her tears of fear and sorrow. 'No, please tell me no, please tell me Bryce didn't – didn't . . . oh God.' She buried her face in her hands and began sobbing deeply, everything that had been pent up inside her for this past week now flooding out.

Glenn Branson produced some tissues for her and she dabbed her eyes, sniffing. 'I'm sorry,' she said. 'I'm really sorry. God. I thought the day I finished with Bryce – threw him out – with PC Spofford's help – I thought that was the day my nightmare had ended. It's starting to feel now like it was the day it began.'

55

Began, baby, you are right on that one! Oh yes, I can promise you that. The day you humiliated me is the day your night-mare began. Although, strictly speaking, nightmare is the wrong word. You wake up from nightmares, you see.

That's not going to happen.

Bryce sat at his desk in his workshop, headphones on, listening to the interview, TweetDeck open in front of him on one of his computer screens. He continued to tap his keyboard while listening. Multitasking. He'd got good at that in these past months. Doing all kinds of stuff, while listening all the time to what was happening with Red. Sometimes smiling, sometimes getting angry.

Nothing had made him so angry as the sounds of Red and the doctor having sex. The sounds she made, the noises, the gasps, the swear words that came out of her mouth, all staccato, as she climaxed.

The same swear words as when she had climaxed with him. As if she had known he was listening and was doing this to taunt him.

He had to stop that, could not let that happen again, it hurt him too much.

He exited TweetDeck. He loved the internet; it was so easy to be anonymous. He was anonymous in real life, too. Creating an identity was easy but it took physical work. Going around to apartment blocks and stealing from the communal mailboxes utility bills, driving licences, tax forms, and all the other kinds of personal stuff that arrived in buff envelopes. Then going through the registry of deaths in the public records office, finding names that matched, but who had died young, too young to have ever applied for driving licences or passports. He had seven real identities – passports, driving licences, bank accounts, credit cards, all registered to different mailbox addresses in Brighton and London. As was his Land Rover.

They had appointed an officer to look after Red. How sweet he was! What fun it might be to tie Red up and then let her watch him slowly cutting bits off PC Spofford in front of her, teaching him not to meddle in private affairs of the heart. It would do the smug bitch Red some good to get a real taste of what he had in store for her. It would be worth all the pain she had put him through, she and her nasty family, if he could see the terror on her face. See it for a long time. Hours. Days. Maybe weeks. As she begged for forgiveness. Pleaded for him to come back, for everything to be how it was with them before. Swore her undying love for him.

Undying love.

He would like to hear those words so much.

In the moments before she died.

But first he had work to do. He opened the animation program, and set to work drawing a boat.

The interview had come to an end. Red was going home. The boat was shaping nicely. He selected Rod Stewart's 'Sailing' from Spotify and clicked to play it. It was one of Red's favourite songs. He smiled. *Sailing.*

A life on the ocean wave. Heigh-ho.

And maybe a death.

He began a Google search of Admiralty charts for the English Channel.

56

It was shortly after eight on a damp October evening when Glenn Branson turned the unmarked car right at the bottom of The Drive, into Church Road.

'Anywhere here's fine,' Red said.

'You sure? I can drop you to your front door. Make sure you're safely home,' he said.

She liked the big, tall, gentle giant, with his kind face. He was enough of a man-mountain to make her feel totally safe, but at the same time she sensed a vulnerability, a deep inner sadness about him. She'd made a couple of attempts at asking him about his personal life on the slow drive through the rush-hour traffic from the CID headquarters, but he'd maintained a total policeman-like focus on how she was to keep alert and safe.

'Thanks, but I need to do some food shopping.'

They were passing the blackened facade of the mini-mart, all boarded up and already stickered with apologetic notices to customers.

'Yeah, well, careful where you go. No more pyrotechnics, okay?'

She gave a wan smile, then pointed across the road to the Tesco superstore. 'If you can drop me there,' she said.

He flipped his right indicator. 'Door-to-door service for madam!'

As he pulled up, Glenn noticed a scruffy, shaven-headed old lag of a villain, in his late forties, lurking near the exterior rubbish bins. Jimmy West. He kept an eye on him, aware of the scam he would be getting up to, of removing a sales receipt from the bin then going into the store, matching groceries up to the receipt and departing. But Jimmy West wasn't his problem right now.

'You're really kind,' Red said, opening the door.

'Yeah, I know!' Glenn grinned.

She grinned back, on the verge of giving him a kiss goodbye, then hesitated, thinking that might not be proper. Instead she gave him a wave of her hand and closed the door.

Glenn continued grinning as he watched her enter the supermarket. She was an attractive lady; he'd seen the hesitation in her face. He'd have liked a kiss from her, he thought. Rather a lot.

He saw West move towards a bin. He hit the button to lower the passenger-door window, leaned across and shouted out, 'Evening, Jimmy! Doing a bit of shopping, are we?'

West looked round at him, flustered for a moment. Then he recognized Glenn's face. 'Oh . . . evening . . . er, Sergeant! Sergeant Bistow!'

'Branson. And it's Inspector now. What you doing here?'

'Oh, er, you know, just passing.'

'Good. Then keep going. Pass right along!'

West raised a finger, signalling his intention to oblige.

Glenn sat there, watching until the man was out of the car park and back on the street. There was a time, he realized, when he would have felt sorry for someone like Jimmy West. Trapped in a spiral, if one of his own making. But just like every cop he had ever spoken to, a few years in the police force changed you, hardened you. You looked for the bad in people, rather than the good. And you didn't often have to look too far to find it.

But Red, he sensed, had good in her. He felt her warmth. He drove out of the car park and pulled up on the opposite side of the road, waiting until she emerged from the store holding two carrier bags. Keeping a discreet distance, he tracked her all the way to her flat, and waited until he saw her safely inside, before driving off back to Sussex House.

57

Wednesday, 30 October

Red punched on the stairwell light, then climbed up warily, holding her two heavy Tesco bags. She stood still, nervous, on the landing and looked along the corridor, checking behind her, down the stairs, before putting the bags down, pulling out her keys, and carefully checking the hair she had stuck at the top of the door jamb. It was still in place.

Relieved, she unlocked all three locks and went in, switching on the hall light and closing the door behind her, locking the deadbolts and pushing home the heavy-duty safety chain. Even so, she still waited for some moments, listening for any sounds. Outside she heard the wail of a siren fading into the distance. She carried her bags along the short corridor, snapping on the lights of the panic room behind its reinforced door and her bedroom light and checking both rooms, before looking in the bathroom and making her way through into the living/kitchen area and dumping the bags on the floor.

She took out the two bottles of Sauvignon Blanc and put one in the fridge and the other into the freezer compartment, then put away the milk, cheese, bread, blueberries and grapes she had bought, put the mixed salad on the table, and ripped the packaging off the fish pie, which she then put into the microwave before setting the timer.

The message light was winking red on her answering

machine, and she hit the play button, peeling off her coat. It was her mother. Why, she wondered, did her dear mother always phone her at home and leave a message there instead of phoning her mobile which she carried with her all the time? She had told her a thousand times, but it made no difference.

'Hi darling. The forecast is good tomorrow, so your father and I are taking the train down to Chichester early in the morning, to sail the boat back to the marina. If you can take the day off, join us – the fresh air might do you good!'

Yeah, Red thought glumly. A day out on the English Channel, freezing her butt off, eating soggy egg and tomato sandwiches and drinking warm beer, whilst enduring a lecture from her well-meaning parents on the disaster that was her life.

She phoned her mother back and told her that, much though she would have loved to join them, she had viewings set up for tomorrow, so skiving off work was, unfortunately, not an option. They confirmed the arrangement to meet at her new flat at midday on Sunday.

Then she flipped up the lid of her laptop and checked first her emails. The usual ton of spam, a message asking if she would be interested in playing lacrosse next Wednesday, to which she replied an enthusiastic yes – no one had organized a game in over a year, and she loved it – and another, an advance warning of a New Year's Eve party, which she logged on her calendar.

Suddenly, an email popped up.

Red Westwood, you have new followers on Twitter.

After three years on Twitter she had a meagre, if respectable, one hundred and thirty-seven followers – despite following over seven thousand people herself, including

Jonathan Ross, Stephen Fry, the Prime Minister, President Obama, and numerous other high-profile people around the world. Not that she worried about it, but it was of course always nice to have new followers.

She clicked to open the link and read with dismay:

The queen of hearts is now following you.

58

Wednesday, 30 October

After his interview with Red Westwood finished, Roy Grace needed no more convincing. He believed her and he felt her pain. He phoned Cleo to tell her he would be delayed, but would get home as soon as he could. She sounded exhausted.

'Please do, darling. Noah's been grizzling all day. I think he's teething.'

Ignoring his guilt, he spent the next hour and a half in his office, first pulling a favour from Tony Case, the Senior Support Officer responsible for Sussex House administration, getting him to clear Major Incident Room One, where there were a few team members of an enquiry which was winding down. Then he began a series of phone calls putting together the team he needed, and setting up the first briefing meeting for 8.30 a.m. the following morning.

On his drive home, shortly after 9 p.m., he continued making calls on his hands-free, and by the time he climbed out of his car, still on his phone, he had the majority of people he wanted in place. He entered the gated courtyard of Cleo's townhouse that he and Cleo were sharing until their hoped-for move to the country within the next couple of months, if the purchase of the house went through okay. And he was cheered by a piece of good news he'd received late this afternoon, a phone call from the estate agent telling him that they had a prospective purchaser for his house, where he had lived with Sandy, and were expecting an offer in the morning.

He slipped the key in the lock and pushed the front door open. All those people who told him that having a baby would change his life were so right, he thought, despite his and Cleo's best efforts. It was inevitable, he realized, because of the enormity of the responsibility the two of them now shared.

Up until the last months of her pregnancy, when he came home from work he would be greeted by the smell of scented candles, music playing and Cleo thrusting an ice-cold vodka martini into his hands, then kissing him passionately.

Today the smell was different. An anodyne, milky smell of baby powder and freshly laundered nappies, which Cleo insisted on using, preferring them to the convenience of disposables. She sat in a loose smock on the sofa, breastfeeding Noah in front of the television, and greeted him with a wan smile.

'Hi darling. How was your day?' she asked.

He wrestled out of his coat, patting an excited Humphrey at the same time. 'Okay . . . well . . . actually, a bit shit. Got a new murder enquiry, which I could do without right now.'

Instantly her face dropped. 'God, is that going to affect our—'

'Absolutely not!' he said, cutting her short in midsentence. 'Nothing's going to affect Saturday, or our honeymoon. How's the little fellow?'

Noah, eyes shut, was sucking away.

'Okay, for the moment. But he's been grizzly all day with the combination feeding. I don't think we're going to get much sleep tonight. Maybe you should go in the spare room.'

He shook his head. 'All for one and one for all!'

She grinned. 'Did you get that from Glenn?'

'Actually, no. *The Three Musketeers* is one of the few books I remember from childhood.' He grinned, then paused to look at the television. 'I need a drink.'

'I've put everything out for you.'

He blew her a kiss, went through into the kitchen and mixed himself a stiff vodka martini, then brought it back into the room and perched on the end of the sofa beside them. He took a sip, and instantly craved a cigarette, but would wait until Noah was in bed.

'If you need to postpone our honeymoon, darling, I'd understand,' Cleo said. 'Even though I've been expressing milk all week.'

'No way.'

'I'd hate for Cassian Pewe to use this against you. Taking off in the middle of a murder enquiry. I can imagine him doing that.'

He shook his head. 'We're well into the investigation. I'm setting everything up and Glenn is perfectly capable of running with it until I'm back. I'm not letting anything get in the way – like I did previously.'

'With Sandy?' The moment she had said the name, she regretted it. 'I'm sorry, I didn't mean that.'

He shrugged. 'That's history. We have our whole lives ahead of us, and I love you so damned much. I'm not going to repeat any mistakes. Okay?' He looked at her with a big smile.

She smiled back. 'Are you still going to have your stag night?'

'It's not exactly going to be a wild occasion. I'm going out for a couple of beers with Glenn and the team tomorrow night, then staying over with him again on Friday. It's meant to be bad luck for the groom to see the bride on the day of the wedding.'

'It's going to be sooooooooo good to have some time alone together,' she said.

'It is! We used to leap on each other all the time. Remember those showers we used to take, soaping each other? God, they made me so damned horny!'

'And me! I promise, next week we'll have showers every night. I'll massage you all over. I can't wait. I still fancy you, Roy Grace, I fancy you like crazy. I'm sorry if I've been too tired recently to show it.'

'And right back at you, my lovely.'

He leaned over and kissed her.

Noah stopped suckling and began crying.

59

Red heard crying. Her eyes sprang open, straight into a dazzling beam of light burning into her retinas like a laser. She closed them. Then opened them again. Saw a face this time.

Bryce.

Staring down at her.

She lay, frozen, staring back up at him. Staring into his eyes. She tried to speak but her voice was muted with fear. She tried again. Then again. Then finally she blurted out a feeble, 'What do you want?'

The light went out and then, suddenly, she was staring into darkness. Listening. Listening for footsteps. Shaking in terror. Was Bryce in the room?

She heard another cry in the darkness. A wail of pain. A howl. A long, tortured, high-pitched scream. The clank of a dustbin. Two cats fighting. Then the wail of a siren. *Police, please!* Brief, then it stopped. The rattle of a taxi. The slam of a car door. Shouting. Two drunks, a man and a potty-mouthed woman, arguing. She hurling obscene insults. He slurring back in a broad Scouse accent.

Was Bryce in the room?

More people outside now, two floors below, all of them sounding drunk. One of them started singing 'Rule Britannia!' Another began shouting, 'Seagulls! Seagulls! Seagulls!'

Football supporters.

She looked at the clock beside her bed. The luminous hands showed it was 2.18 a.m.

'Seagulls!'

'Screw seagulls!'

'I never tried!'

More laughter.

Drunks inflicting their hilarity on everyone sleeping around them.

She was close enough to shout for help. Help from a bunch of drunks? Goosebumps pricked her body. Ran up her legs, her midriff, her arms.

Was Bryce in here?

She reached out her arm, careful not to knock over her water, found the lamp, found the switch and pressed it. The small room flooded with weak light.

She was alone.

Her heart was pounding. She picked up her mobile phone from the bedside table, hovered her thumb over the speed-dial button, number 1, for PC Spofford. Then lay still, listening. The arguing couple moved on, but the drunks remained, starting to sing again, their Seagulls supporters chant.

She wanted to get out of bed and check the flat, but she was too afraid of stepping out of her bedroom door into the corridor. So instead she lay still, listening to the drunks singing and ragging each other. Listening for any sound in her flat beyond the bedroom. Until, suddenly, she heard a male voice.

'One hundred and thirty-four people are feared dead when a railway bridge, one hundred miles north of Calcutta, collapsed in what is reported to be one of India's worst ever rail disasters.'

Red rolled over and stared at the blinking light on her clock/radio. It was just gone 6.30 a.m.

Memories of the night came back, and relief flooded through her. Bryce shining the torch at her, staring down at her, had been a dream. That was all. She closed her eyes and half dozed, half listened to the news, as she did every week-day morning.

Twenty minutes later, she slipped out of bed, naked, and padded through into her bathroom, pushed open the sliding door that closed off the tiny loo, and peed. Then she went through into the kitchen to brew a cup of tea and prepare her breakfast of chopped-up fruit and porridge.

And instantly stopped in her tracks.

Was her memory playing tricks?

She thought back to last night. Her breakfast stuff from the morning had lain unwashed on the draining board. Additionally, she had left the packaging from the fish pie she'd microwaved on the draining board, ready to throw it away in the morning. Along with the dishes she'd used – the plate, the bowl for the salad, and the empty low-fat fruit yoghurt pot.

They had gone.

All the dishes were now clean and lying on the draining board.

She opened the cupboard with the swing bin. The lid rose to reveal a fresh, unused black bin liner.

Her stomach flipped. Fear washed through her. She turned and ran along the corridor to the front door. Then stared for some moments, ensuring she was focused and not dreaming, at the door. The security chain was securely in place.

Bryce could not have been here last night, could he?

No way could he have let himself out of the front door

with that safety chain still in place. It was too high for him to have jumped from a window. She hurried over to each window in turn, and looked down into the faint, breaking light. Not possible. He'd have had to have left something behind if he had gone out of any of the windows. A rope, a cord, a wire. Something.

But if not Bryce, who the hell had done the washing-up then emptied the bin? Had she done it herself? She knew she had drunk far too much last night. Did that explain it? That she had done all of that and forgotten in her drunkenness?

She was so damned sure she had seen Bryce in the middle of the night. But the safety chain was still in place. No one could have come in through the front door. Nor locked it behind them. So how could it have been him?

She had dreamed him, she thought. It was the only possible explanation.

60

At a few minutes before half past eight in the morning, carrying a mug of coffee, Roy Grace left his office and used his pass card to open the door to the Major Crime Suite. He walked along the corridor, the walls lined on both sides with noticeboards pinned with crime-scene photographs, charts and newspaper headlines from recent solved homicides, and entered Major Incident Room One.

MIR-1 was a spacious, modern, airy room furnished with three large oval workstations, around which his team were settling down. Three whiteboards were fixed to the walls. One was stickered with crime-scene photographs from Haywards Heath golf course, with arrows, and hand-writing in red, black and green marker pen. The second displayed a series of portrait photographs of Bryce Laurent. On the third was an association chart of Bryce Laurent, as well as two photographs of Red Westwood. One of these was in Brighton, right in front of the Brighton Oyster & Shellfish Bar. The other was of her on a terrace, overlooking the Mediterranean, with a glass of champagne in her hand.

Someone's mobile phone was ringing with an old-fashioned bell tone. There was a smell of eggs and bacon – Guy Batchelor hunched over a hot breakfast roll from Trudie's mobile cafe, a short walk down the road. As Roy Grace sniffed it, he felt a pang of hunger. The bowl of porridge he'd gulped down at 5.30 a.m. before leaving home seemed a long time ago now.

DS Bella Moy was seated, with the ever-present box of Maltesers in front of her, studying the case notes that had been circulated in advance. Norman Potting sauntered in holding a lidded carton of coffee, and Grace clocked the secretive grin between him and Bella. He smiled to himself, happy to see lost soul Bella at last looking happy; he was pleased for Norman, too. The old sweat's private life had been a series of disasters – particularly the nightmare of his grasping Thai bride of a few months back.

Two young, bright Detective Constables, Alec Davies and Jack Alexander, were present, along with his other stalwarts – DS Jon Exton, recently promoted, DS Guy Batchelor, and Crime Scene Manager David Green. The others in the room included Inspector James Biggs from the Road Policing Unit, HOLMES analyst Keely Scanlan, researcher Becky Davies, Chief Fire Investigation Officer Tony Gurr, and forensic podiatrist Haydn Kelly, whose forensic gait analysis instruments had been invaluable in both of Roy Grace's most recent cases, DI Gordon Graham, a specialist from the Police Financial Investigation Unit, and Ray Packham.

Grace waited until a further two DCs, Francesca Jamieson and Liz Seward, whom he had requested this morning to help on the outside enquiry team, had entered, then seated himself at his own workstation with his policy book and briefing notes, prepared by his assistant, in front of him. He glanced at the notes then opened his policy book and made a note of the date and time.

'Good morning, everyone,' he said. 'Welcome to the first briefing of Operation Aardvark, the investigation into the suspected murder of Dr Karl Thomas Murphy, whose charred body was found on Haywards Heath golf course on the morning of last Thursday, 24 October.'

'Did he count as a movable obstruction, chief, or did the players get a free drop?' Norman Potting said with a chortle. There were a few other titters of laughter, instantly silenced by Grace's glare.

'Thank you, Norman. Save the golfing jokes for another time, okay?'

'Sorry, chief.' Potting turned towards Bella, as if for approval, but she studiously ignored him by reaching forward and helping herself to a chocolate.

Distracted for a moment, Roy Grace noticed the large print from the cartoon film *The Ant and the Aardvark*, with a bright blue, gormless-looking Aardvark standing erect, that some wag had taped to the inside of the door. It had become a Sussex Police tradition for a picture mimicking the title of a major crime operation to be stuck there. This one had appeared faster than usual.

'Before I start,' Roy Grace said, 'I should let you all know that I will be absent from this Saturday until next Friday morning, 8 November, for my marriage to Cleo and our brief honeymoon. DI Branson will deputize for me during this period.'

Glenn, two seats away from him, raised his hand in acknowledgement.

The Detective Superintendent pointed at the whiteboard on which there were a series of photographs of Bryce Laurent. In one he wore a striped T-shirt and shorts; in another he was dressed in a felt graduation cap and ermine gown; another was a US penitentiary photograph of him against a height ruler, with an ID number tag around his neck. 'This man is our prime suspect and we need to find

him urgently. We are also linking him to a number of suspected arson attacks in the city during the past week. We
believe his real name to be Thomas William Cheviot. This
was the name under which he spent three years in a
Philadelphia State Penitentiary for an assault on his girlfriend. According to the detective I spoke to, he beat her up
pretty badly. We're not exactly dealing with Mr Nice Guy
here, okay?'

Then he looked back down at his notes. 'Thomas
Cheviot has any number of possible aliases. His last known
one is Bryce Laurent. Previous ones include Pat Tolley,
Derek Jordan, Michael Andrews and Paul Riley. Thanks to
the cooperation of the Philadelphia police we have his
fingerprints and DNA. He's smart, he dresses well, speaks
with a classy voice, and is a regular charmer in every sense.
He could be anywhere in the world right now. But for
reasons that will become self-evident, I believe he is staying
local and ready to strike at any moment.'

He looked at his notes again. 'What we do know about
Bryce Laurent – we'll refer to him by this name to avoid
confusion – is that he has worked as a close magician, he
has extensive knowledge of pyrotechnics, and he is a total
fantasist. He's passed himself off in the US separately as an
American Airlines captain and an investment banker, and
in the UK as an Air Traffic Controller at Gatwick Airport.
Under one of his aliases, Pat Tolley, he was granted a fireworks manufacturing licence here in the UK. But we've
checked out the address, an industrial site on farmland in
Suffolk, and he's long gone from there. We also know he is
a talented cartoonist.'

He sipped some water. 'I've again engaged the services
of a forensic behavioural psychologist, Dr Julius Proudfoot – some of you will remember he worked with us very

effectively on Operation Houdini, the Shoeman case. He'll be joining future briefings. It is Dr Proudfoot's view that Laurent has an immensely high opinion of himself; that he is displaying all the qualities of a classic narcissist. I wrote down this from him: "Narcissism is a highly dangerous trait, which stems often from people who have been unloved in childhood compensating in later life with grandiose self-belief, arrogance, a tendency to make unreasonable demands, unstable temper and violent mood swings, and, very significantly and dangerously, that familiar attribute of the psychopath – a lack of empathy."'

Grace then brought his team up to speed on Bryce Laurent's relationship with Red Westwood, and what was known so far about the fires. When he had finished, he began to detail the lines of enquiry for his team. First up, he delegated DCs Jack Alexander and Alec Davies to work on the outside enquiry team, interviewing all members of Haywards Heath Golf Club who were present either the afternoon or evening of 23 October, or the morning of 24 October.

Next, he said, 'I need a list of all the non-members who were at Haywards Heath Golf Club that day. Anyone from the general public who paid a green fee, or maybe bought something in the pro shop. All the staff who were there that day. What tradesmen made deliveries. And, this is a big task, we need to find out what mobile phone company masts are in the vicinity – speak to the telecom unit and arrange to secure phone dumps for the relevant time. It's possible the offender phoned someone to say, *job done.* If so, who?'

Norman Potting raised his hand, and Grace nodded at him.

'Are you going to try *Crimewatch*, chief?'

'Yes, we have contacted them, and they're interested.

But they are not on air again for two weeks. We are also planning to issue a reward.' He turned to DS Exton. 'Jon, I'm tasking you with managing the intelligence, which should include what we might get from our covert human intelligence sources.' Next he looked at Potting. 'Norman, we have Bryce Laurent's last known mobile phone number, which was with O2. Go through the Telecoms Unit and see if you can get a plot of his movements, and also find out, crucially, whether the number is still active.'

He sipped some coffee and studied his notes again for a moment. Then he pointed at the two photographs of Red Westwood. 'I've had these analysed. They were taken with a Motorola digital camera. We are able to extrapolate the exact location, the time of the photograph, and the distance the photographer was from his – or her – subject. Ms Westwood told me that Bryce Laurent is a keen photographer. She has dozens taken by him, not just of her, but of landscapes around Sussex and elsewhere. Have her albums looked at and see if you can establish a favoured geographical location for him.'

Potting nodded compliantly.

Grace next looked at DS Moy. 'Bella, if Bryce Laurent has been responsible for these fires, it's possible he might have burned himself in the process. I'm tasking you with checking all hospitals in the surrounding area to see what burns admissions they've had in their A&E departments and whether the dates coincide with what we know about him.'

Then he turned to the forensic podiatrist, Haydn Kelly, who was standing a few metres away facing the room, waiting patiently. 'Haydn, thanks for joining us at such short notice. The night Dr Murphy died was a clear sky, but there had been heavy rain in the previous forty-eight hours. I'm told there are some good footprints.'

'That is correct, yes,' Kelly said. 'But so far I'm unable to obtain a match on any of the databases.'

'But you can still pick out the person who left that footprint, in a crowd, from his gait?' Roy Grace quizzed.

'If there is video footage of the person, then yes, with a high percentage of accuracy.'

Grace turned to the financial investigator, DI Gordon Graham. Suspects were commonly traceable through their finances. Most people today had credit and debit cards. All money movements located and dated them, and, as additional help for the police, fewer establishments still took cash. DI Graham outlined what enquiries he would be getting his star financial investigator, Emily Gaylor, to undertake.

Suddenly, Grace's phone, which he had switched to silent, vibrated. The caller's identity did not show on the display. Ordinarily during a briefing meeting he would take no calls as a matter of principle. But something told him this call was urgent.

He was right. It was Constable Rob Spofford and something had happened. His voice sounded tight with anxiety.

He signalled to Glenn Branson to take over the meeting and stepped away, holding his phone to his ear.

61

Out in the corridor, Roy Grace closed the door to MIR-1 and said to Rob Spofford, 'Tell me.'

'I'm sorry to bother you, sir, but I need to email you something that Red Westwood has just received. There's quite a large attachment with it.'

Grace sometimes had problems reading attachments on his phone. 'I'll go to my office and look on my screen there. Call me back in two minutes on this number.'

He hurried back along the corridor, dismissing his secretary, who wanted a word with him, with a wave of his hand, sat at his desk, and opened his email. Moments later one appeared from Spofford. He clicked on the attachment.

A childlike but elaborate cartoon appeared, part black and white and part in colour. It was a jaunty sketch of a yacht, with two figures in the cockpit, a male and a female, on a choppy sea. Circling around the hull were shark fins. And right in the centre of the boat, rising up, enveloping the mainsail and foresail, were flames. Written in the centre of them was the single word, *BOOM!*

Moments later his phone rang. 'Roy Grace,' he answered.

'Did you get it, sir?'

'Yes, what's this all about?'

'I don't know if Ms Westwood told you, Bryce Laurent is something of a cartoonist?'

'She did, yes.'

'He has a pathological hatred of her parents, in particular her mother. He believes it was her who poisoned their relationship.'

'Because she hired a private detective who found out the truth about him, right?'

'Yes, sir.'

'So what's the significance of this weird cartoon? Some sick joke?'

'I believe it's more than that. Her parents could be in immediate danger. They have a thirty-two-foot yacht, and they're sailing it today from Chichester to Brighton Marina, where they keep it during the winter. This might just be a joke, but in my view he may have placed some form of incendiary device, or even an explosive, on board. We know he has extensive knowledge of bomb-making techniques from his time in the Territorial Army, and he has access to explosives through his firework licence.'

'Do we know where this email's come from?'

'I don't, sir, no. I'm not an expert in these things. Perhaps someone from the High Tech Crime Unit could tell us.'

Grace stared at the cartoon again, and a chill rippled through him. Beneath its childlike simplicity, there was something deeply sinister about it. He hit the command to print the email and attachment.

As the printer chuntered into noisy action he asked, 'Do we know if they've set off yet?'

'Ms Westwood says she tried phoning her parents, knowing they were making an early start. She got a very crackly signal, and briefly heard her mother's voice saying they were going out of phone range.'

'So they're at sea?'

'Sounds like it, sir.'

Grace thought for a moment. 'How long will they be at sea for?'

'Ms Westwood tells me, depending on whether they are using just wind or motor-sailing, about six hours.'

Grace made a mental note about Spofford's efficiency. The constable was sharp and smart. A possible future member of his team. 'What's the name of the yacht?'

'*Red Margot*, sir. Named after the two daughters. I understand her father's rather seriously into wine.'

Yes, and possibly into history, Grace nearly said grimly. 'We can't run the risk of anything happening. We need to get them off the boat right away. Does Ms Westwood have any means of communication with them?'

'They have ship-to-shore radio on board, she told me. But they're not necessarily going to be listening to it.'

Roy Grace had gone on a flotilla sailing holiday with Sandy, around the Greek islands, many years back. From memory, the radio would be down in the cabin. If you were up on deck, you would never hear it – and that was assuming it was even switched on. He was feeling panicky. He stared at the cartoon again. Shit. If it was for real, how long did they have? Minutes? Hours? If it wasn't already too late.

He sprinted along the corridor, entered MIR-1, apologizing to Glenn for interrupting, and thrust the printout at Ray Packham. 'Drop everything you're doing and see if you can find out where this was sent from.' Then he turned to his team. 'Does anyone have any ocean sailing experience?'

Dave Green, the Crime Scene Manager, said, 'Superintendent Nick Sloan does – he has a yacht master's certificate.'

'Where is he?'

'He's gone to Serious and Organized Crime in London.'

'Try to get hold of him and put him through to me. This is an emergency.'

Asking Glenn to come with him, Grace hurried back to his office, briefing him on the way, and picked up his land-line phone, put it on loudspeaker, and dialled Inspector Andy Kille, the duty Ops-1 Controller in the Haywards Heath Control Room.

He quickly apprised Kille of the situation. 'We need to find that boat, fast, and get them off it, Andy. They must have a life raft or dinghy – we've either got to get them into that or airlift them off. Is NPAS 15 available?'

The National Police Air Service helicopter that served Sussex was based at Redhill, having been recently moved from Shoreham.

'It would take them twenty-five minutes to get here, sir,' Kille replied. 'That's if they are available. I think we'd be better off using the Coastguard – their helicopter's down in Lee-on-Solent; they'd be faster and would have winching facilities to get them off the boat. And they'd probably be better able to find them, too. There's a low cloud ceiling over the Channel at the moment, making visibility poor.'

'Okay, get them up.'

'How much information do we have on *Red Margot*'s whereabouts, sir?'

'Very little.'

'Do we have a description of the yacht?'

'One moment.' Grace covered the mouthpiece and turned to Glenn. 'Get Ms Westwood on the line. We need a full description of the boat and the numbers on the sails. It's best you ring because she knows you.'

Branson nodded.

'I'll get you that in a few minutes.'

'Okay, good,' Kille said. 'I ran an operation last year

trying to track a boat suspected of carrying drugs. The UK Border Agency Maritime Division were very helpful. I dealt with their Commander, James Hodge. I'll give you their number.'

'Okay, you get the Coastguard moving and I'll come back to you.'

Grace wrote the number down, hung up, told Glenn to pull up a map of the south coast from Chichester Harbour to Brighton Marina on the computer screen, and then dialled the number.

It took several minutes before James Hodge came on the line, while Grace anxiously drummed on his desk, staring at the map that was now on the screen in front of him. Hodge was a quietly efficient-sounding man. 'How can I assist?' he asked.

'We urgently need to locate a thirty-two-foot yacht sailing between Chichester Harbour and Brighton Marina, with two persons on board who may be in imminent danger from a bomb on the vessel, and get them off. Can you assist?'

'How much information do you have on its whereabouts?'

'Only what I've told you. I would not imagine it's been at sea very long.'

'Vessels over three hundred tons at sea, anywhere in the world, have to carry and keep switched on at all times their AIS – automatic identification system. Those under that weight – which is what this yacht would be – sometimes carry AIS, but it would be unusual for them to leave it on in the daytime, except in fog, because of the drain on the batteries. I guess you've no way of knowing if it's fitted or not?'

'I don't.'

Hodge thought for some moments. 'Sailing from Chichester to Brighton, they would normally take the Looe

Channel, about two miles offshore – unless they're attempting to evade detection.'

'I don't think they would have any reason to do that. They're a respectable retired couple.'

'I'll see if Shoreham Harbour or Brighton Marina breakwater could confirm its track. In the current wind conditions, the yacht as you describe would be travelling between five and six knots. Do we know when they set off?'

'Our best guess would be an hour or so ago,' Grace replied.

'It should be detectable on radar. There's a low cloud ceiling today which is not helpful for a helicopter search. But it sounds as if we could narrow the whereabouts of the yacht down to a few miles. How much time do we have?'

'None,' Grace said emphatically.

His office phone rang. It was Dave Green, telling him Superintendent Sloan was on a boat somewhere in the Atlantic, and unreachable until he radioed in.

Grace stared back at the cartoon. He was feeling helpless, he realized. Finding a small yacht in the Channel with poor visibility was not going to be straightforward. Please God they had AIS and had it switched on.

If it wasn't already too late.

His phone rang. It was Inspector Kille, telling him that the Coastguard helicopter was up and would be over Chichester Harbour mouth within ten minutes. It would then track east along the Looe Channel, below the cloud ceiling. A second helicopter would be along in twenty minutes, and two Coastguard vessels were heading to the area at full speed, but the closest would still be up to an hour.

'An hour?' Grace said.

'Hopefully the helicopter will find them well before then.'

'I've also called out RN EOD,' Kille said. 'Royal Naval Explosive Ordnance Disposal,' he added. 'If we rescue the people from the boat, we could be leaving an unattended drifting bomb.'

If they're not blown to smithereens already, Grace thought, but did not say.

He had a sick feeling of dread in his stomach.

62

Red arrived at her office shortly after 9 a.m. for an urgent meeting she needed to attend. She was worried out of her wits about her parents. PC Spofford had assured her before she left home that he would keep her updated on the search for their yacht.

But his news that the craft, a potential floating bomb in the narrow shipping lanes of the Channel, was causing a major alert did nothing to cheer her. The Navy, in addition to the Coastguard, were carrying out an air search, and a warning had gone out to all shipping in the vicinity to keep well clear of the vessel if sighted. All efforts to contact them by radio had so far failed.

Her parents were on that boat. They might irritate her at times, but she loved them dearly, and was far closer to them than she was to her sister. They were, effectively, all she had in the world. And now they were on board a floating bomb – if indeed they were still alive – and unaware.

Shit. She felt a wrench in her heart. This was all her fault. She'd brought this monster into her family, and he was now destroying them. If only she'd never placed that damned advertisement. If only she had listened to her mother sooner, and never let the relationship with Bryce get as far as it had. Rain lashed the pavement outside. So much for the forecast being good for their sail, she thought, watching an old lady with a wheeled shopping cart, encased in a see-through plastic mac, head bowed beneath a red umbrella, walking grimly past.

You sick bloody bastard, Bryce, she thought to herself as she peeled off her coat and sat down at her desk. She had a stack of particulars on new instructions to mail out to clients, and she had an appointment to go out later this morning to measure up a new property, a small flat in Poet's Corner that was coming on the market. Two viewings this afternoon. But she was in no mood to do anything. She just wanted to sit and wait for her phone to ring. For news from Constable Spofford.

As soon as she was out of the meeting, she logged on and checked her email, scanning through and deleting the endless stream of spam that, as ever, had got through the company's filters and checking for anything that might be from Bryce. To her small relief, there was nothing from him. But really all she could think about was her parents.

Her parents. Her lovely mum and sweet old dad. A hazard to shipping? Just by doing what they loved. Enjoying their retirement.

A floating bomb?

Suddenly, she rushed out of the room, into the ladies' toilet, pushed the door shut, shoved up the seat, and vomited violently into the bowl. Then she stood up, rinsed out her mouth in the basin, splashed cold water on her face, dried it, then headed back to her desk and rummaged in her bag for some chewing gum. As she did so, her mobile phone rang.

'Yes?' she answered instantly, and almost breathlessly.

It was Constable Spofford, and he was sounding sombre. 'Red, I've just heard from DI Branson that your parents' yacht has been found and its identity confirmed.'

'Fantastic!' she said, relief washing through her.

'Well,' he said, not sounding as if he shared any of her enthusiasm, 'I'm afraid there's a problem.'

63

Thursday, 31 October

The Strawberry Fields bed and breakfast was a narrow, bow-fronted Regency building in a terraced square, with communal gardens in the centre, off the Kemp Town seafront. There was a sign beside the bright red front door bearing a picture of a large strawberry, and inside the theme of vivid red and white ran through the communal areas and each of the small, elegant bedrooms.

Most of the guests were overnighters or weekenders. Either discerning tourists on a budget, who wanted something a cut above the traditional seaside bed and breakfast joint, or lovers down in Brighton for a romantic – and frequently illicit – night; there was also a regular stream of honeymoon couples. But there were a few regulars and a handful of long-stay guests, mostly business people, and these were popular with the owners, Jeremy Ogden and Sharon Callaghan, particularly the ones who remained during the thin winter months. And the longest-stay guest of all, the reclusive Paul Millet, had been there for over four months.

Mr Millet – he kept things on a strictly formal basis – came and went at all hours. Sometimes he stayed in his room for days without emerging. On other occasions he would be away for days, and sometimes weeks. But he was punctilious about his payments – always a month in advance. Neither of the owners, nor the Strawberry Fields manager, knew anything about their mysterious but pleasant-natured guest, other than what they saw. They saw a good-looking man in his late thirties, tall, with short black gelled hair, who could have passed as George Clooney's younger brother. He dressed expensively, greeted any of them with a big smile, displaying flawless white teeth, but never engaged in any conversation. And unlike some of their other single guests, to their knowledge, he had never brought anyone home for a night. One thing was for sure, he was obsessively tidy, making his own bed and washing up his mug and glass each day.

They assumed he was conducting business of some kind in the town – whether legitimate or otherwise, they had no idea, but so long as he continued to be polite, to keep his room immaculately tidy, and to pay, they were not unduly concerned. Brighton was Brighton. They'd seen it all in the years they'd owned this place and, to date, he'd done nothing to alarm them.

He was here today, closeted silently in his room, as normal.

Paul Millet sat at the small desk, the horizontal slats of the Venetian blind making him invisible to anyone outside. But from behind them, he had a clear view across the lawn in the centre of the square and down towards the grey water of the English Channel.

Red's parents were on that yacht. Mr and Mrs Westwood. Jeremy and Camilla. *Boom!*

He grinned. *Stand on the riverbank for long enough and the bodies of all your enemies will float past.* Oh yes, Sun Tzu, that old Chinese warrior, knew a thing or two. Well, this wasn't exactly a riverbank but it was the next best thing.

Boom!

He grinned, then peered out and down through the slats again. Checking the street directly below him, he had a clear view of anyone who might enter the front door. He had his escape route planned months ago, the day he had first arrived and gone exploring. Up the back staircase, out through the roof hatch, and down the fire escape to the rear of the building.

On the wooden table to his right was a cute little vanity suitcase, printed with strawberries, the lid open, the interior containing two mugs with cupcakes as a motif, an assortment of teabags and coffee sachets, sugar, sweeteners. It was 9.30 a.m. He stood up, filled the jug kettle and then switched it on. As it heated up, he sat back at the desk and opened an email that had just come in from the private detective agency he had engaged. It had been necessary to do this, because there was too much going on now for him to keep track of it all. And he did not want to miss a thing.

No way. Not on such a glorious day as this! It might be overcast outside today, but not in his heart! Today his heart was filled with sunshine. And hang the cost of the agency. What did money matter? In these last few days of his life? Hell, you couldn't take it with you, so you might as well spend, spend, spend. Have a good time. Enjoy!

Boom!

08.33: Subject leaves property on foot and turns left up Westbourne Terrace towards New Church Road.

08.41: Subject turns right, east, onto New Church Road, south side.

08.53: Subject crosses road and enters Tesco superstore. Purchases a tuna sandwich and an apple, paying £4.10 in cash.

09.03: Subject crosses road and enters offices of estate agents Mishon Mackay.

Paul Millet smiled. *Just an ordinary day, babe. But not so ordinary, hey?*

He listened, through his headset, hearing the anxiety in her voice. And he liked that. Oh yes, he liked that a lot!

'A problem?' he heard Red ask.

'A Coastguard helicopter has made radio contact with your parents.'

'They're okay? They're safe?'

'We've located them, Red, but we have a problem getting them off the boat. Because of the risk of an explosion, the helicopter cannot get permission to hover overhead to lower a winch. They need your parents to abandon the boat either in a life raft, or to jump overboard and swim clear, then they can winch them to safety. So far they're refusing to do either. They are not sure whether your parents are being stubborn or are just too scared.'

'My mother's always been scared of water – particularly the sea,' Red replied. 'Shit.'

'But she sails?' Spofford said.

'Because my dad loves it, she goes along with it. She always has done.'

'Red,' Spofford said, his voice deadly serious. 'They might die if they stay on the boat. Would she listen to you?'

Red was silent, trying to imagine the scenario. Her parents on the yacht, the helicopter hovering close by. 'She's going to bloody have to,' she said.

Moments later, through a crackly ship-to-shore radio link, Paul Millet heard her mother's hateful voice. He grinned again.

Boom!

64

She paid the taxi driver the fare from Heathrow Airport, gave him a generous tip, and climbed out onto the pavement, followed by her ten-year-old son who was neatly dressed in a herringbone overcoat. The driver removed her large overnight bag and her son's backpack from the boot, carried them to the foot of the steps up to the front door, and asked her if she needed help up the steps with them. But she told him she was fine, and he drove off.

In truth, she needed some moments to adjust to being back here. She breathed in the smell of the sea air, and so many memories flooded in. She felt a tug inside her heart. Her son pulled on her arm. 'Mama!' He pointed at a seagull hovering only yards above them. She smiled distantly, then closed her eyes, listening to the cry of the gull and the roar of the traffic.

She was an attractive woman in her late thirties, the fringe of her short black hair visible beneath her peaked leather cap, the collar of her coat turned up, and her eyes concealed behind fashionably large dark glasses, which she was wearing despite the grey morning. Then she opened her eyes again. There was a black railing balustrade to her left, attractive black metal coach lamps, and a large red strawberry on a white background was fixed to the wall like an old-fashioned pub sign. She couldn't see the actual name of the guest house, but this had to be it, she thought, and she liked the elegant look of the place.

She hauled her bag up the steps, pushed the door open, and, followed by her son lugging his backpack, continued through a white door which had a black-and-white sign on it saying *Vacancies,* and then on up the steep, red-carpeted stair treads to the reception desk, hearing the *thump-thump-thump* of her son's bag behind her. A pleasant-looking young woman in a pink blouse greeted them both with a warm smile. 'Hello, do you have a reservation?'

'We do.'

'And what name would that be under?'

'Lohmann,' the woman said.

The receptionist frowned, fingering her way down a printed list. 'Ah, yes! Frau Lohmann and your son, yes?'

'Ja.' After so many years, she responded in German instinctively.

The reception manager handed her the registration book. 'If you could just fill this in and sign it, please.'

The woman studied the required information. First name. Last name.

In the first-name column she wrote, *Sandy.*

65

Thursday, 31 October

I've caused this, was all Red kept thinking, despondently, as she sat in the back of the marked police car beside Detective Inspector Branson. It was being driven at high speed by Tony Omotoso, an officer from the Road Policing Unit, siren wailing, bullying his way through the heavy traffic along past Shoreham Harbour. Branson had assured her the best way to remain covert was to be in a marked car, because no one took much notice of a marked police car travelling on blues and twos.

'Good news that they're safe, yeah?' Glenn Branson said to her.

She nodded gloomily. But the cheery nature of the burly black detective comforted her a little.

'With luck they won't have to blow the yacht up. The Navy have a ship close by keeping all shipping well away from it. Your ex will have calculated the voyage time to be around six hours. So if it gets past twelve hours without a bomb detonating, they may take a view on it and put a line on it to tow it somewhere safe where they can keep an eye on it for a couple of days, and then board to check it. Might all just be a hoax, mightn't it?'

She nodded, but privately did not think so. Bryce delighted in scaring her, but his threats were rarely idle. It was more likely that something had gone wrong with the timer or detonator. She looked at the detective; he made her feel safe, as if nothing bad could happen to her or her family in his presence. 'They love the boat so much. It's been part of our family life for as long as I can remember. That and gardening are the two passions my parents have.'

'You know what I think?' he said.

'No?' She held her breath as they overtook a line of traffic, heading straight towards a massive oncoming tanker. Their driver seemed totally oblivious to its presence, as if somehow the car's siren gave them immunity to death. They squeezed through a gap that simply wasn't there, and she breathed again. Then he pulled back out into the oncoming traffic. She was dimly aware of the power station stack to her left, across the harbour, then the locks, and a row of warehouses. Massive white refinery tanks. Then they were in Shoreham, blasting through a red temporary roadworks light, cars swerving to get out of their way.

They reached a roundabout where Shoreham's Rope-tackle Arts Centre was sited, and she remembered past visits there to talks and to a Sunday morning jazz concert given by Herbie Flowers that Bryce had taken her to in happier times. A minute later they were racing under the tunnel into Shoreham Airport. As they emerged on the far side, passing a row of warehouses and hangars, Red saw a massive red and white liveried helicopter descending.

'That looks like them!' Branson said.

A few hundred yards further, the driver veered the car off the narrow road and pulled up. From a distance, they watched the helicopter touch down, its rotors still spinning, its doors closed. After what seemed an eternity, a rear door opened and a gangway lowered. Then she saw her father's face, above a bulky red lifejacket. But he wasn't looking relieved.

He looked like thunder.

66

Thursday, 31 October

'I'm telling you, if there was a ruddy bomb on the boat, I'd have seen it. I've been sailing her for damned near thirty years and I know every nut, bolt and rivet. There was no bomb. What part of that don't any of your people understand?' her father fulminated at Glenn Branson from the rear seat.

'Darling, you can't be sure,' Red's mother said, trying to pacify him.

'I think it's very nice of Detective Inspector Branson to see you home!' Red said breezily, trying to calm them down.

'So I suppose they're going to blow the ruddy boat up now, are they?' her father said.

They were travelling more slowly now, heading north on the A23 past Pyecombe. 'I don't think so, sir,' Glenn Branson said from the front passenger seat. 'They're going to keep it under observation.'

'It?' her father said. 'Boats are female. They're going to keep *her* under observation – all right?'

'Next left,' Red quietly said to the driver.

They forked off, passing a garage to their right, went over a roundabout, then carried on up an incline. Red turned to her mother. 'How are you feeling, Mummy?'

Her mother, her hair wild and windswept, was looking

traumatized. 'Have you ever tried getting into a life raft?' she responded.

'No.'

'Then being winched up into a helicopter? They had the straps right up in my armpits. I thought I was going to be torn in half!'

'At least you're safe, Mummy.'

'I was quite safe before, thank you, darling. Your father's right, there was no bomb. This is all that dreadful man, isn't it?'

The police had not wanted her parents to return to their house, for safety reasons. But they had been insistent and could not be persuaded otherwise. Like Red, they were not prepared to kowtow to Bryce. Instead, the police were now, reluctantly, having to make preparations for covert surveillance teams to protect the whole family.

They drove through the high street of the village of Henfield in silence, then turned left at the baker's. They wound down, passing the church on their left, over a mini-roundabout, past a pub on their right, some houses on their left, with wide open fields to their right. The road narrowed to a single track.

'Coming up on the left, one hundred yards,' Red said.

A police car, on blues and twos, was coming towards them at high speed. Their driver braked and squeezed over to the left into the hedgerow. But instead, the patrol car turned across them and disappeared.

'Follow him,' Red said, conscious of the sudden prick of anxiety in her throat.

Omotoso turned left into the even narrower country lane. Almost instantly, Red smelled it. Pungent, acrid smoke. Burning paint, timber, plastic. One hundred yards on, as they rounded a bend, the stench growing worse, Red felt a sudden hard knot in her stomach. The lane was blocked with emergency vehicles. Two fire engines, a smaller fire officer's car. Police cars and a motorcycle. An ambulance.

She could see orange flames leaping skywards. Consuming the thatched roof of a house.

Her parents' house.

She pushed open her door before PC Omotoso had even brought the car to a total standstill, and leapt out, running, weaving through the small crowd of onlookers, stepped over two hosepipes, and finally reached the front of the house.

'Please step back,' a female voice said.

She ignored her, lunging on forward. *Oh shit. Oh shit. Oh shit.*

Tears flooded down her face, the hideous smoke stinging her eyes. It seemed that every inch of the house was ablaze. Burning fragments of the straw roof drifted in the air like the dying embers of Chinese lanterns. She turned her head back, towards her parents, then stopped.

She did not want to see their faces. She didn't want to see anyone's face. She covered her own with her hands and sobbed.

Ten miles away, in his room at the Strawberry Fields guest house, Bryce Laurent smiled in satisfaction. He liked to hear Red cry.

It was the best sound in the world.

67

'We're dealing with a ghost,' Roy Grace said to his assembled team at the start of the evening briefing. It was a few minutes past 6.30 p.m., and he had moved the meeting into the conference room of the CID HQ, as MIR-1 was now too small to accommodate all the members of Operation Aardvark. Since the events of this morning, the extra recruits he had drafted in, including the forensic behavioural psychologist Dr Julius Proudfoot, had swelled the number on his team to thirty-six. Proudfoot was a tubby man in his late forties, with small, piggy eyes, dimpled cheeks, and thinning greying hair combed and gelled forward in a manner that did nothing for him or his hair, but his appearance belied his abilities; he came with a fine pedigree in his field.

Most of the room was taken up with an open-centred rectangular table with just enough chairs for everyone present. He had pressure coming down the line, top down. Nicola Roigard, the Police and Crime Commissioner, had raised her concerns about the spate of arson attacks to the Chief Constable, who in turn was leaning on ACC Rigg. And the buck stopped with himself, Roy knew. Every attempt was being made to locate Bryce Laurent, but for the moment he had vanished.

How the hell could he?

Extensive checks were being carried out on all of Bryce Laurent's known aliases. Checks on credit cards, which he would need to stay in most hotels these days. Checks on car rental firms, airline tickets, railway ticket purchases, ferry passengers, fuel purchases, restaurants, food purchases at supermarkets. So far nothing. Checks had also been made on all hospitals in the area for anyone who had gone to casualty with burns of any kind, but they had revealed nothing.

No phone calls had been made for several days on the number Red Westwood had given them, which was no surprise to Roy Grace. Laurent was almost certainly now using untraceable pay-as-you-go phones, paying cash and not accessing the internet to avoid detection.

'Sir, he might already have left the country,' suggested DS Exton. 'He could be anywhere in the world now, couldn't he?'

Grace looked at him. 'What makes you think that, Jon?'

'Because we only know some of his aliases, and he may well have others. He could have slipped abroad without us knowing under another name and passport.'

Out of the corner of his eye, Grace saw Ray Packham from the High Tech Crime Unit slip into the room, mouthing an apology for being late and looking excited. 'I don't think Bryce Laurent has gone anywhere,' Grace said. 'Why would he? What's he doing, and what is he doing it for? Let's look at the pattern – if indeed he is behind it all: he's murdered Red Westwood's new lover. He's torched the restaurant where he took her on their first date – and where Karl Murphy also happened to take her on their first date. Her Volkswagen Beetle car which went up in flames was tampered with – is that correct, Tony?' He looked at Tony Gurr, the Chief Fire Investigator.

'Yes, Roy. We would not ordinarily have examined a car of that age that had caught fire – all too commonly problems with the wiring. But because you asked us to, we looked more closely than normal, and found evidence of very subtle tampering with the car's coil and fuel pipe. Within minutes of the engine running, the coil would have over-heated, with a small amount of petrol spraying on it until it combusted.'

Grace thanked him, then continued. 'Laurent knew how much she loved that car. He then smoked her out of her regular convenience store, and used the smokescreen to put the engagement ring he had originally given her back on her finger. Next he scares her witless with the queen of hearts on the mirror, the cartoon of her parents' boat blow-ing up. And while all attention is diverted on that he sets fire to their house – Red Westwood's family home.' He looked back at DS Exton. 'Do you really think he's finished, Jon? I don't. I think he's on a sick campaign to terrify her by setting fire to everything she loves. But that's not his endgame. He hasn't finished yet. I've been studying patterns of other past cases of obsession, and in my opinion he's only just started. The worst is yet to come. I don't think he'll have gone any-where. He's here, in Brighton. I'd bet the ranch on it.'

'He is, boss,' Ray Packham said. 'I can take you to exactly where he is!'

68

Thursday, 31 October

Red had no appetite and no conversation. She sat having an early supper with her parents in the dining room of the Quincey Hotel on Eastbourne seafront, pushing her grilled plaice around the plate while her father dissected his steak and her mother toyed with her chicken.

'Good piece of beef, this,' her father said.

'Nice chicken,' her mother added.

Then a numbing silence.

The dining room was pleasant enough. A tad old-fashioned, with pleasant, caring staff. A chill draught blew through the windowpane, and there was bleak darkness beyond. And inside Red's heart.

The police had put her parents in here – a safe house, they told them. They'd been booked in under assumed names. If she looked through the window hard enough, she could see a small saloon car parked a short distance along the road with two figures in it, and wondered if they were the covert police. Must be a shit job, she thought, sitting there all night, waiting for something that almost certainly was not going to happen. Bryce wasn't stupid.

She was the stupid one.

Just what the hell had she brought on them all?

Their home razed to the ground. All their memories. Photographs. Everything. Gone.

Her fault.

The only fragment of good news was that the yacht was still intact, towed to an isolated mooring and being kept under observation by a Navy bomb disposal unit for the next forty-eight hours. If nothing exploded, it would be boarded by an expert and checked.

She sipped her wine, a heavily oaked Australian Chardonnay too sweet for her taste, but it was what her mother liked, and her ever dutiful father had ordered it for her. At least the alcohol was helping a bit. But she had to be careful because she was driving home soon, against police advice about returning to her flat.

Home.

Shit.

Fortress Westwood.

She apologized to her parents for the umpteenth time tonight, and both of them lifted their glasses and told her not to blame herself. She half hoped, at any moment, that her father would say, 'Don't worry, darling, things happen.' Instead her mother said, 'We need to know about the boat.'

Her father nodded sadly. As if the house was merely an appendage and the boat was all that mattered in their lives. 'They promised not to blow her up,' he said. 'They were going to keep her under observation.'

'I'm really sorry, you guys,' Red said.

'For what?' her father asked.

'For putting you in this situation. For that bastard setting fire to your house.'

'We don't know that Bryce was responsible,' her mother said.

Red stared at her. Like she had just ridden into town on the back of a truck. 'He is,' she said. 'Believe me.'

'Is madam finished?' the waiter said with a frown, look-ing at her almost untouched dish.

She nodded at him and gave a shrug. She had never felt less hungry in her life.

An hour later she entered her apartment, checking the undisturbed hair she had placed this morning high up on the front door, then slid both safety chains shut behind her. But even so, she checked the bathroom, the loo, her bedroom and then the safe room, leaving the door ajar for a quick entry if she needed it.

Then she went into the living room, poured herself a glass of wine, and lit a cigarette, inhaling the smoke grate-fully. It was a bit pathetic, she thought, but although she was thirty-one years old, her parents did not know she smoked. And she knew they would not approve.

She turned the main light off for a moment, walked over to the window and peered down, always looking for a vehicle she did not recognize that might be Bryce's.

There was no sign of her covert police team, but she presumed they were nearby. To her concern, she saw the front of a small van parked up. That had not been there five minutes ago when she had arrived home.

She felt a cold prickle of fear.

69

Shortly before 8 p.m., Roy Grace turned right at the bottom of Hove Street and drove along Hove seafront, with Glenn Branson, Ray Packham and Norman Potting with him in the unmarked Ford. The wind had risen, buffeting the car. To their left was lawn, the promenade, then the sea beyond; to their right a mix of modern apartments and Victorian terraced mansion blocks. He knew this area well; just a few streets along was where he and Sandy had lived.

'This is one hell of a way to spend your stag night,' Glenn Branson said. 'We're going out for drinks with the lads, however late. Yeah? They're looking forward to it.'

'We'll see,' Grace replied.

'It's not an option,' Branson replied. 'We're getting you wrecked.'

Ignoring him, Roy Grace turned right opposite the bowling club into Westbourne Terrace, a street of elegant detached and semi-detached Victorian houses, mostly painted white, and pulled over to the kerb. There was a narrower road off to the right, Westbourne Terrace Mews, with a small Victorian mansion block on either side.

The street was dark, illuminated only by streetlamps and the ambient light of the city. On their right was another unmarked Ford, with the figures of Rob Spofford and a woman PC inside. Directly in front of them was a plain white van containing a team of eight officers from the LST – the Local Support Team – which Grace had summoned. These were the tough officers, trained in public order, who were the ones equipped with body armour, who bashed doors down and went in first in any potential confrontation. Around the corner, Grace also had a dog unit on standby.

The four detectives, all wearing coats, climbed out into the chill wind, and walked over to Spofford's car. He got out immediately he saw them. 'Good evening, sir,' he said to Grace.

'Evening. Right, so which is Ms Westwood's flat?'

Grace and Spofford walked around the corner and down a cobbled alley into a courtyard off the mews, but remained hidden from view from any of the upstairs windows. Spofford pointed at the small mansion block on the north side of the mews. 'That window on the second floor is her living room.'

Grace stared up. There were lights in some of the other windows, on the other floors, mostly with curtains or blinds drawn. 'Okay.' He looked at Ray Packham. 'How closely can you pinpoint where the photograph of the cartoon was taken?'

He was aware that digital photographs are encoded with the coordinates of the location where they are taken, unless this feature is disabled on cameras and on phone cameras. The cartoon had been photographed and sent as a JPEG, which Packham said was probably the sender's mistaken attempt to mask its origins, because in doing so it had given him another clue: he had obtained the digital coordinates from it.

'Within roughly fifty yards in any direction from where we are standing, boss.'

Grace looked up and around at the dark buildings. Fifty yards covered a mansion block to their left as well as the two buildings to their right, and beyond. 'Can we get more precise, Ray?'

Packham unfolded the Google Earth map he had printed off, and shone a torch beam on it for Grace to see. There was a red circle drawn around one section of it, which encompassed the buildings.

Grace looked up at the buildings pensively. In particular he studied the windows of the block opposite Red's. He was thinking back to a case that involved a massive police operation two years back, when a female doctor had been stalked by a former lover, who had rented an apartment overlooking hers to spy on her. Had Bryce Laurent done the same? he wondered. It seemed from all he had been told that Bryce Laurent had constant close knowledge of Red Westwood's activities. And he could have got that only two ways – by either bugging her flat, or keeping it under surveillance. Or both. A flat overlooking hers would make more sense than trying to spy on it from a car.

The team stayed in the shadows, while Grace walked across to the front entrance and looked at the names on the bell panels; several were blank. He pressed the one for Flat 3, marked *R. Fleuve*. Almost immediately he heard a broken English voice. 'Yes, who is this?'

'I'm sorry to trouble you, sir. This is the police. What floor are you on, please?'

'The second.'

'How many flats on your floor?'

'Two, there are two on each floor.'

'Which way do you face?'

'Across the mews.'

'What number is the other flat on your floor?'

'Four. Do you need to come in?'

'Thank you.'

There was a click and a rasping sound, and Grace pushed the front door open. He turned and signalled to the three detectives, as well as Spofford and the woman police officer, who were hidden, to follow him. They would normally have used a different ruse to enter the building, but they needed the information about the layouts of the flats as this was all happening in fast time.

Then he entered a musty-smelling, dimly lit corridor, the floor littered with flyers from local home delivery pizza, Chinese and Thai restaurants, walked past two padlocked bicycles and pushed a timer button on the wall at the bottom of a narrow staircase. A weak light came on. He climbed the treads, and as he reached the second floor a door opened to his left. A thin young man, with a flop of fair hair and round tortoiseshell glasses, giving him an intellectual air, peered out. He was dressed in a grubby T-shirt and tracksuit bottoms, and was barefoot.

'Mr Fleuve?' Grace asked.

'Oui, yes.'

Grace showed him his warrant card. 'Can you tell me who lives above you on this side of the building?'

He thought for a moment. 'There are two – how do you call? – ladies together in Flat 6.'

'Lezzies?' prompted Norman Potting.

Grace shot him an irritated look.

'Yes, I would say so,' said the Frenchman.

Then Grace asked, 'Can you tell me who lives in Flat 5?'

'I don't see him very much. A man; I think he is on his own. He seems to be away a lot.'

'And above him?'

'Quite an old couple – they are Turkish. And also in Flat 8 is a single lady in her thirties; she works for American Express. She's very nice.'

Grace pulled out his iPhone and showed him a photograph of Bryce Laurent. 'Might this be the man in Flat 5?'

He nodded emphatically. 'Yes, that is him.'

'Flat 5, you are sure?'

'I think so. Flat 5.'

Grace thanked him, then almost sprinted up the stairs, followed by the others, and rapped hard on the door. Two Local Support Team officers, heavily equipped and wearing visors, stood beside him.

There was no answer.

Grace considered his options. He could force an entry now, but his gut feeling was that Bryce Laurent wasn't in the flat. He decided watching and waiting was his best option. Then he radioed the control centre to find out who was the on-call magistrate. It was Juliet Smith, who lived locally. He dispatched Norman Potting to obtain a search warrant. Then, using a paper wedge to keep the front door open, they returned to their vehicles and kept watch on the building, in the hope that Bryce Laurent returned.

It was 8.30 p.m. when Norman Potting came back, triumphantly waving the signed warrant. Grace went over to the van and briefed the Local Support Team. They clambered out, in their blue suits and body armour, one holding the bosher – or the 'big yellow key' as it was called – and another the hydraulic door ram, for stretching the frame on reinforced doors.

Then with two of the members of the LST dispatched to cover the rear fire escape exit of the building, Roy Grace, followed by the others, climbed the staircase behind the other six LST members.

The woman leader of the team rapped hard on the door. 'Mr Laurent, are you in?' she shouted.

As expected, there was no answer.

She stepped aside and a male colleague, gripping the heavy steel battering ram with both hands, turned to his colleagues. Then, bellowing, 'POLICE!' he swung it back, before hurling it with full force at the door lock. With a loud *blam* and a splintering sound, the door flew open. They all burst in, again shouting, 'POLICE! POLICE!' and criss-crossing the darkness with powerful flashlight beams.

Roy Grace, following behind, found a light switch and pressed it.

A bulb, shaded by a paper globe, came on. It revealed a completely empty and almost totally bare room, with cheap-looking, closed curtains. There was an old wheeled typist's chair, a small desk, and one wall was riddled with holes, as if shelves or brackets had been removed. A small breakfast bar led off from the kitchen, which comprised of a sink, work surface, fridge, gas oven and hob, and an ancient microwave, all immaculately clean.

Grace pulled on gloves, then opened the fridge door. The interior was bare. Nothing there at all. 'Shit,' he said.

Even the interior had been cleaned, spotlessly.

He went back out into the living area, and pulled open a shuttered door to reveal a small bedroom, almost filled by a double bed. All the bedding had been removed, leaving a bare, lumpy-looking mattress.

His heart sinking, he went back into the living area, and peered out through a chink in the curtains. One floor below, across the mews and courtyard, he saw Red Westwood pacing around, cigarette and glass of white wine in her hand, talking to someone on the phone.

Who?

70

Thursday, 31 October

Paul Millet, seated at his desk in the Strawberry Fields guest house, knew exactly who. Red's bitch best friend, Raquel Evans.

He was forced to listen to that bitch, Raquel, dishing the dirt on him. All her pent-up feelings about how much she had disliked him the first time they'd met. Disliked him from the get-go.

Really?

So why did you put your arm around me, Raquel, and tell me how good I was for Red? How happy I made her feel?

You damned bitch.

He listened through a microphone he had left behind that they would never find, as Detective Superintendent Roy Grace ordered a forensic team to take the flat apart. There had to be some evidence that Bryce Laurent had been here, he demanded. A fingerprint. A clothing fibre. DNA.

But you won't find anything, Detective Superintendent. I'm always going to be one step ahead of you. Trust me!

Soon after 9 p.m., the voice he recognized as belonging to the black Detective Inspector Glenn Branson said, 'Okay, old timer, we are out of here. Your stag night is now officially beginning. Guy Batchelor, Bella Moy, and all the rest are waiting for you at Bohemia.'

'I'm honestly not in the mood for partying,' Roy Grace replied.

'You think you have an option? Forget it.'

'Yeah?'

'Saturday you are marrying the woman of your dreams. Remember?'

'I remember.'

'So, chill!'

'I wasn't planning to be running a murder enquiry.'

Branson smiled. 'Didn't John Lennon say that life is what happens to you when you are busy making other plans?'

'Something like that.'

'So don't let it.'

'Yeah, right.'

'I'm serious. I can run this enquiry until you are back.'

Quietly, so the others couldn't hear, Grace said, 'Am I mistaken, or are you a bit sweet on Ms Westwood?'

Branson looked coy suddenly. 'What makes you say that?'

'The way you were looking at her in our interview with her.'

'She's nice to look at.'

Grace grinned. He was still grinning as he went back down the stairs, followed by Branson, but then stopped as he walked through the front door to find his path blocked by an attractive fair-haired woman with a reporter's notepad.

'Detective Superintendent Grace? I'm Siobhan Sheldrake from the *Argus*. I wonder if you could tell me about this operation here?'

Grace thought for a moment, then the grin returned. 'This is my colleague, DI Branson. He'll talk to you.'

Then he stepped aside and watched his friend bumble his way through answers to her questions. But in the end he managed to get the right message across. Help from the public was urgently needed to find Bryce Laurent. Full details would be given out at a press conference in the morning. It would be helpful if the paper published his photograph, his name and known aliases, the incident room number and the anonymous Crimestoppers number.

When he had finished and they climbed back into the car, Glenn Branson turned to Grace and said, 'Right, we're off duty. We're now going to take you out and get you nicely pissed.'

Grace decided not to argue. There was nothing he and his immediate team could do now and they could all start again early in the morning. And in truth, he could use a drink; he was starting to feel nervous about the wedding. He loved Cleo very deeply, but felt he was coming to it with so much unresolved baggage. It seemed to him that however happy you might be in life, there was always going to be a dark cloud hovering somewhere above you. And he was scared that the incredible happiness he felt, and had felt for many months with Cleo and now with his son, might too be damaged by something.

71

It all seemed surreal, Roy Grace thought, as he stood next to Glenn Branson outside the entrance porch of Rottingdean church. The bells were ringing loudly above them, and the early afternoon sun was blazing down from a brilliant blue sky, feeling as hot as if it was a summer's day, not late autumn. It was as though someone had turned up a rheostat, making everything feel more intense. Even the flint walls of the Saxon church itself seemed to be glistening with light. Its golden clock shone in the sunlight like an orb. And Grace was trembling with excitement.

Both of them were dressed in top hats and grey morning suits, as the guests streamed up the asphalt path through the graveyard, couples and singles, nodding greetings and then entering the church, and being handed Order of Service sheets by the two ushers, Guy Batchelor and Norman Potting, also in morning suits. 'Bride or groom?' Grace heard each of them asking.

He did not recognize half the guests – family and friends of Cleo. There seemed an impossible number of people attending. Surely they had not invited all of these? He felt a stab of panic over whether they would all fit inside.

Glenn gave him a reassuring pat on the shoulder. 'You bearing up, old timer?'

'Yep.' Grace gave him a nervous smile. Shit, he was shaking all over.

'Feels like we're on the set of *Four Weddings and a Funeral*,' Branson said.

'We can do without the funeral,' he replied with a grin, glad of his mate's support.

Suddenly the Chief Constable, Tom Martinson, resplendent in his dress uniform, and his elegant wife, her outfit topped with an asymmetric grey straw hat with a short veil, were standing right in front of him. Martinson shook his hand. 'Congratulations, Roy. Big day! You've got the weather for it – the gods must be smiling on you!'

'Yes, sir,' he said. 'Thank you.' Then he turned to Mrs Martinson. 'That's a wonderful outfit, if I may say so!'

Then ACC Rigg, in tails, accompanied by his taller, blonde wife, appeared. 'Good stuff, Roy,' he said chirpily. 'Got a glorious day for it!' Then he smiled at Glenn Branson. 'So you're minding the shop for the next week.'

'I am, sir, yes. I'm sorry that you're leaving, but congratulations on your promotion.'

'Well, thank you. I'm sure that ACC Cassian Pewe will prove himself very able,' he replied, studiously avoiding Roy's eyes.

Grace's brand-new white shirt, which Glenn had chosen for him from a shop in the Lanes, felt stiff and uncomfortable, and he cursed himself for not having worn it a couple of times already to soften it a little.

After a few minutes, during which several male and female police officers and support staff who he was sure he had not invited, filed past, each of them thanking him for their invite, Glenn put an arm around his shoulder and gave him a gentle squeeze. 'Your bride'll be here in a minute. Time to rock 'n' roll.'

They went inside. Father Martin, in his cassock with a white stole, gave Roy a firm handshake. 'Remember what I told you, Roy? Relax and enjoy it!'

Grace could not remember ever feeling so nervous in his life. 'I'm trying to!'

Then the clergyman turned to Glenn. 'You've got the rings?'

There was a moment of panic on Branson's face as he dug his hands in his pockets, patting himself down frantically before remembering they were in one of his waistcoat pockets. He gave a reassuring nod.

Then the two detectives walked down the aisle, Grace smiling in acknowledgement at several faces and occasionally raising his hand in a wave. They took their places on the front right-hand pew, and he gave a nervous smile to Cleo's mother and her sister, and some of her other relatives he had met briefly before.

It seemed only a few moments later that 'Pachelbel's Canon' began playing on the organ. He stood and turned, anxiously, and could see Cleo for the first time, looking utterly radiant in a stunning long cream dress, her hair up in a style he had never seen before, but which looked gorgeous. As she and her father slowly walked towards him, followed by three bridesmaids, he realized just how much he loved and adored this incredible person.

Finally he took her hand. 'You look totally stunning,' he whispered.

'You've scrubbed up pretty well yourself!' she replied.

As he stood, with Cleo to his left, facing Father Martin, he heard the clergyman's words only intermittently.

The grace of our Lord Jesus Christ
The love of God
And the fellowship of the Holy Spirit

Be with you.

Then the congregation saying:

And also with you.

The next few minutes passed in a blur. He kept looking sideways at Cleo. Light seemed to be radiating from her.

Marriage is a gift of God in creation . . .

In the delight and tenderness of sexual union . . .

Marriage is a way of life made holy by God . . .

No one should enter it lightly or selfishly

But reverently and responsibly in the sight of almighty God.

Roy and Cleo are now to enter this way of life.

They will each give their consent to the other

And make solemn vows

And in token of this they will each give and receive a ring.

We pray with them that the Holy Spirit will guide and strengthen them

That they may fulfil God's purposes . . .

For the whole of their earthly life together.

There was a long pause. Then he continued.

First, I am required to ask anyone present who knows a reason why these persons may not lawfully marry to declare it now.

There was another long silence. Then a woman's voice suddenly rang out loud and crystal clear from the rear of the church.

'I do!' she said. 'Me. I'm married to him!'

Grace spun round in total shock and horror. And there, at the end of the aisle, was Sandy.

72

Friday, 1 November

Roy Grace snapped open his eyes and stared into darkness. He was gulping down air and shivering. His pillow felt sodden, his hair wet. His whole body was damp with perspiration and the sheet was soaked. He stared around, bewildered and panic-stricken, and had no idea where he was. His mouth was parched and he had a sharp, pounding headache.

Oh shit.

Where the hell was he? The bed was narrow, hard and too short. He was in Glenn's house, he remembered now. He put out a hand for the light switch, struck something hard, and an instant later heard the sound of breaking glass and gurgling water.

Shit.

He found his phone and pushed the command button on it. In the meagre glow from it, he found the bedside light and turned that on, and saw the broken glass lying on its side, water pooling around his watch and soaking his handkerchief.

He was in a tiny room, with a row of teddy bears on the floor and a pink wardrobe. One of Glenn's children's rooms, he realized. The kids were staying over at Glenn's sister's house until Saturday. It was all coming back now.

They'd gone to a private room at the Bohemia bar in

Brighton last night. All his team had been assembled there. Then all the blokes had gone on to a lap-dancing club on North Street called Grace. Drunken, shaven-headed cops shoving tenners and twenty-pound notes down the front of leggy girls' panties. Leching and leering. Endless drinks. What the hell was it about the human psyche that told you if you had one more brandy, you'd feel less shit the next day than if you didn't have it?

The clock on his phone told him it was 4.55 a.m.

He needed water. Paracetamols. A piss.

He wished he was home in bed with Cleo. He lay for some moments in the glow of the light, too tired to move, reflecting, feeling a deep sense of gloom. It had felt so real. Frighteningly real. Sandy standing there. What the hell was his mind trying to tell him?

It was Friday morning. He was getting married tomorrow. And suddenly he felt really scared. What if Sandy was still out there somewhere? What if she really did turn up at their wedding?

Come on, she's been declared legally dead. She is dead.

He was shaking.

But the damned dream had felt so real.

He scrolled to the flashlight app on his iPhone and switched it on. Then he climbed out of bed, padded into the corridor and, using the beam, found the bathroom. He switched on the light, urinated, then opened a cabinet and lucked into a packet of paracetamol. He popped two of them, slung them into his mouth, ran the cold tap and lowered his face under the spout, gulping down the pills with the cold, fresh water. Then he padded back into the bedroom, opened the window with some difficulty, and lay down again, naked, feeling the cooling night air on his face and his body.

Before developing her interest in philosophy, Cleo had studied psychology, and a big part of that had been dream analysis. She'd told him a lot about that. That we all had unresolved problems presented to us in our dreams. That made sense to him. Sandy appearing at his wedding. Of course.

He pushed the dream aside, and all the phantom thoughts that accompanied it. A dangerous creep, alias Bryce Laurent, was out there, a very real threat to Red Westwood. How many sodding aliases did the man have?

Where was he now?

73

Friday, 1 November

Last night had not been a good idea, Roy Grace thought, staring at the sea of tired faces gathered around the conference room table for the 8.30 a.m. morning briefing for Operation Aardvark. Half his Major Enquiry Team out drinking and then fooling around in a lap-dancing club into the small hours, in the middle of a homicide investigation and manhunt.

Guy Batchelor, Jon Exton and Norman Potting all looked pretty bleary-eyed and useless this morning. The normally sharply dressed forensic podiatrist Haydn Kelly was looking like he'd slept the night in a hedge. The only two of his team who had stayed the course and who seemed remotely sparky today were Crime Scene Manager Dave Green and Glenn Branson; the latter, taking his best man duties seriously, had remained on soft drinks all night.

Shit, he hoped Nicola Roigard, the Police and Crime Commissioner, did not get to hear of this; he knew she had strong views on behaviour and commitment to duty. And pernicious Cassian Pewe, who took over responsibility as his boss as the new Assistant Chief Constable next Monday, would have a field day if he found out; but no one had done anything wrong, so far as he knew.

He looked at his watch. Nearly four hours since he had last taken two paracetamols, so it would be safe to take another couple now, he reckoned. He popped them from the blister pack, and gulped them down with a glass of water. Nothing so far was relieving his splitting headache. And he had a deep dread inside him, as if something terrible was about to happen at any moment. Not even the massive, greasy, sizzling fried egg and bacon bap from Trudie's burger van parked a short distance away, which he had forced down, along with a Coke, which normally served as an instant hangover remedy, was having any effect – at least so far.

Christ, man, pull yourself together, he thought. *You're getting married tomorrow to the woman you love.*

He stared down at his notes for the meeting and opened his policy book. A copy of today's *Argus* newspaper lay beside them. The front-page headline shouted, **MANHUNT FOR BRIGHTON ARSONIST**.

Bryce Laurent's photograph and the list of his known aliases were there on the front page, and the story had also appeared on the morning TV news apparently. Hopefully some member of the public would recognize him soon.

'As I informed you yesterday, until I return from honeymoon at the end of next week, I've appointed DI Branson to temporarily take over as SIO on Operation Aardvark, and he will run today's meeting.' He nodded at his colleague.

Glenn Branson said, 'Yeah, right, team, okay.' He paused to look down at his notes. 'Right, last night, following intelligence information from the High Tech Crime Unit, we executed a raid on premises in Westbourne Terrace, Hove, occupied by Bryce Laurent, which we have subsequently been informed he rented under one of his aliases. When we entered it became evident he had cleared out and left – I'm delegating the Outside Enquiry Team to talk to all residents in the area to see if they noticed anyone loading a vehicle either yesterday or any previous days. After making a death threat against Red Westwood's parents, her family home burned down yesterday – it would seem very likely Laurent is the perpetrator. We have to find this man very quickly. Red Westwood is aware of the danger she is in, but is determined to carry on with her daily life. She's refusing to let Bryce Laurent win, as she sees it. The one advantage of this from our standpoint is that by remaining visible, she is a magnet for Laurent. It may provide an opportunity to set a trap for him, but we will deal with that outside of this meeting. I don't think it is remotely likely that Laurent has gone away, but it is possible he's lying low for a bit. One thing is for sure, he has expensive tastes. Wherever he is hiding, he'll be spending money on something. And if he's using credit cards, he'll be leaving a trail.'

He turned to the financial investigator, Gordon Graham. 'Do you have anything to report, Gordon?'

'Yes, I do, sir.' Graham pointed up at the whiteboard showing photographs of both Red Westwood and Bryce Laurent, and the date of their separation in red ink. 'Approximately two months later, Bryce Laurent began withdrawing large cash amounts from his bank account with HSBC in Ditchling Road, Brighton. This money had come from his mother's estate – mostly from the sale of her house. The manager became alarmed and spoke to him about the withdrawals – a professional courtesy – to try to find out if he was being blackmailed or was the victim of a confidence trick, or perhaps a gambling addiction. Laurent told him to mind his own business. By 9 September, he had withdrawn a total of over seven hundred and fifty thousand quid, cleaning out the account, which he then closed down.'

'Did he deposit this money anywhere else, do we know?' Grace asked.

'So far we haven't found anything. We've been running checks on all banks, building societies and post offices across the UK to see which of them have received large cash deposits during this period – and after – and so far no dice.'

'Why would someone withdraw that amount of cash?' DS Batchelor asked, stifling a yawn. 'If it came from his mother's estate, it can't be any form of money laundering.'

'Drugs, sir?' ventured DC Alec Davies.

'Drugs, gambling, blackmail, smuggling it into some country where foreign currency is at a premium,' Graham replied. 'Or to be able to live and travel around without leaving a financial trail. Which so far Laurent seems to have done very successfully. I've been in contact with the City of London Police, who run the biggest financial database in the country, sir,' he said. 'I worked with their Commissioner, Adrian Leppard, when he was a chief officer in Kent. They've been given all Laurent's aliases. All credit card purchases and cash withdrawals made in the name of any of his aliases are being investigated. But it's a mammoth task. Almost all his aliases are common names.'

Dave Green raised his hand, and Glenn nodded at him. 'If Laurent has left his accommodation, and is remaining local, then he has to be staying somewhere, boss.'

'Quite right,' Roy Grace said. 'This morning we need to draft in more uniform officers to visit every hotel, boarding house and letting agency in the city and surrounding area with Laurent's photograph and see if we get a hit on any of the aliases. I have this in hand – Superintendent Watson at John Street is on the case for us. But hearing what you've said, we need to also check out any residents who pay in cash.'

A mobile phone rang. The James Bond theme tune. Blushing, Norman Potting fumbled in his pocket and silenced it.

Then Roy Grace's phone rang. He looked at the screen and saw it was the Control Room. 'Roy Grace,' he answered, as quietly as he could.

'Sir, I have a member of the public urgently wanting to speak to someone about Operation Aardvark. He says he read about it in the *Argus* and may have some important information for you.'

Grace stepped away as she patched the caller through, and slipped out of the door, closing it behind him, speaking into the receiver.

'Detective Superintendent Grace, I'm the Senior Investigating Officer. How can I help you?'

The man's voice sounded confident, and a tad smug. 'I know who your arsonist is, Detective Superintendent,' he said.

'You do?' Roy Grace asked sceptically, not liking the man's voice at all.

'Trust me, I know.'

'What is your name, sir?'

'That doesn't matter. I suggest you take a look at a firefighter at Worthing fire station. Matt Wainwright. He's your man.'

'Tell me more.'

But the line had gone dead.

Grace called the controller back and asked if she had the man's number. But, no surprise, the number was withheld.

He thought for a moment. Tip-offs could be highly valuable, but as often as not they were crank calls that proved to be a huge waste of police resources. It was always hard to gauge whether one was real or not. He hadn't liked the man's voice; there was something deeply unpleasant about it. Could he have been a colleague of the firefighter with a grudge?

The door opened, and Glenn Branson came out. 'You okay, old timer?'

Grace nodded.

'You look green as hell. I think you should go back to bed.'

'I'll be okay.' He held up his phone. 'Just had a response from the *Argus* piece this morning. We've been given a name. A fire officer in Worthing. But the caller sounded odd.'

'Bryce Laurent was a firefighter once.'

'Is there anything Laurent hasn't sodding been?' Grace said. 'Do we know where?'

They went back into the conference room and Grace tasked DC Jack Alexander with contacting Worthing Fire and Rescue to see if they had a Matt Wainwright working there, and a researcher, Becky Davies, to find out if Bryce Laurent had ever worked for the Fire and Rescue Service and, if so, when and where.

As Glenn Branson looked down at his notes to move on to the next item, an internal phone warbled insistently. Guy Batchelor looked at Branson for a nod, then picked up the receiver. 'DS Batchelor, Operation Aardvark.'

There was a moment of silence as all eyes were on the Detective Sergeant, as if sensing from his body language that the call was significant.

It was.

He thanked the caller and replaced the receiver, then turned to Glenn Branson, his eyes moving from him to Roy Grace and back. 'That was an officer called Gwen Barry, from the UK Border Agency at the Eurotunnel terminal in Folkestone. She's got a sighting of Bryce Laurent, using one of his known aliases, Paul Riley, on CCTV footage. He was spotted in the duty-free shop yesterday evening at 11.25 p.m., picking up whisky and cigarettes, then he drove a Toyota, index Golf Victor Zero Six Kilo Bravo November, and boarded a train to Calais.'

'Who's the car registered to?' Grace asked.

'Avis rental. It was picked up from their depot at Gatwick four days ago.'

'Let's see if we can get his ID confirmed from some of the staff there.'

Branson nodded and made a note.

Eurotunnel last night, Grace thought to himself. 11.25. France was an hour ahead, so with the half-hour crossing time the train would have arrived around 1 a.m. Time enough for Bryce Laurent to be anywhere in Europe by now. Or indeed, if he had gone to an airport, anywhere in the world.

But why?

Okay, he had a grudge against Red Westwood's parents, but they were a sideshow compared to his grudge against Red herself, surely? Leaving the country made no sense.

Then he had a thought. Turning to Branson, he said, 'Glenn.'

'Yes, boss.'

'Get Red Westwood on the phone.'

Less than a minute later Branson handed Grace his iPhone.

'Ms Westwood?' he asked.

'Sorry to bother you, but this is urgent. It might seem a strange question, but is Bryce Laurent a smoker?'

'No,' she said. 'Emphatically not. He has a pathological hatred of smoking.'

Grace frowned. 'Okay, what about whisky?'

'Whisky? Like in Scotch?'

'Yes?'

'No, he hates that too. Champagne and fine white wines are all he will touch.'

'Okay, thanks, that's really helpful.' He ended the call and turned to his colleagues, who were frowning.

'Guy, get the Border Agency woman back. I want to know what their CCTV cameras cover, and I want all footage they have of Laurent sent here right away, like now. I want all the footage with him and without him, everything from every camera in and around the duty-free shop from the time he was first sighted. Get on to Kent; ask them to send it to us digitally as soon as possible.'

74

At 10.50 Guy Batchelor phoned Roy Grace, who was in his office trying to clear his email inbox of everything that needed an urgent answer before he left at the end of his final day, to tell him the CCTV footage from Folkestone had come through.

Ten minutes later, Grace sat with Glenn Branson, Guy Batchelor and Ray Packham in a small viewing room in the CID HQ, and Packham started the footage running. The first thing they saw, in reasonable-quality colour, was Bryce Laurent, casually dressed in a leather bomber jacket, slacks and boots, walking across a car park at a leisurely pace towards the Eurotunnel Terminal and the DUTY FREE shopping sign. Laurent paused to look around, turning one way, then another. Not like a shopper getting his bearings, Grace thought, more like someone posing.

'Definitely him?' Batchelor asked.

'From all the pictures I've seen, yes,' Grace said, and looked at Branson for confirmation.

The DS nodded. 'It's him.'

Then Laurent did a strange thing; he turned a full, slow, three hundred and sixty degrees, then carried on, still at his slow pace, as if he had all the time in the world, towards the doors of the building.

'What was all that about?' Branson said. 'The pirouette.'

'I'll tell you, if my hunch is right,' Grace replied.

The next section of footage was from a grainier camera inside the building. After a few moments it picked up Laurent, from the rear, pulling two cartons of cigarettes from a shelf and placing them in a wire shopping basket. He turned slowly around, then back and walked out of shot. Next they saw him, picked up by another camera, again from the rear. He was looking at a selection of whiskies. He made a choice, pulled two bottles out and also placed them in his basket. Then he turned right around again, before once more walking out of sight.

Grace noted down the time showing on the video. 23.33. Then he turned to Packham. 'Ray, can you find the camera covering the checkout desks?'

They saw several other views of the interior of the duty-free shopping area, as Packham scrolled through the cameras. Then a clear view of the checkout tills. Grace looked at the clock. 23.32. He sat for several minutes watching, until 23.38, then said to Packham, 'Okay, Ray, now show me the exterior shot of the duty-free terminal. Pick it up from 23.32.'

A few moments later the camera view came up. 23.32. Then 23.33; 23.34; 23.35. Then at 23.36 Laurent strode out, and walked across the car park. He was empty-handed.

'What's he done with his purchases?' Guy Batchelor asked.

Grace shook his head. 'He didn't buy anything. He doesn't smoke and he doesn't like whisky.'

'Are we missing something here?' Glenn Branson said.

'I don't think we are,' Grace replied. 'No. He just wanted to make sure the cameras saw him. He wanted to make sure we knew he was at Eurotunnel, leaving the country. Because, in my view, he wants us to believe he's gone.'

'But he has, hasn't he?' the DI said. 'There's footage of him driving onto the train.'

'Yep,' Grace said. 'He went to France last night, all right. But I wouldn't be too sure he's still there this morning.'

'You think this is all a ruse to make us think he's gone away?' Batchelor said.

'I wouldn't be surprised if he's not back here already,' Grace said. 'And I think we'd be wise to presume he is.'

75

Friday, 1 November

His beard itched in the warm fug of the transport cafe. The false beard he had glued on, in his rental Toyota, in the darkness of the public car park near to the Eurotunnel station in Calais.

He had googled it in advance and learned from conversation threads online that the car park was free and had no CCTV surveillance. Hundreds of people parked there for their visits on the train to England, so it was likely to be a long time before anyone took any interest in the car, many weeks with luck. By then his job would be done and he would be well gone.

The warmth in here felt good, and the second mug of strong builder's tea was helping his body to thaw and dry out. He'd had a long, cold vigil up on the freezing deck of the ferry, where he had remained throughout the voyage to avoid any risk of being seen. Then his traipse on foot through early morning Dover in the pelting rain. No one would be expecting him to return to England so soon, but even so he had taken every precaution not to be noticed entering the ferry port, or on the ferry, or leaving it.

Wearing a hoodie over his bobble hat, he sat hunched over the tired Formica tabletop, ignored by the handful of other men in here, eating his fry-up, sipping his scalding tea, and making a pretence of reading the *Daily Mail*. The headlines were a spat between the *Mail* and the Labour leader. Politics had never interested him at the best of times. And right now he had plenty of things that interested him much more. Such a busy weekend ahead, so much to do.

Starting with the wedding!

Just how would Red Westwood feel when the detective in charge of hunting him down was felled with a crossbow bolt through his right eye in front of the church where he had just got married? He could just picture the scene. The smiling groom, the radiant bride, all the relatives and friends gathered around. The limousines outside with their white ribbons fluttering. Then . . .

THWANG!

No one would even hear it. It would arc over their heads. The dum-dummed tip slicing through the ball of jelly that was his eye, then piercing his brain and disintegrating into fragments, still at high velocity. Then the screaming would begin!

But it wasn't the screaming at the wedding that he looked forward to hearing. It was the silent screaming inside Red Westwood's head and heart when she realized that no one, not even the county's top detective, was capable of protecting her.

And there would be plenty more screaming from her vocal cords when he had her back in his possession, which was going to happen very soon now. So much screaming and pleading for mercy that she was not going to get. Mercy that was just not going to happen. He was looking forward to that moment. That very long moment that had been a long time coming. It was all he lived for. All he had to live for now.

Soon, baby!

76

Friday, 1 November

Red Westwood sat in the morning management meeting at Mishon Mackay, trying to focus on work but distracted by the strange call she had received on her way here from Detective Superintendent Roy Grace asking her whether Bryce smoked and liked whisky. Why did he need to know that?

Geoff Brady, their gung-ho manager, a burly man in a chalk-striped suit, was pointing at the whiteboard on the wall. At the top was written in purple handwriting the word *COUNTDOWN* and the figure *£146,900*, the amount remaining for their commission target for the year to be achieved with just two months to go. Below was a chart titled, *NEW INSTRUCTIONS, HOT PROPERTIES*, with prices ranging from £179,950 up to £3,500,000.

This was a crucial month, Brady was saying. Still time for people to purchase new homes in time for Christmas. He was urging them all to go for it. Make sure they hit their viewing targets of fifteen per day. They could do it!

She listened to the jargon that she'd had to learn. PTS, which was *preparing to sell.* NOM – *not on market.* U/O – *under offer.* FTB – *first-time buyer.* BTL – *buy to let.*

He held up the thick handwritten ledger in which all instructions and viewings were recorded. Although they were highly computerized, they still kept handwritten

301

information as backup. Each of the agents contributed their updates.

After the meeting ended, Brady arranged for the team to go out for a drink together after work. This was customary on a Friday, their perk for the week before the biggest day of all, Saturday, when they would all be flat out. Red returned to her desk. She looked through her diary at today's booked viewings, and checked her messages, annoyed at the number of cancellations that had come in – over twenty per cent of her bookings. Then she ran her eye down the list of new instructions, noting the ones that might be of interest to clients with whom she had developed a rapport, whom she considered her own, and started making calls to them, following up the successful calls by emailing details and ensuring printed copies were mailed out to them that day.

She was glad of the distraction of work, but equally she was aware she was not firing on all cylinders and that inside she was shaking, and conscious that she was not sounding her usual confident, enthusiastic self. Which of course, she knew, was exactly what Bryce wanted.

And she was determined not to be beaten.

But Christ, it was hard today. She looked over to her right, through the large window onto the street and at the Tesco superstore across the road. A bus went past, then a taxi, and a line of cars. Then a yellow ambulance wailed by. A cyclist, in a yellow sou'wester, pedalled miserably past in the heavy rain. Rain as heavy as her heart.

Her parents had lost their home. She and her sister had lost it, too. All their childhood memories gone. Their childhood photographs turned to ash. Her parents had aged a decade yesterday. All her fault.

Her phone rang and she grabbed the receiver. 'Red Westwood,' she answered, hoping, desperately hoping, that it was Detective Inspector Branson or PC Spofford calling to tell her that Bryce Laurent had been arrested and was in custody. But it wasn't. It was a man with an American accent enquiring about one of their most expensive properties, a secluded house in prestigious Tongdean Avenue, whose owners spent most of their time at another of their homes in Naples, Florida.

'They're asking £3.5 million?' he said.

'That's correct, sir, yes,' she replied politely, her enthusiasm rising a tad, sensing a possible opportunity here. This would be a huge commission for her.

'It's been on the market for several months, I see?'

'It's a fabulous property. We do have a lot of interest,' she fibbed.

'This would suit my family very well – my wife Michele, our son, Brad, and me. I'm a cash buyer but the asking price is a bit of a stretch. Do you think they might be open to offers?'

'I'd strongly recommend a viewing, sir. This is one of the finest residential properties in the city of Brighton and Hove. I'm sure the owners would be prepared to consider an offer.'

She was fibbing again. The owners had left firm instructions that they were in no hurry to sell, and would not budge from the asking price. But this man sounded a real prospect, and if he saw the house, perhaps he would fall in love with it.

'I'm tied up this weekend. What about Monday?'

'What time Monday would suit you, sir? The owners are away so we are flexible on time.'

'Midday?'

'Perfect. My name's Red Westwood. Would you like me to email you or pop the brochure in the post?'

'No, I have everything, thank you.'

'Okay, good, I will meet you there. May I have your name and mobile phone number, please, sir?'

'Andrew Austin,' he replied, and gave her the number.

'I look forward to meeting you, Mr Austin.'

'I look forward to meeting you, too, Ms Westwood.'

And he *was* looking forward to it. She had not recognized his voice! Bryce Laurent, standing outside, the awning of the cafe providing him with scant shelter against the driving rain, was really looking forward to it.

So was Red Westwood. She was required to enter Andrew Austin's name on the computer, his contact details, and the price range he was interested in, so that the other agents could approach him with any new instructions that came in that might suit him. But even though she had only been with Mishon Mackay a short while, she had already started picking up the tricks. So she did enter his details, but she deliberately transposed two of the digits in his phone number. Then she smiled. The sale of a £3.5 million property would be a shitload of commission. And she intended to make sure she got it.

77

THWANG!

Through the cross hairs of the telescopic sight on his Legacy 225 carbon-fibre crossbow, Bryce Laurent watched the flight of the lead-tipped aluminium bolt, flying at 265 feet per second towards the grinning, bright orange pumpkin on a stake in the middle of the field, eighty yards away. The bolt arced several feet over the top and planted itself, with a faint thud, into the wild grass some way beyond.

In *The Day of the Jackal*, one of his favourite films, which he had watched repeatedly in recent weeks, the Jackal, played by Edward Fox, had practised shooting the French President in the head by firing at a watermelon. But with Halloween just over, pumpkins were more readily obtainable. And easier to shape into a face with a Stanley knife.

The face of Detective Superintendent Roy Grace.

Who was getting married tomorrow.

He reloaded, winding the bow back, adjusted the sight, and lined Roy Grace up again in the cross hairs. Centre of his forehead. 'How about this one, Detective Superintendent Grace, Senior Investigating Officer of Operation Aardvark?' He squeezed the trigger, and the powerful weapon kicked in his hands. He kept the cross hairs locked on his target. An instant later, there was an orange blur as it tore through the very top of the pumpkin.

Bryce Laurent grinned with satisfaction. How nice would it be to see the top of Detective Superintendent Roy Grace's scalp fly off, just as he was standing outside the porch of the church tomorrow afternoon, posing for the wedding photographs with his bride? Just like all those images of John F. Kennedy in the back of the Lincoln convertible in Dallas when the sniper's bullet took off the top of his scalp with a little bit of hair.

But there was an image that he liked even better. It was a colour picture in a history book when he was at school, illustrating a scene from the Battle of Hastings in 1066. The scene of the English king, Harold, with an arrow in his right eye. The arrow from an archer that had pierced his brain.

Bryce Laurent reloaded again. He made a small adjustment, then aimed at the slit he had cut to the right of Detective Superintendent Grace's nose. His right eye. He held the cross hairs on it for several moments. He felt so steady. So calm. As if this was part of his destiny.

Gently, as he had been instructed, he squeezed the trigger, taking up the slack. Then a little more. More. More.

THWANG!

The bolt flew. For an instant, in the kick of the weapon, he lost sight of the target. But he found it again almost instantly. Just in time to see it explode, as if a bomb had detonated inside it.

Cutting the front off the lead tips on the arrows had worked, he thought. That made them just as deadly as dum-dum bullets. He smiled, pleased with himself. Incredibly pleased. Actually, beyond pleased.

The pumpkin had disintegrated into a thousand fragments. He'd struck it where he'd aimed from a range of eighty yards. He had already measured out the distance from his intended hiding place to the church porch in

Rottingdean. It was only sixty-seven yards. So he could be even more accurate still!

He walked across to his Land Rover and took another pumpkin from the rear and spiked it on the stake. Until the light failed, on the remote farmland close to his firework factory, he practised on pumpkins. Until he could hit each one in the right eye every time.

78

'The time is 6.30 p.m., Friday, 1 November,' Glenn Branson said to the thirty-five assembled people in the conference room of the Major Crime Suite at Sussex House. 'This is our evening briefing on Operation Aardvark, the investigation into the murder of Dr Karl Murphy, combined with the investigation into a number of arson attacks in and around the city in the past few days, which may be linked.' He shot a glance at Roy Grace.

His mate looked nervous, Grace thought, handling his first briefing on his own. But he was confident in the man. And he was feeling a lot better than this morning, his hangover finally gone, vanquished by a greasy burger and fries, and washed down with another Coke from Trudie's at lunchtime. He was feeling happy and positive about his wedding tomorrow, and his bad dream about Sandy had now faded away. He was fully focused, at this moment, on the investigation, and eager to see how Glenn handled this meeting; he was also excited by the developments of today. Grace gave Branson a reassuring smile and the DI continued after glancing down at his notes.

'At 4 p.m. this afternoon I held a press conference at which I announced we have a suspect in custody.'

There was a quietly raucous cheer from almost the entire assembled company.

Glenn Branson beamed. 'Matt Wainwright, a firefighter at Worthing Fire and Rescue. He was arrested following a tip-off from an anonymous member of the public, and there are a number of elements linking him to our investigation. The first being a cigarette butt found by one of the Crime Scene Investigators yesterday at the scene of a fire in Henfield, at the home of Red Westwood's parents. Wainwright's DNA was fast-track matched to this cigarette.' He paused to let this sink in. 'And we know he is a smoker.'

DS Exton raised his hand. 'And we've had it established that Bryce Laurent was a non-smoker, sir.'

'Yes, exactly,' Branson responded. 'The second element is that a number of shoe prints found at the scene of Dr Karl Murphy's murder match exactly the tread on a pair of boots found in Wainwright's car, which the suspect admitted were one of his two pairs of uniform-issue fire-fighting boots, and which he says had been missing for a fortnight. He had reported their loss, fearing an intruder had taken them, and security had subsequently investigated. But he can't explain how they came to be in his car. He claimed that when on duty, his boots would be placed right next to the appliance he would be riding in, by seat position, and when not on duty they would be kept in the changing room by all the pegs. He has no recollection of putting them in his car, nor can he give any reason why they should be there.'

'Perhaps they walked there by themselves,' Norman Potting said. 'These boots were made for walking . . .' he chortled, then looked around. But met only stony stares back.

Branson turned towards the forensic podiatrist. 'Haydn Kelly is going to be running these through his gait analysis software, and that should give us further confirmation.' He paused again to look down at his notes.

'The third element is traces of petrol found in the boot of the suspect's car. Tests are currently being carried out on this to see if it can be linked to the murder scene – I understand that every batch of petrol has a unique identifier, kind of like DNA.'

'Fuelling suspicion?' Potting said, unhelpfully, with another grin.

Branson ignored him. 'There's another aspect. In addition to being a firefighter, Wainwright is also a professional close magician, and from talking to some of his colleagues today, it appears he harbours an ambition to become a full-time magician. Among Bryce Laurent's numerous apparent careers, he is also a professional close magician. Early intelligence tells us there has been considerable professional competition between them. Which gives us a motive.'

'Stronger than Bryce Laurent's motive to avenge being jilted by Red Westwood?' Grace asked.

'I can only work on the facts we have, boss,' Branson answered him. 'Didn't you once say, *Assumptions are the mother and father of all fuck-ups*?'

There was a titter of laughter. Even Roy Grace himself grinned. 'I did, yes, but go on. Tell us yours.'

'My supposition – and it is only a supposition – is that Bryce Laurent may be a red herring. At this stage we have been assuming it is Laurent behind the murder of Dr Karl Murphy, the fire that destroyed Red Westwood's car, the smoking-out of the convenience store and the burning of her parents' house.'

'What about the cartoon that was sent, of her parents' yacht exploding?' asked DS Exton.

Branson looked at Ray Packham. 'What more have you been able to establish about the sender of that cartoon, Ray?'

'We know the photograph was taken at Laurent's flat, although we've not been able to trace the sender of it. But we are still working on that. Whoever sent it has good knowledge of how to use anonymous email. I'm not sure we will be able to trace it.'

'So it's possible that Wainwright was responsible for it, as part of a plan to set up his magic rival, Laurent. He would have known about *Red Margot* from when the pair worked together at Worthing fire station,' Branson said. 'His personal computer has been seized from his home and your team are working on it. Have you found anything yet?'

'No, we haven't,' Packham said. 'But he could have sent it from anywhere – an internet cafe is one possibility, or his workplace. We're checking those computers now.'

Branson turned to DS Moy. 'Bella, I'm giving you an action to have an outside enquiry team take Matt Wainwright's photograph to all internet cafes in Worthing and the area where he lives to see if anyone recognizes him.'

She nodded and made a note.

Guy Batchelor raised a hand. 'Does Wainwright have any history to indicate he might do something like this?'

'His past is being investigated by our researchers,' Branson said, pointing at the two researchers. Then he turned to the Chief Fire Investigator. 'Tony, would you like to remind the team of your findings on your investigation of Red Westwood's Volkswagen?'

'Yes. After a detailed examination, we found that the coil had been cleverly tampered with to make it short and overheat. At the same time, we found tiny pinholes drilled in the fuel pipe, which would have caused small amounts of petrol to spray out and combust after the engine had been running for some minutes and the wires became hot enough.'

Branson thanked him, looked down briefly at his notes, then continued. 'In the garage of Wainwright's home is a 1970s Volkswagen Beetle car, which he has been restoring. This vehicle is of a similar vintage to Red Westwood's VW, with virtually identical mechanics. He would have known exactly what to do.'

There was a silence. Roy Grace was pensive for some moments. 'If your supposition is correct, Glenn,' he said, 'it would seem that Wainwright has gone to a great deal of trouble and taken a lot of risks.'

'Sleight of hand and distraction techniques are part of the stock-in-trade of a good magician,' the DI replied. 'He's had a wonderful opportunity here, with Bryce Laurent. One presented on a platter to him, perhaps, if he is ruthless enough.'

'But why would he have needed to go to these lengths – what would have made him so desperate?'

'I'm told there is a lot of discontent in the Fire and Rescue Service at the moment, boss. They're talking about strike action for the first time in a generation. There's a big exodus of disenchanted officers from the service. Perhaps Matt Wainwright saw the perfect opportunity to eliminate a key rival for his new career in magic.'

Grace nodded. 'I agree with you, Glenn. There is a lot of evidence suggesting Wainwright is involved in some way. But from what we know about Bryce and his desire for revenge, what if he's being clever and is setting Wainwright up, deflecting the investigation from himself? It's your investigation for the next week. You need to prioritize both these lines of enquiry.'

'On paper, Matt Wainwright ticks a lot of boxes,' Glenn Branson replied. 'But I agree, it could be a red herring.'

Grace smiled. He knew that he had not been as focused

on this job as he should have been because of his impending marriage. He owed it to Cleo to make their wedding day, and their all-too-short honeymoon, a great and happy success. He was aware that his focus on his work had caused friction at times with Sandy, because there had been many occasions when his work had come first, much to her dismay. Sometimes it had been out of his control, but mostly it had been his decision. He always took every murder case personally. Sandy had called him a workaholic, and his response to her had always been to ask her how she would have felt if it was one of her loved ones who had been found dead. She was an intelligent woman, and she had understood. But it had always placed strains on their relationship. However much it pained him, he knew that for the next week he had to let go of the reins on Operation Aardvark.

He remembered a quote that Cleo had read out to him some time back during her studies. *I might disagree with what you say, but I will defend to the death your right to say it.*

'You're the boss. But make sure you articulate your thinking in your policy book – and don't get deflected from finding Laurent as well. It might be Wainwright or both of them together, but I favour Bryce setting up his former colleague, and getting us to divert our resources and waste time. Remember, Red is likely to still be in danger.'

79

Shortly after 1 p.m., Glenn Branson drove Roy Grace, in his clapped-out old Ford Fiesta the colour of a dried-up cow-pat, the short distance to Rottingdean from his Saltdean home, where Grace had spent a second, uncomfortable night in a child's bed before his wedding.

Grace was so preoccupied that for once he hadn't been scared by his mate's driving. He felt uncomfortable in his rented monkey suit, and the collar of the new shirt that Glenn had insisted he buy was rubbing his neck. As they pulled into the car park of the White Horse Hotel, he dug his hand into his inside pocket and pulled out his speech for the third or fourth time, looking at it again to make sure it was his speech and not some other document he'd picked up by mistake.

'You okay, old timer?' Glenn asked.

Grace gave him a nervous nod. His mouth felt dry.

'Remember that film *Four Weddings and a Funeral*, yeah?'

'Why do you want me to remember that?'

''Coz you look like you're going to a fucking funeral, that's why! Come on, man, enjoy! This is the biggest day of your life!'

'The second of the biggest days,' Grace reminded him. 'I've been here before.'

'Groundhog Day?'

'Feels a bit that way.' He touched his shirt collar. Hadn't it felt stiff and scratchy around his neck in his dream?

'Old timer, just for once in your life pack away every-thing to do with work, forget about it, and concentrate on enjoying yourself and cherishing your beautiful bride, yeah? Okay?'

Finally, cowed into submission by his best man's relent-less enthusiasm, Grace mustered a smile.

'You know what you need?' Branson asked.

'No. What do I need?'

'A sodding big drink.'

'I have to make a speech.'

'You'll have sobered up by then.'

They went inside to the bar. Not normally much of a beer drinker, Roy Grace downed a pint of Harvey's, and instantly felt a lot more cheerful. They ordered toasted cheese sandwiches from the menu, then Glenn bought a bottle of Moët & Chandon.

'Hey! We can't drink this!' Roy Grace said.

'We can have a good go!' Branson replied.

'Look, I need to talk to you about Red Westwood,' he tried.

Branson shook his head. 'No. Today you just need to drink.'

When they left the pub, shortly after 2 p.m., the bottle empty, Grace felt slightly tipsy, but relaxed and definitely in a very happy mood now. Glenn Branson strode ahead of him down towards the traffic lights at the start of Rot-tingdean High Street. It was a glorious afternoon, the sun shining from a cloudless sky. Glenn looked magnificent in his top hat and grey tails, he thought, and at least the booze had stopped his damned shirt from itching.

They turned into the High Street. Several people smiled at them; Roy smiled back. He had no idea whether they recognized him or were just amused by their outfits.

Minutes later they were walking up the path to the church. Several people, the men in suits, the women in hats and finery, were already milling around outside. Some, colleagues, he recognized and greeted by name; others, strangers, he presumed were friends or family of Cleo.

It all seemed surreal. The bells were ringing loudly above them, and the early afternoon sun was blazing down from a brilliant blue sky, feeling as hot as if it was a summer's day, not early November. It was as if someone had turned up a rheostat, making everything feel more intense. Even the flint walls of the Saxon church itself seemed to be glistening with light. And he was trembling with excitement. He turned to Glenn.

'You know, this really is Groundhog Day!'

'Yeah?'

Father Martin, plump and cheery in his cassock, with a white stole and buzz cut, suddenly appeared and gave Roy a firm handshake. 'All set?'

Grace felt a sudden lump in his throat. He nodded, his voice deserting him for one of the few times in his life.

Guests were now streaming up the asphalt path through the graveyard, couples and singles, nodding greetings and then entering the church, and being handed Order of Service sheets by his two ushers, Guy Batchelor and Norman Potting, also in morning suits. 'Bride or groom?' he heard each of them asking.

There seemed an impossible number of people attending. Surely they had not invited all of these? He felt a stab of panic over whether they would all fit inside.

And then another stab of panic. This was truly like his

dream. He wished to hell he had not drunk so much, but it was too late now. He smiled and greeted everyone exuberantly, like they were all his long-lost friends and as if the wedding would have been a total disaster without their presence.

Groundhog Day, Glenn had said. This was. Truly. This was exactly like the bloody dream he'd had. Even the weather. The sheen on the church walls.

Glenn gave him a reassuring pat on the shoulder. 'You bearing up, old timer?'

'Yep.' Grace gave him a nervous smile. Shit, he was shaking all over.

This was what Glenn had said to him in the dream.

Suddenly the Chief Constable, Tom Martinson, in a dark suit, and his elegant wife, her outfit topped with a grey hat with a short veil, were standing right in front of him. Martinson shook his hand. 'Congratulations, Roy. Big day! You've got the weather for it – the gods must be smiling on you!'

'Yes, sir,' he said. 'Thank you.' Then he turned to his wife. 'That's a wonderful outfit, if I may say so, Mrs Martinson!'

Then ACC Rigg, in tails, accompanied by his taller, elegant blonde wife, appeared. 'Good stuff, Roy,' he said chirpily. 'Got a glorious day for it!' Then he smiled at Glenn Branson. 'So you're minding the shop for the next week.'

'I am, sir, yes. I'm sorry that you're leaving, but congratulations on your promotion.'

'Well, thank you. I'm sure that ACC Cassian Pewe will prove himself very able,' he replied, studiously avoiding Roy's eyes.

After a few minutes, during which several male and

female police officers and support staff, whom he was sure he had not invited, filed past, each of them thanking him for their invite, Glenn put an arm around his shoulder and gave him a gentle squeeze. 'Your bride'll be here in a minute. Time to rock 'n' roll.'

'I need to speak to you,' Roy Grace said.

'Later, dude.'

'No, now!'

'We have to go in. Cleo's about to arrive!'

'So is Sandy,' Grace hissed urgently.

Branson gave him a sideways look. 'I don't think so.'

They went inside and strode down the aisle together. Grace acknowledged smiling faces with a wave or a cheery smile back. But inside, he was shaking.

Sandy.

The dream.

Was she about to turn up here?

Father Martin greeted Roy in front of the altar with another firm, warm handshake, and immediately Grace felt better. 'Remember what I told you, Roy? Relax and enjoy it!'

Grace frowned. He'd heard those words before in his dream. But, he suddenly remembered, in the dream the Chief Constable had been in his full dress uniform, not a dark suit. He breathed a sigh of relief.

The organ struck up. 'Pachelbel's Canon'!

Roy Grace's heart melted. He turned and stared down the aisle. And saw Cleo, looking utterly beautiful in a cream gown, her hair up, a veil over her face. Slowly, arm in arm with her father, accompanied by the music, she came down the aisle towards him.

No one noticed, nor took any notice at this moment, of

the veiled woman in a broad-brimmed hat and gloves, dressed entirely in funereal black, who slipped in the rear door, accompanied by a neat-looking young boy in a smart herringbone overcoat.

80

'Are those people getting married, Mama?' whispered the boy in German.

Every pew in the church was full. Sandy stood at the rear with her son, clutching the Order of Service sheet. Shaking. Staring.

Staring past the sea of people, strangers, almost all of them. Feeling as if she was on some alien planet. In someone else's world. Staring at Roy Grace, his hair short, cutting an elegant figure in his grey tails, hands clasped behind his back, his bride-to-be to his left. What the fuck was her outfit? She looked like Barbie.

Both of them facing away from her, towards the portly clergyman and the altar. To Roy's right was a tall black man, also in tails, who she did not know. His best man. She wondered who he was. He looked like a cop, perhaps. Of course he would be a cop.

This was all so surreal. Like a dream. A nightmare. Her husband getting married to another woman, in just a few minutes, if she did nothing about it. Her husband with a best man she had never met. Her husband getting married in a church full of people she had never met.

Anger swirled through her, like the first gust of a brewing storm.

'Mama, are they?' the boy whispered. 'Are they getting married?'

'Maybe,' she whispered back.

But maybe not, she thought. *I can stop it.*

'Only *maybe*?' he whispered. 'Why are they standing there if they are not going to get married, Mama?'

The vicar, blocked from her view now by the bride and groom, said, 'The Grace of our Lord Jesus Christ, the love of God and the fellowship of the Holy Spirit be with you.' His name, according to the service sheet, was Father Martin.

There was a quiet response from the congregation. 'And also with you.'

The entire inside of the church became a blur. She felt in total turmoil. Roy looked so confident, so handsome, so mature now. Such a different person from a decade ago. Ten years in which she had thought about him every day. Many times every day. Regretting so much. Burying herself first in one cult, the Scientologists, then another, in Germany. Her relationship with Hans-Jürgen, this cult's founder who turned out to be a control freak who couldn't keep his hands off other women.

Roy had his faults, but in the eight years they were married she was certain, from the deep love he had shown her, that he had never been unfaithful. Indeed she had never, in all that time, even seen him eye another woman. He had told her, many times, that he loved her to bits, that she was his soulmate, that something incredibly powerful had drawn them together. And she had agreed with him each time then. In those early days she had truly believed they would be together for ever.

Until.

She shuddered.

'God is love, and those who live in love live in God and God lives in them,' Father Martin intoned.

In just a few minutes, he would be gone for ever. Married to another woman.

A tear trickled down her cheek.

'Why are you sad, Mama?'

Almost the entire congregation read aloud the words printed on their Order of Service sheet. Sandy clutched her son's hand and held the sheet in the other. On the front was printed *Roy, Cleo*, with the date and a dinky drawing of church bells between them.

She was starting to hyperventilate. Tears were flooding down her cheeks now. She had to stop this. Had to. This lie. This sham. Bigamy was about to happen. She had to stop it. Was duty-bound, surely, to stop it?

And she wanted him back so desperately.

'God of wonder and joy: grace comes from you, and you alone are the source of life and love. Without you, we cannot please you; without your love, our deeds are worth nothing. Send your Holy Spirit and pour into our hearts that most excellent gift of love, that we may worship you now with thankful hearts and serve you always with willing minds; through Jesus Christ our Lord. Amen.'

Grace. The word kept coming up in the service. *Grace.* The name seared her heart. The sight of the man she had once loved so much, and still loved, standing beside his bride-to-be. Sometime tonight they would make love. And again tomorrow, no doubt. Doing all the intimate things they used to do. She knew his moves; his tongue on her skin, and against her lips and deep down in her crevices. The movements of his hands, the places he liked to touch with his fingers. All of that in a few hours' time. On this Barbie doll beside his body.

But she had the power to stop it.

She had come here to stop it.

She would be an accomplice to a criminal act if she did nothing – despite the fact that she had been declared legally dead. But then wouldn't someone notify you if you were legally dead? she wondered.

She thought about that for a moment. The absurdity of that thought.

The organ struck up, the strains of 'Jerusalem'. The congregation began to sing, loudly, lustily; everyone knew and loved this hymn. Their voices rose to the roof of the building and echoed off its walls.

'And did those feet, in ancient time, walk upon England's mountains green? And was the Holy Lamb of God on England's pleasant pastures seen?'

This was the same damned hymn they had sung at their wedding. Roy's favourite, of course, because it was the English rugby anthem. She could remember so very vividly standing at the altar at All Saints Church, Patcham, with Roy to her right, on the happiest day of her life. About to be married to the man she loved, and with whom she wanted, without any question, to spend the rest of her life. Was this Barbie woman standing beside him now as happy as she had felt on her wedding day?

She hoped not. She looked up at the church roof above them, hoping that some fucking lump of masonry would fall from it and crush the smug bitch.

She blinked away the tears, but her eyes were stinging from their saltiness. She felt her son squeeze her hand. She let go, fumbled in her handbag for a tissue, and raising her veil a small amount, dabbed her eyes.

'Mama?'

She silenced him with a raised finger. Then stood still, shaking, listening.

'I will not cease, from mental fight, nor shall my sword sleep in my hand, till we have built Jerusalem in England's green and pleasant land.'

She sniffed, tears streaming down her face. Hans-Jürgen was always spouting meaningful quotations at her. There was one, his favourite, that was resonating now.

For all of us, life is a series of journeys, and at the end of each journey, we arrive back at the place we started from, and know it for the first time.

This was her, now. Here in the church. Listening to the dying sound of the organ, and the echo of their wedding hymn. Realizing just how much she loved this man standing at the altar, and had always loved him.

Knowing it for the first time.

And time was running out.

She had to stop this.

She took a deep breath, then another.

Roy looked so calm, standing so upright, so confident. Was this how the congregation had seen him on their own wedding day? Had he been such an assured man then?

Father Martin began speaking. 'In the presence of God, Father, Son and Holy Spirit, we have come together to witness the marriage of Roy and Cleo, to pray for God's blessing on them, to share their joy and to celebrate their love.'

'Mama, who are they?'

She squeezed his hand and raised a silencing finger again in front of her veiled lips.

'Marriage is a gift of God in creation through which husband and wife may know the grace of God. It is given that as man and woman grow together in love and trust, they shall be united with one another in heart, body and mind, as Christ is united with his bride, the Church.'

She had to stop this. Somehow, she had to find the strength to do it. This was what she had come to do.

'The gift of marriage brings husband and wife together in the delight and tenderness of sexual union.'

She let out a soft weeping sound.

'Mama?' Her son looked at her, alarmed, squeezing her hand tightly with his own tiny one.

'And joyful commitment to the end of their lives. It is given as the foundation of family life in which children are born and nurtured and in which each member of the family, in good times and bad, may find strength, companionship and comfort, and grow to maturity in love.'

More words went over her head as she realized she had never before considered Roy making love to another woman. Doing the same things that he had done to her. He'd been an incredible lover. Always considerate, always determined to pleasure her fully before himself. None of the handful of sexual relationships she had had since had come close. And now, tonight, he would be going to a hotel room, somewhere, and would make love to this blonde stranger, and no doubt do all the things to her they had done. And tell her they were soulmates. And not think for one damned second about her. About all they had once been and once had.

Unless she intervened.

The moment was getting ever closer. Less than a minute or so away. Father Martin continued intoning.

'Roy and Cleo are now to enter this way of life. They will each give their consent to the other and make solemn vows, and in token of this they will each give and receive a ring.'

Sandy twisted the wedding ring that Roy had put on her finger nearly two decades ago.

'We pray with them that the Holy Spirit will guide and strengthen them, that they may fulfil God's purposes for the whole of their earthly life together.'

She took a deep breath. Now. Her moment. Her moment in the sunshine. The chance to change her life. To go back to how it all was. She took another breath. She had it all prepared.

He's already married. To me.

Father Martin said, loudly, 'First, I am required to ask anyone present who knows a reason why these persons may not lawfully marry to declare it now.'

Suddenly, Roy Grace turned and looked back down the aisle, staring at her. Staring straight through the veil into her eyes.

She froze.

He turned back to face the altar.

Her legs turned to jelly. She thought for an instant she was going to throw up. Had he seen her? Did he know she was here? How? It wasn't possible. She had made this journey to stop the wedding, but she couldn't do it. She didn't have the strength. Her mind was a vortex of confusion.

'The vows you are about to take are made in the presence of God, who is judge of all and knows all the secrets of our hearts.'

Sandy gripped her son's hand hard, and dragged him, half running, out of the church and out into the sunlit afternoon.

'Mama!' he protested.

Behind her, she heard the words, 'Therefore if either of you knows a reason why you may not lawfully marry, you must declare it now.'

She stopped to listen. Hoping. Half hoping.

'Mama?'

'Ssshhhh!'

'Roy, will you take Cleo to be your wife? Will you love her, comfort her, honour and protect her, and, forsaking all others, be faithful to her as long as you both shall live?'

Sandy stood still. The silence seemed eternal. Then she heard the whispered words she dreaded. Faint, but distinct enough. Like the whisper of a ghost.

'I will.'

Dragging her son by his hand again, she ran, stumbling, blinded by her tears, down the church path to the road, and back up the hill towards where she had parked her rental car.

81

It really did feel as if God had planted this tree just for him. This massive oak, with its dense golden and red autumn foliage, and a supportive frame around the base, which had made climbing up onto the first branch a doddle.

Bryce Laurent had been here since before dawn had broken this morning, dressed in waterproof camouflage fatigues, thermal underwear and a balaclava. He had found a comfortable, secure perch, and he'd only needed to break a couple of small branches in front of him to give him a clear line of sight of the church porch. And a clear shot.

In his rucksack he carried a dry-cleaner's suit bag, a flask of coffee, sandwiches, a Mars Bar and a bottle to urinate in. He had already drunk most of the coffee and eaten over half his rations, and he felt happy. It had all worked out so well, and he knew he was totally invisible up here – unlike every-one in front of him, who he could see clearly. Such as the woman with the small boy coming out of the church now, well before the service was over.

Who was she? Had she gone to the wrong church? She didn't look like she was dressed for a wedding, all in black like that. But, he thought, she did look familiar.

Then he realized he had seen them, very briefly, at Strawberry Fields. They had crossed on the stairs. He didn't like that. Was she bloody stalking him? He didn't think so.

A few minutes earlier, he had seen her hurrying up the path, almost dragging the small boy, and entering the church after the bride had already gone inside and the organ had struck up. Now they came hurrying back out, almost at a run. She had a look of desperation on her face.

Was she meant to be going to a funeral somewhere else?

Not that he cared a toss. He looked at his watch. Listened to the organ. This could have been himself and Red walking down the aisle, if only things had been different. He felt so sad for a moment. This could have been their wedding. *Oh Red, my love, why did you have to screw it all up?*

A group of about ten uniformed policemen were standing outside the church entrance. Why hadn't they gone in? he wondered. Maybe they were going to form some kind of guard of honour when Detective Superintendent Grace and his bride emerged? Well, they were in for a surprise.

He raised the crossbow carefully, steadied his arms on the sturdy branch in front of him, and stared through the telescopic sight. Holding the cross hairs steady on the wooden doors. The pair of them would be coming through soon, then standing outside, posing for the traditional photographs, the one destined for their mantelpiece. *Thwang!* Well, that would be a different one for the family album! The groom standing there with an arrow sticking out of his right eye.

He lowered the crossbow, imagining the chaos when that happened. He had his escape planned. He would slip down to the ground and sprint away up the road to where his car was parked, well before anyone had figured where the arrow had come from. Oh yes, he liked this so much. What a signal this was going to send to Red!

He waited. Time passed slowly. Then finally, he heard

strains of organ music striking up. And he could not believe his ears. It was Van Morrison's 'Queen of the Slipstream'.

His and Red's song.

You bastards.

You absolute bastards.

He could not believe it.

The doors were opening now. He could see the bride and groom stepping out. His target. He raised the crossbow, shaking in anger still, finding it hard to hold his aim on Roy Grace's face. Then a shadow passed across, blotting out his view. It was a huge double-decker coach pulling up right in front of the church, completely blocking his view.

'Get out the fucking way!' he said.

But the coach did not move. Then he saw a second pull up behind it. Then a third behind that one.

Shit, he thought. *Shit, shit, shit.*

What the fuck was going on the other side of them?

He rammed the crossbow into the dry-cleaner's suit bag he had brought with him and dropped down to the ground. Three sodding, chuntering coaches. He hurried up beside them, and found his view of the church now blocked by a row of limousines. Two of their drivers, their caps removed, were leaning against an old, gleaming black Rolls-Royce, smoking cigarettes. He walked over to them and said, 'They're bad for you, those things. They kill you.' Then, in a strop, he walked off back towards his car.

'Fuck you!' one of them shouted after him.

He raised a hand behind his back and gave him the bird.

82

Sunday, 3 November

Roy Grace woke with a start from a troubled dream. His right arm, curled around Cleo's neck, was numb. But she was sound asleep and he did not want to disturb her. He loved the feeling of her warm naked body against his. Her bum pressed up tight against him. She stirred for an instant, then her rhythmic breathing continued again. Suddenly she snored, for a few moments, and he grinned, loving the sound. Outside was total silence.

That felt strange, but wonderfully peaceful. They were in a suite in Bailiffscourt, a country house hotel and spa twenty miles west of Brighton, secluded and close to the sea, where they were staying before jetting off on honeymoon on Monday. Cleo's parents were in their house looking after Noah.

It was never silent like this in the city. Nor was it ever so pitch dark. He thought back to the events of yesterday. The wedding service had been beautiful, and he had never seen Cleo look so lovely. The reception at the Royal Pavilion had been an intensely happy occasion, surrounded by friends, colleagues and Cleo's family. Her father's speech had been brilliant, and Glenn, bless him, had told a number of jokes of questionable taste that had fallen a little flat, but overall his mate had been generous and witty.

Then Norman Potting, clearly the worse for wear, had

suddenly stood up, despite Bella Moy's attempts to make him sit back down. Potting had raised his glass and announced that he wished to propose a toast to the happy couple.

'Roy and Cleo, I just want to give you one word of advice. Don't buy a bed from Harrods for your new home. I'm told they always stand by their products!'

To an awkward silence, punctuated by a few titters of laughter, he'd sat back down, chortling away to himself.

At least his own speech had gone down well, Grace thought, despite his nerves.

And part of the cause of his nerves had been from the dream he'd had on Thursday night. The dream of Sandy standing at the back of the church, responding to the priest.

Father Martin, saying aloud and clearly, '*First, I am required to ask anyone present who knows a reason why these persons may not lawfully marry to declare it now.*'

Then Sandy's voice, equally clearly, carrying down the aisle.

'*I do! Me. I'm married to him!*'

The dream that had made him turn and stare at the rear of the church yesterday. And see the veiled woman in black, with the small boy standing beside her.

Had he imagined her? Had his mind been playing tricks?

It must have been that. Because when he turned to look again, as Glenn had stepped forward with the rings, she and the boy were no longer there.

Had he imagined it?

He shook suddenly, and shivered. *Someone walking over your grave,* his mother used to say whenever he did that.

'All right, my love?' Cleo murmured.

He kissed her softly on her back. 'Love you,' he said.

'Love you so much,' she replied sleepily.

Then he felt her hand stroking his thigh, gently at first, then more insistently, moving up until her fingers were lightly playing with his genitals. Instantly he began stiffening.

'I thought you were sleeping,' he whispered.

'I thought you were too, but one part of you doesn't seem to be.' She rolled over and her mouth found his. Her breath was sweet, and her lips soft. She stroked his lips with her tongue, then suddenly wriggled down the bed a short distance and began to tease his right nipple with her tongue.

He let out a gasp of pleasure.

She continued teasing it, then moved slowly further down the bed, kissing his chest, then his stomach, then took him softly, so softly in her mouth.

'Christ!' He gasped with pleasure.

After some moments, she slowly slid back up his body, lying on top of him, gripped him firmly but gently, and guided him inside her.

'God, I love you!' he murmured, nuzzling her ear.

'Are you sure, Detective Superintendent Grace?'

'I've never been more sure!'

'That's just as well, isn't it? 'Coz you're really stuck with me now!'

'Yeah, well, I'll just have to get used to that.'

She pinched his nipples, sending frissons of pleasure shooting through him. Then she whispered, 'Didn't your mother ever tell you it's rude to talk with your mouth full?'

'She said that didn't count with tall, leggy blondes.'

She slapped his cheek playfully.

And at that moment, Grace did not think he had ever felt happier, or hornier, or more at peace in all his life. 'I love you to the ends of the earth and back.'

'That all?'

'Bitch!'

'Horny brute!'

They kissed tenderly, then she whispered, 'I love you way, way, way beyond the ends of the earth.'

'And right back at you.'

Deep inside her she squeezed him hard. 'Married life's not total shit, is it?'

He was silent for a moment, then he said, 'Nah, it's not. Not total shit.'

83

Sunday, 3 November

'And this is the master bedroom!' Red said proudly. Her father shambled along behind her, followed by her mother. Although she was elegant, he was wearing stout shoes, baggy denims and the kind of bulky, shapeless anorak he always wore. Years of gardening and sailing after his retirement had long removed any of the fashion consciousness he might once have had. Clothes were functional for him, their purpose to keep out the wet and cold. No more.

Red was fine with that, although she had always secretly hoped that if she ever had a relationship that lasted anything like as long as her parents' that her partner would still bother to make himself look attractive to her. Sometimes she wondered when her parents had last had sex. Looking at her father now, she decided fondly, it must have been several decades ago.

'This is a lovely room, darling!' her mother said.

'Pity about the view, though,' her father added.

He was right about that, Red thought. It was a huge room, large enough for a king-size bed and space either side of it to put in fitted cupboards. But it was at the rear of the flat, with a view straight across an alley to another building, so it would never get any sunlight. 'I'm only going to be using it for sleeping, Daddy,' she said. 'So much of the year it will be dark anyway. It's the living room that I really love.'

To her relief, both her parents nodded approvingly. 'Yes,' her mother said. 'The living room is lovely.'

It was.

The apartment was on the top floor of a mansion block in Kemp Town. It comprised a large living/dining area, with a breakfast bar, an island hob and a generous kitchen, and had a wide sun terrace overlooking the English Channel. In addition to the master bedroom there was a much smaller guest bedroom, and another room, not much bigger than a broom closet, that would take a spare single bed or make a small office.

'I can see you living here!' her father said.

'You can?'

'It's delightful. How many apartments at this price level have a sea view?' he said.

'Very few,' Red replied. 'I can tell you that from work. And thank you again for the loan.'

'Your father and I are always here to help you, darling,' her mother said.

Red smiled. 'I love you guys. As soon as my flat money comes through, I can pay you back.'

'Don't worry about that, darling,' her father said. 'The important thing is for you to have a home you feel safe in.'

'There's something about this place that really does make me feel safe,' Red said. She walked across the bare living room, opened the French doors and stepped out onto the balcony. The fine weather had lasted through the weekend, and Brighton looked at its stunning best. The sea, reflecting the sky, was a deep blue. To her right, she could see the Brighton Eye and the pier beyond. To her left, the west harbour mole of the marina. A mile or so out to sea in front of them, several yachts were taking part in a winter race series, their sails shimmering in the early afternoon sun.

'When do you hope to exchange contracts?' her father asked.

Red shrugged. 'Well, if you are really still happy to lend me the money, bearing in mind what's happened, as soon as possible. But if it's going to be difficult now, please don't worry. I'm okay where I am, I hope.'

'You are not okay where you are, darling,' her mother said. 'We want you out of there as quickly as possible and away from that horrible man.'

'We were well insured, luckily,' her father said. 'Your mother and I will be fine. Your safety is our prime concern now, darling.'

'Just let us know when you need the money,' her mother said. 'And one thing that is terribly important for you is to make sure that horrible man never finds out where you are moving to.'

'I'm making sure of that, as best I can,' Red replied.

'I agree with your mother,' her father said.

None of them took any notice of the small van parked a short distance along on the far side of the street.

84

Sunday, 3 November

'Fuckwits,' said Bryce Laurent, sitting in his little Ford van on the seafront, which shimmied in a strong gust of wind while he listened to the conversation. He was staring at the elegant Regency building that, in former times, would have been a single dwelling with servants' quarters, no doubt, but was now divided into flats.

The kind that would burn easily. Modern apartment blocks were designed to contain fires. Impossible to destroy. But not an old building like this.

He'd looked it up on the internet, and the flat Red was buying was on the top floor. He'd seen them come out onto the terrace and look out at the view. It must be magnificent from up there.

Too bad you'll never get to enjoy it!

Behind him, the rear of the van was nicely kitted out with a mattress and duvets. And a number of restraints he had fitted himself. Along with a bag containing a few implements with which to cause Red a lot of pain, which she richly deserved. Pliers. Razors. A small gas blowtorch. Some piano wire. An electric shock machine. A hood. And a few masks from a joke shop for him to wear.

The gods of justice were surely smiling on him today. There was a Fox and Sons estate agency board fixed beside the front door. GROUND-FLOOR FLAT FOR SALE it read.

He dialled the number and asked when it would be possible to view the ground-floor flat of the Royal Regent mansion block. 'Whenever you like, sir. It's an executor sale, so we have access whenever convenient.'

He thanked the agent and made an appointment for that afternoon.

Such good news!

And it was such good news that Red and her parents liked the top-floor flat so much.

The only bad news right now was the lack of accommodation. Strawberry Fields had suited him rather well. He was left alone there. A breakfast box was delivered to his door every morning. He could be totally anonymous there for as long as needed, and he was fully paid up for two more weeks. But he had seen his photograph on television this morning. A big black detective calling him a dangerous man. Warning the public not to approach him.

Me?

I'm gentle.

Until I get angry. And I am angry now. You'd better believe it.

But now the heat was off. They had Matt Wainwright in custody. How good was that?

Except, that girl on reception was sharp. She had seen his face several times. He could not take the risk that she might call the police. So, sadly, there was no going back there. He would sleep in the van tonight. Then tomorrow the fun would really begin!

He sprang to attention. Red and her parents were coming out of the front door of the building now. Going off to the Grand Hotel for Sunday lunch. Such a nice place! He totally approved.

He did not bother to follow their little Honda SUV, he

just listened to their progress. Heard them being greeted at the restaurant, and shown to their seats.

'Anyone like a snifter?' her idiot father said.

Both her parents ordered gin and tonics. Red ordered a Sauvignon Blanc.

He had to listen to them perusing the menus. Red's stupid mother and imbecilic father ordered the Sunday roast. Red ordered the sea bass option.

Ah, so healthy. Good girl! That's my Red. Be healthy, my angel! I need you healthy to endure all I'm going to put you through. I'd hate to think of you dying before I'm done with you. Really I would! You've got a lot of suffering in front of you. To make up for all you've put me through. Your last words on earth will be, 'I am so sorry, Bryce, I truly love you. I will love you for ever.' I promise, that's what you will say. With your dying breath. Really you will.

Then I will release you. I'm a man of my word.

85

Sunday, 3 November

'I need to warn you in advance about the condition this place is in,' the estate agent said, with a slight French accent, unlocking the front door of the Royal Regent mansion block with a jailer-size bunch of keys. With her free hand she held the particulars.

She was an elegant woman in her mid-forties, with chic blonde hair, a smart navy coat with brass buttons, and an expensive-looking handbag. She had told him her name, but he had forgotten it. Sophie? Sandrine? Suzy? He didn't care, but he didn't like forgetting things. Normally he remembered names scrupulously. He was too distracted, he knew, too much on edge. He needed to calm down and sharpen up.

'It's an executor sale, you see, Mr Millet. The family have been arguing about the valuation for a couple of years, so nothing's been touched – and I'm afraid it was in a pretty neglected state when the owner died.'

'Good,' Bryce Laurent said, scratching his itching chin through his beard. 'I'm looking for a restoration project.'

'Well, this is certainly one. The wiring is frankly in a dangerous state. And the plumbing's pretty ancient.'

Wiring in a dangerous state was music to his ears.

They entered the communal hallway, which appeared to have recently been done up. There was a smell of fresh paint and new carpet, and a row of smart-looking mailbox pigeon holes. Several bicycles stood propped against a wall, and leaflets littered the floor. He noticed the linked fire alarm high up on the wall. City regulations in all apartment buildings. She fumbled with her bunch of keys, found the right one, and unlocked the door to their right, pressed a light switch and they entered.

Bryce wrinkled his nose in disgust at the musty, old-people smell, and the hint of damp and mildew. They were in a tiny hallway, with a framed, embroidered prayer on the wall beside a wooden Victorian coat rack, on which hung a dusty beige mackintosh and a tweed cap. He followed the agent through into the sitting room, a small, drab and sad-feeling space with hideous flock wallpaper, its view through greying net curtains out on to the seafront mostly obscured by iron railings and a row of dustbins. It was furnished with a 1950s three-piece suite, a three-bar electric fire, on an ancient brown flex, in the grate beneath a marble mantel-piece, and a square television that looked like something out of the Ark. A framed replica of Constable's *Hay Wain* was fixed, slightly crooked, to one wall, and a replica Turner seascape on another.

'He had nice taste in art,' Laurent said.

The agent looked at him quizzically, as if unsure whether he meant that or was making a joke. 'Yes,' she said, erring on the side of caution. 'Quite.'

'Great painters.'

'Great painters,' she said. 'I understand from the family that all the contents are for sale by negotiation.'

He smiled. 'Good to know.'

He looked back at the television. It was the television that interested him the most, but he tried not to let that show. He glanced up at the stuccoed ceiling, which was an ochre colour above the dado rail, studying the ancient smoke detector.

'I think he must have been a heavy smoker,' she said, looking up too.

'Smoking kills you,' he replied.

'Quite.'

He looked at the television set again. Stared at it. For as long as he dared.

'Quite an antique, isn't it!' she said, clocking his interest.

'Wonder if it only gets old programmes?'

She gave him another uncertain look, as if she was unable to tell whether he was being humorous or serious.

Then he followed her on a tour of the rest of the gloomy little ground-floor flat. He saw the toilet, with its wooden seat and stained bowl, a small frosted-glass window above it, and the wallpaper bulging near the bottom in one corner, and mottled – a sure sign of damp. He stared at the window for some moments, before following her into the kitchen.

In keeping with the rest of the flat, it was a drab, old-fashioned room, with an ancient Lec fridge and a filthy-looking cloth hanging on a wooden drying rack. 'This is definitely in need of some modernization,' she said.

Some? he thought. There wasn't going to be any need, not for his purposes. But he didn't tell her that. Again he clocked the smoke detector in here. Following her, he peered into the grimy tiled bathroom, with brown stains running down the tub. Then the master bedroom, which had a candlewick bedspread over a narrow double bed. He wondered if anyone had ever had sex in this room, then shuddered in revulsion at the very idea. It was strange that there were no photographs, he thought, but maybe the family had already claimed them. Not that he cared.

The television was the only thing on his mind at this moment.

And the ancient wiring. Oh yes. That was good. So good. Especially the wiring for the fire alarm in the communal areas. None of the furniture in any of the rooms would have passed modern fire regulations, he thought. Perfect. The place was a tinder box waiting to go up.

And it would not have to wait long!

'What about parking?' he asked.

'There is a space that comes with the property, to the rear,' she informed him. 'Behind the toilet there's an alley-way with one space that will accommodate a reasonably-sized car. Quite rare for properties in Kemp Town, actually,' she said, her voice brightening as she pointed it out on the floor plans.

'That's very good,' he said.

'It is!' She sensed his interest. 'I'm sure the family would be open to offers, Mr Millet,' she said. 'It's been empty for a while now and a lot of people I've shown around have been put off by the condition. But with some vision, and a little investment, this could be turned into a very nice flat. You could make it jolly cosy.'

'It's interesting,' he agreed. 'It definitely could be cosy. It has potential!'

'A lot of potential!' she agreed. Then she frowned.

Was she frowning at his beard? He didn't care. The television was the thing. Oh yes! And it was perfectly located in a corner. From his brief time in the fire brigade, before he had been sacked, he had learned quite what a danger old television sets presented. Especially those that caught fire which were located in a corner. The fire would shoot up two walls simultaneously, and rapidly spread from there. Especially with the old dry paper covering the walls.

And no fireproofing between the flats here, he could be sure of that.

And old television sets were a frequent cause of fires. There would be little to be suspicious of with the television being the source.

Yes. Beautiful.

'You're smiling!' she said. 'You like it?'

'I do. I like it a lot!'

She looked at her watch. 'I'll have to move on – I have another appointment to go to. I'll give you my card, if you would like to have a second viewing any time.'

He took it, and glanced down at her name. Sylvie Young.

'Thank you, Sylvie. I just need a quick pee.'

'Of course.'

He hurried back into the toilet, closed and locked the door, then turned his attention to the window. It had a rusted lever handle on it, but, as he had noticed earlier, no lock. He smiled. Simple.

To mask the sound, he pulled the chain flush. Then he yanked the window handle. It was so corroded that for a moment it seemed almost welded to the locking stud. Then, on the second try, it came free. He pushed the window frame, hard. It did not budge. He tried again, then a third time, and finally it opened. A spider scurried down a web outside and out of sight. He peeped out into the alleyway the agent had talked about. Nothing there. He pulled the window almost shut, leaving the lever free.

It was quite big enough for him to crawl through later, under the cover of darkness.

He sauntered back across the flat to the front door, where the agent was waiting a tad impatiently.

'It has potential. Most definitely,' he said.

'It does. It needs someone with a little vision.'
'I have vision,' he replied. 'I have so much vision!'
'I can see that,' she said.
'This is definitely my kind of place.'

86

Monday, 4 November

Norman made her feel safe. She loved to wake curled up beside his plump body, and to smell the stale pipe smoke on his breath. That smell reminded her of her father, who had died over two decades ago, when she was in her early teens. She'd rarely ever seen her father without a pipe in his hand or his mouth. He was always cleaning it, filling it, tamping down the tobacco, lighting it, sending rich blue clouds of sweet-smelling smoke swirling across the room towards her. Just the way Norman did now.

After years of looking after her constantly ailing mother, it had never occurred to her that one day she might fall in love with someone and start a totally new life. But this was how she felt now, lying in Norman Potting's arms, feeling his morning erection against her stomach.

'I have to go, babe,' she whispered.

He rolled over and looked at the radio alarm. 'Briefing's not until 8.30! We've two whole hours. And I'm feeling a bit randy, if you want to know! Go on, let's have a Monday morning quickie!'

'I have to leave early.' She kissed his forehead. 'Isn't there some terrible joke you tell about that? About someone ordering in a restaurant?'

'The bloke in the cafe who orders a quickie? The waitress says it's actually pronounced "quiche", sir.'

Bella giggled. 'I've got to go. I'm not at the main briefing. I have to be at Brighton nick first thing, to brief the Outside Enquiry Team.'

She slipped out of bed.

'Come back, I'm missing you!'

'Missing you, too!' she retorted, and blew him a kiss. God, she didn't understand it. After years of working together and loathing this man. Listening to his terrible jokes and boasts of his conquests, one after another, she could not have imagined in a hundred years that she might fall in love with him.

But gradually her dislike of him had turned to pity. And then to very different sorts of feelings for him. Inside he was a good man who'd had a shit childhood. A bit like her own, after her father had died. And she'd realized, eventually, they were both looking for the same thing, albeit in different directions. They were looking for love. Even now she couldn't work out how it had really happened. Didn't people say sometimes you fell for opposites?

But maybe, she thought, as she stood in the shower, almost regretfully washing his smell off her, it was something else you fell for. She'd been fifteen years in the police. Fifteen years of seeing the shit side of human life. Slowly, gradually, however irritating Norman Potting was, she'd come to see him as a decent man, a good man in a rotten world.

Then he'd been diagnosed with prostate cancer.

He was scared as hell about that. And, she realized, she was scared as hell of losing him. Sure there was an age gap, but at heart he was just a big kid. He made her feel safe. But beneath all his bluff exterior, there was something deeply tender and vulnerable about him that made her want to throw her arms around him and protect him.

Last night, after he had fallen asleep in her arms, she had prayed, as she did often. She'd prayed to God to make his cancer better. To ensure he didn't lose what he was terrified of losing, his *winky action.*

She did not want him to lose that either. She'd not had many lovers in her life, and Norman was the best by a million miles. He knew how to turn her on in ways she had never known. And he took genuine pleasure in that. He cared. He really did. So many colleagues dismissed him as an old sweat, a dinosaur, way past his sell-by date. But they were wrong.

He was in his prime. And she was determined not to let anyone, ever again, dismiss him. That was something she liked about Roy Grace. Unlike so many others, he actually *got* Norman. He realized just how good he was. Maybe, in time, she could change him, she thought. Stop him from making a fool of himself, like the way he had done on Saturday at the wedding. It was insecurity, that was all. If she could make him feel secure then, she was confident, she could soften and change him.

She stepped out of the shower, a towel around her body and another, like a turban, around her head. He had gone back to sleep. She leaned down and kissed his forehead. 'I love you,' she said. 'I love you so much.'

He farted.

87

Monday, 4 November

Building fires had a repellent, noxious smell that was utterly distinctive, Bella thought. She could smell one now, at a quarter to eight in the morning, as she drove her Mini west into Brighton along the clifftop from Norman's home in Peacehaven. It was getting stronger.

The acrid stench of burning paint, plastics, wood, rubber, paper. A smell that was tinged with sadness and tragedy. Any home that burned meant the loss of so much to the occupants. Their photographs, memories, possessions. Gone for ever. As had just happened to Red Westwood's family.

As she negotiated the roundabout above the marina, and headed through the early morning daylight along the road she loved so much, Kemp Town's Marine Parade, with its elegant Regency terraced houses, she saw slivers of strobing blue light. Then, as she neared, over to her right she saw the thick black smoke belching from a ground-floor window, and from the first-floor window above.

She swung across the road and pulled up behind a marked Ford Mondeo, then climbed out of her car, glad of her donkey jacket in the chilly air, and held up her warrant card to the two young male officers. One was tall and thin, the other short, stocky and bespectacled. She didn't recognize either of them. Several bewildered-looking people, residents of the building who had evacuated, she presumed, were gathered on the pavement. Most of them looked as if they had just thrown on any clothes they could find. A young shaven-headed man sporting a goatee beard held a laptop under his arm. A teenage boy was filming the whole scene on his phone.

Suddenly, a panicky-looking woman clad in a dressing gown and slippers, her hair a mess, came running out of the building holding an infant boy in her arms and looking around, in desperation, at the knot of people. She thrust him at another woman, crying, 'Please take him, take Rhys. My daughter's still inside, with the dog. Someone please help me.'

She turned to run back in. The small officer stepped in her path. 'The fire brigade will be here any moment. They'll have equipment and they'll go straight in,' the officer said.

'Do you know where in the building she is?' Bella asked her urgently. In the distance she could hear the faint but distinct wail of multiple sirens. Then, as she looked up, she suddenly saw a dog, frantically barking and leaping against the window on the third floor. A beautiful golden retriever.

'She's in there with the dog! Megan! My daughter's in there. Megan. Megan's in there, she wouldn't leave without him. Rocky. He wouldn't move. The whole place was filled with smoke. I kept calling him and he wouldn't come.' The woman looked up. 'I have to go back, I have to get Megan!' She tried to sidestep the policeman but he blocked her path again.

'No,' the bespectacled police officer said. 'You can't go back in. I can't allow you. My colleague will go.'

'No, I'll go,' Bella said.

'I HAVE TO!' There was utter panic in the woman's voice.

The retriever was getting increasingly frantic. Bella stared at its face, at the poor, helpless creature, and felt a stab in her heart for it. Where the hell was the little girl?

The woman pushed the shorter policeman so hard he almost fell. 'I'm going in! I'll just dash up and grab Megan!' she said, and strode determinedly towards the front door in her slippered feet.

The taller officer ran over and grabbed her arm. 'I'm sorry, madam, I can't allow you to go back inside.'

'Do you know where in the building she is?' Bella asked her again, even more urgently, as she headed towards the front door herself.

'It's my child!' The woman shook her head in bewilderment. 'My child! She's going to die. I can't – I can't leave her. Don't you understand? Let me go!'

'We can't allow you to go in, madam, for your safety,' the officer said. 'The fire brigade will be here in a minute. They'll go in with their breathing apparatus and get her. Meantime my colleague's going in now.'

'It'll be too late!' She raised her voice then shouted hysterically, 'SOMEONE HELP ME! PLEASE, SOMEONE HELP ME GET MY CHILD!' Then she broke free of the officer's grip, and ran towards the door. One slipper came off and she ignored it. He ran after her and seized her arm firmly again. 'I'm sorry, I cannot allow you to go back in.'

'YOU HAVE TO!' she screamed.

Bella called out, 'What flat number?'

'Five,' the woman replied. 'Third floor. Please hurry! Please, please, please hurry!'

Bella looked up at the window, where she could see the dog was physically hurling itself at the glass. She'd been here less than a minute but it seemed already much longer. 'Megan's her name, yes?'

'Yes. And Rocky!'

Bella pushed open the front door. The smell of smoke was faint in here and the stairs looked clear. This wasn't going to be a problem, she thought. She ran up the first flight, calling the girl's name, and immediately entered a thin mist of vile-smelling smoke on the first-floor landing, swirling like tendrils around her. The stairs ahead were in darkness. Above her she could hear the frantic screams of the girl. 'MUMMY! MUMMY! MUMMY!'

Bella threw herself up to the second floor. The smoke was thicker here and she could feel heat coming through the wall to her right. She coughed, her throat stinging, pulled off her coat and held the collar over her face, breathing through it as she ran on up to the next floor, which was in darkness.

The door marked *Number 5* was open, with ghostly whorls of grey smoke, like seahorses, pouring out. 'Megan! MEGAN!' she shouted.

She heard the little girl crying and screaming nearby and the sound of barking. She took a deep breath and entered, feeling instantly disoriented, the smoke stinging her eyes, and shouted out, 'Hello! Megan! Where are you! Call your name so I know where you are!'

She heard the girl shouting her name.

Bella called back, 'Where are you?' Then she gagged. She coughed and felt like she was inhaling oil-soaked cotton; her eyes were watering so much she was virtually blinded. She needed to get out of here, she knew, but she couldn't leave the girl. 'Megan!' she called out again, then coughed, painfully. She stumbled over something in the narrow hall-way, a toy of some kind, then crunched on some pieces of what felt like Lego. Coughing. Coughing. She could hear barking now.

'Megan!'

Coughing again, she fumbled for a light switch, keeping her coat collar firmly over her mouth and nose. The carpet beneath her feet felt warm, as if there was underfloor heating turned up too high. She found a light switch but nothing happened. The smoke momentarily cleared and she could see a closed door in front of her, and she could hear barking on the other side of it.

But she was aware of backdraught danger. Or, she wondered, was it flashover danger? She felt confused about whether or not to open the door. Suddenly, behind her, flames were filling the doorway. Melted, scalding plastic was dripping down onto her. Light fittings and cables were falling around her like scorching tentacles. Bella screamed in pain as one struck her cheek. Get low, she remembered from a previous fire she had attended, talking to the firefighters present afterwards. It wasn't the fire that killed most people, it was inhaling the toxic fumes. She crouched lower and lower. Saw little flashes above her, like angels dancing. Then she saw the edge of a sofa burning, the flames getting increasingly intense.

Christ, how long did she have before flashover?

It sounded like the girl, screaming, and the barking dog were on the other side of the door. Bella seized the handle and carefully pushed it open. From the small amount of daylight in the room, penetrating the increasingly dense, acrid smoke, she could just make out the shape of a little girl cowering in the middle of the floor, holding the dog.

Suddenly the wall to her left began glowing, as if it was covered in red, fluorescent coral. The curtains and wallpaper were on fire, she realized. Christ. She was scared. Had to get out, now. She ran forward and grabbed the girl, and tried to grab the dog, which was whining in terror, but it ran out of reach and disappeared.

Which way?

Then she could see a figure at the window, and realized it must be the fire brigade.

She dragged the girl towards the window, keeping as low as she could, coughing more and more, increasingly blinded by the stinging smoke. The floor beneath her was getting hotter. She reached the sash window, and between her and the firefighter managed to lever it up sufficiently for her to push the girl through into his arms.

Almost instantly there was a deafening roar of flames behind her. She heard a splintering sound, and suddenly she was falling through air. The floor must have collapsed, she realized in her terror. She landed hard and fell forward in agony. It felt as though she had broken her leg. All around her the room was glowing. Her head was spinning. The floor was getting hotter. Her face was burning; she felt as if she was inside a huge oven. She was going to faint. *Keep going. Must keep going.* She lay flat on the floor. Then, suddenly, through the dense smoke above her, she could see flickering lights. Flames, she realized. 'Norman,' she mumbled. 'Please come and get me, Norman, I'm scared.'

She knew she must not panic. Just keep focused. She tried to figure out where the window must be. Something searing hot fell on her face, and she desperately brushed it away, burning her hand. Then something else, hot and stringy. She pulled her coat over her head, sucking frantically through the fibres of the cloth for air, but all that came through were hot, oily fumes. She coughed again. Then again. Panicking from lack of air, totally blinded by smoke and tears now. 'Help me!' she cried out. Then she crawled forward again on all fours, keeping the coat pressed against her face. 'Norman!'

Suddenly, she realized the coat was on fire.

Noooooo. In total panic, she pushed it away from her, and scrabbled forward as fast as she could go. Had to get to a window. Had to. Had to.

Then flames erupted right in front of her.

No. Please no.

She spun round and scrabbled away from them. And suddenly saw an entire wall of flame in front of her.

She spun sideways.

More flames.

Her face felt like it was cooking. She breathed in something that might have been scalding oil. It burned her throat and her lungs. 'Please help me,' she said. 'Oh God, please help me. Where's Norman?'

The floor was cracking beneath her. It was moving. Swaying. She rolled to her right, thrown by sudden movement. It was buckling. The floor was collapsing. She was gasping for air. But all she breathed in were increasing amounts of the oppressive, choking smoke.

Outside in the street there was chaos, with half the road taped off. Inside the cordon were three fire appliances, the fire officer's car, two ambulances and two marked police cars. Water sprayed in through the lower windows from two powerful hoses.

Beyond the cordon stood the gaggle of residents forlornly watching the attempt to save their homes. Mingled with them were several reporters and photographers, and a growing crowd, even at this early hour, photographing or filming the scene with their phones. And some, no doubt, tweeting excitedly, Bryce Laurent thought. He was watching from a safe distance on the far side of Marine Parade, sitting in his van, smiling. Yes. The whole building was well alight now. Helped by the fact it had taken the fire engines so long to arrive. Thanks to his plan.

From his brief time in the fire service, he knew where all the fire appliances that served the city of Brighton and Hove were located. The nearest to here, in Kemp Town, were in Roedean. He had sent those ones going in the opposite direction by a 999 call to say there was a fire in an apartment building on the far side of Rottingdean. The next nearest were in Preston Circus, in central Brighton. He'd sent them to a fire in the AmEx stadium, to the north-east of the city, phoning on a different mobile phone and with a different accent, just in case it was the same operator. The ones that had finally arrived first had come from Hove, nearly ten minutes away. That was all the time that had been needed.

Flames were now leaping out of the window of the top floor, the fourth. The front window of the flat Red had taken her parents to see, that she was so excited to be buying. Where she had come out on the terrace with her parents, and talked excitedly about the view.

Not any more, kiddo.

The elegant front facade of the Royal Regent was already blackened with smoke, and flames were visible in every window. The firefighters had briefly run a ladder up the front, but they'd had to retreat soon after. Of course they had, they were up against a professional! It looked from here as if there might be someone trapped in the building. That was too bad, he thought. Collateral damage. Sad, but shit happened.

The important thing was that Red wasn't going to be moving in here anytime soon. She wasn't going to be moving in here ever! She wasn't going to be moving in anywhere ever again.

He looked at his watch. 8.09 a.m. Time for some break-fast. He had a long and busy day ahead, with a very important appointment at midday.

He was all prepared for it.

Across the road there was a bit of a commotion. The woman in her dressing gown was with the little girl who had come down the ladder, and another child, at the back of an ambulance, was being treated by the paramedics. A camera crew was filming her and several people were gathering around, momentarily obscuring his view. Then, through a gap, he could see a dog. It was one of those golden retriever labrador dogs, wagging its tail. Although this one was far from golden – it looked like it had been rolling in soot.

In happier times, Red had talked excitedly about getting a dog like that. She said they were intelligent, caring pets, which is why they were used so much as guide dogs for the blind.

To him, they had always looked dumb. And that one across the road looked as dumb as they came.

Two firefighters in breathing apparatus and holding thermal-imaging cameras emerged from the front door. They had a defeated air about them. Hardly surprising, Bryce thought. He'd done a good job. No amount of fire-fighters were going to be able to put out what he had started here, he'd seen to that. This building was going to be a demolition project. It would be years before it was rebuilt.

How are you going to feel about that one, Red?

88

Glenn Branson felt a little nervous taking this Monday morning's briefing without Roy Grace present. True, Roy had been absent for both the ones yesterday, but at least he had been near Brighton, and easily contactable. Now the newlyweds would be getting ready to leave for the airport, for their honeymoon, and there was no way he could, or would want to, disturb them.

He'd spent much of yesterday closeted with a senior Surrey homicide detective, Detective Inspector Paul Williamson, reviewing where Operation Aardvark was to date. It was normal to have regular reviews by an outsider, to help the SIO ensure nothing had been overlooked.

Although Williamson agreed that the forensic evidence pointed to Matt Wainwright, he remarked that there was nothing in the man's history to indicate that he would behave in this way. Wainwright's reputation with the fire brigade was exemplary, and he was in a stable, happy family relationship. Yes, he had a motive, but they both felt it was a weak one. They reviewed the recording of Wainwright's first interview, and Glenn had to agree the man's protestations of his innocence were convincing.

Although Wainwright had not been eliminated from the investigation and was out on police bail, the focus remained on finding Bryce Laurent.

'Okay, right,' he said, staring at the sea of faces of his team gathered around the table in the conference room. 'Any overnight developments?'

Haydn Kelly, dressed in a black pinstriped suit, white shirt and brushed silk black tie, raised his hand. 'Glenn,' the forensic podiatrist said. 'I'd like everyone to look at this whiteboard.' He pointed to a new one which had been erected alongside the boards displaying the crime-scene photographs of Dr Karl Murphy's body at the golf course and the association charts.

On the left side of the board, there was a close-up of a single boot print in wet grass, and another photograph of a row of them in the same wet grass. To the right of these, a profile photograph of a firefighter's boot and a zoomed image of the sole of that boot. There were two computer printout graphs beside them, marked A and B.

Using a laser pointer, Kelly put the red dot first on the close-up of the print taken at the golf course. 'Firstly, let's view the single boot print in the grass.' After a few seconds' pause to allow the audience to digest the observations, he then moved the dot onto the image of the firefighter's boot. 'This is a photograph of one of the matching pair of boots found in Fire Officer Matt Wainwright's car.' He swung the dot over to the zoomed image of the sole. 'This is the sole of that boot. This is an exact match of the boot print in the grass taken at the golf course.' He moved the beam to the next photograph of the row of prints. 'And these are an exact match, also. There is no doubt that these prints found at the crime scene were made by this pair of boots.' He paused.

'Which puts Matt Wainwright at the crime scene, right?' DS Batchelor said.

Kelly gave him the kind of benign smile a teacher might give to a pupil who'd had a good but unsuccessful guess at an answer. 'Let's have a look at these two graphs.' He swung the red laser dot onto the one marked 'A'. Then he ran the dot over it, tracing the zigzag pattern. 'I fed CCTV images of Matt Wainwright in the custody block into my forensic gait analysis software, and this graph shows his gait pattern.'

'Looks a bit pissed if you ask me – all that zigzagging!' Norman Potting said. There were a few titters of laughter, and he looked around with a grin.

'I don't think so,' Kelly said, humouring him politely. 'Now, this is where it gets interesting.' He moved the dot across the graph marked 'B', and again traced the zigzag line. 'Quite different, yes?' He gave the team a quizzical look.

Several people nodded.

'There's a reason,' Kelly said. 'As those of you who've been on other recent investigations with Detective Superintendent Grace know from my previous work, we are able to identify the gait of someone from their footprints.' He pointed the laser dot back on graph A. 'This is the gait of the person who left those footprints at the crime scene at Haywards Heath Golf Club. He was wearing Matt Wainwright's boots, for sure.' He paused for emphasis. 'But it wasn't Wainwright who made the prints.'

'So who did?' Dave Green asked.

'Well,' the forensic podiatrist said. 'I'm sorry to rain on your parade, but my guess is it was the killer.'

'Which means Wainwright isn't our man?'

'Quite possibly,' Kelly said, nodding.

It didn't come as a total shock to Glenn, after yesterday's review, and the result of some of their enquiries.

A doctor had been murdered and his body set on fire; a restaurant had been burned to the ground; a supermarket had been torched; a car had been set on fire; a house had been burned down. A yacht that was a potential floating time bomb was in Naval custody. The banner headline of this morning's *Argus* read: **SUSSEX ARSONIST SUSPECT ARRESTED.**

He was now faced with the realization that Red Westwood was still in deadly danger. He asked, 'How certain are you, Haydn? There must be some margin for error, right?'

Before Kelly could answer, an internal phone rang. DC Alexander, who was nearest it, picked it up. 'Yes,' he said. 'Oh, yes, sir. He's right here.' He turned to Branson and passed the receiver over. 'Boss, it's Chief Superintendent Kemp.'

Branson frowned. Nev Kemp was the Divisional Commander of Brighton and Hove. He would be unlikely to be calling him personally unless it was an important matter. Mouthing an apology to the team, he took the receiver. 'DI Branson,' he said deferentially. 'Good morning, sir.'

There was almost total silence in the conference room as he listened to Kemp. Although his current role had him back in uniform, Kemp had at one time been a senior and highly effective Major Crime Team Detective Superintendent.

After some moments of just listening, saying nothing, Glenn felt his insides turning cold. His eyes fell on Norman Potting. He kept looking at the man. He looked away but then his eyes were drawn back to him. 'There's no possible chance, sir?' he asked Kemp.

'I'm afraid not, no,' Kemp replied tersely, his voice close to cracking.

Glenn's own voice was close to cracking, too. He was shaking, fighting off tears. He was trying to keep a focus on his job, despite what he was hearing. He was thinking who needed to be told, what actions needed to be taken, and what the implications for this case were.

The Royal Regent.

Red Westwood had told him just the other day that she was about to exchange contracts on an apartment in this mansion block. Now it was on fire.

Another fire.

But at this moment that took second place to the horrific news that Chief Superintendent Kemp had just given him. He looked back again at Norman Potting.

Shit. Oh shit. Oh God. In the time that he had been in the police force, some of his colleagues had had some close calls, and he'd had one himself last year when he had been shot. But you shrugged them off. Fear was something that came to you after you'd done whatever you had to do. At the time, whether you were trying to disarm a maniac wielding a scimitar, or plunging headlong into a vicious fight where you were outnumbered, or chasing a suspect across a perilous rooftop, you just got on with it, running on adrenaline, doing your job. It was only much later, in the small hours of the morning, that you woke up and thought, *Shit, I could have been killed today.*

Rough and tumble danger was part of what you signed up to when you joined the police. And in truth, many officers signed up for excitement. But you never really, seriously, expected that you might one day actually get killed.

Glenn could not take his eyes off Norman Potting.

Glenn's eyes were watering. 'Yes, thank you, sir. Thank you for informing me,' he said to Kemp. 'I'll be there right away.' He was conscious that his voice was choked. He hung up, blinking away tears.

Oh shit.

He stared at Norman Potting again.

89

Despite all his work distractions, Roy Grace had determined that their honeymoon should be perfect, and memorable, and he had planned every detail meticulously. He had begun by ordering well in advance the best car that Brighton's Streamline Taxis had in their fleet to take them to Gatwick Airport.

And now in the back of the Mercedes, on the M23 motorway heading towards Gatwick, his hand entwined with Cleo's, Roy felt truly relaxed and happy. Confident that Glenn Branson could handle Operation Aardvark competently in his absence, he felt, on one of the few occasions in his life, almost without a care in the world. They were going to have a good time. A damned good time. He leaned over and kissed Cleo on the cheek. 'God, I love you,' he whispered.

'I love you too,' she whispered back, and grinned. She puckered her lips, then added, 'Rather a lot, actually!'

There was an added bonus, which was that he wouldn't be around for Assistant Chief Constable Cassian Pewe's first week. What a shame!

The driver had the news on low. Suddenly he turned his head, for an instant. 'Nasty fire in Brighton,' he said.

Grace felt a prick of anxiety. But determined to let nothing spoil the moment, he only commented non-committally, 'Right.' With all the old buildings in the city, many of them fire hazards, and its population of vagrants and drunks and elderly folk who fell asleep smoking in bed, fires were all too commonplace. Nothing to fret about. He turned his thoughts back to the journey ahead.

For a special treat he'd booked business-class seats on the British Airways flight. They'd got a great deal on a suite at the Cipriani, the most romantic hotel in Venice, his agent at Travel Counsellors had told him. They had dinner reservations for tonight at that hotel, and for the next three nights at different great restaurants in the city that he'd researched carefully on the internet. And before dinner tomorrow night, they would have Bellinis at the fabled Harry's Bar.

'So, you still haven't told me where we are going!' Cleo said.

Roy grinned. 'Have a guess.'

'Scunthorpe?'

'Bugger, you got it! Four nights in the Premier Inn there!'

'You know what, I'd be happy anywhere so long as I was with you.'

'And back at you.'

The morning rush hour had ended and the traffic was light, and there was a clear blue sky above them to add to Grace's sunny mood. He saw the Gatwick Airport turn-off ahead, and the taxi indicated and moved over.

'Scunthorpe has an airport, does it?' Cleo asked in a teasing voice.

'Humberside.'

'So, Detective Superintendent, if we are going on honeymoon in England, why were you so insistent I checked that I had my passport with me?'

'You don't miss much, do you?'

She stroked his thigh suggestively. 'All that bodily

contact we've had – I guess some of your detection skills must have rubbed off on me.' She kissed him again.

'They can be a bit fussy about us southerners, up in the north.'

'Why don't I believe you?'

He shrugged, giving her an innocent expression, stifling a grin.

'Want to know where I really think we are going?' she said. 'In fact, where I *know* we are going?'

'Tell me.'

She kissed him on the cheek again, ran her tongue around his ear, then whispered seductively, 'To bed. Soon.'

Twenty minutes later, Grace stood in his socks and placed his shoes in the security tray, along with his mobile phone, laptop, watch and belt. Then he followed Cleo through the metal detector. To his relief, neither of them pinged it. As he pulled his shoes back on, his excitement was growing. By hanging on to both of their tickets, he'd managed to conceal from her that they were flying in luxury. She would find out in a few minutes, of course, when he took her into the lounge for their first glass of champagne of the day. He could not wait to see her face.

Then his phone rang.

90

Monday, 4 November

Bryce Laurent was in a sunny mood, too, as he drove along Tongdean Avenue shortly before 10.30 a.m., despite his ridiculously itchy beard. His anger that they had played this music in church forgotten, he was humming to Van Morrison's 'Queen of the Slipstream' which was playing on his van's radio, tuned to Radio Sussex. So appropriate, as he was on his way to see his queen!

And this was a street fit for a queen. The swankiest street in all of Brighton and Hove! He passed a big bling house on his right, set well back from the road behind security gates, with a columned facade. Then an equally swanky one on his left, sitting atop a circular drive high above the road. He imagined it would have fine views of the sea over the rooftops to his right and a mile to the south. Oh yes, he could imagine living here. A swanky life. With Red.

Once upon a time.

The music ended and he heard the voice of Danny Pike welcoming back his special guest, Norman Cook, aka Fatboy Slim, who was talking enthusiastically about his new venture, the Big Beach Cafe. But Bryce had too much on his mind to concentrate on chatter right now. 'Sorry, Danny and Norm, catch you later, eh?' He turned the radio off, and then braked to a halt as a learner driver ahead executed a painfully slow three-point turn. The instructor waved him through, so he drove on, looking at the numbers on the left.

But he didn't need a street number to recognize the house he was coming to view, Tongdean Lodge; he recognized it by the ten-foot brick wall running around the perimeter that he had studied, much earlier, on Google Earth.

It was a sodding great wall, like a fortress, and there were wrought-iron gates, closed. He slowed as he passed, then pulled into the kerb and parked his van a short distance on. Thinking. He had a number of plans going on inside his head all at the same time. Plans A, B, C, D. He rehearsed them all carefully in his mind. He had plenty of time. Over an hour and a half before Red would be arriving for her appointment. Ahead he watched another learner driver under instruction also making an absurdly slow three-point turn. And further along the road was yet another learner driver doing a similar manoeuvre. Hmm, he wondered, this would be pretty irritating if he lived here.

He started the engine, turned the van around and drove up to the gates. Then, tugging his baseball cap peak low, he wound down the window and stared at the smart, brass entryphone panel. There was a numerical keypad with a bell button beside it, and the lens of a CCTV camera. The camera did not worry him; it could not see much of his face.

He rang the bell, hard and long. There was no answer. After a minute, he rang again. Still no answer. To be sure, he rang one more time.

Good, good, good, no one home!

He climbed out, clutching a small toolkit, then unscrewed the front plate of the keypad and lifted it off. He studied the wiring beneath for some moments, prodding around with his tiny, insulated screwdriver, working out from his knowledge from his job installing such systems what was what. Then he shorted them out. Moments later the gates swung obligingly open.

He replaced the keypad cover, then drove up the steep, curving tarmac driveway, passing a garage block, with what looked like accommodation above it, to his left. Nice granny annexe, he thought. The driveway formed a loop in front of a large red-brick mansion. Definitely swanky, he thought. He parked the van nose into a yew hedge on the far side of the drive, so it would look like a workman's or a gardener's vehicle, then climbed out.

Just to be sure the house was empty, he walked up to the porch, which seemed even bigger and taller as he approached it, and rang the bell, his story prepared. He was delivering a package, and was at the wrong address if anyone should open the door. But again there was no response. He rapped several times with the brass lion knocker. Again, no response.

This was so good!

He checked his watch, then took a walk around the side of the house. Beautifully trimmed terraced lawns. A swimming pool beneath a blue cover, with a wooden pool house that looked in good condition. A grass tennis court, the net lowered and the markings faded. He checked his watch again, to be sure. Almost an hour before Red was due here. To meet her client, Mr Andrew Austin.

He strode back to the van, opened the rear doors and peered in, checking all was in order, and was pleased with his handiwork. The six restraining straps bolted securely to the sides of the van, and the floor. Then he peered inside the leather holdall, to check all the accessories. Hood. Gag. Blowtorch. Scalpel. Power drill. Folding razor. Pliers. Water bottles. Caffeine tablets to stop her falling asleep. She would need to stay awake, to fully appreciate all that he had planned for her!

Oh, Red, we are going to have such fun. Bringing back all those memories. You lying there as I read out all those texts you sent me. Hundreds of them.

He looked at one, still stored on the phone he had long ago stopped using.

Oh God, I love you, Bryce. Something is missing today . . . and it is deffo you. I so love you, adore you, fancy you, admire you, want you, yearn for you, pine for you, misssssss you soooooooooo much. Can't wait, seriously cannot wait, to see you tonite! To be in your arms. To hold you and taste you. XXXXXXXXXXXXXX

Will you remember this one, Red? I'll make the pain bearable enough so you will. I promise. You are going to be remembering so much in the coming hours.

Sooooooooooo much.

Happy days!

He closed up the van, then walked back around the side of the house looking for a suitable hiding place that would give him a clear view of the driveway. He found a laurel bush that was well sited, and took up a position behind it.

Then he settled down to wait.

91

Monday, 4 November

'I'm sorry, darling,' Roy Grace said, for the third or maybe fourth time, turning to Cleo who was sitting in the back of the marked Traffic Police BMW estate car, as PC Omotoso drove them down the fast lane of the M23, lights blazing and siren wailing.

'I understand,' she said with a wan smile. 'You don't have to apologize. I understand totally. You don't have any option.'

'Not much of a start to your honeymoon, is it, sir?' Omotoso said grimly.

Grace shook his head miserably. 'No.'

At least Cleo did, genuinely, understand, he thought. And, involuntarily, he suddenly found himself thinking about how Sandy would have reacted to this same situation. Not at all well. Nothing like the calm, understanding way in which Cleo was taking it.

She reached out and took his hand, gently massaging it. 'You really didn't have any choice, darling,' she said.

He shrugged. 'I did, I could have ignored the damned phone.'

'And then? We'd have got to Venice and there would have been a message waiting for you at the hotel, and we'd still have had to come back. You wouldn't have been able to stay there, I know you too well. So it's better it happened before we boarded the plane. We'll still have our honeymoon – it's just delayed, that's all.'

He squeezed her hand back, and stared into her eyes. She was incredible. He'd never, ever in his life loved someone more than he loved this woman, and the way she was handling her disappointment made him love her even more – and made him even more determined that yes, they would have their honeymoon soon, and when they did he would make it all up to her.

But for the moment his thoughts were a million miles from the airport lounge and their glass of champagne, and their suite at the Cipriani with the bottle of champagne he had ordered to be waiting on ice for their arrival.

His thoughts were on the fire at the Royal Regent building. Where Red Westwood had been buying a flat.

And where, although it was not yet confirmed, it would appear that one of his best officers had died this morning.

And that he was responsible.

He squeezed Cleo's hand hard, again, for comfort. Tears were rolling down his cheeks.

Twenty minutes later, the siren still wailing, PC Tony Omotoso weaved the BMW through the standstill traffic along Marine Parade. Grace could smell the vile stench of the fire increasingly strongly as they neared the building. Ahead he could see a blaze of blue flashing lights, and as they approached the scene, he saw three fire appliances, two ambulances, the dark green mortuary van with the Coroner's emblem on the side, police cars blocking most of the wide street, and two television outside broadcast vehicles as well as a Radio Sussex outside broadcast car.

Fire hoses were hurtling jets of water through windows on the ground floor and first floor of the blackened building. Thick dark smoke was belching out. Charred debris lay on the pavement. A large number of onlookers, several of them holding up their phone cameras, were crowded around, kept at a safe distance by a cordon of blue and white tape and several police officers.

'Do you mind dropping Cleo home?' Grace asked Tony Omotoso as they pulled up as close as they could get.

'Of course not, sir,' he said.

Grace kissed Cleo, then climbed out into the choking stench of noxious smoke and damp. Almost instantly, and to his horror, he saw the new Assistant Chief Constable, Cassian Pewe, in his full dress uniform and braided cap, striding towards him, followed by the Chief Constable, Tom Martinson, also in full uniform.

'Roy!' Pewe said with a cadaverous smile, his eyes as ever cold as glass, his arm outstretched. They shook hands. Pewe's was, as Grace remembered it from before, damp and limp, and Pewe winced, visibly, under Roy's strong grip. 'It's good to see you again. But what terrible circumstances.'

Grace nodded, blinking away tears, and his voice choked; he could barely get out the word. 'Yes.' Then with difficulty he added, 'Sir.'

'Terrible news,' the Chief Constable said, also shaking Roy's hand.

'It is, sir.'

'Let's not be formal, Roy,' Pewe said, giving Tom Martinson a sideways glance. 'We've had our issues in the past, but let's look forward now, shall we?'

'Good idea,' Grace replied warily. He wondered what bombshell was coming next.

But instead, Pewe said, 'This is one hell of a start to my first day here.'

'And to my honeymoon.'

Pewe nodded. 'It's good of you to come. That must be bloody hard.'

'Not as hard as losing an officer, sir. But are we absolutely sure we have?'

Pewe pointed at the building, then shot a glance at his watch. 'I'm told that Detective Sergeant Bella Moy entered the building to try to save a child around eight this morning. She hasn't come back out, although she saved the child. It is now five to eleven. The Fire Chief has told me no one could survive in there for even just one minute without breathing apparatus.'

'She's smart,' Roy Grace said. 'Maybe she's found an air pocket.' He knew he was clutching at straws. 'Has anyone searched the place?'

Pewe pointed at the building. 'Fire officers have searched as much as they can, with breathing apparatus and with remote cameras. The stairs have all gone. They've been up on the ladders and their opinion is—'

There was a sudden commotion behind them. Both men turned. A man was shouting. 'Let me through! I'm a police officer, let me fucking through, you halfwits. That's my fiancée in there. LET ME THROUGH!'

It was Norman Potting, his face sheet-white, holding up his warrant card, shaking off the hands of a uniformed police officer as he ducked under the tape and began running towards the smoking front door.

'Norman!' Grace shouted, alarmed, then sprinted after him. Two firefighters got there first, restraining the Detective Sergeant by his arms.

'She's in there!' Potting shouted. 'Oh my God, Bella is in there. Let me go and find her. Let me find her. I have to get her out!'

Grace reached them. Potting looked like a crazed animal, his eyes bulging, his whole pallid face pulsing.

'Norman! Let them do their job. If she's in there, they'll find her.'

'I'll find her! She's in there, I'll find her. I know she's all right! She's my Bella. I love her. She's all right. She's safe, I know she is. BELLA!' he shouted at the top of his voice. 'I'M HERE! IT'S NORMAN! I'M COMING TO GET YOU OUT!'

Then he collapsed in tears in Roy's arms. 'Oh God, Roy, please don't let anything have happened to her. I love this woman. She's made me realize I've never truly loved anyone before in my life.' His voice was choked with sobs. 'Please don't let her be taken away from me. We've only just found each other. Please don't. Please, please, please, let me go in and rescue her. She's okay, I know she is. She has to be. Please let me, let me, let me go in. I won't be a moment.'

'Norman,' Grace said gently. 'Listen. Let the firemen find her, they have the equipment. If she's OK, they'll find her. That's what they're trained to do.'

Norman hugged Roy Grace, clinging to him as if he were a life raft in a storm-tossed ocean. 'I love her, Roy. I do, I truly do. Please don't let anything have happened to her. They said the dog came out. She must be okay. If the fucking dog has survived, she must have done, too.'

92

Monday, 4 November

Ever since the phone call on Saturday from Rob Spofford telling her they had a suspect in custody, Red had been feeling uneasy. It just didn't sound right, but she figured the police must know what they were doing, and would not arrest someone unless they had some strong evidence, surely? They were still looking for Bryce, and Rob told her it was not certain that the suspect was involved. In her heart she remained convinced that it was Bryce who was behind all this.

It had to be.

She drove the Mishon Mackay Mini along Tongdean Avenue as fast as she could, conscious that she was nearly ten minutes late. The couple who'd made an appointment to view the house in Coleman Avenue had turned up twenty minutes late, having gone to the wrong street first. To ensure each of the sales team could achieve his or her daily target of fifteen viewings, for most appointments the agency allowed a quarter-of-an-hour viewing slot. But she'd made sure she had nothing booked in after this Tongdean house, because she figured that someone contemplating spending three and a half million pounds might just want a little bit longer than fifteen minutes.

A moment later she was forced to a halt by a learner driver under instruction in a driving-school car, practising his three-point turn. There was another just beyond this one, doing the same. God, it must drive the residents of this exclusive street bananas that every driving school in the city chose to come here – although she could understand why. It was a wide, tree-lined road, with very little traffic normally. She looked at the car clock, then double-checked against her watch. Twelve minutes late.

The instructor at least had the courtesy to wave her past, but just as she started the manoeuvre, the idiot learner suddenly shot forward. How she missed a collision she did not know, and in her anger she raised her hand, giving two fingers. Not a good advert for the company, she knew, with its logo emblazoned all over her car, but she didn't care. She needed to get to the house, and was already perspiring with anxiety. *Please don't give up and leave*, she thought.

She saw the high brick wall ahead, instantly recognizable from the photographs on the glossy brochure on the seat beside her, and the gates, open. She had to stop again, for another full agonizing minute as another learner stalled in the middle of the road ahead of her. The woman driver started, jerked forward a few inches, then stalled again.

Sod you! Red put two wheels over the pavement and drove around, bumping back onto the road, then finally reached the house. The smart gold and black sign by the open gates confirmed its name. *Tongdean Lodge.* She turned in, and drove up the drive, passing the garage block to her left, and reached the top, where the drive became circular, and she could now see the magnificent house to her right. And she breathed out a massive sigh of relief. The client wasn't here yet, she had beaten him to it!

She glanced down at the list of nine names on the lined paper on her clipboard with today's earlier viewings to remind herself of his name. *Andrew Austin.*

The only sign of life was a small white van, parked on the far side of the drive. Probably the gardener, or someone doing maintenance on the property, she assumed. She rummaged through the assortment of keys and found the one for Tongdean Lodge, which also had the gate entry code and alarm code written on its tag. Thoughtful of the gardener, or whoever, to have left the gates open for her, she thought, as she climbed out of the car, closed the door, and walked up to the front door.

She waited there for some moments, and then had a prick of doubt. Andrew Austin was going to turn up, wasn't he? She glanced at her watch. He was now fifteen minutes late. She had his mobile number on her list. Give him another five minutes and she would call him. In the meantime, she thought it would be a good idea to take a walk around the property, to familiarize herself with it a little.

She turned and looked at the stunning view over the rooftops of the houses on the south side of the avenue, right across Hove and down to the English Channel, which sparkled beneath the bright sunshine. It was a perfect day for a viewing – everything looking at its best. There weren't going to be many days like this at this time of the year. *Oh, please turn up, Mr Austin!*

There was a brick archway through into the gardens, with a mature laurel bush beside it. She stepped through it, entranced by the magnificence of the gardens that lay beyond, as if she had entered a secret world. She stared at the neatly manicured, terraced lawns; the swimming pool with a Roman arch at one end; the tennis court further on.

To her left was a wide, magnificent terrace, with a twelve- or even fourteen-seater wrought-iron table in front of French windows. What a glorious spot to eat out on a fine summer's day or evening, she thought, making a mental note to ensure she mentioned this.

She was startled by a sudden soft footfall behind her, and instantly a shadow fell over her. But before she could react, she felt a strong blow on the side of her head, as if she had been struck by a flying brick. A searing flash of white light inside her skull, as if a firework had been set off.

Her legs were collapsing. Her body swaying, her brain spinning her into darkness.

From behind, Bryce put his arms around her, gripping her unconscious body, preventing her from falling to the ground. He did not want her to hurt herself.

He wanted to do all the hurting.

93

Monday, 4 November

It wasn't until shortly after 3 p.m. that the fire at the Royal Regent had been extinguished for sufficient time for the building to be deemed safe for firemen to re-enter.

Two went in while Roy Grace and a numb Norman Potting stayed outside, along with the Chief Constable and Cassian Pewe, watching all that was happening and barely exchanging a word between them. Grace badly needed to get back to the office, but he could not leave Norman Potting in his current state. Instead he called Glenn Branson who came over and updated him and Pewe and the Chief Constable on the events of this morning's briefing.

Glenn had been instructed to step up the manhunt for Bryce Laurent with renewed urgency, and to ensure that Red Westwood was protected.

Both the Chief Constable and Cassian Pewe were being supportive to Grace, neither of his bosses levelling any blame. To his surprise, certainly today, at any rate, given their history, Pewe appeared to hold no grudge. Perhaps because his skin was too thick.

Suddenly, Tom Martinson put an arm around his shoulder. 'Roy,' he said in his kindly voice. 'Sometimes in every police officer's career a really terrible thing happens. When it does, that is the moment we wonder why the hell we are doing this job. But if we are able to be mentally strong enough, it's also the moment when we realize that's why we chose to do this job. Because all our training kicks in. Not many people phone the police because they are happy. We're not here to serve happy people. We're here to make a difference. Occasionally, however tragic it might be, we give up our lives to do that. Human lifespans are not predictable. Don't ever make the mistake of measuring someone by the length of their life. Measure them by the difference they made to this world.'

Roy Grace looked at him and nodded, blinking through his tears. 'I'll try to remember that, sir. Thank you.'

Five minutes later the two firefighters, in their breathing apparatus, came back out. They walked like a pair of space-men, their expressions invisible behind their masks, over to a fire engine, opened a locker in its side, then returned to the building with a quantity of lighting equipment.

Norman Potting let out a low, keening wail, then col-lapsed, weeping, onto the pavement.

Roy Grace knelt beside him with an arm around him, and wept also. He tried desperately to find some words to comfort the old detective, but could find nothing.

They knelt together, two grown men sobbing, oblivious to all around them.

94

Monday, 4 November

Gounod's *Faust* was playing on the radio as Bryce Laurent drove the van across the rough cart track. An idiot rabbit sat upright dead ahead, staring, mesmerized by his headlights. He felt it bump under his front wheel. Then a more violent bump as they jolted through a rut.

He'd holed up in the Brighton station car park until dusk, wanting his approach to his factory to be in the dark, to give the minimum chance of being spotted. He'd spent a highly enjoyable few hours just sitting in the van, reading out loud to Red, in the back, all the texts she had sent him in the months of their courtship. There were some gems, some absolute gems! Too bad he couldn't hear her reaction, because he didn't dare remove the gag in case she tried screaming.

Now they were on their way! He hummed to himself in tune to the music. Opera! He'd never got the damned stuff when he was young. It was only when he'd worked on the runway inspection team at Gatwick Airport that one of his colleagues had explained it to him. Or, rather, un-explained it.

Opera, he had said, *is raw emotion. Forget trying to intellectualize it, just let the emotion carry you along.*

Yep. He had been right. So now, as he drove, he let the *raw emotion* flood through him, raising his arms from the wheel, humming, then singing out loud, 'Rumtitumti-tumtity.' He was so happy. He had Red back. Yesssss!

Raw emotion!

He glanced over his shoulder as they jolted over another rut. 'Soon be there, my baby! Rumtitumtitumtity!'

He sang loudly, his lungs close to bursting. They were almost a mile from the nearest dwelling. His factory was right ahead, just a hundred yards to go. He burst into song again. Copying the French libretto. He had no idea what the words meant, but he sounded good. His mother had once told him he had a beautiful voice, that he could have been an opera singer.

And now he was one!

He looked over his shoulder again to see whether Red was appreciating it. But it was difficult to tell with the gag duct-taped in her mouth and the blindfold duct-taped around her forehead.

'So good to see you again, Red, my angel!' he said. 'You've no idea how good this makes me feel! You and I, with the rest of our lives ahead of us. How good is that?'

95

.

The Monday evening briefing was a sombre event. The death of any police officer in any force throughout the UK was felt with a level of sadness by every serving officer, regardless of where they were. But when it was a member of their own team, the impact was totally devastating. As an indication of how seriously the whole of Sussex Police took this, Cassian Pewe was sitting in on the meeting with them.

Roy Grace had, fortunately, never lost an officer before, and the fact that Bella Moy had been such a long-standing member of his team, someone he had greatly respected and grown fond of, made it all far worse. Norman Potting, bravely, was attending, red-eyed and hunched over the table looking lost. He had wanted to be there, he told Roy, as he couldn't face the alternative of going home and sitting all alone. And besides, this was now personal. Roy agreed he could attend the briefing, but they both decided that he should no longer be part of the investigation.

It was too early for the investigators to tell the cause of the fire that had gutted the Royal Regent, but the coincidence of it being the place Red Westwood had been planning to move to was deeply suspicious to all the team. And the fact that there had been two hoax calls, sending the nearest fire appliances away in opposite directions to the fire, was too coincidental to be ignored.

The investigation into the cause of the fire would begin in earnest tomorrow morning, by which time the building should have cooled down sufficiently to enable structural engineers to enter and make it safe.

'I want to start this evening,' Roy Grace said, 'with one minute's silence in honour of our fallen colleague, Detective Sergeant Bella Moy, one of the very best and nicest officers I have ever worked with. She gave her life to save a small girl.'

He looked at his watch, then closed his eyes. Throughout the ensuing long minute, he could hear Norman Potting sobbing. When he opened his eyes, counting down silently the last few seconds, hardly any of the team had a dry eye.

'Can I suggest Bella be put forward for a medal for bravery, Roy?' Guy Batchelor said.

He nodded. 'Yes, I'm going to talk to the Chief about it.'

Dave Green, the Crime Scene Manager, said grimly, 'So damned tragic.'

Roy Grace said firmly, but gently, 'She saved a child's life.'

'So why didn't Bella come out after doing that?' Green said. 'She must have stayed on to try to get the dog.'

'We don't know that,' Grace said. 'We don't know what happened in there.'

'If it's any consolation,' Haydn Kelly said, 'the sculptor Giacometti was once asked, if he was in a burning house and had the choice of saving a Rembrandt or a cat, which would he save? He replied the cat. He said that in any choice between art or life, he would choose life every time.'

Potting, his face buried in his hands, sobbed even more loudly. Roy Grace stood up, walked over to him, and put his arms around him. 'She did something very brave, Norman,' he said. 'What's happened is terrible and there are no words to describe how we are all feeling – and especially how you must be feeling. She did something that any of us might have done – and might one day have to do. That's why we are police officers, and not clerks sitting behind desks, spending our lives pushing paper around, living in a sterile cocoon of sodding health and safety. Every time we go out, we potentially face a life-threatening situation. I would hope that in the same situation that Bella found herself in, any of us would have the courage to do the same thing, to take that same risk she did.'

He squeezed the Detective Sergeant's shoulders. 'The best possible way we can honour Bella is to ensure she did not die in vain – and that means catching this bastard before he can put any more lives at risk.' He leaned down, kissed Norman Potting on the cheek, then returned to his chair, and looked down at his notes through eyes blurred with tears.

He paused for a moment to dab them with his handkerchief. 'Okay, the first and most urgent item concerns Red Westwood, who has not been seen since she left her office at 10 a.m. today for a number of viewings of residential properties in the Brighton area. Her mother has been trying to get hold of her for several hours. Her last confirmed sighting was at a house in Coleman Avenue, Hove, where she showed a couple around. Then she had an appointment with a client to view a house in Tongdean Avenue.' He looked at DS Exton. 'Jon, you went there. Can you tell us your findings?'

'Yes, sir. I attended with DC Davies. The gates to the property were open, and I found a Mini with the Mishon Mackay logo on it apparently abandoned there. There was no answer when we rang, so we forced entry and searched the house and surrounding grounds, but there was no sign of Red Westwood. I've requested ANPR and all CCTV sightings of her car prior to her arriving at the house, and what I have to date confirms her journey from the previous address to Tongdean Avenue. The surveillance team saw her enter the property, but don't know what happened after that. She just disappeared. They couldn't get too close in such a quiet area, but they did say no one followed her into the grounds of the house. When they were able to move forward safely they found her Mishon Mackay Mini still at the premises, but she was nowhere to be found. Subsequently, on searching the gardens at the rear of the property, officers discovered that a six-foot-wide piece of panelling that fenced the property off from the road on the other side had been removed, and there were tyre marks over the ground. It appeared that a vehicle had left the property by this makeshift exit.'

Grace nodded, annoyed about the loss, but knew from his own past experience that surveillance work could never be one hundred per cent. 'I've taken the step of having Red Westwood's parents temporarily removed from their hotel in Eastbourne, where they've been staying because of their house being torched. I've also ordered a round-the-clock police guard on her best friend, Raquel Evans, and her husband. We've put out an alert to find Ms Westwood and that operation is being run by the Duty Gold, Superintendent Jackson, alongside this investigation.'

As this was now a formal Sussex Police operation, the Gold, Silver and Bronze command structure was in place. Gold had set the strategy, Silver was implementing the strategy, and the Bronze commanders each had their own areas of responsibility, such as investigations, firearms or search.

He looked at DS Batchelor. 'You've checked on her flat, Guy?'

'Yes, sir. There's no sign of her there.'

'So, working back to her last known sighting, which was with . . .' He paused to look down at his notes. 'A Mr and Mrs Morley. They have subsequently been spoken to, correct?' He looked at DC Jack Alexander.

'Yes, sir, I met Mr John Morley at his office, a firm of independent financial advisers, early this afternoon. He said they had arrived late for the viewing because of having gone to the wrong address first, and that Ms Westwood seemed in a slightly agitated state because they had made her late for her next appointment. But she showed them round, was pleasant and helpful.'

'Anything suspicious about him?' Grace quizzed.

'No, sir. He dropped his wife back at Seaford for an amateur dramatic rehearsal at ten past twelve. I checked this out and he was telling me the truth.'

'And what about Morley's movements after then?'

'He had lunch with a client at Topolino's restaurant in Hove. I spoke to one of the owners who confirmed he had arrived shortly after 1 p.m.'

'Good work,' Grace said.

'Ms Westwood's manager at Mishon Mackay informed me that her next appointment, the last before she was due to return to the office, was for midday, at a house in Tongdean Avenue called Tongdean Lodge. The appointment was with a Mr Andrew Austin. He was a new client, with a wife and son, looking for a prestigious property, and she had noted down the phone number on the log she had written in the ledger and entered on the computer. This is a procedure carried out by all estate agents ever since the disappearance of Suzy Lamplugh.'

Suzy Lamplugh was an estate agent who went missing, presumed murdered, in south London in 1986. She had gone to show a client, who had given his name as Mr Kipper, around a secluded property, and was never seen again.

'Has someone phoned Mr Austin?' Grace asked.

'Yes, sir. The manager tried the number, and I tried it also. It's answered by an elderly man on holiday in Tenerife in the Canary Isles. I contacted the phone provider, O2, and they've confirmed his name as the subscriber, and I've phoned the hotel where he claimed to be staying and they've confirmed he and his wife are there.'

'Tongdean Lodge is on for three and a half million pounds, sir,' DC Alexander said.

Grace was pensive for some moments. 'Andrew Austin. Someone who can afford a house of that value has to be pretty seriously wealthy. Have you tried Googling him? Looking him up on Wikipedia?'

'Both, sir,' Alexander replied. 'There are hundreds of them.'

'What about the owners of Tongdean Lodge?'

'They're away at a second home they own in Florida.' Jack Alexander checked his notes. 'They have a couple who clean, called Mark and Debbie Brown, but they were not there today. The gardener comes on a Friday. There would not have been anyone at the property.'

Grace looked down at some jottings he had made on his pad. 'So Red was last seen apparently on her way to meet a man who might not exist, who gave a false phone number?' He looked around the grimly silent sea of faces. 'I don't like the sound of this. Not one bit.'

'Presumably someone has checked again that she's not lying somewhere in the grounds?' Guy Batchelor asked.

'Yes,' Alexander replied. 'The grounds have been searched and she's not there.'

Grace looked back down at his pad. This day, which he thought could not possibly get any worse, had suddenly got a whole lot worse.

96

Monday, 4 November

Red had a splitting headache, made worse by the smell of exhaust fumes and the jolting of the vehicle. Her mouth and throat were parched and she was desperate for water. And the pounding inside her head was making it hard for her to think clearly. She should be afraid, she knew, but instead she was angry. Angry at herself for having walked into this trap.

Angry at Bryce.

She tried yet again to move her numb arms and then her legs, but he'd done a good job on them, and she could not even bring her legs together; she felt like a manacled animal. And she desperately needed to pee. She was not going to be able to hold on much longer. The vehicle, presumably the white van she had seen at the house, lurched again over something – a rut or a rock.

'Guess you must be thirsty? Need the loo? You could never go very long without needing to pee, could you, Red? Using the *facilities,* as you always so delicately called them. You'll be needing the *facilities* now, I'll bet, eh?'

Then he picked up her mobile phone from the passenger seat. 'I'd so love to switch this on, Red. Your phone I'm holding! I had to switch it off, same as I did mine, because phones give out a location position, even when they're idle. Be nice to switch it on, though, and see who's been missing you. Your mummy and daddy, I'll bet. Wonder what she would say if she could see the two of us now, eh? The happy couple. We would have been, we both know that, if she hadn't meddled so much. She just didn't get it, did she? She didn't get *us*. She was all obsessed about my past. Hey, who hasn't bigged themselves up just a little? We've all told little porkies – do you think there's a politician in the world who hasn't? That's all I did, and she destroyed us for that. You heard all those texts you sent me. They were from your heart, Red. Surely, you meant all you said in them? Because you loved me for what I was, not all the shit I had once been. If only your mother could have seen that, everything would be so very different now.'

He smiled and looked in the mirror, although he could see only darkness reflected in it. 'We're nearly there. I'll take your gag off and your blindfold and we'll see what you have to say for yourself. I do keep thinking that maybe I should give you one more chance – if you're willing to give it a go. But then I realize all the bad stuff I've done just recently, that's going to catch up with me, and where's that going to leave us? Me in prison, knowing you are out there screwing a new man? It's one hell of a dilemma, eh, Red?'

He halted the van outside the cluster of farm buildings, climbed out, leaving the engine running, and jerked open the two barn doors of the old grain store beside his workshop, drove in, and stopped, then switched off the engine and lights. Then he opened his door. The hot engine ticked and pinged noisily in the silence. The barn was cold and smelled of old straw and, at this moment, exhaust fumes from the van.

He turned his head to gaze at his prisoner, in the weak glow of the roof light. 'Oh, Red, how different it could have been, eh? How very different. I'm quite sad, really. This is not what I had planned for you, all that time back, on our first date. It really isn't. I'm sure this isn't how either of us wanted to end up, is it?'

She lay motionless.

'Red?' he said. Then he became alarmed. 'Red? Red?'

He ran around to the rear of the van, opened the doors and climbed in. 'Red?'

She lay as still as a corpse.

97

Monday, 4 November

Roy Grace's mother used to look at the clock on their kitchen wall at home and say, 'How's the enemy?'

Time was always the enemy to her, to the end, finally running out on her in the cancer ward at the Royal Sussex County Hospital. Time was everyone's enemy, he thought more acutely than ever at this moment, checking his watch in the conference room of Sussex House. It was 6.45 p.m. Right now the enquiry was in 'fast time', where every second counted. If Red Westwood had been taken at the house, by the mysterious Andrew Austin, that would have been shortly after midday. Over six hours ago.

It was a grim fact that most victims of abductions were murdered within three hours. But if Andrew Austin was indeed Bryce Laurent, which seemed the most likely scenario, then there was a good chance she was still alive. Grace had no real idea what Laurent would want with her, or hope to gain by abducting her, and a number of dark scenarios crossed his mind.

Normally his team were sparking with thoughts and ideas at briefings, but this evening they were all so damned quiet. He suddenly clapped his hands together, really loudly. 'Listen, everyone! I know we're all in shock, but that's not going to help save Red Westwood's life if, I just hope to hell, she is still alive now. Okay? Right now, forget Bella, however tough that is for all of us. We have a very serious and urgent job to do.'

He looked around at his team and was greeted by nods. They understood; he sensed the distinct sudden mood change in the room. As if something had been unblocked, and everyone had got their energy supply back.

'We had a number of sightings of Bryce Laurent called in following our appeals in the press and media,' Becky Davies, the researcher, said. 'We've had a response from a bed and breakfast hotel called Strawberry Fields, saying they had a long-stay guest who checked out suddenly, yesterday, who they say looks like Bryce Laurent. His name was Paul Millet and they have a credit card imprint in his name as, fortunately for us, they insist on payment by credit card.'

Grace turned to the HOLMES analyst, Keely Scanlan. 'Give that name to the financial investigators, see what it throws up.'

'Yes, sir.'

Jon Exton raised a hand. 'I took a call earlier this morning from the manager of Cuba Libre restaurant, who'd seen the photograph of Bryce Laurent. He's convinced that he was working for him on the day of the fire.'

'Bryce Laurent? Working in the restaurant?' Grace said.

'Yes, as a busboy. He'd started there three days earlier.'

Grace frowned. 'Under what name?'

'Jason Benfield.'

Grace looked up at the whiteboard on which all of Laurent's known aliases were listed. 'I don't see this one there, but that doesn't mean a thing. Do we have any idea yet of the cause of that fire?'

Tony Gurr, the Chief Fire Investigator, said, 'Yes, Roy. It looks to us that it was caused by stacking tea towels and other kitchen laundry items.'

The detective superintendent gave him a quizzical look. 'Stacking tea towels?'

'Cotton laundry,' Gurr explained, 'such as chefs' whites, aprons, tea towels and cloths are normally contaminated with organic cooking oils. These can self-combust – spontaneously – if they are taken out of the tumble dryer and stacked before they've had a chance to cool first.'

'Do many people know this?'

'Someone working in the catering trade should. And a fire officer should know – most will have attended fires started this way.'

'Bryce Laurent was in the fire brigade for a short time,' Glenn Branson said.

'Seems a bit too coincidental for him to be working there,' DS Batchelor said. 'Particularly to have just started working there. Three days. Enough time for him to have become familiar with how everything worked.'

Grace nodded. 'Yes, I agree.' He made a note. It was more evidence of Bryce's obsession and determination to ruin everything to do with Red Westwood's life.

'Is there any job this guy has not done?' said a new recruit to the team, DC Danielle Goodman. 'I had a call this morning from a man called Paul Davison, who runs a headhunting agency called SLM Search and Selection – the full name is Shortlist-Me. They're based in Leeds, but operate nationwide. He told me he recognized Laurent from the photograph – he had worked for his company for a brief while, under his alias of Paul Millet. I went to talk to him at his Brighton office earlier this afternoon.'

'He worked as a headhunter?' Grace asked.

'Yes, sir. Mr Davison told me he recognized him as a narcissist right away, and someone with a serious lack of empathy – a sociopath, in other words. But he took him because he had an extremely impressive CV and references. Davison said he was quite a successful headhunter because he was never emotionally attached to his clients but ultimately grew concerned because he became too manipulative – manoeuvring his clients like pawns on a chessboard – in his words.'

'How long did Laurent – sorry, Millet – work for Short-list-Me?' Grace asked.

'Just over three months. Paul Davison started noticing anger management issues, especially when anyone tried asking him too many questions about his past. That made Davison suspicious, so he began looking more deeply into the references Millet had provided. He also looked in his briefcase one day.'

'In his briefcase?' Glenn Branson said, with a frown. 'Was he nicking things from the office?'

'No, sir,' DC Goodman said. 'Apparently Millet used to come into the office every day with a really swanky briefcase – when he really had no need for one at all. Davison said he looked in it one time when Millet was in a meeting with a client and found it contained a hairdryer, foundation, toothbrush, toothpaste, different coloured contact lenses, hair gel, and a book on how to become a top sales person.'

'I've always wondered what was in your bag, Glenn,' Guy Batchelor ribbed him. 'Does that all sound familiar?'

There was a ripple of laughter, and Grace was glad to hear it. Even Glenn Branson grinned. Laughter was a major coping mechanism for all police officers when confronted with horror. The day you couldn't laugh, no matter how grim the situation, was a dangerous day for your mental state. 'Okay, the picture I'm getting more and more clearly of Bryce Laurent is that of a highly intelligent man, a chameleon, with anger issues and the inability to hold down a job. But none of this is helping us with what we urgently need right now, which is to find him. We need to know his vehicle, and then start looking at what ANPR cameras he's pinged, or what CCTV footage of it there might be.'

Dave Green raised his hand. 'Boss,' he said to Roy. 'I've had the result of the analysis on the petrol in the can found at Haywards Heath Golf Club. It is one produced by BP – the regular unleaded. There are dozens and dozens of BP filling stations across the county; we'd need to look at CCTV from each one of them, going back weeks, in the hope of spotting Bryce Laurent.'

Grace thought about it for a moment, wrote *BP* on his pad, and made a circle around it. 'If we can't find this bastard any other way, we may have to resort to this, Dave. But it's a massive task and one that will take days, if not weeks. That's not going to help us save Red Westwood.'

Another DC, Martha Ritchie, raised her hand. 'I've spoken to the charity Rise, for abused women, where Red went during her relationship with Laurent. They gave me the name of her counsellor, Judith Biddlestone, who I called this afternoon to see if she might have any idea, from what Red told her, where Bryce Laurent might be located. Apparently he had a secret location where he went to practise some of his conjuring tricks, particularly the ones involving fire and explosives.'

Glenn Branson responded. 'We know that under his alias Pat Tolley he was granted a fireworks licence and operated for a time out of a farm building in Suffolk. But he has long vacated those premises, and we haven't been able to establish from where he is currently operating that business, if he still is at all.'

The door opened, and Ray Packham from the High Tech

Crime Unit entered. 'I'm sorry I'm late, chief,' he said. 'But I have something that might be of interest.'

'Yes? Tell us,' Roy Grace said.

Packham had a wry smile on his face. 'Would the words *Geotec* or *IrfanView* mean anything to anyone here?'

The Crime Scene Manager raised his hand. 'Something to do with locating coordinates of places in photographs.'

'Exactly,' Ray Packham said. 'Last week, Ms Westwood received a cartoon, through email, of sharks circling around the hull of a yacht. It was sent as a JPEG file, which I identi-fied at the time as having been taken from a camera phone – which is very helpful. You see, as I explained before, unless the location option is switched off when a digital camera takes a photograph, it embeds in the photograph the exact time it was taken, as well as the compass coordinates, which are accurate to within fifty feet.' He hesitated.

'And?' Grace said.

'Further research reveals that the phone used has been in a static position for several days since then. Triangulation from mobile phone masts gives us a position approximately half a mile south of the Dyke Golf Club.'

They all looked at one whiteboard, to which was pinned a large-scale map of the county of Sussex.

Grace stood up and went over to the map. He looked at the scale indicator, then ran his finger over a section of green, on which was marked a cluster of buildings. 'In here?' he said.

'That's where the photograph was taken, sir,' Packham said.

'How sure are you?' Grace asked.

'One hundred per cent.'

Grace picked up the phone to the Silver commander and updated him with the information. The Silver commander then rang Andy Kille, the duty Ops-1, and requested the helicopter NPAS 15. He read out the coordinates that Roy Grace had given him, requested cars to get close to the scene, with a fast but silent approach, and to stand by but remain as inconspicuous as possible in that area. He wanted to begin to tighten the net around the location that was looking good for where Bryce was holding his victim. He also updated Gold, who was running the suspected abduction operation, with this new information.

98

In the back of the van, with the rear doors open, Bryce shook Red. 'Are you okay? Red? My love! Are you okay? Red! Red!'

She still did not move.

He stared down at the ligature around her throat. Had he made it too tight? Had she choked or strangled to death? *Oh shit, no, please God, no. Please, no.*

'Red!' he shouted, shaking her hard.

There was no response.

'Red!'

Nothing.

Christ.

He tried to think clearly, to think back. To slugging her on the head at Tongdean. Oh shit, had he hit her too hard? Caused a haemorrhage? No. It was just a tap, surely just a tap, hard enough to knock her out, but that was all. Surely?

Surely?

He shook her. 'Red? Red, my love, my angel. Are you okay? Please wake up, please. Please wake up! Don't do this to me. I have so much planned for us! Really I do. Don't be a bitch and deprive me, please, don't do that! I have so much pain lined up for you! You hear me, you bitch? YOU HEAR ME?'

He kissed her on the cheek. Smelled her hair. It smelled the way it always had when they were lovers. A faint scent of coconut. Lemongrass. He nuzzled his face in it. 'Wake up, my darling, my angel, please wake up. I love you so much. Wake up! I love you! Wake up!'

She lay limp, her eyes closed.

He held her wrist, trying to take her pulse. But his heart-beat had gone crazy. He heard the roaring of his own blood in his ears. Felt the pulse through his body. His pulse. 'Red!' he said, urgently. 'Wake up, my darling. Wake up! We have so much to talk about. Wake up, it's me, Bryce. I love you. I love you so much! Sooooo damned much! Wake up!'

Was he imagining it or was her body turning cold?

'Red! Please don't die on me! Don't die on me until I'm ready. Don't cheat me, please!'

He tore at the straps restraining her, undoing them one at a time. 'Red, oh Red, my darling, my angel, my beautiful. Come back to me. Come back to Bryce. Come back to me.'

When her arms and legs were free, he began chest com-pressions.

Still nothing.

He gently pulled the duct tape from her mouth with shaky hands. Pressed his lips to hers and began the com-pressions again.

Then felt an agonizing pain as she bit right through his lower lip. And jammed her fingers in his eyes, so hard she was starting to gouge them out.

He screamed, momentarily blinded, thrashing at her with his hands.

She bit harder. He tasted blood. He could see nothing. He squirmed, wriggled, but her fingers, nails sharp, kept pushing into his sockets. She was wriggling beneath him. Suddenly, he could no longer feel her.

Silence.

His eyes were in agony.

He raised his fingers and felt fluid. Lights flashed all around him. Green, yellow, blue, orange, bright red.

'Noooooooooo!' he screamed. 'Nooooooo, you fucking bitch!' He clamped his hand over his left eye, which was stinging as if it had been sprayed with acid. All he could see through it were streaks of colour. He swung himself around in the darkness. 'COME BACK! COME HERE, RED!'

His head struck something hard. The roof of the van, he realized. He stared with his good eye at the roof light, which burned as bright as a laser and shot shards of brilliant white in all directions. 'RED!' he screamed. 'RED!'

He grabbed his crossbow off the front seat. Beside it lay the night-sight. He lifted that to his right eye, his good eye. And saw her.

Running away.

She was running across the field.

He snapped off the day-sight and slipped on the night-sight. Now he could see her clearly, against a green landscape. He took careful aim. She was already quite a distance away. A good eighty yards, he estimated.

Eighty yards was the distance he had practised on for Rottingdean church.

Slowly, much more calmly than he felt inside, he brought the cross hairs of the sight down to the middle of her back. Then he squeezed the trigger.

99

Roy Grace stared at his watch, and cursed the damned budget cuts. Sussex Police, in line with all the nation's other forty-two forces, was required to reduce its annual expenditure by twenty per cent. A government edict. One of the savings had been to lose the county's combined police and air ambulance helicopter, Hotel 900, located at Shoreham Airport, which had the capability to be anywhere in the city of Brighton and Hove in under three minutes. Now with the advent of the National Police Air Service, the helicopter allocated to them, NPAS 15, was shared with Surrey, Kent and Hampshire, and located at Redhill. It took a minimum of fifteen minutes for the helicopter to reach Brighton – providing it was even available. Fortunately tonight it was.

He sat at his allocated workstation in MIR-1 rather than return to his office, watching the time with growing frustration. The helicopter was still ten minutes away. There was no certainty that Bryce Laurent was in one of those farm buildings south of the Dyke Golf Club, but it was all they had to go on at this moment and it seemed probable to him. If Laurent had abducted Red Westwood, he would have needed to take her somewhere remote and isolated. This place looked suitable, and Laurent would have known it.

Grace was thinking fast. The first priority was to locate the two of them. But the even greater priority was to get Red away from Laurent, unharmed. That was going to be harder. Grace had spoken with Silver, who wanted the helicopter to overfly the farm buildings where he had a feeling Bryce Laurent had taken Red Westwood, using its thermal-imaging camera to establish whether there was anyone in the buildings. He had requested it fly at as high an altitude as possible to try to avoid alerting Bryce Laurent. He was awaiting a call back.

Then he turned to the forensic behavioural analyst, Dr Julius Proudfoot, who was at this moment rummaging for something inside his tan man-bag. He retrieved a bottle of First Defence nose drops and pulled off the cap.

'So if we are right in our assumption that Laurent has seized Red Westwood and is holding her captive, what in your view is his next step going to be, Julius?' Grace asked him.

Proudfoot shot two squirts of drops up each of his nostrils, sniffed, then replaced the bottle in his bag. 'Sorry,' he said in an unusually nasally voice. 'Got a cold coming on.'

Instinctively, Grace leaned back a little, getting as far from the man's breath as he could.

Proudfoot placed his elbows on his workstation, steepled his pudgy fingers and stared over the tops of them at an empty chair on the other side of the workstation for some moments. 'What I don't like, Roy, is what we learned last Friday about Laurent's cash withdrawals from his bank. Cleaning out his account. People only use cash these days when they want to be untraceable. So the first question I would ask is what reason does Laurent have for wanting to be untraceable?'

'He's committed murder and a number of arson attacks against Red Westwood, and her family, and wants to go to ground to evade arrest?'

'He's a game player. The cartoon of the parents' sailing boat? He's aloof and arrogant. In his own mind he is far too clever to get arrested. I don't think it's his next step we should be focusing on, Roy, we need to try to establish his endgame. That will give us all his steps.'

'So what do you think his endgame is?' Grace asked.

'Killing Red Westwood, after he's enjoyed himself torturing her mentally or physically – and possibly both – then either killing himself or disappearing. However, the fact that he has emptied his bank account indicates he has plans beyond avenging Red – to leave the UK for somewhere further afield, either under one of his identities or by creating an entirely new one.'

'Torturing her first, you say?'

'Oh yes. He's been systematically destroying her world – setting fire to everything dear to her. He hasn't gone to all this trouble to capture her just to kill her right away. He's going to have his sport with her. He'll be driven by his ego, wanting her to grovel, to apologize, probably to beg him to start over with her again. He will want absolute power over her.'

'She's smart,' Roy Grace said. 'I'm sure she'll play whatever game she needs to. Even to the point of pretending she'll take him back, if needs be.'

'The problem is, I don't think he's going to accept her offering to take him back. My guess is that he actually won't want her back now. She and her parents have humiliated him. I've seen the texts that Red and he exchanged. She was pretty loved up with him, and then turned overnight.'

'She turned for a good reason,' Grace said. 'She found out everything about his past was a lie and that he had a history of violence.'

'Yes, but he doesn't see it that way, you can be sure.

He's not capable of accepting he's done anything wrong. In his mind, he's the injured party, and now he has her in his power. I can't predict the outcome, but it's not going to be good. The only positive is that you have a little time. Certainly some hours, and possibly a few days. He's not going to kill her quickly, that's for sure. He's going to want to have his day in the sun with her first.'

Grace looked at his watch again. Red Westwood would have met Laurent at the house in Tongdean Avenue around midday. More than six hours ago. The buildings near the Dyke golf course would have been a ten-minute drive, if he went straight there. Or maybe, to be safe, he might have waited somewhere until after dark. In which case he'd have been there not that long ago. If Proudfoot was right – and what he said made sense – whatever might be happening to the woman, she was still alive now. With luck.

'Julius, if Bryce Laurent is where we think, with Red Westwood, and we surround him, what's he likely to do?'

'He has to win, there's no other possible option for him. He would kill Red and then himself, and see that as a grand act of defiance against you.' He sneezed into his hand, then hastily dug a handkerchief out of his pocket. As he did so, he sneezed again.

'Bless you,' Grace said. Then his phone rang. It was the duty Ops-1 Controller, Andy Kille. The helicopter was two minutes away from the target position.

100

Monday, 4 November

She was running blind through starless darkness, unable to see a thing in front of her other than the weak glow of the lights of the city several miles away. The ground felt soft and claggy, the mud sticking to the soles of her court shoes, making them heavier with each step and trying to suck them free of her feet. She heard a constant crunching that sounded like she was running through corn stubble. Then she stumbled and fell forward, and something sharp lanced her cheek painfully.

How far was Bryce behind her?

In panic, she frantically scrambled back onto her feet, and stumbled on. She was trying as best she could to head well away from the cart track, and towards the orange glow of the lights of Brighton and Hove. *Have to keep away from the track and the road*, she thought. *Run across the fields. Keep going across the fields. Keep going. Going.*

Then she slammed into something sharp and unyielding, and cried out in shock, feeling painful pricks in her knee, leg, stomach and hands. A barbed-wire fence, she realized.

Overhead, she suddenly heard the *thwock, thwock, thwock* of an approaching helicopter. She looked up for an instant, gulping down air, and saw navigation lights high above her moving quickly through the sky. She began to climb over the fence, feeling gingerly with her hands for the barbs. Her skirt snagged, and she jerked hard, hearing the fabric rip; then she felt a pain in her right leg as it caught on something sharp. She stretched her left leg down to the ground on the far side, and part of the fencing collapsed. She fell sideways, and as she did, she heard a sharp, hissing *swoosh* sound, felt a rush of air past her right ear, then heard a thud a short distance ahead, like a rock being thrown.

Or a missile of some kind.

A chill rippled through her as she remembered something about Bryce. One of his hobbies was crossbow shooting. He'd won prizes, he told her, and one of his many unfulfilled promises to her had been to give her a lesson.

Was he shooting at her now?

From somewhere, maybe a movie she had seen, she remembered that it was harder to hit a zigzagging target. That made sense. She began to run on, changing direction every few paces. A short way ahead she saw headlights, growing brighter. She heard the roar of a car, driving fast. The lights passed in front of her and then she saw the red glow of tail lights. The main road, she realized. She veered to the right, stumbling on so that she would be parallel to it, not reaching it. Bryce had brought her in a van, and that could not get across the fields and especially not through a barbed-wire fence. But he could chase her along the road.

Shit, shit, shit. She stumbled on, the mud heavier, her pace slowing despite her efforts as her shoes became as heavy as lead.

Then she heard the *thwock, thwock, thwock* of the helicopter returning, sounding louder, lower. An instant later she was illuminated, for a brief second, by a blinding pool of light. 'Go away!' she screamed, waving her arms, gesticulating angrily. 'Go away, you idiots!'

The light swept over her, then momentarily lit up the ground ahead of her. A field full of a short green crop – some kind of cattle field, she could see. Then the light swept around in a brilliant, dazzling arc and came back towards her, the *thwock, thwock, thwock* almost deafeningly loud, and suddenly she was lit up again, like a diva on a stage. 'Get away, you fucking idiots!' she screamed. Then her foot caught in something, a rabbit hole, twisting agonizingly, and she fell flat on her face again.

As she scrambled to her feet, panting and crying in terror, there was another thud, right by her face. And now in the light she could see the feathered steel crossbow bolt sticking out of the earth. She turned and looked over her shoulder, and saw two distant bright white headlight beams. And what looked like the shadow of a figure standing between them, legs apart.

She stood still for a moment, watching. Mercifully the helicopter moved away, leaving her back in darkness. She watched the beam of its searchlight moving across the field, illuminating briefly the fence she had clambered over. Then it was right over the white van, brilliantly illuminating it and the figure in front of it, holding something. Bryce, holding his crossbow.

She buried her face against the mud, bracing herself, waiting. It was harder to hit a target lying flat. She'd heard that or read that somewhere. An instant later she heard another thud, over to her right. *Oh Jesus.*

What the hell was the helicopter doing?

Then she saw it was circling above the white van.

She stumbled on, her chest hurting, a painful stitch in her side. One of her shoes came off, but she didn't care, she broke into a sprint, stifling a scream of pain as her stockinged right foot struck something hard and sharp;

she kept on going, then stopped dead again as she struck another fence.

No, please no. Ignoring the barbs, she scrambled over it, ran on a few paces, then her legs banged agonizingly into something solid, metallic, and she fell forward, her arms plunging into icy, foul-smelling water, her chin striking metal. A cattle trough, she realized.

She looked back over her shoulder and saw the helicopter still hovering in the same place, in front of farm buildings, above the white van. Suddenly, it made a sharp movement to the right, and banked steeply, its beam travelling up the buildings' walls. Then it banked even more steeply, and despite the danger she was in, she watched, mesmerized for an instant, as it started to climb, then suddenly began to drop, almost on its side now.

Plunging sideways.

Not right, surely not right?

No, please God, no, she pleaded, silently.

It was dropping faster, plunging sideways towards the ground.

She stared, as the gap between the helicopter and the ground reduced, as if she was watching something unravelling in a nightmare. Then, suddenly, she heard a deep, hollow, metallic bang. Seconds later, the entire helicopter erupted into a massive ball of flame.

This could not be happening. It could not be. She was shaking. This could not be happening. *Please, no. No. No.*

In the halo of the flames she could see dense black smoke billowing before being swallowed into the darkness of the night. She stood, rooted to the spot, in utter, numb horror, feeling as if her innards had been scooped out. No one ran from the wreckage. Christ.

What the hell had happened?

But she knew exactly what must have happened.

Then she saw a powerful flashlight beam glinting towards her.

Tears streaming down her face, she turned and ran painfully on, gulping down air, and after a few paces, she lost her left shoe, also. But she was beyond caring. All she could see was the image of the plunging helicopter. The fireball. Light rain was starting to fall, cooling her face. She stumbled on, heard distant sirens, her feet cold, almost numb, squelching through the mud, every few paces she yelped in pain as one or the other struck something sharp and hard.

Then in the distance, ahead to her left, she saw strobing blue lights. Getting closer. An entire convoy of them hurtling down the road which was a good half a mile away. A succession of police cars.

She altered her course, for a wild, crazy instant thinking she might be able to get there before they passed and flag them down.

Then the ground disappeared beneath her. With a yelp of fear she fell several feet, into a wet ditch, her face slamming into the bank. She closed her eyes for a moment, wondering how much more she could take. But she had to go on, she knew. She could not let that brute win. She felt a sudden rage at him. How dare he, the bastard? How dare he do all he had done? How dare he set fire to her parents' house? Her car?

And suddenly, she was not afraid any more, she was just angry. Driven by a fury. She would get this bastard, pay him back somehow. Oh yes. He would pay for this.

The rain was hardening. She didn't care. She was in the middle of nowhere, several miles from the city, but she didn't care. She heard the sirens wail past, but she didn't care.

You bastard.

She hauled herself up the far side of the ditch. If only she had her phone, she thought, she would get some small amount of light from that. But it was back in the van somewhere.

At least the police were on their way. They would get him. And then?

He'd spend a few years in prison, before being released. To do what? Come after her again? Or find someone else to abuse and terrorize?

She ran on, the rain hardening with every step she took, heading towards the main road now. She would flag down a police car when she got there.

Shit, fuck, shit!

She had run into a gorse bush.

Almost beyond feeling pain now, she backed away, then walked slowly forward. Only a short distance in front of her now she saw headlights moving from left to right.

Another car went past.

Then another.

Then two cars, in close succession, heading in the opposite direction. Towards the helicopter?

A few minutes later, headlights were approaching, very close now. In the beam she could see a rail-and-post fence. Close to exhaustion, she clambered over it. Then she stood still in the darkness. Waiting.

After what seemed an eternity, she heard the roar of a motorcycle, saw the beam of light and watched it hurtle past at high speed. Over to her left she could see the red glow of the burning helicopter. She was barely aware of the rain any more. Nor of her isolation. She just felt a burning deep inside her.

A burning rage.

And helplessness.

She was shivering with cold.

Then she saw headlights. A large car coming along, slowly. When it was close enough for her to be sure it was not a white van, she hobbled out in front of it, her arms raised in the air. For an instant she thought it was going to run her over. Then, to her relief, it indicated left and slowed to a halt. It was a large, elderly Jaguar, with an equally elderly man behind the wheel. She ran round to the passenger side and the window lowered. He peered at her, looking clearly a little sloshed. 'You all right, my dear?'

She burst into tears. Sobbing, she asked, 'Could you take me to the police?'

He squinted at her. She could see his face in the green glow of the instruments, ruddy and flaccid; he was wearing a tie with crossed golf clubs on it, and a checked shirt. 'Well, to be honest wish you,' he slurred, 'I was rather hoping to avoid them.' He squinted again. 'Your face is bleeding. Have you been attacked?'

She burst into tears again.

He leaned over and opened the door for her. She climbed in and pulled it shut, grateful for the warmth inside the car, inhaling the comforting smell of old leather, as well as the smell of booze. 'I've been kidnapped,' she blurted. 'I've just escaped.'

'Someone's having a bonfire over there,' he replied, jerking his thumb towards his rear window, not registering what she had said.

'It's a helicopter that's crashed,' she said, pulling down the sun visor and peering in the mirror. In its weak light she could see her face clearly. It was streaked with mud and blood.

'Never fancied one myself,' he replied. 'I'm a fixed-wing

414

man. Bloody deathtraps, helicopters. Engine packs up in those, you've got one and a half seconds to react or you're toast. Roast – toast. You're a pilot, are you?'

'No,' she said, casting an anxious glance behind her. Was Bryce somewhere out there, coming for her? She wished this man would drive on, quickly. 'Could you take me into Brighton? Just drop me anywhere.'

'You need to go to hospital?'

'Sure,' she said. 'Hospital would be good.' Anywhere but here, right now, she thought, would be good. Even being driven by a drunk, right now, would be good.

101

Roy Grace, seated at the workstation in MIR-1, listened to the voice of Inspector Andy Kille down the phone in disbelief. 'Gone down? The helicopter? What the hell happened, Andy?'

'We don't know yet, sir. We have the emergency services at the scene now. We do know the helicopter had picked up through their infrared camera that a man with a crossbow was at that location. Silver has sent armed Response units there as well as covert Response support.'

'What about the crew?'

'Information I have is that it's a fireball. Doesn't sound like there are any survivors.'

'Would there have been a crew of three?'

'Yes.'

'One of them a police officer?'

'That's correct, Roy.'

'God.' He balled his fists and knocked his knuckles together. Two officers killed on this operation. If he hadn't gone on honeymoon, maybe Bella would not have been where she was at that time. If he hadn't come back, maybe things would have been different with the helicopter, he wondered.

He put down the receiver and buried his face in his hands, thinking.

'What's happened?' Glenn Branson asked.

'Shit's happened,' he replied. He picked the receiver back up and called Gold, Superintendent Jackson. 'I'm on my way to the crash site, to ensure we don't lose evidence, as this is a crime scene. Can you give me the exact location? Also, is there any other helicopter attending?'

'I can try, but NPAS 15 is really our only one,' Gold said. 'Every unit we have is looking for Red Westwood; we need to find her urgently. I'm organizing roadblocks with at least ten more vehicles making their way from all over the county. I want every exit onto the main roads from the Dyke manned and to have them stop and search every vehicle approaching from the Dyke, and further afield I want a roadblock ring of steel around the whole city. Silver is implementing this strategy.'

Grace agreed, and updated him on what his own team were doing.

'No one in Brighton and Hove Police is to go off-duty tonight – neither uniform nor CID,' Gold continued.

'I'll send that instruction straight out.' Grace put the phone down.

Glenn Branson said, 'Did I hear right? The helicopter?'

'You did. NPAS 15's gone down at the scene.'

'Shit.'

Two minutes later, ignoring his misgivings about his colleague's driving, Roy Grace sat cradling his phone in the passenger seat of the unmarked Ford estate car, and tightening his seat belt, as Glenn Branson drove them down the ramp at the front entrance of Sussex House.

Switching on the blue lights and siren, the DI pulled straight out in front of a bus, narrowly missing being hit by a car coming the other way, and accelerated the Ford up the hill. 'What information do we have on this, Roy?' he said, nonchalantly hurtling over the roundabout almost under the wheels of a truck that had right of way. Branson never seemed to understand that driving on blues and twos did not grant you automatic right of way – it was a request for that, no more.

Grace, holding his breath, took a moment to reply as they hurtled down the slip road and straight out into the heavy evening traffic on the A27 dual carriageway, the wipers clouting away the heavy rain. 'The chopper crew reported two people – one stationary, the other running away. Sounds like Bryce Laurent and Red Westwood. They reported that he appeared to be shooting at her.'

Grace's phone rang. Then he heard the voice of the Ops-1 Controller. 'Chief, I've just listened to the recording from NPAS 15. The sergeant on board is saying that the man on the ground is pointing a weapon at them. Then she's screaming that the pilot's been shot. Then it goes silent.'

'Christ. Who's the sergeant on board?'

'Amanda Morrison.'

'Amanda Morrison? I don't know her. What's happened to her and anyone else on board?'

'I don't have any information yet. I'll keep you updated.'

'We'll be there in five.' Grace nearly added *with luck,* as he gripped the grab handle. Branson came off the A27 and slewed the car into the roundabout at the top of the hill. Grace felt the tail slide out and for a moment thought they were going to spin. He gave Glenn Branson a nervous look.

'Relax, old timer!' he said, see-sawing the steering wheel one way then the other, as the car fishtailed twice, then somehow, seemingly defying the laws of physics again over a second roundabout and onto the dark, narrow road that led towards the Dyke Golf Club. Flashes of blue light streaked the hedgerows. They hurtled past a travellers' encampment to their right. Headlights were coming towards them, on full beam, dazzling them.

Glenn flashed his lights back twice. 'Bloody idiot!' he said.

Almost at the last moment, the lights of the oncoming car dimmed. Grace peered at it as it passed, checking it wasn't a white van. But it was a large saloon, an old Jag, perhaps. He stared ahead, and could see a red glow, like a bonfire, in the distance. He had a knot in his gullet, praying silently that the crew were all right. But knowing in his heart that a helicopter going down was never going to be good news.

Then his phone rang again. He answered and his heart sank even further. It was his new boss, Assistant Chief Constable Cassian Pewe. He was not a happy man. 'What the hell's going on, Roy?'

'My sentiments exactly, sir,' he replied, mirroring his acidity.

102

Monday, 4 November

Red saw the blue flashing lights approaching, then hurtling past.

'Played a blinder today,' the old man said. 'And birdied the eighteenth! How's that for a finish? Damned near got an eagle on the twelfth – went into the hole and damned well rolled out. You a golfer?' he asked again.

She shook her head.

'Read about that terrible thing at Haywards Heath last week? Week before?'

'That was my boyfriend,' she replied, staring at the approaching roundabout, and the welcoming street lights of the city only a couple of hundred yards ahead of them. She was not sure that her driver, who was looking more at her than at the road, had noticed yet, but she felt strangely detached, not caring if they had a wipeout smash or not at this moment. Everything was surreal, as if she were a passive observer in a bad dream.

He braked sharply, at the last possible moment, throwing her forward against her seat belt. Jolting her awake and to her senses.

'Sorry about that, don't remember that being there. Not exactly there.' His face furrowed into a frown. 'You play at Haywards Heath?' he asked, navigating the roundabout uncertainly.

She turned and looked over her shoulder, and to her relief the road behind was in darkness. 'I'm not a golfer,' she replied, thinking hard about what she should do. Go to the hospital, where she would be safe? John Street police station? Would that still be open at this hour? She could not be sure. Hadn't there been stuff in the papers about all the police cuts, and many stations either closing or cutting down their hours?

Where would Bryce be expecting her to go?

As her thoughts began to clarify, she suddenly realized that he would have the keys to her flat, which were in her handbag. Would he go to the flat? Could she get there before him and get the locks changed?

She suddenly felt leadenly tired. Yet strangely alert at the same time. If she went to the Royal Sussex County Hospital, she could find herself sitting in the Accident and Emergency department for several hours. But if her drunk rescuer dropped her at John Street police station, which he was clearly reluctant to do in any event, and she found it closed, what then, without any money for a taxi home?

She wanted to phone Rob Spofford, but she couldn't remember his number. She'd had it on speed dial for so long, she had never looked at it. *Shit.*

They were heading down Dyke Road Avenue, one of the smartest streets in the city. 'I live just over there.' He pointed at a huge mansion behind wrought-iron gates, slowing to a halt. 'Where would you like to go?'

She thought for a moment, and knew she should go to the police, but the only place she could feel safe at that moment was in her safe room in the flat, and that's where she needed to get to. She just wanted to shower, get into fresh clothes and get safe.

She noticed a glow to her right and saw an iPhone

nestling in a charger cradle. 'Could I borrow your phone for a second?'

'For a damsel in distress, anything!'

She picked it up, and saw it had no security code. She went to the Google app and entered, *Locksmiths in Brighton.*

Fifteen minutes later, she thanked her gallant, if somewhat inebriated, white knight, gave him a peck on the cheek and climbed out of the Jaguar, which he had pulled up in front of her building.

'Sure you're okay?'

She nodded. 'I can never thank you enough.'

'Any time you fancy a round of golf. No pressure!'

'I'll remember that!'

He raised his pinkie and winked at her. 'Got to get home now, to she-who-must-be-obeyed.'

She stood in the rain, looking around her, warily, as the Jaguar drove off up Westbourne Terrace, its tail lights fading and blurring. No sign of any white van. She glanced at her watch. 7.58 p.m. She felt conspicuous standing here. A lorry rattled along the Kingsway, followed by a number of cars, their tyres sluicing across the wet tarmac, then a noisy motor-cycle. She was shaking, she realized, from her ordeal, from the sickening image of the crashing and burning helicopter, and from the icy wind blowing straight off the Channel, just a couple of hundred yards south of her. Her ankle hurt like hell, and her left hand and her cheek. Her eyes darted in all directions.

Her brain darted in all directions, too. Thinking. Thinking.

Where was Bryce?

Why hadn't she had her rescuer drive her to Raquel

Evans's house? Or just phone the police? Why had she come back here?

But she knew the reason. Because the bastard had made her a victim. A bedraggled, cut and bleeding victim. All the time she was in this state he had won. She wanted to clean herself up, have a bath, dress her wounds, put on fresh clothes. Be ready for battle.

I'm coming after you now, you bastard.

Where the hell was the locksmith?

A car was driving down Westbourne Terrace. Her hopes rose that it was the locksmith, but then she saw the little Nissan Micra pass, with an elderly-looking man at the wheel. The woman who had answered the locksmith's phone number said he would be there within fifteen minutes. Still five to go yet.

Please come quickly.

In the distance she heard a siren. Then it faded away. She looked around her in all directions, staring at the shadows, convinced, for an instant, that she saw one move. She felt a dry prick of anxiety in her throat. Watched the shadow. Watched. Shivering. Ready to break into a run.

Then she heard a vehicle approaching, swinging into Westbourne Terrace from the seafront. The lights of a tall, dark van dazzled her fleetingly. An instant later, she could read the words emblazoned above the windscreen: 24-HOUR LOCK-UP!

She stepped forward, raising her hands in the air, and it pulled over beside her. A tall, wiry guy, with a Mohican haircut and a ring through his bottom lip, lowered his window and peered out. 'Mrs Westwood?' he asked. She could see him frowning at her appearance. At her victim appearance. He looked strong and tough enough to deal with anyone who crossed him.

'Yes,' she said, shooting a glance at the shadow she thought had moved. But now in the beam of the headlights she could see nothing there. Just the side entrance to a house and some bins.

'You're locked out?'

'Yes, but I need to replace the locks, please. The lady on the phone said you can do that, right?'

'Yes, I can, but I'll need some proof it's your property.'

'I have stuff in the flat – I can show you when we go inside.'

'I can't do that – I'll need proof first, I'm afraid. What ID do you have on you?'

'None.'

'The thing is, I'm not allowed to open up any property without knowing I have consent from the owner.' He was staring at her more closely now.

'I've just been abducted – kidnapped – by my ex. He's got my handbag with everything in it. I need to change the locks before he – he – ' Her eyes welled with tears. 'Please,' she said. 'Please help me.'

She could see through her blurred eyes that he was wavering. 'The thing is, I need to know it's your property, lady. It's more than my job's worth.'

'Come on, you don't look like a jobsworth to me. You must have this all the time – I can't believe that everyone who gets locked out of their home has ID with them, surely?'

She turned, wiping away her tears, and stared warily around. Looking back at where she thought she had seen the shadow moving. But the street was deserted. 'Please help me, please.'

'Is there one of your neighbours who could vouch for you?' he asked, more friendly now.

She shook her head. 'I haven't been here very long . . .

you see . . .' She hesitated, unsure whether to tell him. But she couldn't see any option. 'This is . . . well, the thing is, I'm being stalked by my ex. This is a police safe house. The Sanctuary Scheme arranged this for me.'

'Okay, so could we phone the police and have someone come down?'

'I don't have my phone. He kidnapped me and I escaped.' She raised her arms. 'Look at me, look at the state I'm in. I've just escaped – I've run over fields near the Dyke. He shot down a police helicopter. Some kind stranger gave me a lift here. There's an officer who looks after me, PC Spofford, at Brighton police station – John Street.'

'You look frozen,' he said. 'Tell you what, jump in, and I'll phone him and put you on.'

She climbed gratefully into the dry warmth of the van. There was a strong reek of tobacco. As she pulled the door shut she said, 'What's your name?'

'Mal Oxley,' he said.

'Do you have a ciggie I could bum, Mal?'

'How do you know I smoke?'

'I can smell it on you.'

Mal Oxley grinned. 'I've only got roll-ups.'

'A roll-up would be fine.'

He picked up his phone from the dashboard cradle. 'Do you know PC Stafford's number?'

'Spofford,' she said. 'Just dial 999 and ask for the police – that's what I've been told to do in any emergency.'

He dialled, put the phone on loudspeaker and jammed it back in the cradle. Moments later an operator answered.

'Emergency, which service do you require?'

'Police,' he said, then rummaged in his pocket and pro-duced a tobacco pouch and a pack of Rizla cigarette papers.

'Sussex Police,' a stern male voice answered moments later. 'May I have your name and number, please.'

'I have a very distressed lady with me who needs to speak urgently to a PC . . . er . . . Stanford.'

'Spofford!' Red corrected him.

'I'm sorry, that should be PC Spofford.'

'What is the lady's name, please?'

Red leaned forward. 'My name's Red Westwood.'

There was a brief silence; she heard the putter of a keypad, then the change in tone of the operator's voice. 'I'll try to reach him for you, Ms Westwood. We've been looking for you – are you safe now?'

'Yes.' She began crying again.

'Can you give me your location?'

'I'm outside my flat.' She gave him the address. 'I've just been kidnapped and escaped, but I can't get inside because I don't have my keys.'

'I'll try to contact PC Spofford, but in the meantime I'll have a car with you within a few minutes. Are you safe for the moment?'

She looked at the locksmith, who was engrossed in laying a filter at one end of the brown cigarette paper. 'Yes, thank you, I am.' She peered nervously through the windscreen.

'Can we contact you via this number?' He was sounding kindly now, so kindly that her tears worsened.

'Yes,' she said, and sniffed.

'If it makes you more comfortable, I'll stay on the line until someone is with you.'

'Thank you,' she said. 'Thank you very much. I'm in a van marked with a locksmith name.' She looked at her companion.

'24-Hour Lock-up,' he said clearly, into the phone. 'We're

parked on Westbourne Terrace just to the north of the Kingsway.'

With his large, grubby hands, he laid thick, golden strands of tobacco along the length of the paper, added more to it, then brought it to his lips, licked along the length, and rolled it. Then he handed the thin, slightly creased, but well-formed tube to her. 'Get me into trouble, smoking in the workplace,' he grinned, then held up the flame of a plastic lighter.

She inhaled the sweet smoke gratefully. As she did so, she was aware of what she assumed was an unmarked police car pulling up alongside, and suddenly she felt better, safer.

She opened the door and jumped down onto the road. Two uniformed officers climbed out of the car. One was a sturdily built woman in her late twenties, with brown curly hair and a friendly face; the other was a male, in his forties, tall and thin, holding a torch.

'Ms Westwood?' the woman asked, looking at her sympathetically.

Red nodded.

'PC Holiday and PC Roberts. We're on the Neighbourhood Team, with PC Spofford, so we know all about you. You look injured – do you need to go to hospital?'

'I'm okay,' Red said, wiping away her tears with the back of her hand, then pressing it against each of her eyes in turn to stop the stinging. She was aware of the cigarette in her left hand.

'Have you just been up near the Dyke?'

Red nodded.

'We need to get you to hospital.'

'No, I'm okay – I – I ran into a barbed-wire fence, just cut myself a bit. I want to get into my flat, I have to get cleaned up. What's happened – to the helicopter? I saw it – I saw it on fire.'

The two officers shot a glance at each other. 'We don't have any information yet,' PC Roberts said. 'We were just down the road when we got the call to come here.'

'Thank you,' Red said.

'Were you with Bryce Laurent?'

She nodded. 'I went to show a prospective client around a property at lunchtime. Then next thing I knew I was tied up in the back of a van being driven by Bryce. We went into some kind of car park for . . . I don't know how long. Then out to the Dyke. I managed to escape. He was shooting at me – with a crossbow, I think. I was able to get to the road and flag down a car – the driver kindly dropped me here.'

'Why didn't you call us then?'

Red began crying again. 'I – I don't know. I – I just wanted to get home. I had no phone or money; I was just terrified, not thinking straight. But I realized I don't have my keys or anything.' She jerked a finger at the van. 'And he won't open the door for me without ID.'

'Okay, we'll speak to him,' PC Holiday said. 'But we really need to take you to the Victim Suite, where you can be made comfortable, receive medical attention, and we can give you an opportunity to provide an account of what's happened.'

Red replied, 'I know, but I'm not going anywhere right now. I want to go into my flat.' She burst into tears.

Two minutes later the four of them headed towards the front door of Red's building, the locksmith carrying a metal toolbox.

103

Monday, 4 November

Roy Grace on the radio to Cassian Pewe said, 'I'm making my way to the RV point, which has been set up for emergency vehicles, sir. I'll then go closer to the crash site and meet Bronze at the Forward Control Point, which is being set up. Silver's in the Control Room and my role is as the Senior Investigating Officer, nothing else. I've given Silver my investigative requirement, which has been approved by Force Gold. My team at Sussex House are also feeding up-to-date intel to him. Everyone is focused on finding Laurent and Ms Westwood.'

He could see the red glow in the distance, over to their left, in the middle of the farmland that extended a mile south from here to the Hangleton residential district of Brighton. The lights of the houses and the distant sprawl of the city beyond were faint through the driving rain.

He looked down at his phone, trying to read the text he had received with directions to the scene, but it was hard at the speed they were travelling on the uneven country road. 'I think we make a left, opposite where the road turns right up towards the Dyke,' he said to Glenn Branson.

'Copy.'

'I think this is it,' Glenn said, the headlights picking out the sign to a farm and a track to the left. DYKE GRANGE FARM.

He swung the car onto it and they hurtled down a steep,

potholed incline, then around the back of a cluster of build-ings, far too fast. The car bounced, and Grace could feel the rear end losing traction, swinging out to the left, as Glenn sawed at the wheel. They swung violently to the right, and this time, the phone flying out of his hand, Grace was certain they were going to spin. At the last possible moment the car swung back the other way, then in the opposite direction again. Then somehow they were going in a straight line once more.

'Sorry about that,' Glenn said. 'Bit of a tank-slapper!'

Grace leaned forward to retrieve his phone from the footwell, and his face slammed into the dash as they bounced over a ridge on the cart track.

'I think we could slow down now, Lewis,' he said.

'Yeah, you see, Hamilton and me, we're good in the wet. Am I scaring you?'

'No more than usual.' Roy Grace could smell an increas-ingly strong, acrid odour of burning plastic and paint. It reminded him of torched cars he had attended.

'It's all about keeping the car balanced. Basic physics, yeah?'

'I thought it was all about getting to your destination alive.' Then, staring at the cluster of police, fire and am-bulance vehicles they could now see in the beam of the headlights, Grace fell into a grim silence. They had obviously arrived at the RV point. In the almost ethereal red glow, two uniformed officers in hi-viz jackets were putting up a tape barrier. Firefighters were jetting water onto the burning wreckage in the distance.

As they pulled up behind a fire appliance, another car hurtled down the track behind them. Grace and Branson climbed out, instantly feeling the heat on their faces. They were greeted by Inspector Roy Apps, in his hi-viz jacket and police hat. The red glow gave him a slightly demonic appearance. An experienced police officer, Apps was the current Golf 99 – Duty Inspector for Brighton and Hove. A wiry man in his early fifties, he had started life as a game-keeper before joining Sussex Police. This rural setting was strangely appropriate for him.

'Hi Roy, what's the update?' Grace asked him. The stench of burning was even stronger now, laced with the reek of spent aviation fuel. He could feel the heat on his face even more intensely.

Normally a cheery man, unfazed by most things he encountered, the inspector had a sad countenance tonight. 'It's bad news, chief. NPAS 15 down and no sign of any sur-vivors. The information I have is that there are three on board: the pilot, a police officer, Sergeant Amanda Morri-son, and a paramedic. The standard crew. We believe they're still in the helicopter, but the blaze is too fierce for anyone to get close enough to determine that. There's an air crash investigation team coming down, but I don't know when they are due.'

Grace shot a glance at the burning hulk beyond him, with a sick feeling in the pit of his stomach. He was trying to shut out of his mind the thought of three humans inciner-ated in the inferno. But he could not shut out the knowledge that today two police officers involved with his investigation had been killed.

Then he heard the nasally voice of Assistant Chief Constable Cassian Pewe right behind him. 'This is dreadful, Roy!'

He turned, and saw Pewe in his full dress uniform and braided cap.

'This is the second tragedy we've had in the city today,' Pewe said.

At that moment, out of thin air, a fair-haired young woman appeared, holding a shorthand notepad. 'Amy Gee from the *Argus*. You're the new Assistant Chief Constable, sir?'

'Yes.'

'Is there anything you'd like to say to the people of Brighton and Hove about this terrible tragedy?'

'It's not safe here. We will have something to say, but for now you must get back to safety.'

She turned to Roy Grace. 'Detective Superintendent, I understand that DS Bella Moy, who died in a house fire on Marine Parade this morning, was one of your team investigating Operation Aardvark?'

'Yes,' he said tersely, not wanting to be rude.

'And this police helicopter crash occurred during your operation. Unconfirmed reports are that a woman police sergeant has died in the crash.'

'I don't have enough information at this stage to be able to comment,' he replied. 'I will be holding a press conference tomorrow morning. You need to leave now.'

'Can I just ask you which of the fires in the city you are currently linking to the arsonist, Detective Superintendent?'

'I hope to be able to give that information tomorrow,' he said. 'I'm sorry, don't think me rude, one of my officers will escort you away.'

There were more headlights behind him now. He saw a television van and a Radio Sussex van approaching.

He turned to Roy Apps. 'Is there a scene guard yet?'

'I'll have one in place in a few minutes.'

'It needs to be sorted now – I want these bloody media people kept away. This is a crime scene, for Chrissake!'

'Yes, sir. It's being put in place as we speak. I'll speed it up.'

'Do we have any witnesses?'

'There's a local farmer.' He pointed to a man who was on his mobile phone. 'He's just speaking to somebody and he'll be back in a minute.'

Grace jerked a finger back at the approaching vehicles. 'Keep them all at a safe distance.'

'I will.'

Grace ducked under the tape, followed by Glenn Branson, and immediately saw the figure of Tony McCord, the Chief Fire Officer, heading towards him, looking solemn. He was a quiet, calm man, never easily perturbed, with film-star good looks. Grace had met him several times on past cases and he always thought that if he were a casting director looking for a handsome Fire Chief, McCord would fit the bill perfectly.

'Good evening, Roy,' he said.

'Not looking good is it, Tony?'

'No,' he said. 'We've got more units on the way, but – ' He shrugged.

'Roy!' Inspector Apps called out. 'Eddie Naylor's here now – the farmer!'

Grace turned. 'Okay!' He ducked back under the tape and walked up to the tall, grizzled-looking man, in a tweed cap, tattered Barbour over a chunky sweater, dungarees and work boots.

Apps said, 'Mr Naylor, this is Detective Superintendent Grace, the Senior Investigating Officer.'

Grace shook the farmer's massive, strong hand. 'Good evening, sir,' he said. 'I apologize for any disruption we're causing you.'

'No, none at all,' he said affably, in a deep voice that was much posher than his appearance. 'Dreadful thing, this.'

'Can you tell me anything you saw this evening?'

'Yes, well, those buildings over there, you see them?' He jerked a finger at a distant cluster of farm buildings.

'Yes.'

'I rent them out, been a couple of years or so now, to a bit of a strange fellow. His name is Paul Riley.'

'Paul Riley?' Grace said, his interest piqued. Paul Riley was one of Bryce Laurent's known aliases.

'Yes.'

'Can you describe him?'

'Well, to be honest, I haven't seen him in a while. Pops the rent through my letterbox every three months, always well in advance of the due date. Quite a tall fellow – short dark hair, in his late thirties or early forties, I'd say. Quite well dressed – more of a city type than a countryman.'

'What does he use the premises for?'

'He told me he has a business making bespoke fire-works. He needed somewhere remote where he could experiment without bothering anyone. He's been no trouble at all, apart from a few pretty big bangs every now and then, and the odd ball of flame that we can see from our house.'

'How does he pay you?'

The farmer hesitated then gave an awkward smile. 'Cash. It's useful to have a bit of cash in hand, if you know what I mean.'

Grace detected the nervousness in his answer. 'Don't worry, I don't work for the Revenue. I'm not interested in anything other than finding this man. Do you know what vehicle he drives?'

'He's had an old Land Rover most of the times I've seen him. But tonight I saw a white van. I was just going out rabbiting when I heard the helicopter, then the explosion. It was a few minutes after, this small white van went past at high speed, and out onto the road.'

'Could you see what make it was?'

'I'm pretty sure it was a Renault. I had one a while ago; it's got a bit of a distinctive bonnet shape. I don't know why, but something made me suspicious, so I tried to remember the licence plate. I wanted to write it down but my ruddy pen was out of ink. I ran inside, repeating it to myself, but to be honest I could only remember two numbers and two letters.'

'What were they?'

He rummaged in the pocket of his jacket and pulled out a crumpled sheet of paper, then a torch which he switched on. He shone the beam onto the paper and held it out to Roy Grace.

'Four Seven Charlie Papa,' Grace read aloud. 'You don't remember any of the others?'

'The third one might have been an N. But I can't swear to that.'

'Not CPN – Charlie Papa November?' CPN, Grace knew, was a common Brighton registration number.

'It's possible, Detective Superintendent. But I'd be lying if I said I was sure. He went by very fast, and it was hard to see through the rain, in the dark.'

'Of course. Can you remember as accurately as possible what time you saw this vehicle?'

Eddie Naylor looked pensive. Then he pulled up his sleeve and studied his wristwatch. 'About half an hour ago. Twenty to eight, I would say.'

'How certain are you?'

'Give or take five minutes.'

'Did you by chance get a glimpse of the driver? Could you positively identify that it was Paul Riley driving?'

'I couldn't say that for sure, no. It was too dark.'

'Anyone else in the vehicle with him?'

'I couldn't say. I didn't notice anyone, but really, it was too dark. Can you tell me what's happened? Do you know why the helicopter came down?'

'We don't at this point, no, sir.'

'I heard that there were three people on board.'

'I'm afraid so, but I can't give you any more information than that.'

'Dangerous things, helicopters. A mate of mine was killed in one a few years ago. Went down in conditions like this.'

Grace thanked him, turned to Glenn and said, 'Talk to anyone you can find here who might have seen that Renault and see if you can get more of the index – and a description of who was in it. Then meet me back at the car.'

As he hurried through the rain, he dialled the number for MIR-1. DS Exton answered.

'Jon, good, just who I wanted to speak to. I need to know about small Renault vans. How many different models are sold in the UK? And get me a list of every one that has the digits and letters Four Seven Charlie Papa in the index.'

'Yes, sir. I may not be able to find out the amount of vehicles sold, and the breakdown of those in Sussex, until office hours tomorrow, but I'll see if I can find someone to talk to at the DVLA who can conduct some enquiries on the details we have, or else make enquiries to get you the information on the different models.'

'Good man.' Roy reached the car and climbed in, shut the door, and sat for a moment, doing some mental calculations. How far could someone drive in forty minutes? At an average speed of, say, fifty miles an hour. Forty-five miles easily, which could take them into another county. But if it was Bryce Laurent, where would he be going? Would he be fleeing?

He didn't think so. He'd be looking for Red locally. Waiting for her somewhere in Brighton. Perhaps at her flat? More importantly at the moment, where was Red Westwood? The report from the helicopter was that a figure was shooting at someone. Bryce Laurent shooting at Red Westwood, who was running away? So if he hadn't hit her, would he be letting her go?

No way.

But had she got away? If so, she was somewhere on foot out there in the dark. Unless she was lying wounded or dead out in the fields.

His phone rang. 'Roy Grace,' he answered.

'Sir, it's PC Spofford. I've just been contacted by one of our Neighbourhood Policing teams who are with Red Westwood. She was apparently kidnapped by Bryce Laurent earlier today, around lunchtime, and taken to a farm out near the Devil's Dyke. She managed to escape and is now back at her home, with two officers attending, and a locksmith who is changing her locks. Apparently she's in a pretty bad state emotionally, but she's not seriously hurt.'

'Thank God she's safe,' Grace said. He thanked Spofford and then rang Silver, updating him with the information he had been given.

'I'll put a twenty-four-hour police guard on her until further notice – a covert car outside her home – and make sure she is not left without a police presence nearby for one second. We can't make her leave the flat, but we'll do all we can.'

'Yes, thanks,' Grace replied. He ended the call and immediately called Andy Kille. 'We're looking for a small white van, possibly a Renault, with the following digits in its index: Four Seven Charlie Papa. We need to find this van urgently. We believe it was in the Tongdean Road area of the city around midday and more recently in the vicinity of Dyke Grange Farm near the Devil's Dyke, up until forty-five minutes ago. I want an ANPR check and a careful study of all CCTV footage that would pick up a vehicle travelling between those two areas. And also run through the partials on PNC.'

'Four Seven Charlie Papa?' Kille repeated calmly.

'Yes, yes.'

'I've only got three RPU units available now, sir,' Kille said. 'I'll see what Brighton Response have. And we have other county units making for Brighton.'

'This has to have priority over everything, Andy.'

Grace ended the conversation and immediately called MIR-1. Norman Potting answered.

'Norman, is Haydn Kelly still there by any chance?'

'No, chief,' he replied gloomily. 'He went home.'

'You should go home, too, Norman.'

'I'd rather stay here, if it's all right, sir?' he asked plaintively.

'Of course. Okay, I need you to get hold of Haydn and ask him to come out here to the Dyke right away. I need some footprint analysis done very fast.'

'Leave it with me,' Potting said.

There was a rap on the window. Grace looked up and saw Cassian Pewe's face glaring in at him. He lowered the window.

'Sheltering from the rain, are we, Roy? Nothing better to do?'

104

Monday, 4 November

The locksmith worked on each of Red's front door locks in turn, using a long, thin spindle with what looked like a small square tooth at the end. Red and the two police officers stood back, watching as Mal Oxley wiggled his tool one way and then the other, his ear close to the door, listening.

Then, within a couple of minutes, he pushed the door open.

'I thought these locks were meant to be unpickable?' Red quizzed him, entering the hallway gratefully and switching on the light.

'There are unpickable locks,' he grinned. 'People invent them all the time. Particularly the automotive industry. Lock yourself out of some modern cars and your only way back in is with a new key from the dealer. But most domestic residential locks are pickable – luckily for people like you who lock themselves out.'

'Great,' she said. 'So how do I make my home secure?'

'Put on the safety chain whenever you are in.' He pointed to the one on the inside of her door. 'That's substantial; no one's getting in here with that in place, without bolt-cutters. You can sleep tight with that.'

'But I can't stop someone who's determined from getting in here when I'm out?'

'You can make it so difficult for them that only a pro will get in. You'll never keep a pro out, no one will.'

Red thought back to some of the findings of the private detective her mother had hired to look into Bryce's background. Bryce had had a job, for a brief time, installing security systems in buildings. One of his magic acts was picking locks. 'Thanks,' she said. 'I'll remember that.'

'What you have here are quality locks, both of them. You can't do better. I'll replace the cylinders.'

'We are going to take a look around, Red,' PC Susi Holiday said. 'Check everything is in order.'

'Yes, thank you.'

The two police officers walked down the hall, intermittent, muffled snatches of dialogue emitting from their radios. 'Charlie Romeo Four,' Red heard, then a moment later, 'We have a report of a male acting suspiciously in Trafalgar Gate.'

She was starting to realize the enormity of what losing her bag, with her purse in it, meant. She now had no credit cards and no means of drawing out any cash, certainly not tonight anyway. She'd have to wait until the morning when the banks were open. 'I'm sorry,' she told the locksmith, 'I can't pay you tonight.' She realized she was still holding his roll-up.

'That's all right,' he said with a smile. 'I know where you live.' He gave her a light, then departed cheerily. 'They'll post you an invoice and some spare keys.'

'I really appreciate your help,' she said.

'Anytime,' he said with a grin. 'For a fellow smoker!'

She let him out, then closed the door and walked towards the sitting room. She heard voices from the police radio coming from inside the safe room and went in. It was a small space, with a chair and a simple wooden table, with louvred doors to a toilet and tiny washbasin, fashioned out of what had originally been the spare bedroom. There were smoke and fireproof seals on the window and around the door frame. On the table sat a mobile phone, with the 999 number and PC Spofford's number both programmed in on speed dial.

Susi Holiday ran her fingers along the edge of the six-inch-wide steel door, which was as thick as a bank vault, with a large round wheel-handle on the inside to double lock it. There was no handle on the outside. 'This should make you feel pretty secure,' she said.

'It does,' Red agreed.

'What would happen if you passed out in here?' PC Roberts asked her. 'How would the emergency services get to you?'

'Well, I think that's the point of it,' Red said. 'Once I'm in here, no one can get in. The window is triple-glazed and sealed shut. There is a window lock key on the ledge above it.' She pointed. 'I guess in a worst-case scenario, if I did pass out, the fire brigade could get to me through this window.'

Susi Holiday peered through it. 'What's down below?'

'It's the alley at the rear of the building; there are some lock-up garages and the bin store.'

'You don't know where Bryce Laurent is currently?' Holiday asked.

'Last time I saw him was an hour and a half or so ago, maybe longer, firing a crossbow at me. I don't know where he is now.'

'I really think it would be better for you to come with us to Brighton police station, where you can be looked after.'

'I've lost a whole afternoon,' Red said. 'I'm trying to build a new career as an estate agent, and I have a ton of work to do. I feel pretty safe here. If there's anything I'm not happy about, I'll lock myself in this room and phone you.' Tears welled in her eyes. 'I'm not leaving here now. Please don't force me.'

'It's okay, we can't force you,' PC Holiday said gently. 'But could you at least let us have all your clothes so they can be forensically examined?'

'Okay,' Red said, 'sure. I'll go and change.'

Five minutes later she returned, in a dressing gown, with her clothes in the separate bags the police had provided her with.

'We're on lates tonight,' Susi Holiday said. 'We're around until midnight. And there's going to be a police car outside your front entrance all night. But we'll also make sure we stay local to you. If there's anything you are not happy about, just call 999. Anything at all – don't worry how trivial you think it might be. We want to keep you safe, okay? Detectives are on their way to your flat now.'

Red nodded, feeling tears welling in her eyes again at the kindness of these officers. 'Thank you,' she said.

'Charlie Romeo Zero Two?' the voice from Susi Holiday's radio said.

She tilted her head and spoke into it, 'Charlie Romeo Zero Two.'

'Charlie Romeo Zero Two, an alarm's gone off at the Big Beach Cafe on the Hove Lagoon. There's a report of two intruders on the premises. Are you free to investigate?'

'No,' she replied, and explained why not. She turned back to Red. 'We'll be close by all evening.'

Red thanked her. She closed the door, pushed home the safety chain and the top and bottom bolts. Then she went into the kitchen, took a bottle of Albarino out of the fridge, poured herself a large glass of the white wine, and picked her ashtray up off the draining board. She went through into the sitting room, sat down on the sofa, took a large gulp of wine, and relit the roll-up which had gone out again. Then she stared out of the window at the darkness and the lights of the apartment block across the courtyard and picked up the television remote.

Her hand was shaking. Shaking so much she was unable to push the green power button. She put the remote back down, dragged on her cigarette and drained her glass. Then she got up and went through to the kitchen to pour herself a refill, and carried the bottle back into the sitting room.

The wine was calming her down. She drank some more, then used her landline to dial her mother's mobile phone, her hand a little calmer now, and was relieved to hear her answer after two rings.

'Darling, are you all right?' Her mother sounded desperately anxious.

'Yes, I'm home, I'm safe, the police are just outside. What about you and Dad?'

'We're safe as well, and we just heard the news. A police helicopter has crashed just outside Brighton, and apparently three people are feared dead. A nice police officer outside in the corridor who is guarding us said that this was an incident involving you. Your father and I have been worried out of our wits.'

'I'm fine, I'm safe. God, where are you?'

Her mother sounded hesitant suddenly and her voice lowered to almost a whisper. 'Well, the thing is, darling, we're not allowed to tell anyone. They've moved us from the hotel, but I can't tell you where in case – it sounds ridiculous, I know – but in case Bryce is listening. But you're okay? You are safe?'

'Yes. I have police guards outside the flat. I'm safe.'

'Keep in touch, darling. Phone us every hour until you go to bed, all right?'

Red promised she would, ended the call and then phoned Raquel Evans's mobile.

It went to voicemail. 'Hi, this is Raquel. I'm sorry I can't take your call right now. Leave a message and I'll get back to you as soon as I can.'

'Hi Raq,' Red said. 'It's me. Give me a call when you get this if not too late.'

She poured herself another glass of wine, then lit another cigarette, a Silk Cut. It tasted feeble after the strong tobacco of the locksmith's roll-up. She stubbed it out, picked up her glass, walked through into her bedroom and stripped off, then went into the bathroom, turned on the shower and waited for it to warm up. The police had asked her not to shower because of potential forensic evidence on her body, but she had refused; she just felt dirty and was beyond caring.

She stepped inside and despite the stinging of her wounds, stayed a long time, luxuriating in the hot jets of water and, helped by the wine, finally relaxing a little. Yet her fear remained.

Images of the film *Psycho* played in her mind. The knife blade ripping through the shower curtain.

What if Bryce had let himself in somehow? She'd never hear him with the water running.

Feeling far too vulnerable, she stepped out again, shivering with cold and fear, dried herself tenderly, dabbed some antiseptic on the worst cuts and grazes, then pulled on her towelling dressing gown and padded along the corridor, past the safe room and up to the front door. Everything seemed to be as she had left it. The safety chain was securely in place. She peered through the spyhole, and all she could see was the dimly lit, silent landing outside.

Her phone was ringing. She hurried back into her sitting room and saw the caller was Raquel Evans. She snatched the receiver off the cradle.

'Hi!' she said.

'Red, you okay?'

'I've been better.'

'What's going on? Paul and I are so worried.'

'It's been a bit shit today, to be honest. But what about you?'

'We've been told we have to have a police guard, that Bryce is out there somewhere trying to hurt people close to you. I just went out to collect a takeaway curry and had a police officer come with me in the car. Do you want to come over here and stay with us?'

'I'm so sorry to put you and Paul through this, Raq.'

'Don't worry about us. It's you we're worried about. Do you want me to come over and pick you up?'

'No, I'm okay. I'm fine, honest.'

'You don't sound at all fine.'

'I've just had the locks changed and I have a police car outside. I've had one hell of a day and I'm shattered. I just want to try to calm down and get some sleep. I'm okay, really, thanks.'

'Do you want me to come over and stay with you?'

'No, I'm good, honestly.'

'What a bastard. Unbelievable. I never liked him. But, you know, you seemed happy and it was good seeing you like that, so I didn't say too much. But, shit . . .'

'They'll catch him soon. The whole of Sussex Police is hunting for him. They'll find him, and then all this will be over, Raq. I feel confident about it.'

'I'm here for you, at the end of the phone, all night. Call anytime. Doesn't matter how late, okay?'

'Love you,' Red said.

'Love you too.'

105

And I love you, too, both of you, Bryce Laurent said silently, listening to the conversation in his van. *I love you to death. So sweet, Raquel, so sweet, Red. I'll deal with you later, Raquel, and your smug little husband, Paul. I know you never liked me. Well, you want to know a secret? I never liked you, either. But hey, what's a little hatred between friends? Eh, Raq?*

So you love Red? Did you ever love her the way I loved her and she loved me? Did she ever send you a text like this? He looked down at his iPhone, at the texts he had been scrolling through for the past twenty minutes, until he came to one of his favourites. One of the fantasies that he and Red used to text each other constantly. *This one, Raquel?*

So we hire out a cute cottage in the Cotswolds which we are driving to. You are driving. We've got some music on and you have your hand on me all the time you can. I pick up your arm and begin to kiss it; I suck your fingers and lick the back of your hand before placing it on my chest, smiling. You start to stroke my breasts and squeeze my nipples, which gets me so horny. I look over and down; I can see how hard you are and I put my hand on you. You are pulsing with excitement and are telling me that you are going to have to stop the car. You pull in at the next opportunity and lustfully take my face in your

hands and kiss me passionately while your hand slips down into my knickers and you press your fingers inside me, working me to a mind-blowing orgasm and making me crazily hungry for you.

Did you get a text like this from her, Raquel? I don't think so. But me, I did, daily. Sometimes several times a day.

Until her bitch mother intervened and ruined it all.

Perhaps I should send you the whole list of her texts and then you might begin to understand the feelings we once had for each other. The deepest love two human beings could have.

Then you might be able to understand why I'm just a tiny bit unhappy.

Actually, I'm lying. I'm really more than a tiny bit unhappy. As Red is going to find out very soon now.

He pulled out of his pocket a pay-as-you-go mobile phone he had bought some days ago and dialled 999. When the operator answered, asking which service he required, he said, 'Police, please. It's very urgent!'

106

Monday, 4 November

All thoughts of his honeymoon had long been gone from his mind. Shortly after 9.30 p.m., when he should have been in Venice with Cleo, Roy Grace sat in the windowless CCTV room on the third floor of John Street police station, with Glenn Branson, Cassian Pewe and Nev Kemp, the Divisional Commander of Brighton and Hove Police. In front of them was a bank of CCTV monitors, and each of them was focusing intently on one screen.

There were currently four hundred and three cameras covering the city of Brighton and Hove. Most of them were concentrated on the downtown areas, where the majority of the city's problems occurred, but the outlying areas were also covered, particularly the exit routes from the city.

A civilian controller, Jon Pumfrey, a neatly dressed and quietly efficient man, was operating the playbacks for them. He was fast-forwarding, on the four monitors in front of them, footage from cameras that were located in the Tongdean and Dyke Road Avenue areas from midday until early evening today. So far there had been no sighting of a van answering the description of the one they were looking for.

Pumfrey took a swig of coffee from a thermos, then unwrapped a sandwich, all the time eyeing the screens. The synchronized time clock on them reached 19.32.

'Can you freeze them, please,' Grace asked, suddenly.

Pumfrey leaned forward and tapped some keys on the large control panel in front of him.

Roy knew he could have delegated this task, but he wanted to see for himself this CCTV footage whilst the search for Bryce Laurent continued.

Camera Three was showing the top of Dyke Road Avenue. 'That's the obvious way Laurent would have gone to the Dyke from Tongdean Avenue,' Grace said.

'Yes,' Pumfrey concurred.

'The less obvious route would have been to detour via the A23 London Road,' Grace said. 'Let's see the footage from that.'

'I'll put it up on Camera Three, sir.'

Roy Grace's phone rang. It was an operator from the control room. 'Detective Superintendent, I've a man on the line who insists he speak to you. He says he gave a lift to someone answering Red Westwood's description earlier this evening.'

'Put him through.'

Moments later, he heard a voice that sounded a little the worse for wear from drink. 'Detective Superintendent Grace?'

'Yes, who am I speaking to?'

'I . . . my name's Marcus Cunningham, detective. Listen, I gave a lift to a lady – on my way back, near the Dyke. She – she stepped out in front of me, looking in a pretty bad state. You know?'

'I don't know. Tell me?'

'Just driving home from the Dyke . . . Golf Club. She flagged me down, needing a lift. She was covered – just covered – in mud and blood. She asked me to drive her home to the bottom of Westbourne Terrace. I took her there.

She said she'd be fine. Then I went home and saw the news. I decided to come back down here and see if she's all right.'

'Where are you now, sir?' Grace asked, sounding more patient than he felt.

'Well, the thing is, I popped back down here . . .'coz I felt a bit bad 'bout leaving her on the street. But no sign of her. So I thought I should phone the police. Make sure she's okay.'

'Are you near her residence, sir?'

'Where I dropped her off. Down Westbourne Terrace.'

'What time was that?'

'Just before eight o'clock. I would have stayed, you see, but my wife . . . had supper ready . . . promised her I'd be home by seven. But then we were watching Sky News Live, and there was her photograph. I thought you might want to know.'

'Very much,' Grace said. 'I'm very grateful to you. You say you are in Westbourne Terrace now?'

'Yes. I did escort her to the front door of her building, to make sure she got home safe.'

'And you're aware from the news that she had been abducted?'

'Yes, saw on the television. But she's safe now?'

'She's safe, sir, thank you. Out of interest, can you tell me what you can see from where you are?'

'Yes. A police car pulling out of a side street. Blue lights on. Just whizzing up Westbourne Terrace now. In a bit of a hurry. Oh, and it said on the news that you are looking for a small white Renault van?'

'Yes, we are.'

'If it's of interest, I just passed one on my way here. Parked near the top of Westbourne Terrace.'

107

Monday, 4 November

Red was awoken, confused, by a sharp ringing sound. The doorbell? Where the hell was she?

The ringing continued.

On the television she saw the youthful figure of the Secretary of State for Health, talking defensively about cuts in health benefits to visitors to the UK. She'd fallen asleep on the sofa, she realized. It was the phone ringing. She lunged forward and grabbed the receiver. 'Hello?' She felt leadenly tired.

'Red Westwood?'

She recognized the friendly male voice, but could not immediately place it.

'Yes, who is this?'

'Detective Inspector Glenn Branson. How are you doing?'

Her head felt muzzy, as if she wasn't quite together yet. She saw the empty bottle of wine on the coffee table, and the equally empty glass beside it, and the ashtray studded with butts. Shit, had she drunk the entire bottle? And smoked all of those? 'Yes, I'm okay, thanks,' she said.

'Listen, Red, I don't want to panic you, but we've just had a report that a van that might belong to Bryce Laurent has been seen in your road.'

She broke out into goosebumps. 'I – I thought you – you were protecting me all night?'

'Don't worry, we are. But for your protection, we'd like you to lock yourself in your safe room for a little while. Just until we've had a chance to investigate the van and search the area. Can you do that?'

Suddenly, she was thinking clearly again. 'Yes, I suppose so. Is it really necessary? The locks have been changed, and I'm pretty secure.'

'I'd feel happier if you did,' he said. 'It won't be for long. Just until we know you are safe. Hopefully we are close to arresting him.'

Despite the chill of her fear, she yawned. 'Okay, I'm going there now.'

'I have the number of the phone in there. I'll call you as soon as it's all right for you to come out, okay?'

'Okay.'

She hung up and padded out into the hallway, and again looked down towards the front door, checking that the safety chain was in position, as she had left it. Feeling more comfortable, she entered the safe room, switched on the light, then pushed the heavy door shut. She wound the locking wheel, one turn, two, then three, until she couldn't move it any more.

Then she noticed something lying on the floor – something that had not been there earlier.

It was a playing card, face up. The queen of hearts.

She felt suddenly enveloped by a cold, paralysing swirl of fear. She heard the click of the louvred door behind her, then her hands were jerked, violently, behind her back.

Then his voice, quiet and calm.

'Now we're all alone, Red.'

108

Roy Grace raced down the three flights of stairs, closely followed by Glenn Branson. They ran out of the rear door, across the car park in the pouring rain, and into the Ford. Branson sat behind the wheel, and both men belted themselves in, on the move, as Branson steered past a row of police vans and patrol cars.

They pulled out of the front entrance and Branson reached forward to switch on the blue lights and siren.

'Just the lights,' Grace said. 'We'll turn them off when we get near – don't want to alert him. Covert armed units are on their way and will be in place soon.'

The DI nodded, driving down the steep slope at too high a speed, Grace thought, unsure whether they were going to be able to stop at the bottom, at the junction with the A23, on the wet, slippery road. But Branson didn't bother stopping, he just pulled straight out, trusting too much to the blue lights, Grace thought, but did not say, his mind focused on the task ahead. His phone rang. It was Andy Kille.

'Sir, unmarked units are in place at the top and bottom of Westbourne Terrace – one on New Church Road and the other on the Kingsway, out of sight of anyone in Westbourne Terrace,' Kille continued. 'If they see a white Renault van, with index containing the digits and letters Four Seven Charlie Papa, they are to stop it immediately and disable it

454

however they can. Silver has authorized them to use any necessary tactics to stop the vehicle.'

'Understood,' Grace replied.

Branson drove at high speed past the Royal Pavilion, which was to their right, then negotiated the roundabout in front of Brighton Pier and west along the seafront, weaving through the traffic. Grace's phone rang. It was PC Spofford.

'Sir, I'm not getting any reply from the landline in Red Westwood's flat.'

'We're absolutely sure she's still in there?'

'Not one hundred per cent, no, sir. But if she'd gone out, she would have been seen by the officers outside.'

They were passing the Peace Statue on their left, which marked the border between the former separate towns of Brighton and Hove. They were about a minute and a half away from Red Westwood's flat, at the speed at which Glenn was driving, he calculated. 'Have you tried the safe room number?' he asked Spofford.

'Yes I have, sir. I've called it every couple of minutes.'

Grace knew the type of policeman Spofford was. Conscientious, hardworking, caring, decent.

'My number is programmed on that phone, on speed dial, sir. If she has a reason to enter the safe room and lock herself in, the plan is for her to call me instantly.'

Branson slowed for a red light at the bottom of Grand Avenue, then accelerated hard through it. He turned to Roy. 'She should be in the safe room. I told her to go there before we left.'

'Call that safe room number again, please, Rob.'

'Yes, sir. I'll have to use this phone, so I'll phone you back.'

Grace thought, *A white Renault van at the top of West-bourne Terrace.* His phone rang.

'Roy Grace?' he answered.

It was DS Exton, with information he had been able to obtain about Renault van models. 'Kangoo, Trafic and Master, sir.'

Grace made a mental note of them, then heard his phone beeping with an incoming call. Hastily thanking the DS, he switched over, hoping it would be Spofford.

It was. But his news wasn't good.

109

Monday, 4 November

'We have a whole hour, Red! It's not as long as I would have liked to spend with you, because we've so much catching up to do. But still, there is a lot we can do in an hour, hey? And who of us in life has the luxury of time, hey? You're shaking, Red, I can feel you. Nervous, aren't you? Not so confident as earlier, in my van, when you jammed your sharp little fingers in my eyes. You've blinded me in one eye – hopefully just temporarily. That's my dominant eye, too. Lucky for you. I'd never have missed if I'd aimed with that eye, I'd have got you with the first shot. But that's history now. Like you. Like me. Soon we're both going to be history.'

Red was silent. He was gripping her wrists so hard they were hurting. The mobile phone on the desk in front of her began ringing. A soft, persistent warble. Four rings; five; six.

It stopped.

'We could of course have much longer than an hour, Red, if I could trust you.'

She could feel the heat of his breath on her neck, and a minty smell as if he had just brushed his teeth. Her brain was racing, trying to think what to do. What options she had. What to say to him.

The phone began warbling again.

'I know all about this room,' he went on. 'Your *safe* room. Designed to give you one hour of protection. Impenetrable for one whole hour! That's how long it would take anyone to get the door open. Even your new best friend Detective Inspector Branson and his eager little boss, Detective Superintendent Grace, would take an hour to break in here, throwing everything they've got at the door. Well, I'll tell you something about your options. Would you like to know your options?'

'I'd like to know how you got in here.'

'I bet you would, Red. I'm an escapologist, I'm the best.'

'I know you're the best,' she said. Maybe pandering to his narcissism would lower his guard? she wondered. 'You're brilliant.'

'If an escapologist can get out of something, he can also get into it. Yes?'

'So how did you?'

'Easy, Red. Your neighbours in the flat above are away. I went in, and cut a panel out of the ceiling. So convenient – I cut away the one right above your toilet in this safe room. I knew no one was ever going to look up and spot the joins, you see; the plod aren't that smart. You think they could protect you? Well, you've just learned a big lesson. I know the police think they're protecting you by surrounding the flat, but they can't see into the one above you. I'm not worried about telling you that little secret, because you are not going to be around to share it with anyone. Ever.'

The phone stopped ringing.

'Know what I think, Red?'

'About what?'

'I think that phone's going to start ringing again in a minute.'

'You never told me you were psychic.'

Instantly she regretted saying that. His response was filled with vitriol.

'There are a lot of things you never knew about me, you stupid, stupid girl. So much. You never gave me a chance, did you? You and your mother and your moronic yes-man father.'

She stayed silent.

'It's not going to take your police friends long to figure out where you are – and that I'm in here with you, Red. That's why they're ringing this phone – because you're not answering the landline. They'll have seen my van out in the street and phoned you to tell you to come in here. If you don't answer and tell them you are fine, they'll start breaking in. One hour, it will take them. And you know what they will find when they do?'

Through her terror, Red tried to think what she could say to him. To play for time somehow.

'Did you ever see *Romeo and Juliet*, Red? Or maybe you acted in it in a school play, perhaps? It's a terrible tragedy of misunderstanding between lovers. You and I, we're like a modern-day version of that story, aren't we? Do you remember the last line, as they both lay dead? *For never was a story of more woe, than this of Juliet and her Romeo.*'

Still she said nothing.

'So very sad, Red. They died so needlessly. Just like you and I are going to die needlessly. Unless . . .'

'Unless what?' she replied, sensing the smallest window of hope.

110

'Twice?' Roy Grace said to PC Spofford, as Glenn Branson swung the car right into Westbourne Terrace, blue lights off now, and slowed as they saw the marked patrol car in the side street, with two officers in it.

'Yes, sir,' Spofford replied. 'I've rung it twice and there's no answer.'

'Try it one more time,' Grace said, then turned to Branson. 'Drive up the street, I want to see if the van's still here.'

As they neared the top, at the junction with the wide, residential street New Church Road, they both saw a white Renault van parked on the right. Branson halted alongside it. Grace pulled a torch out of the glove compartment and jumped out. He shone the torch on the front number plate, and instantly picked out the numbers and letters 47 CP.

In the beam of his torch he could see three mobile phones lying on the passenger seat. Then he shone it at the rear compartment, but it was curtained off. He went round to the back of the van, which had blacked-out windows, and saw the door handle had been removed, leaving a small hole. There was also a small gap between the doors. He was tempted to break into the vehicle, but knowing Laurent's history with incendiary devices he knew it was unsafe to do so, and in any case, it did not appear there was anyone inside.

Suddenly he became aware of a cyclist alongside him.

'Detective Superintendent Grace! I'm Adam Triming-ham from the *Argus*. I live nearby. Something going on?'

'Boy, you guys get everywhere!' Glenn Branson said to the elderly journalist, as Grace shone his torch into the rear, through the gap in the doors, and squinted through the handle hole.

'Shit!' Grace said. In the beam he could see what looked like a torture chamber. There was a mattress, with arm and leg restraints bolted to the floor on either side. A saw. A holdall lying on its side from which had spilled pliers and a small blowtorch. A transformer, connected to a car battery, with calipers on long cables. Several horror masks. And an angle grinder.

'Oh Jesus!' Glenn Branson said, peering over Grace's shoulder.

Then a flash of light startled both detectives. The journalist had taken a photograph.

111

'Unless . . .' Bryce said, with a taunt in his voice. 'Unless, Red . . .'

The phone began warbling again.

'Unless you answer it and tell them you're fine, that there's no problem, no problem at all. Then we'll have a little longer! How does that sound to you?'

The fourth ring began.

Then the fifth.

'Okay,' she said. 'Okay, I'll do it.'

'Smart girl.'

Red felt her arms released. She stepped forward, picked up the phone from its charger cradle and pressed the green answer button, thinking fast. She heard Rob Spofford's voice.

'Red? Are you okay?'

'I'm fine,' she said. 'Never better. Is there a problem?'

'You're not answering your phones. I was worried.'

Then she screamed, 'Help me!' spinning round as she did, and seeing Bryce for the first time. He was dressed all in black, with a hoodie. In one swift movement, catching him off-guard, she stabbed the phone as hard as she could into his good eye.

He staggered back. She twisted her wrist right and left, ground it in further, trying to gouge his eye out, hearing his

462

grunt of pain, then brought her knee up as hard as she could between his legs, slamming it up into his groin.

With a gasp, he staggered backwards and fell over. She leapt onto him, hammering at his head as hard as she could with the phone, feeling the plastic crack in her hand, but still continuing. Pounding him. Pounding. Again, again, again. Then suddenly, as if he had found some superhuman strength, she felt herself being levered up off the floor and propelled backwards. She fell painfully against the edge of the table. An instant later, leering with rage, Bryce was standing over her, red weals around his eyes, holding a boning knife in his hand. He was blinking wildly, his mouth filled with spittle. 'You bitch, fucking little bitch. I'm going to kill you. You stupid fucking bitch.'

She lashed out with her foot, and felt a searing pain as the blade cut into her ankle. She squirmed sideways, grabbing the chair, and held it up in front of her as he stabbed down hard, the blade thudding into the underside of the seat.

'Help me!' she screamed, hoping the phone line was still connected. Hoping someone was listening, that someone was coming to help her.

'An hour, bitch! A whole hour!'

She swung the chair, striking him on his hands, knocking the knife out of them, then swung it the other way, striking his knees. He took a pained step back.

The knife lay on the floor, midway between them. 'Scream all you like, bitch,' he said. 'They'll be listening and they're helpless. They're going to have to listen to me killing you – but only after I've tortured you first. I'm sure they'll enjoy your screams, but not as much as I will.'

He lunged for the knife.

112

Roy Grace's phone rang. 'Yes?'

'She's in there with him,' Spofford said. 'We have to get in there, fast, sir.'

'How do we get through the sodding door?' Grace asked. 'Is there no other way in?'

'There's a window, sir, accessible from the rear. But she's two floors up.'

'So how the hell did he get in?' Grace said. Then he thought for a moment. The man was cunning. He was a magician. A lot of magic tricks worked by distraction. The conjuror focused your attention away from the pocket he was going to pick, or the coin he was going to slip up his sleeve. Bryce Laurent would have seen the safe apartment as a challenge. He was remembering the words of the behavioural psychologist, Julius Proudfoot.

He has to win, there's no other possible option for him. He would kill Red and then himself, and see that as a grand act of defiance against you.

One hour.

Laurent had equipped his van to capture and torture Red. Was he aware it would take one hour for them to get into that safe room? If so, was he planning to use every minute of it? To torture her or torment her until the end? For better or worse, that at least gave them a bit of time.

'Call the fire brigade,' he instructed. 'I want a ladder that will reach that window – and tell them no sirens or lights.'

There was a fire station barely a mile away. They could be here within five minutes easily, he thought. He turned to Branson, jerking a finger at his car. 'Spin her round, get us back down to the front of her building.'

Less than a minute later, he jumped out, before it had come to a full halt, ran over to the police car and jerked open the passenger door, flashing his warrant card.

'Yes, sir?' DC Susi Holiday said.

'Come with me to the rear of the building, please.'

He looked at his watch. By his calculation, twenty minutes had elapsed. Every single second was critical. He wondered what the hell was happening inside that safe room right now.

And he just had to hope to hell that Red was still alive. He was thinking hard, trying to work out how Bryce had got in with police outside the door. And then, suddenly, he knew the answer.

113

Monday, 4 November

As Bryce's hand reached the boning knife, Red threw the chair at him in desperation. The seat struck him squarely on the head, sending him reeling. He crashed into the louvred door, splintering it, and fell backwards into the toilet, and lay there, motionless.

Red launched herself at the knife, seized it, clamped it under her armpit and began frantically turning the wheel. But she only managed half a turn when she heard a noise behind her. She spun round and saw Bryce lumbering, enraged, towards her, blinking furiously.

She gripped the knife in her right hand and held it up, threatening.

'You stupid girl. Think I'm afraid of you with that knife? Come on, stab me! Come on, stab me!'

She stood her ground, the blade held out in front of her, and she could see, despite her terror, that it was worrying him. She lunged forward, in a feint, and he stepped back, almost losing his balance. She lunged forward again, another feint, and now his back was against the busted toilet door. He grinned at her.

'Okay, Red, you have the knife. But you won't have it for long, I promise you. Have you thought about where you are going to stick it in me? Like, you've got one chance, right? Do you understand that? Straight through the heart. Anywhere else, you're just going to wound me. And if you do that, I'm going to get very angry. You don't like me being angry, do you? Remember all those times when we were together and you made me angry? I'm not a nice person when I'm angry.'

'I'm not a nice person with a knife, Bryce,' she said.

He pouted his lips, mocking. 'Oooh, fighting talk!' Suddenly he took a step towards her. A big step. She jumped back in fear.

'Brave girl!' he taunted, holding up his hands in a gesture to show he was unarmed. 'Perhaps you're not as brave as you think, Red. Are you? I'm not sure you have the guts to stick that in me, even to save your life. Shall we put it to the test?' He took another step towards her.

She was shaking so much, she could feel the weapon jiggling in her hand. Christ. Where were the police? Why couldn't she hear anyone trying to open the door right behind her?

Bryce glanced down at his watch. 'It's okay, we've plenty of time, Red. They haven't even started on the door yet. That's when the countdown's really going to begin. And what a sight they're going to find in here, eh? I'll tell you what I'm thinking would be nice.' He smiled, showing his immaculate white teeth. 'How about the police finally break down the door and they find your severed head on the table, staring at them, with me lying on my back on the floor, with the knife through my heart? How good would that be? Eh, Red? Eh? Eh, Red?'

He took another step towards her.

She held the knife out determinedly. 'Stay where you are!' she commanded. 'You killed Karl. Don't push me, Bryce. I'll kill you with pleasure.'

He took another step forward. Now he was just two feet from her.

Before she could react, he grabbed her arm holding the knife and wrenched it so hard she screamed in pain; the knife fell to the floor with a clatter.

'Ooops!' he said. 'Clumsy monkey!'

They stared at each other in a momentary face-off. Red felt her terror return. She had to get that knife back. Had to. Had to. Somehow.

Suddenly he lashed out with his foot and kicked the knife, sending it skittering across the floor to the wall. Out of reach.

'So who's the big, brave girl now?' he taunted. 'Where is Mummy now? Why isn't Mummy here to protect you? Mummy who hired the private dick to spy on her little girl's new beau? Eh? Perhaps your daddy's going to come through the door with that pea-shooter of an airgun he uses to kill bunnies in his garden, do you think? Eh?'

Red stared at him. She felt paralysed with fear.

''Coz I don't think he is, Red. Mummy and Daddy are nicely tucked up in their *safe* place, probably watching a movie.' He then mimicked her mother's voice.

'Well, the thing is, darling, we're not allowed to tell anyone. They've moved us from the hotel, but I can't tell you where in case – it sounds ridiculous, I know – but in case Bryce is listening. But you're okay? You are safe?'

She stared at him in shock, at the realization. He had heard their conversation. How many more had he heard?

'Are you safe, Red?'

She stared at him, then glanced at the knife. Thinking. Trying to find a way through to him. She was never going to beat him through physical strength, she knew. But maybe she could find a way to reason with him. To keep him talking for long enough. The police had to be on their way, surely? She was so terrified it was hard to think straight. She had to keep calm somehow. Had to.

Had to think clearly.

'It's sharp, Red. Sharp enough to cut off your head. Or mine. Shall we have a race to see who gets to it first?'

'Would that make you happy, cutting off my head, Bryce?'

'Very.'

'I wouldn't want to cut yours off,' she said.

'No?' He gave her a mocking grin.

'Really I wouldn't. It's the most beautiful head I've ever seen. Why would I want to destroy such a beautiful person?'

He stared at her and, for an instant, she wondered if she might have got through to something in his core.

'Really?'

'God, yes, really, Bryce.'

Then he shot a glance at his watch. 'Hmm, keep going, Red. Keep going.'

She shrugged. 'I really did love you.'

'I know you did. I really loved you, too. But didn't Oscar Wilde say in "The Ballad of Reading Gaol" that each man kills the thing he loves?'

'You're in a very literary mood tonight.'

'I am, yes. I've been doing a lot of reading lately.' He shot a glance towards the knife. 'Much nicer to die with beautiful words in our heads, don't you think, Red?'

She saw him lunge at the knife, and threw herself at it at the same time. They collided on the floor. He had it in his hand and raised it. She jabbed her fingers at his eyes, but he jerked back his head, then she bit hard into his wrist. He screamed in pain and she heard the clatter of the knife falling to the floor.

'You bitch!' he screamed.

Somewhere behind him, she heard a sound, like a door slamming, as they both grappled for the knife. She touched it, fleetingly, then he had it in his hand again, and an instant later he was kneeling over her, pinning her to the floor, the knife raised above her.

There was a crazed gleam in his eyes. 'Who's Daddy's girl now?' he said. 'Which eye would you like me to cut out first, Red? Your right or your left? Eh?'

She tried to move but he once again seemed to be fuelled by some superhuman strength. 'Please, Bryce, let's talk some more.'

'I don't think so.'

She saw the knife hurtling down towards her. Then, suddenly, it stopped in mid-air and flew out of his hand. She heard a crackling sound, like electrical static.

He began to shake violently, as if he were having an epileptic fit, twisting and turning in a macabre dance. An instant later he was on the floor, jerking, a trail of twined coiled wires running from his back and through into the toilet.

A voice shouted urgently, 'Red, are you okay?'

She switched from the twitching body to the face of Detective Superintendent Roy Grace, clambering down from the loft hatch above the toilet before standing next to a man in blue body armour, a helmet and visor, who was holding what looked like a pistol with wires running from it. Grace hurried over to her, casting a quick look at the twitching figure of Bryce. 'You okay?'

She stared into Grace's cool blue eyes. Her heart was pounding, her head throbbing. For a moment she found it hard to speak. 'Yes, yes, thank you. I'm okay.'

More people were coming down through the hatch now, also wearing helmets and visors.

'You're safe, Red,' Grace said gently. 'It's all over.'

They were the sweetest-sounding words she had ever heard.

114

Roy Grace knelt by his open suitcase, carefully folding a white shirt and laying it in. Cleo put a vodka martini down on the bedside table. 'Thought you might like a little celebratory drink!'

'Thank you.' He took a sip of the ice-cold liquid; it was so strong it almost burned going down. 'Mmm, you're getting really rather good at these.'

'It's been my father's favourite drink for years, remember?'

'Yes, his are killer ones.'

'Meaning this isn't strong enough?'

He grinned. 'It's plenty strong enough. A few more sips of this and I've no idea what I'll be packing.'

'There's only one thing I really need you to bring.' She put her arms around his neck and nuzzled his ear. 'And the way I'm feeling about you right now, he's not going to fit into your suitcase.' She nuzzled his ear again.

'You're wicked and I love you.'

'You're a horny beast and I love you, Detective Superintendent Grace.' She lifted the glass off the table, took a sip herself, pressed her lips against his, and let the vodka martini slowly slip into his mouth.

'Mmmmnn!' he said.

'So we really are off tomorrow, darling?'

'Only a week later than scheduled.' He reached up and held her hand, brought it to his lips and kissed each of the fingers. 'I love you so much.'

'I love you too.'

He smelled her scent and the warmth of her breath, and pulled her arm tighter around him.

'How's the poor woman, Red Westwood, doing?' she asked.

'She's okay, she's a plucky lady. I popped into her office yesterday to see how she's getting on and to ask her a couple of things, and she seemed remarkably perky, considering. But she has one big worry, which is Laurent being released.'

'Surely he'll be kept in custody?'

'For now, yes. But he might not be in jail for ever. If he gets life, he still might get out one day, and Red knows that.'

'God, poor woman. To have that hanging over you. And the constant fear of him being released – or worse, escaping.'

'I don't imagine she's going to be joining another dating agency any time soon.'

'I don't blame her!'

There was a massive explosion outside their window. Both of them jumped.

'Shit, what the hell was—?' Roy said. Downstairs they heard a yelp from Humphrey.

Then he realized. It had been the fifth of November, Bonfire Night, a few days ago. It was probably people still letting off fireworks.

Noah began screaming. Cleo leapt to her feet and hurried through into the baby's room, almost tripping over Humphrey, who came hurtling up the stairs and into their room like a hairy black rocket, whining and whimpering, his tail down. He was sopping wet from recently being out on the terrace in the pouring rain, where he had been furiously barking at a neighbour's cat on the wall.

'It's okay, Humphrey! It's okay!'

There was another massive explosion, and a shower of brilliant white lights outside the window. With a yelp, Humphrey shot past Roy Grace and jumped straight into the open suitcase, turning himself round and round on top of his owner's white shirt.

'Hey! Hey! Get off, you idiot dog!'

The dog gave him a reproachful look, as if to say, *You're leaving me, and with these explosions?*

Noah's screams increased in volume.

'That's my best damned shirt!'

Cleo came back into the room, cradling Noah in her arms in his blue and white striped sleepsuit. He was bawling his eyes out.

'Look at the sodding dog!' Grace said. 'Look what he's done to my shirt!'

Cleo grinned. 'Welcome to domestic bliss, my darling. Still sure you want to go away?'

For his answer, Grace picked up the glass and downed the rest of his drink in one gulp.

115

Monday, 11 November

Alan Setterington, one of the Governors of Lewes Prison, stepped out of the shower in the changing area, towelled himself dry, then dressed in his dark grey suit, white shirt, and one of the selection of bright ties he liked to wear. It was 7 a.m. and he was invigorated after his ninety-minute cycle ride through mostly back roads of Sussex from his home to here, his daily commute.

He was a tall man in his forties, with boyish good looks and the lean figure of an athlete, who had spent his entire career in Her Majesty's Prison Service, rising at a relatively early age to his current position. In his previous roles he had served at several of the UK's maximum security prisons, and had had the dubious pleasure of meeting some of the most notorious criminals of his generation.

Setterington still retained enthusiasm for his job, not letting any of his residents bother him too much, and rarely losing sleep over any of them. But today he was a tad tired. A few days ago a character, Bryce Laurent, had been remanded in custody on murder and arson charges. There was a coldness in Laurent's eyes that he had seen on just a few occasions in life. A darkness, as if he had looked into some unfathomable depth of inhumanity.

Visitors always found prisons uncomfortable places, and Lewes, built in Victorian times, was as formidable as they came. Grey cement floors, stark, bare walls, and the smell all prisons had, which he had never fully been able to describe – a mixture of disinfectant, institutional soap, stale clothes, sweat and despair.

Information was the prison currency. Everywhere you walked you would see prisoners, in their crimson tunics, loitering, listening. Seeing what information they could eavesdrop. Which was why no sensible prison officer ever said where he or she lived, or what car they drove, or where they were going on holiday. You never knew who might one day be out for revenge against you.

Setterington went into his office and switched on the kettle to make himself a cappuccino, then sat at his desk and unwrapped the egg and tomato sandwich and carrot cake his wife, Lisa, had made him. The office was stark and functional, with a window that looked down, through the rain, onto the sodden exercise yard. In addition to enabling him to keep an eye on the prisoners, he could also see from here the occasional package of contraband that was lobbed over the wall from outside – containing usually either drugs or mobile phones.

Guarding seven hundred and twenty prisoners, many of them highly cunning, was not an easy task. Setterington did not like it, but it was a fact of life he had to live with: that stuff always had been smuggled into prisons and always would be. Thrown over the walls, exchanged in contact between loved ones during visits, sometimes mouth to mouth. If a prisoner wanted something brought in from outside badly enough, he could usually get it.

The governor logged on to his computer and began running through the mountain of overnight emails, noting concerns that officers had about particular prisoners, security risks and details about impending construction work to modernize the remand wing, which would be commencing in a few weeks. He was interrupted by a knock on the door.

'Come in!' he called out.

One of his officers entered, a burly man called Jack Willis, keys dangling from a chain on his belt. 'Morning, guv,' he said. 'Sorry to bother you so early, but I've got a prisoner on the remand wing who's asking to speak to you – says it's very urgent.'

'Did he tell you what it's about?'

'Wouldn't say, sir. He's a bit nervous.'

Prisoners giving information about fellow prisoners could be highly valuable. But at the same time, all of them were worried about being seen as snitches. Punishments meted out to those suspected by their fellow prisoners were brutal. There was an elaborate procedure in place, where they would be seen in an interview room, rather than be observed going to the staff office. Any contact between a prisoner and a senior staff member was noted by other prisoners, and queried rigorously.

'Okay, bring him along to an interview room.'

Ten minutes later, Setterington sat behind a small table, in a room well away from the prying eyes of any other prisoners. The officer showed in a gangly, wiry man, with a shaven head and stooped posture, who Setterington had known for many years.

Darren Spicer was in his early forties, and looked two decades older, thanks to most of his life being spent in prison, and he smelt of cigarette smoke. A career high-end house burglar, he was a true recidivist – what they termed here as a revolving door prisoner. He had a string of previous convictions for drug dealing and burglary, and regularly ensured he got arrested around this time of year so that he could spend Christmas in prison.

Although he never became emotionally attached to any of his prisoners, Setterington had time for this man. For all his sins, life had dealt Spicer a shitty hand, and he was a model prisoner. Brought up in a single-parent family of third-generation dole scroungers and petty villains, he'd never had a role model in his life. Burgling was all he knew, and in all likelihood, all he ever would. Yet he had, in his own distorted way, moral principles. And he was a keen reader, which was why he never seemed to mind being incarcerated. He was currently on remand after being caught breaking into Brighton's Royal Pavilion, trying to steal one of its most valuable paintings.

Setterington gestured for him to sit.

Spicer gave him a sheepish grin. 'Nice to see you again, sir.'

'It would be nicer not to see you here, Darren. But it doesn't seem that's ever going to happen, does it?'

He hunched his shoulders, lowering his head and peering up at Setterington in an almost childlike manner. 'Yeah, well. You know, sir, I have my dream. To be married again, have kids, live in a nice house, have a nice car, but it's not going to happen, is it?'

'You've told me that before. So why not?'

'I got over one hundred and seventy previous. Who's going to give me a chance?'

'Didn't you get a nice lump of money about a year ago, Darren? Fifty thousand quid reward through Crimestoppers. Couldn't that have set you up?'

Spicer shrugged, then sniffed and pointed to his nose. 'That's where most of it went, to tell you the truth. I prefer being inside – I like it in here.'

The Governor nodded. 'I know, you've told me your reasons before. You like the food, you've got everything paid for, and most of your friends are here, right?'

'Yeah. And I like the Christmas dinner especially.'

'Fifty grand could have bought you a lot of Christmas dinners.'

'Yeah. Yeah, you're right.' He nodded and for an instant the governor detected a wistful look in the man's eyes.

'So, you have something to tell me that's urgent?'

Spicer looked around furtively, and up towards the ceiling, as if worried there were other people in the room. Then he leaned forward, and lowered his voice to a whisper. 'It's about a bloke I've been chatting with on the remand wing, see.'

'Who's that?'

'His name's Bryce Laurent.'

Suddenly, Spicer had Setterington's full attention. 'Okay, what about him?'

'Well, the thing is . . . I don't want to be a snitch, right?'

'The conversation we're having is private, Darren. There are no microphones or cameras in here. You can talk freely.'

'Yeah, well, the thing is, he's trying to hire a hitman.'

'A hitman? To do what?'

'To kill his ex. Get revenge. Her name's Red. Red Westwood, I think he said. Thing is, he's got a stash, a very big stash.'

'How much?'

'Over half a million quid. In folding.'

'Cash?'

'Yeah, cash. And he's offering fifty grand for the hit.'

'And has he found any hitmen yet?'

'Well, there's quite a few people in here interested, he told me. I ain't surprised. That's big money, that is.'

'So why haven't you had a go for it yourself?'

Spicer grinned. 'I have. I told him I knew just the bloke. But that I wanted to know the dough was real first.'

'Has he told you where?'

'He is willing to tell me where some of it is. The fifty's spread over two different bank security boxes. He'll pay half now to show he's real. The balance on completion.'

'And has he told you where these boxes are, Darren?'

'No, but he will tell me where the first one is, if I can confirm I have someone.'

'And I suppose you want a cut if you tell the police, right?'

'Yeah. That's it. A cut.' He shrugged. 'Someone's going to do it for that money, Mr Setterington, sir. That's a lot of money, that is.'

116

Roy Grace had one thing to do this Monday morning, before setting off on honeymoon. Although they were due to leave for the airport in just over three hours, he left his casual clothes, which he had laid out the night before on the chair in the bedroom, put on a shirt and tie and donned a work suit. Then he gulped down a quick bowl of porridge and a mug of tea, and kissed Cleo, who was breastfeeding Noah, on the cheek, and promised he would be back in plenty of time. Then he kissed his son on the forehead.

'When are your parents arriving?' he asked.

'They said they'd be here by nine to collect Noah.'

'You sure you're not going to miss him?' He stifled a yawn, and glanced at his watch. 7.20 a.m. He needed to leave now to make the 8 a.m. meeting in good time. And he dared not be late.

She gave him a tired smile. 'After he managed to keep us awake most of the night? Yes, of course I will. But I'm so much looking forward to spending time with you, I'll get over it!'

He grinned and kissed Noah again. 'Bye, my noisy little prince,' he said to him. 'Daddy's going to miss you, too. But you're going to be spoiled rotten, I'm not sure you'll miss us at all!' He grabbed his keys and hurried out to his car.

*

Twenty-five minutes later he drove through the security barrier of Malling House, the police HQ on the outskirts of Lewes, parked in the visitors' car park, then hurried over to the Queen Anne building which housed the top brass. As ever when entering this building, he was taken straight back to memories of being at school and being summoned to the headmaster's study.

He was taken straight up to Tom Martinson's office, by his assistant, and shown in. The Chief Constable was standing there, in dark uniform trousers, a white short-sleeve shirt with epaulettes featuring the crown and cross-tipped staves, and black tie, alongside ACC Cassian Pewe in his full uniform.

Both men shook hands with him. 'Roy,' Martinson said. 'It's good of you to make the time to come and see us – I'm aware you're in a hurry. What time is your plane?'

'Two o'clock from Gatwick, sir,' he said. He smiled, trying not to show his nerves. He had been wondering what this meeting was all about ever since getting the call from the Chief himself last night. He had a pretty good idea. Two officers were dead. Both working on an operation he was involved in.

Someone was going to have to be held to account.

Himself?

'This won't take long, Roy,' Martinson said, and glanced at Cassian Pewe, who nodded his confirmation. 'Some tea or coffee?'

'Thank you, sir, I'd love a coffee.'

Martinson picked up the phone on his vast, spotless desk, and requested three coffees, then directed Grace to one of the two sofas. The Chief and the ACC sat on the other. Grace studied their body language, but could read no sinister message in the relaxed way they sat.

Cassian Pewe brought his hands together on his lap. 'Roy, the Chief and I wanted to see you before you went off, because we know you must be feeling pretty bad about the loss of Sergeant Moy. We're aware you knew her personally and that you had a long professional history together. We're sure you are also feeling bad about the loss of Sergeant Morrison on the helicopter, as we all are. This has been a really difficult week for everyone in Sussex Police – and one hell of a start to my role here. There are going to be a lot of questions asked, but we felt it was important to keep a perspective.' He fell silent.

Grace waited for him to continue, wondering when the sting in his tail was going to strike.

'You've had a damned tough job with this case, dealing with a monster, and the Chief and I want to congratulate you on your handling of it. Your quick thinking undoubtedly saved the life of Ms Westwood and resulted in a highly dangerous man being brought into custody. We don't want you to blame yourself for what happened. We are both right behind you.' Pewe looked at Martinson.

'I'd like to echo that, Roy,' the Chief Constable said. 'Sergeant Moy died in an act of supreme bravery, which she undertook of her own accord, whilst off-duty, saving the life of a child, and you can in no way be blamed for her death. I also do not believe that you should feel responsible for the downing of NPAS 15 and the loss of life of the personnel on board. That's really what we wanted to say to you. You aborted your honeymoon to take over command of a situation that had become life-threatening to Ms Westwood, and I commend you for that. I want you now to go and enjoy your delayed honeymoon with a clear conscience.'

Grace stared back at him, amazed, and very relieved. 'Thank you, sir,' he said. Then he turned to Cassian Pewe.

Was he a changed man? He doubted it. Playing Mr Nice Guy in front of the Chief to show him that Roy had nothing to worry about, that their past antagonistic history was just that now, history? More likely. 'I'm very grateful for your support, sir.'

Pewe smiled at him with what seemed, despite his reptilian smile, genuine warmth. 'Absolutely, Roy.'

'What's going to happen regarding the funerals?'

'It will be a while before their bodies are released by the Coroner,' Tom Martinson said. 'Neither will take place until well after you are back. So we want you to go with a clear conscience that you did your duty, and relax and enjoy. Focus on cherishing your very beautiful and delightful bride.'

The assistant came in with a tray laden with their coffee and a plate of biscuits.

'I'll try,' Grace said. 'I can assure you of that.'

'I think you know that Detective Chief Superintendent Skerritt is planning to retire next year, Roy,' Martinson said.

'Yes, sir, I had heard.'

'Well, I hope you'll apply for his job. I'd like to see you in that role.' He looked at Cassian Pewe.

'I endorse that, Roy.'

Grace stared at both men in turn. With Martinson he felt it was genuine. With Cassian Pewe, he wondered whether he might be being handed a poisoned chalice. He was already doing some of this role, but was still able to be hands-on with cases when he wanted to be. Stepping into Skerritt's shoes would make that harder – particularly given all the politics now involved since the Surrey and Sussex Major Crime Teams were merged. But it was good to be asked.

'I'll certainly think about it,' he said. 'Thank you. I'm very grateful for your support. I think the one thing that is going to worry me, above all else, is the knowledge that whatever sentence Bryce Laurent receives, he might not be kept behind bars for ever. The nightmare is never going to really end for Red Westwood, is it? She's always going to have to live with the fear that he might escape one day, or get released.'

'Roy, you've given her a Warning Notice,' Tom Martinson said. 'You've offered for the police to help her change identity and move to another part of the country. She's chosen not to take that advice. All of us have to make decisions in life, based on weighing up all the information we have. You've done all any police officer could to protect her. If, God forbid, Laurent is ever released, then we – and she – will have to make decisions based on what we know at that time. But for now, it's job done. Okay?'

Twenty minutes later, despite all the emotions running through his mind from the past few days, Roy Grace walked back to his car with a spring in his step and a smile in his heart.

117

Red sipped her second cup of coffee of the morning and stared at the list of nine appointments she had for viewings today. Last week already seemed a long time ago.

And the best news, to start this new week, was that the husband of the couple she had shown around the house in Portland Avenue last week, who had originally told her they had seen somewhere they liked more, had just phoned to say that they had changed their minds again, and would now like to proceed to purchase the property.

She had the forms in front of her, and they were coming in to sign this afternoon. And they were cash buyers! All being well, within a couple of days the Mishon Mackay FOR SALE board outside the house would have a banner across it announcing, SALE AGREED.

Her first sale! Her new career was on its way.

Despite the nightmare of her ordeal at Tongdean Lodge, she was really enjoying her job, and felt she had the right qualities for it.

A new email pinged up on her screen, with a JPEG attachment. She did not recognize the sender's name, but she opened the email and read it.

'I have a very special attachment for a very special lady!' it said.

She double clicked on the attachment, and saw a cartoon.

And froze.

118

In the furnished consulting room in Schwabing, close to Munich's Isar river, the attractive woman in her late thirties, with her black hair cropped short in a boyish fringe, lay prostrate on the psychiatrist's couch.

'Tell me, how did you feel in the church, Sandy?' the psychiatrist, Dr Eberstark, asked.

She was silent for some moments, then she said, 'I felt like an alien. I realized I didn't know his world any more. And I kept thinking what a mistake I'd made. I watched him turn and gaze at his bride as she walked down the aisle on the arm of someone – I guess her father. And it made me think so much of the time, almost twenty years or so ago, when I walked down the aisle on the arm of my father, and he'd turned and smiled at me – and I'd never felt so happy or proud in all my life.' She paused and let out a sob. 'Such a big bloody mistake. When I realized that, I wanted him back so much, I wanted to be there, I wanted to be that woman.'

'Yet you left him.'

'Yes. I left him. I guess I didn't know then what I know now. I wanted him back so badly. Really, at that moment when the priest guy – the vicar – asked if anyone knew any reason why they should not be joined together in Holy matrimony, I nearly shouted out that I did. Really,

488

I so nearly did. That's what I had gone there intending to do.'
She shrugged.

The psychiatrist waited silently.

'Looking at him, I realized what a mistake I'd made. I wanted him back. I still do. I feel I've screwed up my life. Every day I wake up in the morning and I lie to my son. He asks me about his father and I don't tell him the truth. I'm scared I'm going to screw him up. What the hell should I do?'

'What do you think you should do?'

'Some days I think I should kill myself.'

'Do you think about the consequence of that for Bruno?'

'Bruno. Yes, I think sometimes that I should mail Roy a letter, telling him the truth, and telling him that by the time he gets it, I will be dead. He always wanted to have children. He could come here and take his son back to England.'

She continued to talk for a few minutes before Dr Eberstark glanced at the clock on the wall.

'We'll have to leave it there,' he said. 'I'll see you on Thursday. Is that okay with you?'

After she closed the front door of Dr Eberstark's building, Sandy walked out onto the pavement alongside the four lanes of heavy traffic on Widenmayerstrasse, and stopped, staring at the wide grass bank of the Isar river across the busy street, collecting her thoughts.

Reflecting on her session. How many sessions had she had? Where were they getting her? Sometimes she left the psychiatrist's office feeling strong, but other times, like now, she left feeling more confused than ever.

As the traffic thundered past in front of her, she wondered if now really was the time, finally, to tell Roy about Bruno. Their son.

That would sure as hell throw a spanner into his newly-wed bliss.

How would his blonde bimbo take the news?

How would he take it?

She had an idea; he was a kind man at heart. A responsible person. He would take responsibility, he would have no option. But how much did he care for the bimbo, really? He'd kept telling her, during their life together, that he could not live without her. Well, he seemed to be doing pretty well.

She decided a walk along the bank of the Isar, towards the Englischergarten, would do her some good, clear her head.

Her sodding confused head.

For an instant she was back in Brighton, in England. Where the traffic drove on the opposite side of the road. She looked to the right, and the road was clear. She stepped out. Heard the blare of a horn. The scream of tyres on dry tarmac.

Then the cream Mercedes taxi hit her broadside.

119

It felt like another Groundhog Day, as Roy Grace stood in his socks and placed his shoes in one of the Gatwick Airport security trays, along with his jacket, mobile phone, laptop, watch and belt. He had done exactly the same thing a week ago, to the hour, if not almost to the minute.

He followed Cleo through the metal detector, and to his relief, again neither of them pinged it. As he pulled his shoes back on, his excitement was growing. By hanging onto both of their tickets again, this time around, he'd managed to keep from her that they were flying in luxury.

If anything, he was even more excited than a week ago. His excitement fuelled by his determination that this time, nothing was going to stop them.

Then his phone rang.

He looked at Cleo and she grinned.

He picked it up out of the grey tray and stared at the display. The *number withheld* message meant almost certainly that it was work.

'I'm not answering it!'

'You will!' she said, with a grin, and kissed him.

'No, I won't!' He killed the call.

Moments later the phone rang again. He hesitated. It could be any number of people calling him for any number of reasons. But he didn't care, he really did not care this time.

Whatever the problem – if there was a problem – for the next few days it was not his.

'Roy Grace,' he answered.

'See!' Cleo said gleefully.

He grinned and blew a silent kiss at her.

It was Glenn Branson. 'Where are you, old timer? On a gondola on the Rialto?'

'Very funny. You want me to buy you a Cornetto?'

'Just-ah-one!'

'Listen, I'm just finishing going through security at Gatwick. Can I call you back?'

'Yeah, but I don't want to disturb your honeymoon.'

'You just have. What's up?'

'Well, here's the thing. Bryce Laurent's on remand in Lewes Prison on murder charges, right? Which means no bail, so he'll be there until the end of his trial. But he's trying to get at her. I had a call from her a little while ago, very upset. She's had a cartoon emailed to her – by, it would seem, Laurent.'

'I thought prisoners didn't have access to email in Lewes Prison, mate?' He signalled an apology to Cleo. 'What was the cartoon?'

'It depicted her in a cross hair gun-sight, wearing an eye-patch, surrounded by flames and swirling wind. It was captioned, *To the Queen of the Slipstream. Enjoy your last days on earth.*'

'Van Morrison,' Grace said.

'Van Morrison?'

'The song.'

'Enjoy your last days on earth?' Branson queried

'No! Queen of the Slipstream! I thought you knew your music.'

'Yeah, I do – but not your trashy white man stuff.'

'It played at the wedding – did you have your thumbs in your ear or something?' Grinning, Grace removed his belt from the tray and, holding the phone to his ear with his shoulder, began threading it back through the loops on his trousers. 'Okay, so tell me more about the cartoon.'

'I spoke to the Deputy Governor at Lewes, Alan Setterington. He says it's possible it could have been sent from within the prison, despite the ban on internet connections, or maybe Laurent had someone outside do it. But I thought you should know something of concern: Setterington told me a prisoner informed him this morning that Laurent's trying to hire a hitman to kill Red. He's put out word that he's offering around fifty grand cash for a result.'

'Has he found a taker?'

'Doesn't sound like it yet. The man Laurent thinks might do it told Setterington earlier today.'

'So what are your thoughts?'

'If we could find that fifty grand stash, then we'll have spiked Laurent's guns.'

'My thoughts exactly,' said Grace. 'We're on the same page. Setterington had better get his colleagues eavesdropping on Laurent. We need to listen to every conversation he has. Correction, *you* need to listen.'

'You don't sound as worried as you might, boss,' Glenn Branson said.

'No, I'm not, because you're in charge and I've got every faith in you! Have a good week. I'll see you next Monday morning.'

'Yeah, but . . . hang on, old timer—'

Roy Grace hung up. Then he switched his phone off altogether. He'd worked his butt off to keep the city of Brighton and Hove – and the whole of Sussex – safe for the past twenty years. It would now have to cope for one week without him.

'I've never, ever, seen you do that before,' Cleo said, with a massive smile.

'Yep, well, I've never been on honeymoon with you before.' He slipped his arm around her. 'And I don't intend wasting another second of it.'

She looked at him with a huge, warm grin. 'Now, why don't I believe that? You without your phone on?' She shook her head. 'It's not going to happen!'

'It is!'

'You're not going to pick up your messages for the whole time?'

'Well . . . maybe I'll check them . . . just occasionally. In case . . .'

'See, you can't, can you? And I wouldn't want you to. I don't want to change you, Roy, I love you as you are.' She put her arms around his neck and kissed him.

120

Tuesday, 12 November

The sodding towel he had put up over the window, to block out the glare from the security lights outside, had fallen down, and the tiny cell was filled with a weak yellow glow. How the fuck could anyone sleep on this hard, absurdly narrow bed, and with this bloody light? Bryce Laurent thought.

He rolled over for the umpteenth time, feeling the coarse blanket against his face and shivering with cold. His left eye was bandaged and still hurt like hell from where that bitch had dug her nails in. The prison doctor was arranging for him to see a specialist because he was worried about the extent of damage, expressing concerns that it might be permanent and irreversible. Blind in one eye.

He was so going to get even with Red for that.

Somewhere in the block he heard another prisoner shouting out in his sleep. Having a damned nightmare. This place was a nightmare. So much swirled through his head, an angry mist of thoughts. And plans. Oh yes, he had plans. New plans forming all the time. He was working on one now. It was a beautiful one. Masterly! It would ensure Red never, ever, felt safe again. For the rest of her life.

Although, if all went well, that was going to be a very short time.

Suddenly, he noticed the sound of trickling water. As if

someone had left a tap running. Who? Where? In the next-door cell? How long had it been going on? Had he left the tap running in here, or was it the cistern of his toilet?

He closed his eyes to shut it out, but it seemed to be getting worse, louder, running faster. A distinct gurgling sound now, almost echoing in the silence of the night.

Then he smelled petrol.

He frowned.

Petrol?

Who had petrol in here? Were they using it in a heater?

The smell was getting stronger.

He now heard a sound like lapping water running up a beach.

And suddenly, in anxiety, he swung his legs off his bunk and onto the floor.

They splashed into something wet.

He took a tentative step forward. *Shit*. The floor was wet. With petrol. *Shit. Oh Shit.*

The gurgling sound continued. More was pouring in every second.

What the hell was going on?

Outside prisoner 076569's cell door, another prisoner of Lewes's remand wing continued to squeeze the reservoir bag of the water pouch, which was designed for cyclists, letting all three pints of petrol pour, via the drinking tube, through the cell inundation point in Bryce Laurent's cell door.

'Hey!' Laurent said, his voice panicky. 'Hey, what's going on?'

'It's nearly lighting up time!' his antagonist replied, in a soft Irish lilt. Then he switched on a torch and shone the beam at his own face, which was close to the grille. 'Boo!'

He laughed as Laurent recoiled in shock. 'Who the hell are you?' Laurent asked, fumbling for the light switch in his cell but momentarily unable to find it.

'A friend of a friend who doesn't like you. We're like-minded, him and I. We don't like men who hurt women. You've got a pretty long track record of hurting women, I'd say. You like playing with fire, don't you?'

'Warder!' Laurent shouted, scared now. Then, remembering they didn't like being called that, he shouted, in a panic-stricken voice, 'Officer! Officer!'

'There's only one prison officer on duty on this floor,' the Irishman said. 'He doesn't like you very much either. You see, you murdered his cousin and set fire to his body just a couple of weeks back. Remember him? Up at the golf course? Dr Karl Murphy?'

'Officer!' Laurent shouted.

'Relax, Bryce, he's not interested! He'll come when I call him, to lock me back in my cell. Then he'll open yours and throw in this water pouch. Whatever remains of it for the forensics boys, everyone will think, with all you've been saying about killing yourself, that you smuggled it in yourself. I mean, I would! Hey, I *do*!'

'Officer!' Laurent screamed in terror. 'Officer, officer, officer!'

The Irishman suddenly stuck a cigarette in his mouth, and flicked the wheel of a plastic lighter, then lit the cigarette from the flame.

Laurent jumped back into the darkness of his cell at the sight of it. The Irishman dragged on his cigarette again.

'Put that out! For God's sake, put it out!'

'Relax! Tut, tut, I'm surprised at an experienced pyromaniac like you, Bryce, all surrounded by petrol, being scared of a cigarette. Don't you know your basics, Bryce?

Everyone who's ever tried knows that a cigarette doesn't burn hot enough to ignite petrol.' He took another drag.

'But, you shitty little woman-abuser,' he went on, 'a lighted cigarette with a tiny strip of magnesium in the middle will – just as soon as the flame hits the magnesium. Which in this case will be in about five seconds.'

Then he pushed the half-smoked cigarette through the grille.

ACKNOWLEDGEMENTS

This novel came after I heard about an interesting investigation led by Chief Superintendent Nev Kemp, now Divisional Commander of Brighton and Hove. I contacted Nev and he told me about the case which inspired this story. I owe an incalculable debt to him for his help in setting me off on the journey that was to become *Want You Dead*.

Former Detective Chief Superintendent Dave Gaylor has, as ever, given me the most enormous help, not just in so many areas of research for this novel, but in the plotting and editorial processes. I also need to single out Chief Inspector Jason Tingley, who gave me many introductions to those people and organizations involved in the White Ribbon campaign in Sussex against domestic abuse.

There are so many other officers and support staff of Sussex Police, who give me such constant and enthusiastic help and advice, to whom I am immensely grateful. Starting with the very recently retired Chief Constable, Martin Richards, QPM. The Police and Crime Commissioner, Katy Bourne. Former Chief Superintendent Graham Bartlett. Detective Superintendent Paul Furnell. Detective Chief Inspector Nick May. Inspector Andy Kille. Inspector Steve Grace. Sgt Jonathan Hartley. PC Andrew Dunkling. Sgt Phil Taylor and Ray Packham of the High Tech Crime Unit. PC Tony Omotoso. Colin Voice.

I owe huge thanks to Alan Setterington, former Deputy Governor of Lewes Prison, pyrotechnic expert Mike Sansom, and to many people in the Sussex Fire and Rescue Services: Matt Wainwright, who not only opened the doors to Worthing fire station for me, but who also taught me so much about close magic. Very especially Tony McCord, Borough Commander of East Sussex Fire and Rescue Service, and his wife Jan McCord. Both have been immeasurably helpful to me. Tony Gurr, Chief Fire Investigator. Mark Hobbs. Julie Gilbert-King. Sharon Milner. Roy Barraclough, Group Station Manager, Worthing fire station. Watch Commander Darren Wickens.

And to many of those involved in the struggle against domestic abuse. Lindsay Jordan, team manager of the Southdown Housing Association. Sarah Findlay, Head of Housing Strategy, Lewes District Council, who gave me the information on the Sanctuary Scheme. Tracy O'Rourke Burr. Suzy Ridgwell. Penny Butler. Fin Castle. Kate Dale, Naomi Bos and Carys Jenkins of Rise. Tricia Bernal, who was prepared to so openly and candidly talk to me about the tragic death of her daughter, Clare, at the hands of her stalker ex-boyfriend. Former Chief Magistrate of Brighton and Hove, Juliet Smith. Psychologist Zoe Lodrick, who incredibly generously gave me many hours of her time helping me on key chapters.

Pathologists Mark Howard, Ben Swift and Nigel Kirkham. Forensic Podiatrist Haydn Kelly. Julie Frith of Mishon Mackay. Graham Rand of Rand & Co. Nick Fitzherbert. Nick Bonner.

As ever, my boundless gratitude to tireless Chris Webb of MacService for coaxing my Mac back to life on the many occasions it appeared to have died during the writing of this book.

Very big and special thanks to Helen Shenston and Anna-Lisa Hancock. And to Sue Ansell, who has read and helped me so much, editorially, with every single book I have written; very many thanks also to Martin and Jane Diplock, and Nicola Mitchell.

A huge debt of gratitude also to my agent and wonderful friend Carole Blake. And to Tony Mulliken, Sophie Ransom and Becky Short of Midas PR. To list everyone at Pan Macmillan would be impossible, but thank you Geoff Duffield, Anna Bond, Sara Lloyd, my wonderful and lovely publishing director, Wayne Brookes, and my incredibly patient editor, Susan Opie. And of course my great US team: Andy Martin, my editor Marc Resnick, my publicists Hector DeJean and Paul Hochman of Minotaur, Elena Stokes and Tanya Farrell of Wunderkind and all the rest at Team James USA!

An extremely special thanks to my brilliant PA, Linda Buckley, who has worked with me, tirelessly, on endless drafts and revisions and corrections on this manuscript, and is always bright and cheerful.

Phoebe, Oscar and Coco, as ever have been the model of all patience – above and beyond all duty for dogs! For waiting around the foot of my desk for the slightest hint that I'm going to take a break and walk them before they go wonderfully crazy with excitement – and for reminding me that sometimes there is a life beyond my keyboard and screen . . .

Fond memories of my friend Jim Herbert, who was so supportive to me and sadly died during the time I was writing this book.

Thank you, my readers. Your emails, tweets, Facebook and blog posts give me such constant encouragement!

Peter James
Sussex, England
scary@pavilion.co.uk
www.peterjames.com
www.facebook.com/peterjames.roygrace
www.twitter.com/peterjamesuk

THE TELLTALE SIGNS OF PSYCHOLOGICAL ABUSE ARE LISTED BELOW:

Many women suffer horrific psychological violence without showing any obvious symptoms.

To learn more about how to spot non-violent abuse visit **whiteribboncampaign.co.uk**